Man and His Surroundings

Fazil Iskander

Man and His Surroundings

Fazil Iskander

Translated by
Alexander Rojavin

BOSTON
2023

Library of Congress Cataloging-in-Publication Data

Names: Iskander, Fazil′, author. | Rojavin, Alexander, translator.
Title: Man and his surroundings / Fazil Iskander ; translated by Alexander Rojavin.
Other titles: Chelovek i ego okrestnosti. English (Rojavin)
Description: Boston : Academic Studies Press, 2023.
Identifiers: LCCN 2022054279 (print) | LCCN 2022054280 (ebook) | ISBN 9798887191041 (hardback) | ISBN 9798887191058 (paperback) | ISBN 9798887191065 (adobe pdf) | ISBN 9798887191072 (epub)
Subjects: LCGFT: Fiction.
Classification: LCC PG3482.S5 C4813 2023 (print) | LCC PG3482.S5 (ebook) | DDC 891.73/44--dc23/eng/20221121

LC record available at https://lccn.loc.gov/2022054279
LC ebook record available at https://lccn.loc.gov/2022054280

ISBN 9798887191041 (hardback)
ISBN 9798887191058 (paperback)
ISBN 9798887191065 (adobe pdf)
ISBN 9798887191072 (epub)

Cover design by Ivan Grave
Book design by Kryon Publishing Services

Published by Cherry Orchard Books, an imprint of Academic Studies Press.
1577 Beacon Street
Brookline, MA 02446, USA
press@academicstudiespress.com
www.academicstudiespress.com

Contents

Translator's Introduction

"Humor is the last reality of optimism," writes Iskander. I would disagree. Humor is the frontline of hope. Humor is the backbone of resilience. In the fight between good and evil, humor favors the former. Humor is, in fact, incomprehensible to the latter. "Power, violence, authority never speak the language of laughter," wrote Bakhtin.[1] Tyranny does not understand humor. Tyranny fears humor, for humor is its undoing.

Fazil Iskander understood this acutely. Born in 1929, Iskander witnessed it all: the terror of the Stalin years, the illusory promise of the Khrushchev Thaw, the aimlessness of the Brezhnev era, the accelerated liberalization of Gorbachev's perestroika, the creeping oligarchy of Yeltsin's '90s, and, finally, the consolidated kleptocracy of the 2000s and 2010s. For several decades, Iskander's works held up a mirror to each era's surreal shortcomings and, by reflecting them, rendered them powerless. By reflecting them, Iskander also underscored the idiosyncratic historical qualities that some peoples of the Soviet Union were unable to escape.

Today is March 16, 2022. I write this as Russian bombs sow death in Ukrainian cities. The fields, woods, and urban jungles of Ukraine are serving as a battleground for a fight between a people defending a hard-won democracy and a people held in the thrall of an authoritarian regime unleashing the genocidal spasms of its late-stage senility. Russia's looming military defeat and the obstinate resilience of the Ukrainian people should not have come as a surprise. Had the West better grasped the mindsets of the different peoples occupying post-Soviet space, perhaps it would not have. This translation of a work by one of the most beloved late Soviet writers should help bridge that gap.

To the astute onlooker, this war should have revealed a key difference between Kremlin-Mordor's attacking horde and the Ukrainians, ordinary and extraordinary, standing sentinel on democracy's border. That key difference is a sense of humor. From grandmothers, standing on the side of the road

---

1   Mikhail Bakhtin, *Rabelais and His World* (Moscow: Khudozhestvennaya Literatura, 1990), 104.

laughing at Russian orcs driving by in their tanks, to Ukrainian television anchors, who spent the first week of the war cracking wise on air in parking garages and basements. Their levity in the face of an adversary with genocidal objectives has been unfailing. And it has revealed that the Russian horde's attempt to conquer the unconquerable is laughable. It is savage, barbaric, inhuman, genocidal, helpless, borne of a single insignificant man's psychotic envy—envy of Ukraine's freedom, envy of Ukraine's quality of life, envy of Ukraine's confidence. But it is always laughable, because it has always been doomed to failure.

As Iskander's works show, all such attempts ultimately are.

As the October Revolution—and the endemic absurdity of the Soviet Union and post-Soviet Russia—was fated to be. And nobody simultaneously captured, illuminated, subverted, and ultimately neutered this absurdity better than Fazil Iskander. The seemingly effortless wit and humor of his oeuvre, which spanned over forty years, proved so potent a remedy to the absurd tyranny of Soviet and post-Soviet times that he often had to publish his books in the United States first prior to re-importing them to the USSR.

It is a sadly appropriate coincidence that this translation of Iskander's *Man and His Surroundings* should come out after the war. "The function of laughter is to reveal, uncover the truth, untether reality from the cover of etiquette, ceremonialism, artificial inequality."[2] Iskander's pathos-less wit and casual irony strip away the near-endless layers of falsehood that have clouded both Soviet and post-Soviet Russian realities. This book reveals the cultural pathologies that have taken such powerful root over the centuries, from the birth of imperial Russia through the darkness of the Soviet Union to the genocidal senility of post-Yeltsin Russia. These are pathologies in which lie the causes of many of the woes plaguing modern Russia—and those in whose lives modern Russian has interfered, often lethally. Iskander's light-handed humor lays bare the foundation of modern Russia's criminality—and its impending unraveling.

As Ukraine, even twenty-one days into this war, maintains its sense of humor, waves of actors, satirists, and stand-up comedians are fleeing Russia, passports in hand. The last sources of laughter are quitting the country while Roskomnadzor cleans up the remaining vestiges of liberal-adjacent

---

2   Dmitry Likhachev, *Historical Poetics of Russian Literature* (St. Petersburg: Aleteya, 1977), 350.

thought in Russia's information space. In this war, it is not difficult to figure out which—invader or defender—is immune to humor. No, not immune— *terrified*. Just as the Soviet authorities were always terrified of Iskander and the humor that he wielded, humor that so effectively revealed the regime's emptiness when little else could.

It is my hope that this translation endows English-speaking audiences with a little more understanding of the worldviews, mindsets, tendencies, and psycho-cultural realities of some of the peoples who occupied Soviet territories and who now occupy post-Soviet territories. It is my hope that readers of this book will understand that there is nothing surprising about the current war or about what is currently happening in Russia, Ukraine, Georgia, Belarus. It is my hope that readers will realize that this war was preventable, had the West acted a little differently, a little more decisively. It is my fervent hope that readers will value the role that humor must play in a thriving democracy.

Humor is not the last reality of optimism. But it can be the last thing that authoritarianism ever hears.

May laughter ring throughout the cities of Russia—however little territory it occupies—soon.

— Alexander Rojavin

Instead of a Foreword

Man and His Surroundings is my last work. Every writer thinks his last work is his best. That makes sense. He wouldn't write it otherwise. Gyrating on a dialectical spiral, he believes that he's finally gotten his hands on the juiciest cluster of grapes and has managed to squeeze it out in its entirety onto the manuscript. Naturally, his own intoxication doesn't affect anything, and time alone will tell how successful the book is.

The chapter on Lenin seems to be seminal for the whole book. Everything that takes place in the subsequent chapters up through the semi-disintegration of our government is a natural function of the triumph of Leninism.

I knew a madman once who dedicated his whole life to Lenin and sometimes posed as him. That's what helped me engage Lenin in what was a fairly tiring dialogue and what ultimately allowed me to write this chapter.

I rewrote it for the final time right before the August Putsch. I was still in bed when my wife told me about what had happened. I didn't get up. My first thought was: it's over, no one will publish it now. I'll have to publish it in another country, like *Sandro*, if the danger won't be too great.

Still in bed, but listening to the door's slightest movements, I thought it unlikely that a string of high-profile arrests would follow. But I was sure there would likely be a great famine.

Still in bed, I remembered my madman and was surprised that after reinventing himself as Lenin, he said several times during our last conversation that a coup was in the works and transparently hinted at how analogous his own role would be to his role in 1917.

That's when the phone rang, and I was forced to get up. This was all happening at my summer home. It was my nephew calling. He was passing through Moscow and had stopped at my apartment. He said that some man had just come by asking for me. Judging by the man's description, I instantly figured out who he was talking about. It was an extraordinary coincidence. Of all my noble acquaintances, he was the one we always suspected the most of working for them. What those people wanted from us is unclear. Since then, he himself disappeared without a trace.

So, let's get back to the hero of my tale. Judging by how the failed revolt was organized, it seemed entirely plausible that he really *was* in charge of it. I won't go over the crude military errors that even I noticed for reasons that the reader can figure out independently. Especially since he's also dropped off the face of the earth. I mean my literary hero, not the reader, of course. Though these days, anything is possible.

It's possible that he's gone deep underground and is planning a new revolt. Let's hope that it will be equally "successful." At any rate, we must remain vigilant, and the publisher should quickly set about publishing this book.

But if everything turns out *very* poorly, then I'll take advantage of my old relationship with my tale's hero, and I'll try to shield myself and the publisher. I'll assure him that he was called a madman exclusively for censorship reasons, and as for Lenin's ideas—well, I never disfigured them. For some reason, I first wrote "you can't disfigure them." A Freudian slip, and one that rhymes with my name. What could that mean? No, he won't believe me. That's for sure.

1

Lenin at the Amra

Humor is the last reality of optimism. So, let's take advantage of this (I almost wrote "sad") reality.

They said that Lenin had showed up in town. They said that he rode around on a bike and that he didn't preach too openly, but that he didn't shy away from the near future's impending revolt. They said that he did so at the Amra, the roofless top floor of a restaurant where many locals and out-of-towners eat ice cream and drink coffee—and maybe even something stronger.

Let me specify right away that I'm talking about the seaside restaurant Amra that's on the ancient wharf in the town called Mukhus. If someone has in mind some other restaurant called "Amra" in some other town, even if its name sounds similar to my Mukhus, they should abstain from any protestations. "That's not how they serve food in our Amra." "Our barista's nose is completely different." "The author's got it all wrong, and the architecture's wrong too." I will repeat myself right now: I am talking about my Amra in my Mukhus. Everything in it looks exactly as I say, and the barista's nose looks exactly like I say it does, if I even choose to say anything about it at all.

So. They said that Lenin had showed up in town. Obviously, I'm talking about the crazy person that sometimes masqueraded as Lenin and sometimes didn't. Though they said that he wasn't posing as Lenin himself, but as the foremost expert on Lenin's biography, and that he could answer any question on the subject.

Though he was born in Mukhus and his poor mother is still alive, he spent his entire adult life working in Moscow. He taught Marxism in one of Moscow's universities and spent many years writing a book in which he reconstructed Lenin's life not just by the day, but sometimes by the hour.

He made many desperate attempts to publish it. First under Khrush-chev, then under Brezhnev. But neither the Khrushchev nor the Brezhnev governments wanted anything to do with such a detailed biography of Lenin. According to hearsay, that's when he went right off the deep end.

As odd as it may seem, almost everything that people would say about him afterwards proved correct. But does anybody truly understand the secrets of the human psyche? Nobody knows when exactly he went off the deep end: was it when his thirty years of work were rejected by every single publisher he contacted, or was it when he began the work in the first place?

You know, could it have been his own name that inspired him to take up this pursuit?

The thing is that his name was, unfortunately, Stepan Timofeyevich, just like the famous Volga bandit, Stepan Razin, whom our historians have morphed into a nonconformist revolutionary.[1]

Though, all things considered, long before the Bolsheviks, people had already made him their idol, writing legends and songs in his honor. Not a single people in history has failed to elegize its outlaws, but every people has done so differently.

The famous song on Stepan Razin praises the fact that he threw his gorgeous Persian girl overboard as a noble deed. Why? Because he heard his crew murmuring behind his back: "Did he just replace us with some broad?" Of course, the problem isn't that he exchanged his cutthroats for a broad, but that he has a beautiful Persian girl and they don't. How unjust.

Our people are willing to commit the most heinous crime so long as they're assured that they'll be equal in their banditry. They understand and accept solidarity and equality before banditry. But they don't understand, nor do they accept equality before the law. They've never had a law like that, and what they did have that tried to pass itself off as such a law was always a boldfaced lie. A yearning for equality resulted in the fleeting equality of banditry.

Banditry turns into a moment of truth. Dreams of equality before banditry enthrall them so much that not only do they not pity their victims,

---

1   Stepan Razin (or Stenka Razin) was a seventeenth-century Cossack leader who led an uprising against the nobility in 1670–1671. He was mythologized in multiple Russian and Soviet works of art, including poems, songs, and one of the very first Russian narrative films (1908). Aside from leading an uprising, he is most famous in popular culture for throwing a captive princess overboard into the Volga River.

they're confident ahead of time about their guilt, if only because the poor victims are soulless in their eyes, like swine, and consequently they can be cut down like swine.

Equality before banditry doesn't mean that everyone will profit the same. Everyone has an equal opportunity before banditry, but it's worth saying that a lot hinges on one's agility, cunning, ruthlessness, and luck.

Banditry, as paradoxical as it may seem, sates one's thirst for seeing enterprise be justly rewarded. In places where times of peace don't see enterprise naturally rewarded—in other words, an absence of bourgeois law—this thirst is sated by banditry and the moment in which banditry occurs.

As an ideal folk hero, Stepan Razin surmises the fierce might of his companions' displeasure just in time. He was the one to ignore the rules of the game—not them. If it were a barrel of gold next to him instead of a beautiful Persian girl, he'd pour it out to his companions, and everything would be fine. But you can't divide a Persian princess like that. So what's left?

Overboard she goes.

Right into the inbound wave.

The grim splendor of equal distribution. If nobody gets any, that means everybody gets none. The line "right into the inbound wave" is surprising in its brilliant simplicity. The wave, bounding up to the ship, does so like a faithful dog bounding to its master. Nature itself approves of such a just act. Harmony is restored. And nature's approval belies the secret will of God. It's as if he observes everything from above and smiles: "You're on the right path, comrades. You're doing good."

What do you call an eastern overlord that orders silver coins to be thrown into the crowd when he stands before his people? What do you call a merchant who rolls out a barrel of wine for his employees? What do you call a celebratory feast in honor of a minister's years of service? And what do you call the outbreak of collectivization, and what do you call 1937? These are all varied attempts to unite us and restore our unity through our common brigandish proto-memories. But let's not get ahead of ourselves and instead return to my countryman, who once reached the conclusion that he was Lenin.

There's a half-philosopher, half-mystic that lives in Mukhus (you can find anything in Mukhus), who explains what happened as follows. He says that our countryman, having poured his soul into Lenin's biography, literally restored Lenin's spirit, and that this grateful spirit evidently preferred the mortal coil of our hard-working kinsman to all other mortal coils. (Why the spirit didn't head for the Mausoleum will become clear later, if I manage to guide this story to its end.)

It's odd that Lenin never really concerned me as a character during my life as a writer. Stalin interested and drew me to him. I had the feeling that in him lay the secret of what it was to be a great villain. But I passed by Lenin without a second glance. "So he might be a fanatic, he might be a rationalist, so what?" I thought. "There's no deep, secret personality to uncover."

I was in America in a Russian summer school in Vermont. Together with my wife and kid, I lived in that school for a month and a half, occasionally giving lectures to the students studying Russian literature, but more often roaming around its verdant, hilly surroundings.

There was an old man there who was ninety-plus years old who happened to be the school's founder. His last name was Pervushin. He came to my lectures, and not only mine—a few Muscovite writers had come there with me. Old man Pervushin listened to us with a spry interest that was surprising for his age and even asked us questions fairly often.

Turned out that he was related to Lenin. In fact, he was so closely related, or at least their families were, that with the help of Lenin's brother Dmitry Ulyanov, he managed to forge Lenin's signature on a document ostensibly allowing him to go to some made-up conference and flee Russia.

This was obviously when Lenin was still alive. I took note of a particular detail. Old man Pervushin said that at the time, Ulyanov's last name alone was enough for the Cheka.[2] Apparently, right after the revolution, Lenin hadn't yet begun signing his name like we're used to seeing in his facsimile—Ulyanov-Lenin. He would, by quite understandable habit, sign his name as he always had since his youth.

Having explained whom he has to thank for fleeing the country, the old man laughed a quiet, cooing laugh. His laugh could be interpreted like this: "I realized that it's not worth getting too close to history, and that's why I'm still alive. And where are those that decided to get too intimate with it? Exactly!"

---

2   The acronym ChK (ЧК in Russian) stands for Emergency Committee. Headed by "Iron" Felix Dzerzhinsky, it was the predecessor to the NKVD, which preceded the KGB, which preceded the FSB.

It was very amiable laughter. Sadly, I didn't ask the old man anything else about his famous relative. I hadn't even asked him about this. He just told us on his own. I regret it, but alas, it's too late now.

Having come back to Moscow and plunged into our restless, harried, hysterical life that so resembles pre-October Russia, I finally decided to read Lenin's works that I hadn't touched since my student days.

I stubbornly read him for a solid month. It wasn't easy reading, in the sense that it was difficult trying to get over how dull it was. He writes in endless circles, occasionally performing rhetorical zigzags that would make a professional ice skater blush, but he does it all monotonously, all on one, unchanging plane.

But what's self-evident to an ice skater isn't evident to a thinker. A thinker is intriguing because we see him go deeper and deeper, step by step in his search for the truth. We're interested in this deepening path, because it is art, because he himself has no idea where his next step will take him. We see how he feels around for firm ground, finds it, and moves on.

Lenin knows ahead of time that there's nowhere deeper to go and no reason to do so. He's smart, of course, but in a limited sense. Lenin is consistently sensible within the chaos of the general idea. What's fascinating is the contradiction between the energy of his mind and the banality of his thought. Typically, great thinkers astound us with a combination of mental energy and grand ideas. This seems natural. It's the mental energy that allows the idea to soar to unimaginable heights.

But maybe there are exceptions? This question is interesting when divorced from Lenin. Could you imagine a singer of Chaliapin's[3] caliber hear the Marseillaise, fall in love with it, and perform nothing else for the rest of his life, even if he sang thousands of variations?

Can you imagine a writer of Lev Tolstoy's caliber spend his life doing low-quality journalism and never writing a single short story worthy of his innate talent just because he happened to be poor or burdened with a large family?

It's practically impossible to imagine this. It would seem that a person's thoughts about another person correspond to his innate ability to understand people. Ethical hearing is like musical hearing—you can hone it slightly, but you're still stuck with what you're born.

---

3   Fyodor Chaliapin (1873–1938) was a world-famous Russian opera singer.

It would be inaccurate to say that Lenin's massive revolutionary undertaking distracted him and limited his comprehension of his fellow man. On the contrary, his massive revolutionary work was the result of his limited comprehension of human nature. It released in his soul the dreadful and joyful energy of destruction.

Let's imagine a card player who's developed a credible theory on how to win. But this theory requires big games and big money that he doesn't have. Let's imagine that he reveals this theory to a very wealthy person who agrees to let him play using his money, on some conditions.

And he sits down to play. But it turns out that the theory is wrong. And yet he plays and plays and eventually loses everything. Why didn't he stop after sensing that the theory was wrong? Because he was in the heat of the moment, and, more importantly, because he wasn't losing his own money.

Our great revolutionary is the same. He's playing with somebody else's money. A joke concerning Wilhelm's money isn't appropriate here. He's playing with millions of lives. If he had had the thought beforehand that he might lose, that hordes of people might die for nothing, he wouldn't have begun his revolution. But why doesn't this thought pay him a visit? Because of his limited comprehension of human nature. But where is this limited comprehension of human nature from? If we boil his own nature down to its very essence, we'll be left with this—moral stupidity.

Given his rage and the frightful temperament with which he constantly hammers away at the old morality, dreaming of creating a new socialist human, did he really fail to understand that even if it were possible to create a new morality, more perfect than the old one, it would be the fruit of *millennia* of work? And how can you begin a new life with the destruction of the old morality that was also forged over millennia? It's no different from planting the shoot of a breadfruit tree and immediately burning the nearby, albeit not yet entirely mature, wheat field.

There is no wisdom in Lenin's writings. He's always rushing, always biased. Apparently, to be wise, you have to think a lot, but lazily. Only he who thinks but forgets what he thinks about can get his thoughts somewhere significant. In order to think, you have to remove yourself from life. The philosopher's strength is the ability to remove himself from life while hanging on to his memories of it.

I'll take it on myself to dispute Marx's famous aphorism: up to this point, philosophers have explained the world, but the trick is to change it. As soon as a philosopher begins changing life, he loses the ability to judge it impartially because he becomes a part of life's stream. And the more he changes the stream's direction after entering its flow, the more misguided are his judgments about what is happening. And now, the only person who can properly evaluate what's going on in the world, which our philosopher is changing and splashing about in, is another philosopher who's sitting on the beach, observing what's going on.

But if, after seeing his colleague splashing around, he dives in after him to explain his errors, everything he tells him will be inaccurate, because in entering the stream himself, he has once again altered its properties.

Which is how poor Martov[4] would dive into the stream that Lenin was splashing around in, and then get out and yell at him about his errors from the beach, but to no avail—they were already destined never to understand each other. Meanwhile, Lenin was paddling aimlessly inside a whirlpool, interpreting each lap around the watery cyclone as a new dialectical spiral, right up to the point when he convulsively choked to death.

Put short, reading Lenin brought up a lot of bewildered questions. Oh, and I also noticed his powerful human traits. For example, disciplined self-control, at least in his writings. The more tragic the situation was, the more furiously and unswervingly he would dictate his will. No panic, no confusion.

I wrote and printed an essay in which I expressed serious doubts about his ideas and train of thought. I mention this because it is relevant to what I'm going to tell.

So, Lenin showed up in Mukhus. I was standing with my cousin Kemal, a former military pilot and current senior citizen, on a neat, little street, planted all over with old sycamores. I was asking him about this man. My cousin would reluctantly respond. He clearly didn't approve of my curiosity.

"An insolent son of a bitch," he called him.

"Why?" I asked.

"He got groceries at the same veterans' store we did," my cousin said. "But then it turned out that he was never in the war . . . A strange guy . . . Oh, here he is!"

My cousin nodded in the direction of a man that appeared out from behind the corner on a bicycle. I instantly recognized him, and he instantly recognized me.

---

4   Julius Martov (1873–1923), born Tsederbaum, was a politician and leader of the Mensheviks. He was also a close friend of Lenin.

"What a pair of wonder-brothers I see!" he shouted out and then added after raising his hand: "I read your article! I fundamentally disagree! We'll duke it out on the idiot box!"

With that, he caught the wiggling handlebars and zoomed by us. He was wearing a short-sleeved, blue-and-white sailor's shirt that showed off surprisingly strong, viselike arms. He had a familiar, very tanned, thickset face with bright eyes and a large forehead with a hairline that wasn't even remotely receding. I knew him well, of course, but I'd just forgotten about him. Some fifteen years ago in Moscow, he'd come to me with some verse he had written. He called me by phone, said that he was my countryman, and asked me to read his poetry.

When I answered the doorbell, a heavyset, bright-eyed man with a large forehead stood in the door, and he looked absolutely nothing like Lenin. Head slightly inclined, he examined me and curtly stated his impressions:

"You look like him. Definitely. Though not really. Slightly worse for the wear."

"Who do I look like?" I asked, wary.

"Like your pilot cousin!" he joyfully exclaimed, lurched towards me, hugged me, and even managed to land a kiss on my cheek. Then, as if having proven our kinship, he quickly undressed and began telling me about himself, all the while glancing in the mirror and combing his curly, light brown hair.

This is how you behave with a very old friend in a very familiar home. Right, I forgot to add that, before this, he handed me a red folder full of his verse with a sense of relief. Like an idiot, I took it and became a little stricter, as if in light of the responsibility he had just heaved upon me. I decided to be curter with him and at least do away with the familial ardor.

He was infinitely friendly. He would laugh at the drop of a hat. He'd jump up, sit back down, joke around. Then I read his verse while he strolled next to the bookshelves, greeting some books like old friends, as if unobtrusively demonstrating his class.

His verse turned out to be fairly grammatical and fairly insipid. The main theme was the Revolution. For the most part they were poems about Lenin. I gave him a pretty sour review, but to make the pill sweeter to swallow, I told him to bring me some more. He wasn't at all offended by my response, and I liked that.

Then he told me that he was planning to publish his life's work—the Leniniana. This didn't surprise me at all. Just about every single Marxism teacher dreams of writing a book on Marx or Lenin. Or on Engels at the very least.

However, I stopped that train of thought right in its tracks, getting the sense that this person had far too much energy. We'd spend more than enough time just talking about the innocent eccentricities of our mutual acquaintances, even if those eccentricities sometimes turned into inexplicable oddities. That said, he did make one more attempt to break through and cried out:

"When Lenin's one hundred and twenty-seven love letters to Ines Armand are published, the world will know that this fiery revolutionary could love like no one else!"

"Why didn't he marry her, then?" I inquired, but letting him know with my tone that I didn't want a novel in response. And he understood that.

"He couldn't leave Nadezhda Konstantinovna!" came the heated response. "She had Graves' Disease, and he couldn't leave a sick wife! The man's nobility is incredible. The world has to know!"

Both the world and I already knew a little something about the man's nobility, but I kept quiet. In short, I gave him a sour response to his verse and told him that he should show me something else. He visited me several times over the course of two years. The poems changed, but the subject matter narrowed and, as I now understand, menacingly concentrated on Lenin. They didn't really differ from the usual graphomaniacal poems about Lenin. Everyone wrote about how Lenin was metaphorically alive. But my countryman focused on the idea of the people somehow, miraculously meeting Lenin anew: "Lenin is Coming," "Lenin is Among Us," "Lenin Will Be Here Soon," and the like. Again, these motifs weren't new, but my kinsman was clearly overdoing it.

"I'm tired of trying to get the Leniniana published," he said to me once, winking at me meaningfully. "I'm prepared to split the royalties with whoever manages to push my book through. Tit for tat, sound good?"

"No," I said. "That won't work for me."

"Does tit for tat not suit you?" he sounded surprised and said: "Ok, how about this: one third of royalties go to me, one third goes to you, and one third to the publisher's director?"

"Do you really not see the monstrous contradiction here?" I said, surgically getting angry. "You live in Lenin's kingdom, you glorify Lenin with your book, but nobody wants to publish it? What do you call that in your dialectic: the negation of a negative?"

"There's no contradiction!" he exclaimed. "Stalin organized a quiet, counterrevolutionary coup! We have to launch a new attack. My Leniniana is the algebra of revolution—that's why they don't want to publish it."

I kept silent. Who the hell was this guy! Could he have been . . . one of them? After all, why couldn't they use oddballs like him? That had already happened to me. After my uncensored *Sandro* came out in America, I waited for something bad to happen. And suddenly an old acquaintance of mine showed up, and after a short conversation that didn't obligate anyone to do anything, he led me out to my own balcony, as if wary of listening devices in the room, and told me that a friend of his just came back from Europe, a dependable friend, and that I could send a manuscript that wouldn't make it past the censorship with him to the West.

"There's no need," I told him coldly.

I had the feeling that he sighed with relief: he both fulfilled his assignment and didn't actually betray anyone. We went back inside.

"What's this for?" he nodded towards the desk where there lay an Abkhazian shepherd's knife next to my typewriter, solemnly guarding that minstrel of the shepherd's way of life.

"That's in case anyone tries anything funny," I said very clearly so that the people who worked where he came from could hear me too. He left quickly and never came back. At the time, I felt like I played that round well and won. I still feel like that, but I can never be completely sure that he really came from where I think he did. At any rate, those were our realities back then.

One way or another, I'd had enough of my countryman, and I decided to get rid of him by pretending to help. I decided to write a recommendatory note to the editors of a relatively liberal journal where I'd been published and where they knew me well. Let *them* deal with writers like this, they actually get paid for it.

I felt that I had written a cleverly disguised, ironic note, recommending an aspiring poet and a well-known teacher of Marxism. (Well known to whom? Lenin would have put an ironic "sic!" here.) Noting the aspiring poet's literary naiveté on one hand, I complimented his stubborn efforts to laud the purity of revolutionary ideals.

I was pleased. I felt that the note would slip past the censors. I was sure that my friends over at the journal would instantly understand that it was a joke. And he wouldn't. I gave him the note and relaxed in the quiet and joyful anticipation of our little romance coming to an end.

He read the note, looked up at me, and unexpectedly gave me a savory kiss right on the lips. God damn him! I had relaxed and couldn't take advantage of an ancient piece of writer's wisdom: if a graphomaniac tries to kiss you on the lips, give him your cheek.

But he left without any further sentiments. I was even a little hurt. I absolutely wanted him to leave as quickly as humanly possible. But I wanted him to leave after shuffling about gratefully. But it was as if by grabbing the note and rewarding me with a juicy kiss, he paid me back tenfold and had no intention of wasting another second with me.

I had a bad feeling that the kiss wasn't a portent of good fortune. And that turned out to be exactly true. Three months later, the journal published his verse, prefacing them with my recommendation. This shouldn't have happened, but it did. I had taken everything into account except for the rampant insanity of the world we live in, which is what I should've accounted for first and foremost.

I later called my friend who worked at the journal, a fairly liberal writer who had dealt with the poems. Turns out that my countryman's verse with my note stapled to it was lying on his table when the chief editor walked into his office. He automatically took the poems, saw the note stapled to them, and took them away to his own office like a hawk flapping away with its prey.

The thing is that criticism of the journal's editor sometimes pushed him in a certain direction, and he decided to use these poems to reinforce the journal's ideological platform. He himself wasn't very liberal, but he went with the flow of the Khrushchev era. The editor's armchair would sometimes float up too high, but rock pleasantly. Whereas he dreamed of stability. He wanted the armchair to rock pleasantly, but not float up too high.

"Of course I took your hint right away," my friend defended himself over the phone. "It just happened. The editor flew in and took away the poems with your note. Usually, he holds his nose when dealing with poems that we *do* recommend, but this time he took everything himself and sent them off to be typed up. Don't worry! The top brass said that you turned out better than they thought you would. That'll come in handy!"

After my countryman got published, I stopped getting calls from him. I tried to forget about the man's existence and was resoundingly successful.

Some two years later, maybe a bit more, a psychiatrist I knew invited me over for a little lunch and some Sunday cross-country skiing. He lived and worked outside the city. Thinking that I would turn him down, he figured he'd lure me in with the promise of showing me a patient whose mania was so sensitive that he couldn't tell me about it over the phone.

He was an exceptionally kind and hospitable man. I leapt at the invitation. One bright and frosty day, I exited the commuter train and went off in the direction of the hospital. At an intersection of the provincial roads, I saw a sled with two people, a passenger and the driver. They were seemingly mulling over which direction they should be going in. Both were bundled up in many layers. I approached them and, insuring my question by pointing in the direction from which they came, asked:

"Is the hospital that way?"

"Tell this simpleton," said the passenger through the scarf wrapped around his face, his breath frosting in front of him, "that my estate is that way! What do they need? I haven't been in politics since 1916! Go!"

The last word was clearly meant for the driver. The driver managed to nod, but after hearing the passenger's word, I could confidently follow the sled tracks. The passenger's voice seemed familiar, but I didn't pay any attention to it then. I set off, mulling over what he said and finding much hidden humor in it.

He meant, of course, that he was being hunted by the police. By saying that he hasn't been in politics since 1916, he wanted to instill in me that he didn't have anything to do with the revolution in 1917. The revolution, it seemed, had been squashed. Its instigators were hunted. This one was waiting it out in his estate, naming 1916 as an alibi. Why so close to 1917? He was too notable a revolutionary, it would've been unrealistic to name an earlier year.

That's how I deciphered what he said as I approached a dreary building that, alas, the poor fellow must have considered his estate. My kindly host, who looked like a mighty warrior, a *bogatyr*[5] of yore, led me to his office and gave me a small drink to warm me up after the cold. His colleagues came too, and we started chewing the fat. Oh, and he wanted to show me a patient who believed himself to be Lenin, but I wasn't even remotely interested in him.

"You've already written about Stalin," said my kindhearted host. "I thought you were interested in Lenin now."

"No," I said. "I had a matter to settle with Stalin. Lenin was too long ago."

---

5   In Slavic myth, *bogatyrs* are powerful warriors, the Slavic equivalent of medieval knights-errant.

And then one old psychiatrist sitting at our table said a curious thing. He said that under Stalin, people feared him so much that not a single mentally ill person with delusions of grandeur dared pose as him.

If that really were true, that would mean that the kernel of fear sitting in the mentally ill person's head sat so deeply that it still affected the person even after the illness took root.

The party inconspicuously moved to my friend's apartment. I kept drinking, though it later turned out that I really should have been stopped. The problem was that we were all going at the same speed, so nobody was qualified to be on stopping duty. Apparently, even when we were still in his office, I got onto the windowsill and yelled out the window:

"A Soviet psycho is the most normal psycho in the world!"

It's worth noting that this drunken sentence that I wanted to and, in fact, did yell out to the world, would also have slipped past the censors. So, I can confirm the old psychiatrist's observation. To a certain extent, inebriation can be considered a benign form of insanity. So, we witnessed a lighter version of the same scenario.

The morning was hard. But, attempting to overcome my hangover, I tried to get on the skis. My bogatyr of a host suddenly grabbed my hand:

"Lemme feel your pulse!" He felt it and said: "Time to go home. To bed."

We came back to his home, and I lay down in bed, even though I didn't really feel anything beyond the gloom of being hungover. But seeing as this gloom with its bleary haziness resembled the bleak feeling of guilt with regard to what was happening in the country, I was quite used to it and kept my calm.

I lay in bed while my host guiltily grabbed his head, possibly succumbing to post-drunken theatrics, and kept saying:

"How could I forget about this!" It turned out the medical alcohol we had been drinking had gone bad a few years back. The drinking medical professionals had adapted to the spirit, but I was a novice. I did drink spirit many years ago in Siberia, but it probably hadn't yet been spoiled by additives used in later times.

Then I had a thought: if the spirit that, by its very nature, was supposed to stop something else from spoiling had itself managed to spoil, then we were in a pretty bad spot. Meanwhile, my restless host had summoned some doctors armed with various instruments that evaluated the state of your heart, and these instruments—also broken, as it later turned out—maliciously pointed to only one possible explanation for my condition: I was having a heart attack!

Thankfully, knock on wood, the heart attack never came. But I can imagine how my host must have worried before we found out that the instruments were playing us for fools. Naturally, he didn't give me any sign of it then.

I was up and about by the evening, and he took me to Moscow in his car. So, I never found out if his patient was my very own countryman or someone different. And I can't ask him now because my *bogatyr* is in Israel. Given his mighty frame, I didn't expect such a change of course from him or such a perfect landing in so small a country. Then again, maybe he himself didn't suspect that such agility lay dormant inside him.

Here's what happened. One night, he was accompanying his friend to the train station after some heavy libations. They were apparently having so much fun that while they were strolling along the platform, they let a few trains go by. But in Russia, you can't forget where you are. Especially when you're having fun, and *especially* when you're having fun on a provincial train platform at night.

Apparently, while they were strolling about the platform, a couple of local thugs got them in their sights. My loving host finally put his friend on the train and went home. A *bogatyr*, by his very *bogatyr*-ness, is just asking for any would-be attackers to strike while his back is turned. And so, someone struck him from behind with something heavy, and he lost consciousness. When he came to, he found himself lying in the snow, his pockets empty, his hat and coat gone. By the time he crawled back home, he must have remembered that his mother was half-Jewish.

And suddenly he was in a rush to go to Israel, even though he never had any such intention previously—I didn't even know that he had the opportunity. So, he took his whole family to Israel, leaving his psychos God knows in whose care.

Hospitality is a wonderful quality, but this was too much. It's now clear that he was using his Jewish energy to expand his Russian opportunities. But would Israel help in this case? Who knows. As long as nobody takes his coat anymore.

The reader might ask: what does all this have to do with what I'm going to tell you about? My answer will be curt, even snippy: if it's on the page, it means something.

. . . And so, I'm sitting at a table on the top floor of the restaurant Amra. Thank God everything here's like it always was. Only the prices leapt up and froze mid-jump, so that no one would be any the wiser. I sat facing the entrance so as not to miss him, admiring the town of my youth against my will.

Heavens be praised, it was the same shoreline, the same towering, drab eucalyptuses on the seaside boulevard, the same white houses could be seen through the lush greenery, the same seaside hotel looked as comfortable as ever, so long as you didn't know, of course, that a fire had destroyed everything inside. Seeing as the instigator of the fire was never found, everyone thought that he carelessly burned to death with the hotel. They said that it was being rebuilt by migrants from Turkey and Poland. In Moscow and in Leningrad, many famous buildings were being rebuilt by migrants from Turkey and Finland. The thing that seems like a side effect of a dying empire—the disappearance of master craftsmen—is in reality its main symptom.

Closer to the exit, to my right, next to the railing enclosing the entire floor, sat three young men. Two of them wore blindingly white shirts, the third had on a magenta silk shirt, fluttering effervescently in the breeze. He had clearly gotten it very recently, because every now and then he'd stop what he was doing and admire the scintillating red silk. They were drinking coffee, telling each other jolly tales, and glancing at the girls wandering by. There was quite a crowd in the restaurant. It was hot, but the sun was warded off by shade-giving tents. And as usual, there weren't enough tables beneath the tents. Those sitting beneath the tents clearly weren't in a hurry to leave especially because some restaurant-goers were stubbornly awaiting their liberation.

The sound of an approaching hydroplane could suddenly be heard from the sea. The noise cut off abruptly right in the restaurant wharves.

"Bocho's here!" said one of the guys, leaning over the railings to look down.

"You won't find a funnier guy in town," added the proud wearer of the magenta shirt.

"Let's see what he'll say," put in the third.

A few minutes later, a curly-haired head with a tan face could be seen bobbing above the restaurant railings. He had climbed up to the top floor on an iron ladder on the side of the restaurant.

"Where my ladies at?" he called loudly. "Get in line for a nautical adventure while I'm here! It's summer season, I'll accept any clientele age twenty to forty! Older than forty, and you can stay in your seats—the winter season's just around the corner!"

Young girls from all parts of the restaurant made a dash for him. One woman got up, but hearing the end of his invitation, hesitated, as if trying to remember her age. After successfully recalling it, she sat back down in resignation.

Young restaurant-goers, of course, caught her moment of enterprising and, nodding in her direction, started dying of laughter. Six girls were already standing next to the hydroplane pilot.

"You! You! You! You!" he picked out four girls and waved the rest away: "You wait for when I get back!"

The pilot got off the ladder onto the wooden deck on other side of the railing. Hanging on to the railing with one hand, he helped the girls get over it and descend the narrow iron ladder with the other. At the same time, he glanced around the restaurant deck with a cheerful, predatory gaze. Noticing the guys sitting to my right, he yelled out to them, all the while helping the girls:

"You guys'll die laughing. My family's having dinner at home yesterday. The woman living next door comes up to the window and yells: 'Natasha, you're home. What're you doing?'

"'I'm having dinner,' my wife responds.

"'Go on, you go ahead and have your dinner!' our neighbor yells. 'Meanwhile, your husband and my idiot took two vacationing bimbos and went on a trip to New Aphon. But you go ahead and have dinner with your kids!'

"I'm dying laughing, my wife's looking at me like she's ready to kill me. Finally I yell to our neighbor:

"'I haven't seen your idiot in three days!'

"'Wait, you're back already?' the neighbor says and goes away just like that. She suddenly decided to feel shame.

"'See,' I say to my wife, 'the gossip that people spread about our happy, wonderful family. Women are jealous of you, they're trying to drive a wedge between us.' I'll tell you another one when I get back."

"Bocho, what'd you do with the girls you were giving a ride to?" asked the proud wearer of the magenta shirt.

"What do you mean 'what did I do with them?'" Bocho gave a start. "I took them to the maternity ward!"

The guys busted up. The last girl clambering over the railing jerked her head to look at Bocho.

"Don't worry, young miss," he called jovially, still holding her hand with his own. "I let them get off on the beach. Anybody who jokes around like this wouldn't lay a finger on you. And whoever has roaming fingers would never joke around."

The girl laughed and climbed all the way over the railing.

"All that's left is to figure out whether I'm joking!" Bocho called down after her as she descended the ladder. Winking to the guys, the joker went down the ladder after her.

A minute later the engine roared to life, and the hydroplane left for the sea.

"What a guy!" mused the proud wearer of the magenta shirt admiringly.

"Does he fool around, though?" another asked.

"I don't think so," said the third. "I had a girlfriend from out of town visiting with a friend. I had loads of cash too. I run into Bocho and tell him what's up. I tell him we're loaded. I ask him if he'd look after my girlfriend's friend. Sure thing, he says. We get to the restaurant. I order everything I can. Bocho's laying it on thick, he's joking up a storm, the girls are dying. Even mine starts inching towards him. I swear! But I can't even be mad—it's Bocho! As soon as we finish dinner, he gets up and says 'Bye, ladies. Thank you for the company, but my beautiful wife is waiting for me!'"

"His wife really is a beauty," sighed the guy who asked the question.

"That's not the point," the proud wearer of the magenta shirt noted. "Keep in mind, he fools around on the down low."

Meanwhile, I had gotten so caught up in the lives of these youths that I didn't even notice how the person I was waiting for had shown up.

"I fundamentally and categorically disagree," a cheerful and firm voice said above my head.

I came to. It was him. In the same sleeveless sailor's shirt, black corduroy pants, and pristinely white canvas shoes. They had clearly been bleached not too long ago. There he stood before me, thickset, stocky. His muscular arms were crossed. His tanned, tough face signaled that he was ready for action, as did his small, bright, lively eyes. The metallic top of the pen that was clipped to his shirt caught and reflected the sunlight.

"Have a seat," I said. "Coffee, cognac?"

"What kind of freedom is this?" he said, vehemently sitting down and vehemently leaning towards me, his bright, bullet-like eyes boring right into me. "You're denying a great person the right to do an experiment that people have been awaiting for millennia! What kind of freedom is that, my dear man?"

"Yes, that's exactly what I'm doing," I said. "A man can experiment on himself. All things considered, people that shared his mindset could've bought a large piece of land in Russia or Europe, populated it, and done their social experiments there without bothering anybody else."

"My dear man, socialism in a laboratory is garbage!" he cried out, waving his arms above the table. "Therein lies the drama of great Lenin: the fact that he understood the vast consequences that a historical shift would bring, but did it anyway! And he'll do it again when he has to!"

"Ok, but, please," I told him, "if you could refrain from using all these little words: my dear man, nope, hmmm. I especially despise hmmm."

"Hmmm," he said immediately, as if to assert his rights right on the spot.

I recalled how, in my youth, if somebody were to firmly shut the door on their way out of the room, my crazy uncle would jump up and throw the door wide open to demonstrate that nobody had the right to lock him up, even though nobody ever locked anything.

"I can't forbid you to do anything," I said peaceably, "but please try, if you can."

"I didn't say 'hmmm' on purpose," he explained. "I expressed my doubts about how democratic your character is."

"So say that instead: I doubt your democratic nature."

"Why should I say so many words when I can quickly just say 'hmmm?'"

"That 'hmmm,'" I said, trying to be straightforward, "belies a certain malevolent arrogance. As if you're so much better than your conversation partner that he doesn't deserve your words."

"Hmmm," he said again, but then added, realizing what he did: "That wasn't with regard to our conversation, but to what you consider arrogance."

I realized that this tiny skirmish could go on indefinitely.

"Ok, do as you like," I said, and then, trying to catch him at the very instant of his deviation into insanity, asked: "What do you mean 'Lenin will do it again?' Will a new Lenin rise up?"

His gaze became stricter. But I got the impression that he had gotten a hold of himself.

"Not new, but renewed by fresh historical conditions," he said evasively, but also firmly.

I called over a waitress that was standing off to the side, shooting us hurt glances for some reason. She came over.

"Do you drink?" I asked him.

"I dabble," he responded animatedly.

The waitress frowned.

"Two coffees and three hundred grams of cognac," I said and added, addressing him: "Maybe something else too?"

"Ice cream," he said curtly. "Mental work requires sweets."

I recalled that my crazy uncle liked sweets too. Back in my childhood, I would only sometimes be allowed to bring him a little lemonade.

"Maybe three portions?" I asked.

"Three! Three!" he flared up. "You guessed my norm! I like dealing with perceptive people, though I never back away from my principles."

The waitress's frown deepened and, having written down our order, she said to me:

"You're new here, I'm begging you if Uncle Styopa starts saying that he's Lenin, stop him or call me. I'll ask him to leave. I know that it's a new age of freedom now, but it's shameful . . . And he makes you feel sorry for Lenin . . ."

"The Leniniana continues," my companion remarked enigmatically.

"You're at it again?" she asked with bitter pity.

"My dear, don't forget that I'm a former Moscow university dean," my companion said with a degree of arrogance.

"Exactly—*former*," the waitress noted vengefully.

"Overboard she goes right into the inbound wave," my companion suddenly sang in a surprisingly well-defined baritone. He sang looking at the waitress, and his singing was partly a joking threat aimed at her and partly a promise to grant her request by staying within the boundaries of Stepan Razin.

"For God's sake, leave it alone," the waitress said and left.

I didn't want to argue with him. But I wanted to ask him something, since he knew so much about Lenin's life. The thing is, when I was abroad, I had read a book that insisted that Fanny Kaplan's assassination attempt on Lenin was organized by Stalin and Dzerzhinsky. The author didn't bring any convincing evidence to the table, and it all didn't really seem like it could be true. But there were some things that I thought were indisputable.

Citing the newspaper *Izvestiya*,[6] which covered the assassination attempt, the author wrote that gunshots were heard coming from different

---

6   Literally, "News."

directions. He couldn't have made that up, considering that that could so easily be disproved. But maybe *Izvestiya* were given that information in the heat of the moment, with nothing to back it up but hearsay. Could there have been a refutation or elaboration of this information in *Izvestiya* later on?

The author wrote that after firing several shots at Lenin as he stood before a crowd of workers, Fanny Kaplan made her way through the crowd, got to a train station that was fairly far away from the factory, and only there was she arrested, and accidentally at that. If that's true, then what can we conclude about the factory workers' attitude towards Lenin?

And also, Fanny Kaplan was executed far too quickly. That probably supports the author's version of events. As liberal as the government was back then with punishments, executing a socialist revolutionary that shot at the head of state just a day or two after the fact doesn't make a lot of sense. Could it have been the threat of Moscow being taken over by the Whites?[7] No, that didn't happen. Then what was the reason? The government itself would only have benefited from a thorough investigation. Who rushed to execute Fanny Kaplan, and why?

I told him about my doubts. He carefully heard me out and exclaimed abruptly:

"So you know about that too!"

And then, as if afraid that he'd later forget something without which my information would be impermissibly incomplete, he added feverishly:

"Only, Dzerzhinsky had nothing to do with it! Remember that! Remember that! Remember that!"

"Then how did it happen, if you know?"

He looked around suspiciously. His eyes were on fire. He leaned in and whispered:

"I'll tell you everything. You're one of us, even though you just don't know it yet."

"How do you mean?"

"Literally. You offered us some invaluable aid in our time of need."

It seemed like he'd calmed down. He sat up straight again, at any rate.

"What kind of help?"

"You helped me publish my poems, which had been rejected by every other publisher. That way, you helped me sustain the spirit of the people,

---

7   The White Army, as opposed to the Reds, or Bolsheviks.

who have been losing all semblance of hope. The people are waiting for Lenin. You're one of us. Didn't you use to love revolutionary songs in your childhood?

His gaze pierced me. I grew cold, a monstrous suspicion seeping through me. How could he know? That information was from the first chapter of my new work! Nobody had seen it yet! I left it in Moscow on my desk! It was stolen! Stolen! He had never been crazy! He's one of *them*! And the Lenin poems were just a test of my loyalty! But I accidentally dodged that bullet! What do they want? Are they testing my resolve when faced with a crazy person? Rubbish! Get a hold of yourself!

"Yes," I said, trying to hide my worry. "I did like revolutionary songs in my childhood. But how do you know that?"

"I know everything," he said, looking at me mockingly. "But why are you all tense? Are you ashamed? Remember this: whoever didn't like revolutionary songs in his childhood is a scumbag. I loved them too! Nobody loved them like I did!"

With that, the fire in his eyes dimmed and was replaced by a yearning, begging desire for reason. Oh, I knew that look in his eyes so well from my uncle! I would sometimes put on somebody else's clothes and make fun of him. He would look at me, recognizing me and not recognizing me, and his eyes would show how his mind was scrambling to make sense of what he was seeing, how he was appealing to what vestiges of reason he still had in an attempt to understand what was going on. God forgive me!

And now I had the feeling that Lenin's double, in his extraordinary yearning for reason, was hinting at the cause of his craziness and hiding behind the actual Lenin, trying to convince me that his errors had the same noble cause.

No, buddy, that won't work. As for the songs—he was right. It's true: whoever didn't like revolutionary songs in his childhood is a scumbag! And he's an idiot who, having grown up, doesn't understand that a good revolutionary song reflects a religious yearning for brotherhood and a renewal of life. Life isn't responsible for the bloody farce of the revolution.

And you can't blame it, even if it does encourage revolutionary passions. What's the boundary? There is no boundary! It's the same as blaming reason for other people gazing too deeply into the future and seeing only their own graves. Is reason to blame, even though if reason didn't exist, man wouldn't know that he was mortal? He has to find balance between the abyss of life and the abyss of oblivion. As with art, as with song.

My companion once again looked around warily and leaned in close, inviting me to respond in kind.

"Look here. Only for you," he said confidentially.

With two strong, tan fingers, he pulled back the sailor's shirt from his neck, inviting me to take a look. I saw two pink scars on his pale shoulder. There were no doubts left about what he was insinuating.

"Quiet! Someone's coming! Not a word!" he hissed, and, letting go of his shirt, sat up straight.

Our furious waitress quickly came up to us.

"You're at it again, aren't you!" she screamed. "I saw what you were showing! I'll kick you out of here!"

"What was I showing?" my companion spread his arms out in surprise. "I was showing him what's left of a few boils. When Marx was working on his *Kapital*, he suffered from boils too. 'My boils will cost the bourgeoisie dearly,' he used to say back then."

"So you've moved on to Marx then!" the waitress said, quieting down a bit. "God, what an unbearable man!"

She left, coming to terms with the lesser of two evils.

"Conspiracy, conspiracy, and yet more conspiracy," said my companion, clearly pleased with himself.

"So *you* were shot?"

"Who else could it have been?"

"But it's been such a long time," I said sensibly. "Do you look like a person who's over a hundred years old?"

He smiled the smile of a grownup hearing children babbling.

"My real biological age," he said, enunciating clearly, "consists of the years I lived before I was frozen and those I lived after I was thawed out."

"Thawed out?"

"Of course. It's a long story. But you're one of us, you'll serve our proletarian cause. The uprising is coming, though I can't tell even you the time and place. But it's imminent . . . The crisis has gone on too long . . ."

"What, is there a party in congress I don't know about?" I asked him suddenly, trying to catch him off-guard.

"There is! There is!" he replied, not only defensively, but happily opening up. "But it's deep underground right now."

He started quickly scooping up ice cream with a spoon, sending it into his big-lipped mouth. And now it seemed like he was sensing the sweetness of revolution in the sweetness of the ice cream.

"Who froze you and who thawed you out?" I asked, trying to enunciate as clearly as possible.

His eyes burned decisively and grimly. He abruptly swept aside the empty ice cream bowl.

"It's a long story," he began softly. "What is the tragedy of Lenin? He didn't take into account how much the Bolsheviks loved power. According to Lenin's plan, the revolution had to have two stages: destruction and creation. In the beginning, the fighters take center stage. They take power. But then come the builders. And as soon as Lenin tried to begin the shift in focus, the assassination attempt happened . . . Which is how I became intimately acquainted with those bullets . . ."

He stopped, looked at me with glassy eyes, and suddenly asked:

"By the way, is Plekhanov[8] still alive?"

He answered himself before I even opened my mouth:

"He's dead! Dead! My memory's been acting up since they thawed me out. Sometimes, it feels like events that I lived through were actually just relayed to me by somebody else. And things that happened while I was frozen seem like they happened before my very eyes . . . So that's why they shot me . . . But there were loyal people too. Especially among my German friends. After the wound, I lay in my Kremlin chambers. When I grew healthier, they put some worker from Sormovo who looked a lot like me in my place. As for me, they extracted me to Germany to save my life and help out the local revolution."

"Is it really possible," I asked, "that the war chiefs of October could have confused you with some worker from Sormovo? That's impossible!"

"Of course," he agreed. "But what were they to do? The politburo had a meeting. Stalin said, 'This worker from Sormovo will pretend to be Lenin. His tenure won't be tedious. And meanwhile, we'll search for the real Lenin and his kidnappers. We'll have to eliminate Kamo.[9] He's uncontrollable; he'll shout to anybody who'll listen *I knew Lenin! That's not the real Lenin!*'"

At that point, one of the guys sitting to our right came up to our table. It was the proud wearer of the magenta shirt. Addressing my companion with respect that hinged on insolence, he asked:

---

8   Georgi Plekhanov (1856–1918) was a self-proclaimed Marxist and an outspoken critic of Lenin's politics.

9   A Bolshevik of Armenian-Georgian descent. He was convinced by his Russian tutor, Stalin, to join the revolutionary cause.

"Local students are wondering, could you please tell us what Lenin was doing on September 1st, 1917?"

It was as if my companion suddenly surfaced after being deep underwater. He readily turned to the guy and spoke heatedly and sensibly— at least, as sensibly as possible within the framework of Lenin's teachings.

"Young man, you couldn't have asked a more relevant question!" he exclaimed. "Listen well and remember this—we might as well be talking about the present! On September 1st, 1917, the newspaper *Proletariat* published an article written by Lenin in which he criticized Martov's speech at the Soviet Central Electoral Commission.

"See, Martov was saying that the Soviets couldn't fight for power at that particular historical moment because they were at war with Germany. According to Martov, a power struggle could lead to a civil war.

"Well, well, well! Look at the little upstart, the itty-bitty spider! So according to Martov, we revolutionary democrats should counter-pressure the government against the pressure from the right. Well, well!

"Do you see the parallel to contemporary liberals, young man? It turns out that the government fights both extremes—left *and* right! As if the government isn't completely in the right's clutches! That's the philistine wisdom, that's the lesson for today's rights and centrists! Lenin called on people to take power into their own hands, silly little Martov's philistine wisdom notwithstanding! Do you understand Lenin's point, young man?"

"Yes, of course," said the proud wearer of the magenta shirt. "I'll tell the guys what you said."

As he monologued, the young man listened with unbridled mocking respect. His friends were convulsing in silent laughter. The guy that was facing me was hiding behind the guy whose back was turned to me. It was nice and surprising that they were at least somewhat ashamed of their mockery.

"They're our only hope," my companion nodded towards the departing magenta shirt. "Let's drink to their health."

I poured the cognac. We raised our glasses when he suddenly recalled:

"He found a kindred soul in Martov, our patriot did . . . He said the same thing . . . Says . . ."

"What patriot?" I missed something.

"Plekhanov, Georgi Valentinovich," my companion explained. "He stood through the entire world war . . . and still stands . . . No, stood, he's not standing any longer . . ."

His eyes fogged over with the sheen of madness. He looked at me with a gaze that was begging and ashamed of the fact that he was begging:

"Is he alive?"

"He died," I said as simply as I could, so as not to traumatize him. I said it as if he had died just a few days back, and he simply might not have heard yet.

He quickly put his glass down and slammed the table with both hands.

"Yes!" he exclaimed as his hands hit the table, reason flaring up in him again. "How could I forget! The man couldn't live with the sailors being searched! Let's drink to the youth that's storming the future!"

We drank, and for some reason I thought that my companion's sailor's shirt was somehow connected to the sailors' search that Plekhanov couldn't handle. Putting down his glass, he lightly fluttered back from his last point of madness to the previous one and continued:

"That's when we made the call. We wouldn't tell the people that Lenin was kidnapped. The people could rise up against the government that let Lenin be kidnapped. We outsmarted Stalin."

"Did Krupskaya[10] know about this?"

"Sure. I gave dear Nadya a Party-sanctioned mission to acknowledge the new Lenin as the old one and teach him on the down-low how Lenin was supposed to live both in Shushenskoye[11] and abroad. He easily got the hang of the Shushenskoye way of life. By analogy. But life abroad posed a challenge."

"Did Stalin know that Krupskaya knew about the kidnapping?"

"Sure, he had his suspicions," he nodded, loudly slurping the melted ice cream from the second bowl. "He blackmailed her, tried to get her to tell him where I was hiding. 'It turns out that Lenin has a real wife and real children in Sormovo,' Stalin told her, painfully insinuating Ines Armand. 'Either you give us the real Lenin's whereabouts, or the bigamist gets liquidated.' But dear Nadya kept silent like a partisan. He tried especially hard to get her to fess up if Grisha played a part in my kidnapping."

"What Grisha?"

"Grigory Zinoviev."[12]

---

10 Nadezhda Krupskaya (1869–1939) was Lenin's wife and comrade.

11 A settlement in central Russia where Lenin spent his exile from 1897 to 1900.

12 Grigory Zinoviev (1883–1936), born Hirsch Apfelbaum, was one of the seven members, alongside Lenin, Stalin, and Trotsky, of the original politburo. Stalin had him executed after a show trial in 1936, which marked the beginning of the Terror.

"Wait, he took part in the kidnapping?"

"He knew about it, but he didn't participate."

"What about Kamenev?"[13]

"He knew about it and took part. We couldn't have done it without his technical expertise."

"What about Trotsky?"

"No, no, and no! I never trusted him. He was a talented man, but he wasn't one of us."

"What were you doing in Germany, then?"

"I was buried in work. On one hand, I was preparing encoded instructions for my Sormovo double. On the other hand, after the squashed rebellion, I was preparing Germany's working class to assume power peacefully. Don't be surprised. The situation was exceedingly difficult. Only two people knew that I was Lenin. For my German comrades I was a Russian revolutionary from the Lenin school in Longjumeau.[14] It was a tragedy worthy of Shakespeare!

"The real Lenin is teaching his German comrades that the new conditions of the Weimar Republic allow for a peaceful path to power by allying with the social democrats. But they're telling me, 'Nein, Lenin taught us to hate the social democrats!' I tell them: 'Lenin changes in accordance with the dialectic!' And they shoot back: 'Nein, nein, Lenin never changes!' And so while we were arguing, Hitler took power.

"After Hitler assumed power, a communist German scientist used Einstein's formula to freeze me until a new revolutionary surge. They kept me in Hamburg in a safe house ..."

He suddenly stopped, looked at me with his bright-eyed gaze, and said:

"Aren't you a congressman? You could help me find an empty apartment! You could pretend to be helping my old mother, she lives in a communal apartment. I need a safe house."

"No," I said firmly. "The local councils should be in charge of that."

I had gotten burned offering that kind of help before. A woman had come to my home once, complaining about her living situation. She had a kid who was thoroughly worn out by sleepless nights spent wherever they could

---

13 Lev Kamenev (1883–1936), born Lev Rozenfeld, was also one of the seven members of the original politburo. Stalin had him executed alongside Zinoviev.

14 A Parisian suburb where Lenin opened a school in 1911 that was intended to train Party functionaries.

lie down peacefully. It turned out she came up from the country often and stayed in the city for long periods of time, lugging her kid and her complaints around various government offices. The city council took away one of the rooms in her apartment because they decided she hadn't obtained it by the most legal of means. I did everything that I could for her. I contacted her town council, wrote a letter to the Supreme Soviet; they sent a committee to her town. But nothing helped. Either her efforts didn't have a solid enough legal foundation, or it was just the usual red tape.

But she demanded that I organize a meeting with the chair of the Supreme Soviet. I obviously couldn't do that and denied her request. At that, she suddenly started calling me just about every day and would shout monstrous obscenities over the phone.

I got tired of these phone calls and told an acquaintance who worked somewhere in the administration about them. He gave me the phone of a police service that ostensibly dealt with problems like this. I called them and, without naming the woman, told them about the invasive phone calls. The person I was talking to became so rapaciously interested in the situation that I backpedaled. I pitied the woman—she was probably just ill. I said that it probably wasn't worth dealing with yet, but that if she called again, I'd contact him.

And suddenly those vile phone calls that had gone on for more than a month magically stopped. What was I supposed to think? That it was a coincidence? Or did someone who knew about my conversation say to her: "Enough?"

"Hitler looked for me all over Germany and couldn't find me," my companion went on. "And after the war, Stalin searched for me by pretending to search for Hitler's corpse, but didn't find me either and warded himself off with the Berlin Wall . . ."

The magenta shirt came up to us again. This time, apologizing for interrupting us, he looked at us both, and I felt that the radius of mockery had grown wider.

"Forgive me for interrupting your scientific discussion," he said, "but we students are curious as to what Lenin was doing on March 9th, 1909."

"Equally topical!" my companion exclaimed happily and waved his hand, as if to say that you could point at any day in Lenin's life, and it would always be full of imminent significance. "That day, Lenin wrote a letter to his older sister Anna Ilyinichna. He had recently come to Paris from Nice, where he had had a relaxing vacation, which rarely happened to him.

His sister was the editor of his book *Materialism and Empirio-Criticism*, which was being published by *Krumbugel*. Even then Lenin already fought against sacerdotalism and asked his sister not to soften his attacks against Bogdanov and Lunacharsky.

"But then, the sacerdotalism flooded our press. A former Bolshevik had just recently been shown on TV standing in front of a church holding a candle like a halfwit. And he wasn't just a rank-and-file Bolshevik. Let me ask you, if you're a Bolshevik, what do you need a church for? And if you're one of the faithful, then what kind of Bolshevik are you? It's apples and oranges. Though, on the other hand, the reason our ideological orchard is so full of apples is because all the oranges went over the hill and far away. But don't you worry! They'll be back! We'll weed out the bad apples, we'll mercilessly weed them out! You tell your friends!"

"I will, thank you."

He turned around and went back to his friends, trying to keep a steady pace. His friends were already convulsing in fits of laughter.

It suddenly dawned on me to ask my companion to explain his presence in our little southern town.

"Tell me," I said, "after being frozen, you show up in this town, and this takes nobody by surprise: how did you get here? Who are you? Where did you come from?"

"You mean how am I registered?" he asked and laughed. "Registration isn't an obstacle for somebody who's lying low. The fee here is five thousand rubles."

"No, no, not your registration," I said, trying to be as clear as possible, "You're new here, but everybody treats you like an old-timer."

"Oh, that's easy," he said, surprised at my surprise. "Stepan Timofeyevich was and still is a real person, and I'm here in his stead. He's frozen now."

"Ok, but even if others accept you as Stepan Timofeyevich, his mother couldn't have made that mistake, right?" I asked, sensing that I was getting drawn deeper into his madness and was already going in circles.

He sat back and again gave that childlike laugh Lenin was famous for. Having laughed it out, he wiped his tears away with a fist and said:

"There's no mother! My senior secretary is living with me and posing as his mother. She's ninety-six—she was twenty and change back then.

She had her own little drama. That banshee Kollontai[15] had stolen her beloved from her. She used to cry on my shoulder. But what could I do? I summoned Kollontai and talked to her. But being the iron bitch that she was, she said, 'The revolution has no bearing on personal life. If you bring this issue up in the politburo, I'll answer in kind! Why did you leave Ines Armand after the revolution? That's not very chivalrous.'

"How could I explain to her that the chair of the Council of People's Commissars isn't just some émigré revolutionary? The whole world is looking at him—a world that is still too bourgeois to understand the new, revolutionary morality. 'Alright, go on,' I told her. What could I do? I had to make a detestable truce with Kollontai.

"I sometimes remind my old lady about those glory days and she, poor soul, quietly sobs and wails: 'Dear little Styopa, what did the Bolsheviks do to you? Why did I let you go to the institute? Why did I go nights without sleeping, laundering for the neighbors? Curse your history teacher! He said "Styopa has an extraordinary memory. He'll be a great scholar." Where did your memory go, my boy? What did the Bolsheviks do to you?'

"'Not the Bolsheviks, mom' I say. 'The Thermidor. Wait until we win. Soon. Stalin will get what's coming to him, and Kollontai too. I'll write an article about Kollontai's mistakes.'

"But she just puts her head in her hands and weeps:

"'Oh, my little boy, what did the Bolsheviks do to you!'

"And finally I lose my temper.

"'Mommy dear, let's not confuse the Bolsheviks with the Thermidor. That's a gross error. And mommy dear, you're not my dear mommy. My mother has long been resting in the Volkov cemetery in Leningrad!'

"'It would be better if I were resting in the Volkov cemetery,' she wails, 'and she was here and saw all this.'"

"Ok," I said, trying to interrupt him. "But where's Stepan Timofeyevich's real mother?"

15　Alexandra Kollontai (1872–1952) was a Menshevik-turned-Bolshevik with whom Lenin would have political spats.

"She's frozen," he said cheerfully and added: "As soon as we win, we'll thaw out Stepan Timofeyevich and give him the Order of Lenin. He deserves it."

"What about his mother?" I asked.

"It wouldn't be economical to thaw out his mother," he said, spreading his arms. "She's almost eighty-five."

Afraid that he would begin divulging less-than-savory details about the freezing process, I figured I'd get the conversation back on track.

"So, after Kaplan's assassination attempt and until your death in Gorki, you weren't running the country?"

"No, of course not, but it was run according to my instructions. My double did do a little improvising, but he was generally headed in the right direction as far as the NEP[16] was concerned . . ."

I couldn't take it anymore. "You know, you could at least keep quiet about the NEP. Is that really the reform of a great government official? It's like if a shepherd comes into his sheep pen, sees the sheep huddling in one corner with the wolves in another, and says: 'My dear wolves, you shouldn't be eating the sheep. It's much more advantageous to shear them, sell the wool, and buy meat. The NEP is here to stay.' But as soon as he leaves, the wolves slaughter the sheep. What do they need wool for? There's easy, juicy meat right in front of them. A truly great government official is great because he creates laws and methods of management that can't be easily undone."

Throughout my speech, he listened to me, nodding rewardingly, sometimes inclining his head as if to help me get a bit closer to the truth. What's amazing is that his rewarding nods actually did help me formulate what I wanted to say, even though my words were directed against him.

"You're right on the money with the wolves and sheep," he said. "Let me write that down. I'll use that analogy in my very first report after the coup. Especially since I agree with it."

He whipped out the mechanical pen clipped to his collar, took a notepad out of his pocket, and quickly started jotting something down. I felt that I was getting very tired of him and poured more cognac. He shut the notepad with a concise snap, put it back in his pocket, and fixed the pen onto his shirt. We drank without clinking glasses.

---

16 NEP—Lenin's New Economic Policy, which intended to create a mixed economy that allowed limited private enterprise.

"Wolves," he said suddenly and morosely, putting his glass on the table. "But how can you take power without wolves? My instructions were constantly bungled—my encoder in Germany would make a mistake, or the decoder in Moscow would be arrested . . . Only, for the love of God, don't say anything about collectivization, the famine, 1937 . . . I'm tired of talking about it all. I can show you documents with Ernst Thälmann's[17] signature testifying to the fact that I was frozen at the time and knew nothing about any of it . . . Do you know where Stalin is right now?"

"What do you mean, where?" I said. "In a grave next to the Kremlin wall, where they moved him from the Mausoleum where he lay next to Lenin . . ."

I fell silent and looked at him, grasping the slight awkwardness and even tactlessness of what I said, given the context. He immediately understood why I stopped talking and burst out laughing with that childlike laugh Lenin was famous for.

"My dear man, you know nothing!" he managed to get out, beaming, his eyes twinkling. "He never lay in the Mausoleum with Lenin or without Lenin, especially since Lenin himself was never there. I couldn't be in the Mausoleum and frozen in Hamburg at the same time, could I? It's absurd! The man lying there is that same comrade from Sormovo. And Stalin himself put him there. As for Stalin, he's in the Pentagon right now . . ."

"In the Pentagon?" Clearly, I was missing something.

"In deep freeze," he said. "But when America needs to, they'll thaw him out, maybe even do some plastic surgery, and let him loose here if our revolt succeeds. And it's destined to succeed. The fight will be unbelievable. I'll clash with him one last time and have my revenge."

With that, he lowered his gaze and took out an ancient silver pocket watch. He clicked open the lid, making the reflected sunlight bounce off the table, and checked the time. He then clicked it shut and put the watch away.

"I need to make a phone call on that very subject right now," he said. "Then I'll tell you how Stalin fled from Beria to Franco, and how he was frozen there. Wait here and remember that you're one of us. You'll still be useful to our proletarian cause."

"I am so lost right now," I said and shivered, feeling a creeping chill I couldn't quite place.

---

17 Ernst Thälmann (1886–1944) was the leader of the Communist Party of Germany during the Weimar Republic.

"If you rush with words, you'll be late with deeds," he said mysteriously, swiftly got up, and headed for the exit, the striped shirt rippling in the sun.

* * *

His thick, muscular back, tightly straining against his shirt, was decisively getting farther and farther away. Looking at him, I thought: the world is fueled by the energy of madmen.

But if the world is somehow still alive, then there's got to be another energy, another comprehension of human nature. Possibly the most amazing thing of all is that in the teachings of Christ, comprehension of human nature is high, but not exaggerated.

Preachers can preach whatever they like, but I think that Christ came up with his teachings as a man, and not as a God. There is nothing in his teachings that couldn't be confirmed by human experience. If there was anything godlike in his teachings, it's the precision of his comprehension of man's actual capabilities.

It would be odd and inconsistent if he, the Son of God, accepted death as a man, and if the teachings that he left humanity were the result of divine enlightenment. It's because he based his teachings on a foundation of experience that may have been genius, but still human, that he accepted death as a man—unwillingly, languishing spiritually, grieving.

To employ the methods of the Ancient Greeks, let's imagine this is what happened. God said to his son:

"You know, I've stopped understanding humans. One idiot of a fisherman can tangle the fishing line so badly that ten smart fishermen won't be able to untangle it. Go to the humans and walk the human path as a man. Teach them a lesson and return to me. But if even that doesn't help them, I'm closing down shop."

It seems like Christ's deeds would have been much more convincing if he were born a man, but forgot that he was God, leading the people to learn about it only after his resurrection. But it only seems that way.

If Christ didn't know that he was Jesus Christ, then not only would he not have died heroically, the Strong would not have heroically condescended to the Weak in order to help them restore their strength of spirit. It's a lesson in patience and love, especially since we understand that given the exceeding stupidity of his students, he could've interrupted his lesson at any point and left humanity to fend for itself. But he didn't—instead, they interrupted him.

Mankind really doesn't like to condescend. And the more stubbornly it clambers upwards, tearing its knees on the mountainside, the less willingly it condescends to those that are still below. But the stronger mankind is, the more easily it scales those heights, the more easily it condescends to the weak. We can judge man's true measure by the facility with which he condescends to the weak.

Despite its ostensible simplicity, Christ's teachings deftly account for the nature of man, lending him a hand when he falls and restraining him from vanity when he rises.

Man walks through life predominantly by taking guidance either from pangs of conscience or from utilitarian logic, no matter how broadly it's implemented.

Pangs of conscience slow life down, they force you to retreat, to zigzag down the road of life. But it's a real life, one without deception and self-deception, where slow and steady wins the race.

Someone who primarily takes guidance from utilitarian logic isn't inclined to pay attention to pangs of conscience. And it's worth noting that the more beneficiaries this utilitarian logic tries to service—for example, let's say it's ostensibly for the good of all mankind—the duller are the pangs of conscience. Someone who takes guidance from utilitarian logic sees clear, arrow-like road signs, without once suspecting that they're cunningly outstretched snakes, capable only of leading them to a snake pit.

A rationalistic organization of society is the same utilitarian logic spread wide. It always boils down to the idea that before you can bring someone up, you first have to step on them.

But if a rationalistic model of society boils down to the idea that you have to step on someone, then isn't the very desire to step on someone already subconsciously there? And isn't the rest of the model of a reasoning society the pseudo-scientific justification for that desire?

In her remarkably dull recollections about Lenin, Krupskaya recounts the following. Exile in Siberia. Lenin, ever a gambler at heart, entertains himself by going hunting. The Yenisei River in the fall. It's hailing quietly. Lenin and a fellow exile are taking a boat out to a little island which is full of stranded, white-furred hares. They shoot at the hares. The hares run around the island. They have nowhere to go. They dart back and forth like sheep, as Krupskaya writes innocently. This means that the island must have been *very* small, because hares and sheep run very differently. But in this situation, the hares aimlessly run around, condemned to die, just like sheep. Hence the comparison.

The hunters shoot at the hares relentlessly. They pack their boat full of hares, as Krupskaya writes. You can tell that this happens often. So it wasn't an accident that Lenin went nuts after seeing an armada of hares. Let's keep this in mind.

Any hunt assumes that the hunter has a chance to kill his prey. And there's also a chance that the prey can fly or run away. In this case, the hares didn't have such a chance. It was a slaughter. A prototype of the Russia that was to come.

Vladimir Ulyanov was a nobleman. An educated man. We can't really say that he knew not what he did. We see, more or less, a complete Lenin. The essential Lenin.

But when did he become himself? I have a hard time thinking that once he hit a certain reflective age, he never noticed how he would often get carried away. Not necessarily externally, like with these hares, but internally. After cooling down, he had to have felt revulsion, if not from his actions—he might not have done anything yet—then from his scornful or even baleful thoughts about somebody or other.

At the same time, being incredibly conceited, he couldn't fail to notice that he was much more talented than many others in school. This gave him wings and consoled him. Occasionally, maybe already suffering from his future temperament, he would attempt to draw a parallel between his talent and his scorn for people and, in doing so, justify it. He probably had this desire, but he couldn't completely smooth out its contradictory nature. The upbringing he got from his family got in the way.

Marx's teachings had to have astounded him. They must have led to a veritable eruption of gleeful self-justification! From that point on, until the end of his days, he would gratefully and zealously serve the liberator of his conscience.

If the history of mankind is a class struggle and the harmonious society of the future is the result of the proletariat's victory over the bourgeoisie, then what kind of eternal or panhuman morality can there possibly be? It'll just be one giant fight! That's why your hands were always itching to smack someone on the head! It's the biological endowment of a natural revolutionary.

In the desert of history, the caravan of mankind must reach the oasis of socialism. But the caravan has every right to split up, make stops, turn aside.

What's necessary is a good teamster with a firm whip. Lenin decided that he would be the great caravan teamster! Leave your conscience behind and never look back! I know what to do, when to do it, and where to do it! That's what his writings and speeches all scream about.

The sad fate of Alexander, his executed older brother, makes us forget that he was a man who was cold-bloodedly and methodically planning to kill the tsar. He was a murderer who accidentally didn't see his plan through.

Rather than guess, like my Chegemites, whether Lenin was seeking vengeance for his brother, it's much more realistic to assume that they had a similar temperament. It's no wonder that they were such avid chess players and were so overjoyed when they surpassed their father in skill.

What I call the comprehension of mankind granted by nature or ethical hearing leads to a specific kind of consciousness. Just as Hamlet's endless reflection forced out his ability to act decisively, there is an opposite kind of consciousness in which one's readiness to act leaves no room for reflection.

I would call this a criminal's kind of consciousness. Think of Lenin's naïve admiration of the bandit Kamo, of Koba[18] (until he became Stalin and started posing a threat), of the provocateur Malinovsky,[19] even if he didn't know that he was a provocateur. This all shows his true colors. Mental primitivism and a trigger finger for punishment always enraptured him. This is evident in his letters and notes.

The only thought capable of going through a hardened criminal's mind is how to better rob a bank, but think as he might, it's still not reflection—merely an attempt to master the technology of his scheme. Lenin had a criminal consciousness. Neither his fairly extensive education, nor his grandiose social revolt should blind us to this truth.

Once in my youth, I was astounded by how much a made-up, seventeen-year-old Lenin looked like Pugachev.[20] The same slanting eyes and deep-seated cunning. But back then, I didn't think much about either Lenin or Pugachev. What's most surprising about our history isn't that it was most often ruled by criminals. No, it's that it was occasionally ruled by noble people too.

---

18 "Koba" was one of Stalin's nicknames.
19 Roman Malinovsky (1876–1918) was a Bolshevik politician infamous for being a provocateur.
20 Yemelyan Pugachev (1742–1775) was a Cossack who led the famous but unsuccessful Cossack Rebellion against Catherine II.

* * *

As I thought about Lenin while waiting for his insane counterpart, a pretty young woman with a stroller came into the Amra. She stopped by the entrance, examining the tables. She was clearly looking for someone.

"Boys, look!" said one of the young men. "It's Bocho's wife. If she sees him come back with no one but girls, there'll be hell to pay. Get down, don't let her see you. Maybe she'll leave."

"She already saw us!"

"Zurik, take your shirt off and wave at him, tell him to stay away!"

"He won't understand!"

"Yes he will! He'll understand! Quickly!"

The guy in the magenta shirt half-heartedly stood up, went to the railings, took off his shirt and started waving it around in the air. The woman, wheeling the stroller in front of her, came up to the guys. She stopped at their table, greeted them, and asked:

"Boys, have you seen Bocho?"

"No, why?"

"I need him. He moonlights here sometimes."

"No, he hasn't been here. He's probably moonlighting over on the beach."

The woman sat down in the magenta shirt's seat. He, meanwhile, kept lazily waving his fiery shirt. It was obvious that he didn't buy into the plan's success.

"Natasha, is it true that you and Bocho are opening a coffee shop?" asked one of the guys.

"It is. Daur, get me a coffee."

The guy quietly got up and went to order a coffee.

"My dad gave us money," said the young woman and stretched out her bare, graceful arms to fix something in the stroller. "Bocho is looking for a place to rent. What do you think, will it work?"

"Sure," said both guys. Then one of them added:

"Don't worry, Natasha. If Bocho wants to open a coffee house, all the people here will find their way there. People will pay just to hear his stories. Your husband is the golden boy of the town. You should be proud."

"Sure, but . . ." said the young woman, looking at the stroller, "it's time to get serious. Thirty years old, two kids, and all he can think about are stories."

The guy that went to get the coffee brought back a cup of the steaming drink and carefully put it down in front of the woman.

"Thanks, Daur," said the young woman. She picked up the cup and carefully took a sip. "Our coffee will be better," she said.

The sound of an approaching hydroplane spread through the air. The flame of the shirt being waved around by the guy next to the railings started feverishly flickering back and forth, as if a sudden wind had risen up.

"You'll have the best coffee shop in town!" the guy who had been speaking with her said ardently. He too heard the sound of the approaching hydroplane.

"Best or no, we'll give it a shot," said the young woman and took another sip.

"All of town will only come to your shop!" enthusiastically said the guy who had been speaking with her. "There's no better pick-me-up than just listening to Bocho!"

The sound of the hydroplane grew closer. The fire of the shirt was being hurled back and forth as if by a hurricane.

"He tries too hard to get everyone to like him," the woman said contemplatively. "That's no good either. You have to pay more attention to your family."

The sound of the hydroplane grew louder. The guy waving the shirt now looked as if he was using a fiery brand to beat back a rabid animal. The woman felt something and looked out at the sea. But, apparently deciding that her husband's hydroplane isn't the only one in the wharf, she relocated her gaze back to the stroller.

"All the guys know that Bocho is a faithful husband!" her conversation partner exclaimed. "He doesn't sleep around."

"Oh, he could try," said the young woman fiercely, again paying attention to the noise from the hydroplane, as if directing her words there as well.

The noise from the hydroplane stopped with a screech right at the Amra's wharf. The fiery shirt hung limply and helplessly from the signaler's hand.

"The whole town is proud of your husband!" the guy who was consoling Bocho's wife yelled out desperately.

Bocho's head popped up over the Amra's railings. Not noticing his wife, he happily called out:

"Where my ladies at?"

A few young girls ran up to him. His wife, leaning over the stroller, froze. She was a young panther waiting to pounce. Waiting for the girls to run up to her husband, she let loose and flew in his direction, screaming:

"What ladies, you son of a bitch!"

Sweeping the girls out of her way, she grabbed her husband by the hair and, yelling something, dragged him out onto the restaurant floor. The other guys ran after her. She had already managed to drag him over the railings. She kept shaking him, holding his hair in her fist.

"What are you doing? What're you doing?" he said, sounding bewildered. "I'm working! I'm making money for the kids!"

"'Where my ladies at?'" she screamed, mocking him scornfully, yanking his hair back as if she were trying to scalp him. The guys ran up to them, finally got them separated, and led them back to the table.

Bocho was at a complete loss. His hair was intact, but disheveled.

"I slave the whole day for my family and this is the gratitude that I get," he said, taking a seat.

"Then why do you need 'ladies?'" said his wife, still breathing deeply and looking at him furiously. "What, do they pay more? Are you a pimp?"

"Alright, Natasha, calm down," said the guy that had previously been consoling her.

He took her by the hand and sat her down next to him.

"Listen, the man is thirty years old. He has two kids," she said, sitting, but still seething. "And all he can offer is 'Where my ladies at?'"

"Alright, Natasha, let's drink a cup of coffee and calm down," said the guy that had previously been consoling her. "Are you in any position to be jealous? You're a beauty!"

"That's not the point. I need to go to the clinic, but I can't get the stroller up to the third floor by myself. So I come to find my husband and get 'Where my ladies at' instead."

"Leave the stroller downstairs," said Bocho, already looking around merrily. "You're ruining my business with your behavior."

"'Leave it downstairs,'" she repeated mockingly. "Somebody like you would steal it. Get up, we're leaving."

She stood up suddenly, got a comb out of the stroller, went up to her husband, and started reining in his hair.

"So pretty and yet so jealous," the guy that had previously been consoling her noted plaintively.

"And what are you going on about! 'Pretty,' 'beautiful!'" said Bocho, clearly delighting beneath his wife's comb as if he were taking a hot shower. "You probably asked her out on a date while I wasn't here. Got a date with your friend's wife! Look at that! And to think I was going to trust you to make chebureks[21] at our coffee shop. Somebody who asks his friend's wife out on a date can't be trusted with chebureks."

Everybody laughed.

"If you act like that," said his wife, bringing her combing to a close, "someone might actually take me out. Come on, get up, we don't have time. Ciao, boys."

Bocho got up. He looked into the stroller and said:

"The heir to the best coffee shop in Mukhus. His money's already trickling in, and all he does is sleep."

Bocho took the stroller by the handles, and they left. As soon as they were gone, the guys started laughing at the proud wearer of the magenta shirt.

"Bocho is flying in on a hydroplane and you're waving your shirt around. Like a matador," said Daur.

"What was I supposed to do?" the other guy responded, brushing an invisible speck of dust off his shirt, though he had shaken it out so hard that there couldn't have been a single speck of dust left on it.

"You should've thrown it in the water. Then Bocho would've understood: something terrible's happened since you threw your shirt into the water."

"And what if my shirt had sunk?" asked Zurik.

"We know how to swim," replied Daur. "Or we'd call a scuba diver."

"The current could've carried it away," shot back the proud owner of the shirt with mock seriousness and brushed off another invisible speck of dust.

---

21 Chebureks are a staple of Caucasian cuisine—deep-fried turnovers filled with meat and onions.

2

The Rapier

"For those who are lost in the desert, water distribution becomes most unfair when someone yells: 'I know where there's an oasis! I'll lead you there!'"

I started when I heard the familiar voice. About five meters to my left, two people sat at a table: the artist Andrei Tarkilov and Yura Zvanba, who was known in local intelligentsia[22] and especially in non-intelligentsia circles by the moniker Mystic-Philosopher.

I've already talked about Andrei Tarkilov and his *Trio in Blue Raincoats* in *Sandro from Chegem*. So anybody interested in him can turn to that book. Modesty forbids my spoiling your future reading endeavors with any kind of advertising.

For now, I'd like to tell you about Yuri Alekseyevich (and I won't use his patronymic anymore. We're tight. It's how we do things), and, if possible, where the moniker Mystic-Philosopher came from.

By the way, Yura's father was Abkhazian, and his mother was Kazakh. I point this out to immediately frighten away any lovers of pure blood— hell only knows how many of them have spread throughout this country.

So. I never noticed anything mystical in his philosophical reasoning, although he did like to use that word. He probably earned the nickname not because what he said was too unclear, but because he never really adhered to anything he said.

---

22 In the nineteenth century, when the word first appeared in Russia, the intelligentsia was initially a social layer of intellectuals who were in opposition to the government—a stance that the intelligentsia maintained throughout the Soviet Union. The Russian intelligentsia were marked not only by their educated status, but also by an acute sense of morality and ethical responsibility, and put great stock in decent behavior.

They were sitting at the table, drinking cognac and coffee. Obviously, Yura was the one speaking. Looking at his thin, slightly big-nosed face (by the way, from time to time, he would comically throw his head back, as if demonstrating his superiority over the weight of his horn-rimmed glasses), looking at his slouched figure, shrouded in an old, but imported shirt (a faded symbol of past glory days), looking at all this, especially next to the short, but powerful-looking Andrei Tarkilov, it was difficult to believe that he, Yura, was that same brilliant fencer—a master of the sport since youth—that had triumphantly toured Europe, clearing the way with his rapier. That was so long ago! Now he was a research associate at the institute of ethnography. He makes very little, but he doesn't despair and, as always, has his nose buried in one book or another.

His wife, who had apparently waited patiently for the glint of the rapier to be traded in for the glint of coin, but who had suddenly noticed that after throwing his rapier into the closet, he buried himself even deeper in books, decided that he would never unearth anything that even remotely resembled the glint of coin and abruptly left him for another.

Furiously smacking her stubborn older son and carrying the younger one, they say she left for a man who had, through primitive, but reliable means, attained that elusive glint many times over. He did so gradually, but with increasing speed, rubbing two coins together, which invariably leads to a third joyously leaping out from beneath the lower one. Coins are created just like people, which is why people love them so much. For that matter, this all seems almost like a direct quote from Yura's tale.

We don't know how Yura reacted to his wife leaving him, but on the outside, as an athlete and a philosopher, he held himself stoically. One would even like to think that he held himself then much as he did now—raising his head slightly, overcoming the weight of his large, horn-rimmed glasses, gazing after her, trying to grasp whatever logic lay behind her departure and being surprised at the fact that he couldn't understand that logic, try as he would. That may have been when he said for the first time: "It's a mystery!"—as he couldn't consider the man for whom his wife left him his rival.

That's not only because they were classmates. The thing is, when the other guy was still a boy, he lived very close to Yura's beloved, who had a very strict father—an old Abkhazian duke. And Yura's love notes had to get to her via his classmate.

"I don't get it," Yura would say once the storm had passed. "Why did he spend three years ferrying my love notes over to her if he had such far-reaching plans?"

The question of whether his future rival read his love notes was never raised. But even if he did, how could he divine from them that he could steal her away from Yura after the second child and then, employing the same method that Yura had shown to be rather reliable, add two more of his own? That truly remains a mystery.

Some of Yura's friends say that it's all because of the rapier. If he hadn't tossed it into the closet, but kept on using it, even if only as a trainer, nothing would've happened. The moneyman wouldn't have dared steal her away.

But instead, she told him. Or rather, she probably sent him a note: "The rapier's in the closet"—and he picked up what she was laying down. Maybe, as a rule, a rapier whose tour has ended loses its strength forever. Oh, poor Hamlet!

Speaking of, Yura did look a bit like a cross between a Hamlet who had accidentally survived his duel and a librarian from a large, imposing library. And this hints that Hamlet truly belongs in the royal library, not on the royal throne.

Sometimes, with restrained frustration, Yura would recall his rival's youth. According to Yura, he was already reading Nietzsche as a schoolboy when the other guy, smacking his lips, had only just made his way (and not altogether successfully) to the fairy tales of the Brothers Grimm. The rapier was neither here nor there, Yura said. What rapier could there be when that cornstalk of a ninth grader once almost fainted from being stung by a wasp.

"Wait, what do I mean, 'almost!'" he would angrily correct himself. "He would've fainted if I hadn't held him together!"

"What rapier could there be," Yura would fire himself up, "if when I was already on the Abkhazian fencing team, he had never held anything sharper than a fork!"

However, even if that's true, he had managed to spear quite a few things with his fork. He really is quite wealthy and called himself a businessman long before the Perestroika.

A rapier's strength wanes forever, but Yura got his hands on a gun and called the guy to a duel. Duels in Abkhazia occasionally happen as a transitional, civilized way of settling a blood feud.

The moneyman turned out to be more complicated than one would've thought. After welcoming Yura's second in his estate, he instantly agreed to the duel and asked for a month to take care of his affairs and make sure his kids from a previous marriage would be taken care of in case the result of the duel proved tragic.

He confessed that he had always loved the girl to whom he carried Yura's love notes. But Yura had enthralled her with his rapier while still in school. And her father, the old Abkhazian duke, looked right through him without noticing him. Meanwhile, he took up business right after school and successfully shipped a large batch of laurel leaves to Siberia.

But no, the menacing feudal lord still didn't notice him! In fact, in spite of all his strictness, the menacing feudal lord only took notice of Yura, though, of course, he didn't know about the love notes. He noticed Yura, his heart mellowing as his rapier sent sparks flying, possibly viewing this as a symbol of vassal-like loyalty to the good old blade-centric traditions.

But the years passed. The old feudal lord died and now lies in a little village graveyard. The glint of Yura's rapier faded as the glint of the businessman's coins shone brighter.

"He couldn't turn glory into money," said the businessman. "But I could make glory out of money."

And that's when he explained the bitter offence done to him by Yura. Apparently, wind of him fainting because of a wasp sting had made its way into certain business circles. Apparently, somebody had started spreading the tale. Apparently, someone said that it was dangerous to do business with him. The local attorney need only show him a wasp with a pair of tweezers, even a dead one, and he instantly breaks and sells everybody out.

It was a frivolous tale, but bad for business. How could he, a respectable businessman, tell anyone who'd listen that if faced by such an attorney, he could just grab the tweezers and use those very tweezers to rip out of his wife's ears her diamond earrings, which the attorney would take away even without the tweezers.

And who started the tale? Yura. Even though what had happened in reality? A group of kids from school went out for a picnic. And he drank for the first time in his life. And to make things even better, it was vodka. And he got sick. And then a wasp stung him. And then he got very sick. And that's it! But Yura only talks about the wasp, without bringing up anything that happened before the wasp. Well, if he wants a duel, he'll get a duel! But it should happen in that glen where he got stung by the wasp—he would agree to no other location. But he would need a month to tie up his affairs first.

"I have property," he said helplessly, as if talking about some fatal weight on his soul. "Yura's got it easy. He gives his rapier away to a coal heaver to poke around in the furnace, and all's fine! But I have property to think about!"

Yura agreed to have the duel be in that same glen, gave the businessman a month to prop up his property, and it was probably all for nothing.

Two weeks later, Cheka agents had him in their sights. It's worth noting that they had already been keeping tabs on him. They declared that, according to their sources, he was in the illegal possession of a lethal weapon, and that if he didn't give it up voluntarily, they would be forced to search him and his place of residence.

"The rapier's in the closet," Yura said calmly. "You can have it."

"The gun," the ranking officer corrected him and suddenly sat at his table, as if waiting for Yura to get it, though he may have been just waiting for a conciliatory bite to eat.

The lower-ranking officer went into the kitchen, either to evaluate the stores of provisions and the possibility for a peaceful meal, or to pass through it to the closet, where the gun may have been amicably neighboring with the rapier. Though, all things considered, one didn't exclude the other.

Yura didn't worry about the gun. It was lying on the colorful lampshade hanging in the middle of the room, right above the comfortably seated chief Cheka agent. Yura was certain that none of them would think to shake down the lampshade so that the gun would plop onto the floor. And he was completely right.

But the lowest-ranking officer (there were three of them altogether) went to the bookshelf, as if searching for the book in which he could've hid the gun. During his trips abroad, Yura managed to get his hands on forbidden books, which he would give to reliable friends to read and which he kept in the attic.

But as fate would have it, one of his friends (his second-to-be for the duel) had recently returned Avtorkhanov's *A Study in the Technology of Power*, and Yura, discussing with him the technology of his duel, carelessly put it on the bookshelf, meaning to transfer it to his hidey hole later, but he completely forgot about it.

And now, it wasn't so much standing on the shelf, as much as bodily falling onto the floor and lying at the young Cheka agent's feet, and front cover up, as ill luck would have it.

As soon as Yura noticed this, a chill seeping through him, the young Cheka agent, as if feeling his gaze, looked down at his feet and saw Yura's favorite trophy from all his travels.

And what did he do? Listen carefully. As if examining the books on the shelves, he repositioned himself so as to block the book from the senior Cheka agent's view, and then quietly pushed it under the bookcase with his foot.

Bravo! Bravo! This happened, and we have to be faithful to history. The young Cheka agent turned out to be a true patriot of ours. He had to try to save his famous countryman. In those years, if you got caught with *A Study in the Technology of Power* out in the province, you could get up to five years. Maybe Yura's gloriously representing the Motherland with a rapier could save him three years. But two years in a labor camp isn't a picnic either.

Just as the young Cheka agent moved his philanthropic foot, the other agent that had gone through the kitchen to the closet rushed back in. He was furious and was holding Yura's rapier like some kind of mine detector.

It was unlikely that the cause of his infuriation was his failure to find the gun lying happily next to the rapier, like two old war companions reminiscing about their military conquests. He was most likely infuriated by Yura's empty refrigerator, because he expressively flung out his arms and said:

"Nothing."

At the same time, his hand clutching the rapier handle flew back so carelessly that the tip of the rapier hit the lampshade, which wobbled. Yura hastened to take the rapier away, and decisively placed it in the closest corner, as if by doing so he was making another argument in his case, rather than just hinting at his past achievements.

Hearing his assistant's depressingly short report, the chief agent's expression darkened, and he assumed a much more official pose at the table.

"Search everything, turn the place inside out!" he ordered.

The exhaustive search began with the bookshelves. According to Yura, they used the gun as a pretense to look for illegal books, which they used as a pretense to look for dollars, which, by the way, he would never bring back, exchanging them for books or clothes for his wife.

Yura was sure that they were looking for dollars, because every book that they took from the shelves would be shaken out over the floor, and the two younger agents would virtuously go through this procedure over and over, all in the senior agent's field of view. Such a procedure was clearly superfluous if they were only searching for a gun hidden in a book, rather than searching for dollars hidden between the pages.

When they had shaken out half the books in his library and the dollar bills still hadn't peppered the floor in a criminally beautiful constellation, but the air in the room had filled with pensive, or maybe even wrathful dust shaken awake from old books, the chief started coughing furiously. Growing red in the face, trying to overcome his cough, he roared:

"Search each page individually!"

He must have decided that Yura was gluing each separate dollar to the book pages. The second half of the library was searched on a page-by-page basis. At first, the two agents ponderously leafed through each individual page, but they then quickly grew accustomed to flipping through the pages from front cover to back.

In short, they found neither the dollars, nor the gun, even though the gun was hiding on the colorful lampshade, like Han-Girey on an elevated bed with his nine houris (for the gun held nine rounds).

By the way, according to Yura, the chief agent sometimes looked up at the lampshade, which was a pretty fancy gift from his feudal lord of a father-in-law for their wedding. And these gazes started making Yura slightly nervous, because out of the corner of his eye, made sharper by the looming danger, he noticed that the lampshade was ever so slightly off-center beneath the weight of the gun.

During one of the chief's looks, the lampshade suddenly leaned in his direction, but then changed its mind and re-centered itself. Yura grew uneasy. He couldn't understand what was causing the slight rocking—telepathic signals (whose? The gun's? The agent's?) or the light breeze through the window?

Yura wanted to shut the window to definitively determine what power was forcing the lampshade's pensive rocking, but saw the danger in doing that. The chief might pick up on the cause of his unease. Yura would remember that the agent's strange looks at the lampshade's mysterious rocking were the most uncomfortable moments of the search. Poor Yura! His worry about the looks at the lampshade bear witness to the fact that he's a representative of the generation after mine.

The chief, a man getting on his years, probably just liked that lampshade. And, gazing at it, he nostalgically recalled those idyllic times of Chekism when he could have simply taken the lampshade and left, without even noticing Han-Girey lounging lazily on top of it.

And vice versa. Here in Moscow, during Brezhnev's time, I had happened on another generation of Cheka agents, complete with a psychology that was thoroughly unfamiliar to me.

After we had signed another collective letter defending those who were illegally arrested, someone's patience burst, and I was summoned for a chat in a gloomy little room in an imposing hotel. The chat was long and unpleasant.

You're putting your publisher in a difficult position. Some author comes to him and says that, see, you publish this writer that signs anti-governmental letters, but you don't publish me. You're putting all publishers in a difficult position. They have no defense. They can grow tired of it.

Where did you hear that the hearing was closed? That's nonsense. There wasn't enough room for everyone to fit. And we can't have court hearings in a stadium, now can we?

And finally, the main argument. How is it that you address your letters to the government, but they first make their way to ill-willed radio personalities? I wanted to say that you yourself send them there to have that argument in your back pocket. But I didn't say that. In essence, they could have done that and probably did, but I couldn't prove it.

One of them, considerately demonstrating his knowledge of my body of work, would say every now and then:

"Good old Uncle Sandro wouldn't approve of your actions."

All things considered, his observation was neither foolish nor incorrect. But I shuddered internally when he called him "good old" Uncle Sandro. It was a twisted literary torture technique, but I'm sure that he was aware of that. Which made it all the more powerful.

Seeing as I had imbibed quite a bit not long before this chat (it was coincidental for me, but was it for them?), several times during the conversation I took a glass to the bathroom for a drink of water.

Taking note of my thirst, the representatives of the new, young generation of Cheka agents (there were two of them) asked me several times, even begged me, to let them order dinner and some wine, transparently insinuating that it had no relation to the attempt to deviate me from my views.

"It'll simultaneously help us soften the conversation," the older agent would assure me. "In parallel!"

"Good old Uncle Sandro liked sharing good meals," the other would add cajolingly.

But I wasn't satisfied with either parallel. I knew that any line moving in parallel with that of the security apparatus would sooner or later intersect with it. I repeatedly refused. And this upset them at first, then demeaned them, then sharpened their ideological frustration. The slight threat that they leveled my way at the end of our conversation didn't affect me in the least, and I think that the threat's origin wasn't so much ideological as it was gastronomical. The thing I was most afraid of was that if the younger guy said, "In your place, good old Uncle Sandro . . ." one more time, I would drop to the floor. And then scientists would have to divine the new, diabolical weapon used by the Cheka, who can apparently blow a dart at the departing victim's retreating back and instantly cause brain spasms. But, thank God, he didn't say anything.

The fact that they simply wanted to have dinner and wine at the Cheka's expense was obvious to me even then. But I did have the following thought just now. Let's try to work through it.

I left, leaving them alone in the room. Could they then have pretended that there were still three of us and ordered dinner and wine anyway? Is the dinner's opulence dependent on their guest's budget? I'd like to think that I represented a fairly serious budget. In which case they must have been even more loathe to let such a dinner pass them by.

So what can they do? Those hotel rooms are indisputably bugged, with someone listening in. And the listeners probably don't answer to them. They too are being listened in on. But such a repetitive temptation would of course inspire a resourceful and perceptive Russian citizen find a way to get his hands on a free dinner.

Here's my theory. Keeping in mind that the tape is recording everything they say, one of them approaches the door, opens it, and bangs it shut. Turns out their guest came back. The second agent says, "Come in, come in, don't be shy! Let's sit, chat a little, have some dinner. We're all people, we're all patriots, thank God. I knew you'd come back. Here, have a seat, here's today's newspaper. I'll go get some dinner."

He orders some dinner by phone. The snitch of a waitress brings dinner for three. She sets the table. For now, the missing third person isn't suspicious. Especially since the water's running in the empty bathroom. It couldn't be the shower. That would be too much. But a confident stream from the sink will do the trick. Clearly, their guest is washing his hands in anticipation of sullying his soul, hoping that he'll be able to clean it just as he can his hands. Hence the powerful stream! More cheerfulness!

And then? The tape recorder is on. Where's their guest? At first, his silence can be explained by his ravenous appetite. He's nobly allowing himself to be ridiculed. He worried so much, that he came without having any breakfast. How many times can you keep saying that these are different times, a different Cheka? Can't you at least clink glasses while I'm eating? We then hear the savory clink of glasses. It's possible they'd risk imitating their guest trying to speak with a full mouth. Alright, alright, go ahead and eat. That piece there has your name written all over it. More clinking, more clinking . . . But how long can this last? A scandal is brewing. Your prolonged silence is quite strange. Could it be that he's spiting us? The gall! He comes here, gorges himself, drinks himself half to death, and refuses to say a word. What? You're leaving? Silently? Well I never!

This is followed by a more emotional, but equally indistinct, threat than the first one. The door slams. The last thing recorded caught by the tape: "He ruined everything, the bastard!"

But the con needs to be executed perfectly. The third plate is suspiciously untouched. And the snitch of a waitress is going to show up any minute now. They eliminate the third plate. Obviously, they engage the third pair of utensils. Oh right, they almost forgot—the third wine glass is emptied. Sure, you could pretend that the guest left without finishing his last glass. But these days, people like that are suspicious, so there's no need to take any chances. Finally, the cherry on top is the crumpled up third napkin thrown next to the invisible guest's plate with artistic carelessness. Now it should go off without a hitch.

Incidentally, the reader can come up with his own version of events. On one condition—the guest's silence needs to be realistic in all scenarios. Scenarios can be sent to our publisher. The best scenario will earn a reward determined by the publisher's financial situation, which, quite frankly, is catastrophic. In fact, never mind. The scenario that they choked the guest to death and then had dinner interspersed with realistic shouts, groans, and moans will be declined without further examination on the grounds that it is unrefined and smacks too much of the early Socialist period.

However, we've gotten off track. We've gotten off track because the search wasn't very fruitful. And the reader knows full well that there is nothing more boring than a fruitless search. Especially if the fruitless search is offensive to the government. Which is why when they went to search something, farsighted Cheka agents would often bring with them the damning evidence that they had to find in the possession of whomever they had to take down. But this time they screwed up thanks to the range of their scheme: a gun, books, dollar bills. By throwing the net so wide, they were confident that they'd get *something.* And they could have quite easily caught the aforementioned book, but here it turned out that there was disunity within their own ranks. The search dragged on so long that Yura was considering digging around in the folds of the old coat and suit he used to wear while abroad. Maybe he could find some cents, centimes, or pfennigs, or pesets at least that were still there after all that time. He could get them and give them to the agents so that they'd leave. They couldn't put him away for such a minor crime, but they could slap him on the wrist with the sense of a job well done. However, he decided against it and did the right thing, because back then, the government was still proud enough to consider such an act of conscience as a covert form of charity.

"Do you at least have any Borjomi?" the senior agent finally implored, dispirited by the abundance of bleak impressions. But it turned out there wasn't any Borjomi either, and he turned down the plain water Yura offered, probably because of complex, subordinate reasons. In short, failing to find anything, his guests went home empty-handed.

Yura got out from under the bookcase Avtorkhanov's *A Study of the Technology of Power*, blew off the comradely dust from the agent's shoe, hugged the book to his chest (he loved it dearly at the time), and set about dealing with his library.

"If not for the lampshade," Yura said, "I would have forced them to put every book back where they got it. But the lampshade was acting strange. I couldn't risk it. I had a duel to think about."

. . . It was spring. There was ubiquitous warbling, from swallows up above and rivers down below. The cool flame of purple wisterias stretched out towards the wooden balconies lining the houses. Mimosas bent under the fluffy, virginal weight of their feathery gold.

The rejuvenating verdant hills played host to inquisitive snowdrops, reaching out, seemingly asking: "Where's the snow? Where's the snow?" as they had never seen snow before. And then there were violets, forgotten by the poets of our time, the violets of Flaubert, guarding the charm of women of centuries long past, bloomed, casting their eyes towards the ground.

Meanwhile, hundreds of pomegranate trees constellated the orchards. And it felt like their furious, wet, crimson stars were a second away from bursting, from exploding into God knows how many pieces! Right onto the delicately albescent cherry plum! Where, oh where is its latent, ripe acidity coming from?! Right into the direction of the pink cloud of flowering peach trees, colloquially called "angel's breath." Or else their scarlet buckshot will fall right on a careless dove! Worry not, little dove, you'll hatch a valiant, redheaded hawk, he'll protect you! . . . And in the meantime, or maybe even because of . . .

Invited guests were gathering for the duel. There weren't many of them, but there were some. One Volga and two Mercedes from the businessman's side, while a Moskvich and two Zhiguli[23] marked Yura's supporters.

The cars raced on, scraping the asphalt because of their speed, at times overtaking each other and meekly ceding way to the other cars, as if superstitiously obeying the command of some mysterious apparition, some sign from above that signaled that the faster driver must outstrip the other, only to then cede the way to the other driver once *he* got the signal from above to put pedal to the metal, which he would then do, urging his car onwards.

These were all friends of the duelists. They had put in herculean efforts to keep them from dueling, but once they failed to do so, they decided that they, and only they, deserved to witness the spectacle—as compensation for their wearisome attempts.

The cars, speed holding steady, descended under a bridge in the Gumistinsky Preserve and stopped in the green floodplain, which once hosted the ill-fated picnic and where a lone wasp sting proved to be imbued with such long-lasting venom.

The cars stopped, and everyone but the duelists poured out onto the glen, delightfully shifting around, squinting at the glint of the river, and guiltily relishing the fact that they weren't in harm's way and that they could stomp around the dear earth (say what you will) for a long time still. Only one among their number anxiously looked first at his watch, then at the bridge, and back. Why he was so anxious and kept looking at the bridge will soon become clear.

What's interesting is that everybody poured out onto the glen except for the duelists. Like Abkhazian grooms, who traditionally never show up to their own weddings, instead lurking somewhere nearby, the duelists stayed in their cars for the time being. It was as if they had sworn never again to step on the earth to experience the commotion of life, but would only set foot on it to tread the shortest possible path to the ritual of death.

---

23 The Zhiguli and Moskvich were car models made in the Soviet Union from 1970 to 1988 and from 1946 to 1991 respectively.

As the reader can easily surmise, Yura had his share of romantic leanings. Which is why Yura's second stood among the guests, holding his rapier, like a newly arrived Shakespearean land surveyor on his way to the spadesman. Yura remembered what the businessman said about how he failed to make money out of glory, while his rival turned money into glory. Well, it was to be an instrument of selfless glory that would measure the distance between the two adversaries. The businessman didn't argue when Yura determined the distance to be twelve lengths of the blade.

At this moment, Yura's second was throwing glances at the rival's second, who, in turn, threw glances at the car that held the businessman, who was pointing out the window, yelling out where exactly the wasp had stung him. Yura, observing everything from his own car, smiled venomously.

After extensive elaborations, the location of the wasp sting was identified, if, that is, we are to believe him who was stung. Yura's second carefully began measuring out with the rapier the distance at which the rivals were to duel.

When the hilt of the rapier connected with the earth on the spot where the sting happened, the guests crowded around it, peering into the grass, as if trying to find some trace of what had happened, maybe the remains of the fateful wasp. However, failing to find any trace, they accompanied the second, bending and following the careful flips of the rapier with their eyes, evaluating them to ensure that the accuracy of the distance was unimpeachable. And it was entirely unclear which of the duelists would be aided or harmed if the distance was not perfectly exact.

In short, the whole company was so caught up in this activity that they didn't notice how a beat up little village bus descended, tripping and wobbling, into the flood plain, and only when, stuttering and rattling, it stopped nearby did they turn around.

The door of the bus flung open and out spilled a gaggle of old men, like beans from an especially dried out pod. They were all ceremonially dressed in chokhas and sheepskin hats, and daggers glinted on every single man's belt. They looked like some kind of centenarian choir that was preparing to be filmed by a visiting film crew.

As it turned out, the rather vociferous choir was headed by Yura's grandfather, who lived in the village Lykhna. The band of elders, yelling fiercely and rhetorically grabbing their daggers (pretty dangerous rhetoric), threw themselves at the crowd, searching for the duelists and failing to find them, and growing even more furious because of it, as if they suspected that the worst had already happened and they were too late.

The duelists were forced to exit their cars and, heads hung in shame, they approached the elders. But then, either because he was overjoyed that they were still alive or because he was unable to bridle his fury, one old man looked at Yura's second, who was leaning on the rapier, and interpreting his pose as a call for the bloodshed to commence, yelled: "This rattle-brain is to blame!" and threw himself at him. He grabbed the rapier and managed to smack the completely innocent second several times on the backside. The second tried to elude him, doing everything in his power to hide his backside and trying to convey to everyone that out of respect for the elder's age, he simply cannot turn his back to him and is thus forced to hop around.

And that is when something completely unexpected happened. It turns out that the mocking manner in which the second hid his backside, trying to pass it off as respect, reminded one of the elders that the guy was his very own great-nephew, who, as a little boy, would try to dodge his great-uncle the very same way.

"Who do you think you're lifting your hand against!" yelled the old man, offended by familial extension, and, drawing his dagger, rushed to defend his little boy.

The elder, so inopportunely pursuing the second's mocking backside, was forced to defend himself against the dagger with the rapier. The old men managed to cross blades a few times in their extraordinary one-on-one, but then the other elders rushed in and separated them.

Such a deafening clamor rose up that the driver of the village bus, who had prudently kept his seat, turned on the engine, as if sensing that things could devolve into a bloodbath at any moment and readying himself to either warn the police or simply to retreat back to his village so as to have plausible deniability.

Hearing the treacherous stutter of the engine, the elders instantly quieted down, scared to death that they would have to trudge all the way home on foot. Ever since our elders were denied their horses, they developed a superstitious dependence on the engine.

Needless to say, they immediately shut up and turned around to look at the chauffeur. The chauffeur imperiously kept the engine running for a little bit more, giving them a chance to cool off. Then he got out, but the engine kept smoking for another five minutes. And the elders kept glancing warily at the billows of foul-smelling smoke, basing their caution on centuries of experience with a campfire that went out, but kept smoking, and would sometimes even come back to life on its own.

The smoke finally died out, at which point the elders quietly and wisely set about their business.

Thank God that the influence of elders is still great in Abkhazia. What they said, how they demonstrated the superior proportions of eternity over the proportions of discord I have no idea. No, let's not get carried away, the adversaries didn't make peace. But at that point in time, it was impossible to proceed with their duel, and any future engagement they could plan was rendered impossible by the comical conclusion of this one.

Poor Yura! To make up for it, he took out his gun and emptied it at a distance of about ten steps into an old tin can lying in the glen. Whether the can was a rusty witness of that bygone picnic or whether it was present at more peaceful lunches on the grass will remain a mystery.

Having emptied his gun, Yura approached his target, bent over without reaching for it, folded his arms behind his back, and coldly examined the result of his marksmanship.

Then he straightened and gestured for his second to come closer. Continuing to examine the can without turning around, Yura took his rapier, hooked the can with the blade, shook it a bit to make sure that it was hooked steadfastly enough, and launched it to land at the feet of the businessman and his friends. One of the businessman's friends picked the can up and counted the holes, trying not to mix up the entry and exit holes.

But nobody understood the far-reaching significance of his fastidiously refusing to pick up the can and of his tossing it away like the perforated stub of a former love. Thankfully, the businessman didn't understand it either.

The elders were shocked by the accuracy of the shots.

"Now you shoot," one of them told the businessman, "and we'll see who the real hero is."

But the businessman merely shrugged contemptuously, letting everyone know that he had already spent too much time on useless things, and silently headed for his car. Everyone got into their cars and went home.

And that is how Yura was left alone in town. His mother and father had died long ago, though his grandpa and large clan of relatives still lived in the village. Yura's ex-wife didn't let his kids see him. The only thing keeping him warm now were books and the little flame of bygone glory.

However, something resembling retribution did catch up with his wife. Their older son, the one who had to get slapped so that he wouldn't dig in his feet on the way to her new husband's house, grew to hate his father-in-law's home after losing his real father.

Some three years later, he ran away from home, bumbled around Russia, and then came in contact with the criminal underworld, and here's where the subject of the rapier comes up again, ruthlessly shattered to the size of a pocket knife. He's under arrest now, living it out in Siberia.

If not for this one circumstance, Yura's story could be considered a sad tale with a just ending. The rapier stood up for its owner.

They say that one evening, Yura lay smoking on a windowsill, gazing out at the street. It was warm, and the windows were open in his first-story apartment.

At that point, a tall, beautiful woman appeared at the end of the street, holding an athletic suitcase in one hand and using her other to tug along a small boy in glasses who was trying to keep up with her, holding with his free hand a rapier whose blade clinked and chinked, plowing the unpaved sidewalk. Clearly, as a result of the stultifying contact the blade was experiencing with the apathetic ground, the blade felt demeaned, like an Arabian racer that was unjustly harnessed to a plow.

The first person to witness this scene was Yura's neighbor, who stopped as if thunderstruck. Obviously, it wasn't the denigrated blade that astounded him. A woman with a suitcase and her glasses-wearing, rapier-dragging little boy were closing in on the home of the glasses-wearing master of fencing.

"Yura, you got guests! They want something!" yelled the dazed neighbor, running up to the window. He managed to run ahead of the woman and figured that there was still time to do something.

Instead of shutting the window and hiding, Yura stretched out on the windowsill, looked out, and calmly waited for the approaching woman. Then he calmly said to the neighbor, who stood thunderstruck yet again:

"I always knew that that woman could stop a train in its tracks!"

In reality, everything was much simpler and more complex. Many years ago, Yura trained a capable young girl and (possibly) accidentally pierced her heart with his rapier. She then moved to Russia, leaving no trace behind. Turns out that in the span of seven years, she managed to marry, have a child, and divorce. The last years, she lived in Kharkiv. There are women who, regardless of whatever fate has in store for them, fall in love only once in their lives. She was one such woman. Her name was Lyusia.

How they found each other I haven't the foggiest. I suspect that she found him. True, they were already writing to one another, and he was waiting for her, but she arrived unannounced.

The story of how a tall, beautiful woman (Yura himself was of average height) had come to Yura's home, her son in tow, who in turn lugged his father's rapier all the way from the train station so that he would recall where he left the blade and acknowledge him as his son—though, after taking one look at the boy, only an scoundrel would refuse to accept fatherhood—this story, accompanied either by Homeric laughter or by sentimental sighs, made its rounds through all of Mukhus.

People would say different things. One time, I heard the following:

"I just want to know one thing. I know for sure that our Yura's little boy is exactly six years old. And the newcomer is also six. How could have made them at the same time?"

"Easy. He flew away, left his rapier there, and flew back."

"Our Yura's become so Russified. They say when he saw her, he said 'She'll stop a train in its tracks.' Why didn't he say: 'She'll stop a horse in its tracks?' That would be more appropriate for us."

"His mother's Kazakh, his wife's a Pole," said another. "What does that make him? Is he one of us or not?"

"His wife's Russian. Let's not get carried away."

"Carried away where?"

"As if you don't know where."

"Yura's boy has kid glasses. They can't break. I remember them. Since first grade, Yura and I . . ."

"Since first grade," a sober-sounding voice mocked him. "I never even saw you in our school. Yura started wearing glasses when he was twenty-five. He read too much. Yura's the pride of us all."

"Yes, but I can't figure out whether he's a patriot or not."

"Yura was thundering through all of Europe with his rapier while the patriotic likes of you were sneaking into the sports stadium without a ticket."

"But why won't he just say, 'Yes, I'm a patriot?'"

Echoes of this gossip sometimes reached Yura, but he would just smile as his wife's face shone with the tired radiance of delayed joy. Additionally, the boy remembered his father so vaguely that he couldn't catch with his thirsting love that which he barely remembered, and so he instantly turned his thirst to Yura and started calling him dad right away, even before Yura got the kid's name down.

The boy's name was Mitya. He did his part in supporting hearsay that pleased him with regard to Yura's fatherhood. Local tricksters took advantage of that, believing that they were using the boy to uncover some great secret.

In these cases, the boy would typically smile, nod, and repeat the same phrase in a well-mannered fashion:

"Yes, everybody finds that we look alike."

In reality, they looked nothing alike. He was a pure-blooded, Russian, blue-eyed little boy. And he wore glasses not because he was nearsighted. He was slightly cross-eyed.

Right, I almost forgot. They say that when Yura's ex-wife found out that he married some woman with a son and that the son called him dad, she summarily caused a scandal for her husband and suddenly allowed Yura to see his natural son.

I doubt that she all of a sudden started worrying about her son's welfare after he had been without his father's care for some years. Much more likely she concluded that if Yura were to devote attention to his own son, he'd spend more time neglecting his stepson. That was the key motivator.

Some two years later, in the summer, when the boy was vacationing with Yura's grandfather, Yura, his wife, our mutual friend who owned a car, and I went to the village.

Everybody went to Yura's grandpa's home to get some wine for our impending escape into the nature, while I stayed in the car, watching local youths play soccer on a nearby lawn. Mitya was with them. He was playing without his glasses. The lawn was humming with heated voices. In Abkhazian valley villages, the kids speak pretty good Russian.

It was one of those charming, August days when nature is in a state of serene, familial joy. The earth was happy with the sky, and the sky was pleased with the earth. And within this joy, unfettered by this joy, quick-footed youths were running around with a ball, kicking it, pounding it with their heads, falling to the ground, and laughing.

"Mitya!" I called from the car. "Come here for a minute!"

He ran over. He was breathing heavily, his eyes aflame.

"Do you like it here?"

"Yeah!" he exclaimed, his good upbringing rearing its head as he resisted the urge to run back to the game.

"Where do you like it better, Kharkiv or here?" I asked for some reason. It's always interesting to find out why somebody is happy. Even if it's a kid— then you get the chance to try and untangle the knot from the very beginning.

"Here!" he yelled, demonstrating even more of his good upbringing by continuing to refuse to run back to the game.

"Why, Mitya?" I asked very seriously. "Only think first . . ."

And he understood me. His eyes grew more serious.

"Because...Because..." he repeated, concentrating on finding the right words. "I got it! Here, everyone is family!"

And he rushed back to the guys, knowing full well that he couldn't have said it better. And that was an instant of joy for me.

Everyone is family! It was so clear. A little boy, who grew up with a lonely mother in a large city where everyone is lonely suddenly found himself in another life, which still hung on to the customs of a patriarchal clan: whichever house the boys play soccer next to, that'll be the one into which they'll be called to have lunch.

* * *

In short, that's the story of our Mystic-Philosopher. Now let's get back to the Amra, where, as the reader will recall, he's sitting at a table together with the artist Andrei Tarkilov.

Aside from a jug of cognac and cups of coffee, the table also held a small bottle of Pepsi-Cola and an unfinished cup of it. Since there was only one cup, I figured that Yura was here with one of his boys and started looking around for him.

There's little Aslan, his son. The tanned kid, wearing a red shirt and imported, blue shorts, stood next to the restaurant's railings, throwing bits of bread to the seagulls flapping about and shrieking moronically.

The gulls, emboldened by their greed, had gone so ballistic that, in urging the boy on, they had just about begun squatting on his head. He yelled, trying to wave them off. The gulls reluctantly retreated, and the boy cackled, pleased with his power over them. His swarthy, muscular legs looked rather comical. Like the shrunken, muscular legs of an Ancient Greek warrior statue. Yura probably trained him along with his stepson.

"For those who are lost in the desert, water distribution becomes most unfair when someone yells: 'I know where there's an oasis! I'll lead you there.' The psychological foundation for the possibility of accepting such unfairness is fairly straightforward," Yura continued. He raised his head, as if demonstrating his superiority over the weight of his large, horn-rimmed glasses. And then, noticing me, he stopped for a moment. He nodded at me in greeting and invited me to join them by gesturing at their table.

"I'm waiting," I said curtly so as to preempt repeat invitations.

"Got it," Yura nodded. "The Messiah's coming."

His sarcasm flowed strong, but it wasn't clear if he knew whom I was waiting for. It wasn't the first time that day that Andrei and I had already seen each other. He winked at me with the eye that was farther away from Yura. It signaled: we were probably going to hear quite a few outlandish things today, but we didn't have to take everything seriously.

I hadn't seen him in many years, though he lives in Moscow now. He is well known. He is invited to tour in many countries. He's got the same serious gaze beneath his heavyset lids, the same strong, combative face, though the face had grown pallid and unhealthy: something had taken its toll on him—either life in Moscow or his incessant travels, together with his familiarity with many different drinks, or his constant back-breaking work in the poisonous workshop air. He was wearing a fashionable blue shirt, an earthly sign of latent success, which parodically enveloped his too-strong shoulders and too-bitter fate—at least for those who knew about it.

"A tribe that is lost in the desert quickly comes to terms with the unfair distribution of water to the benefit of whomever proposes to take them to an oasis," Yura continued. "The significance of the promise outweighs the unfairness. You can rob somebody for a whole lot if you promise him the world. Everybody thinks: we'll get to the oasis, we'll drink our fill, and then there'll be equality in plenty.

"The most monstrous kinds of inequality use as a foundation the chimerical possibility of total equality. We'll leave equality before the law. That's bourgeois law, that's obvious."

He raised his head, again demonstrating his superiority over the weight of his glasses, and he looked at me, as if asking: are you happy that I left in equality before the law? But know, there won't any other kind of equality.

"But this kind of equality has been and continues to be negated within the folds of history," he kept going. "Mankind's dream of everybody being equal to everybody else is ineradicable. What's tragic is that mankind cognizes this religious instinct on an everyday level. The desire is ineradicable, but we have to eradicate it! It's a mystery!

"In the best moments of his life, a normal person truly wants everyone to be happy, himself included, of course. He wants the kind of life where he wouldn't burn up from envy for the lives of others, and where others wouldn't envy him.

"And is that bad? That's beautiful, but that beauty can feasibly transform into something horrifying. If a person doesn't have this desire at all, then he's a scumbag. But if he tries to insert this desire into real life with the help of some outrageously glorious theory, then he's a monster. Another mystery! Take a step to the right, he's a scumbag. A step to left, and he's a monster.

"Why is he a scumbag? Because he doesn't care for his fellow man. Why a monster? Because he tries to resolve people's fates for them, fates that he should have no power over. A man's fate is resolvable independently of principle, only by virtue of one's own will to do good. It always hinges on somebody's own will. I personally willed to give something of mine away, and I did . . ."

It was then that a large group of tourists headed by a tour guide came up to the top floor of the Amra. While the tour guide told the story of how the restaurant came to be on the wharf, trying to make odd, Venetian parallels, the tourists listened to him suspiciously, simultaneously looking around to see what they could buy in the restaurant. But there was little enough that caught their eye.

Two or three tourists went to halfheartedly order some ice cream . . . And then it was as if a clarion call rippled through them: it's the last day to get ice cream in the whole country! And everybody rushed to form an efficient line. The tour guide, pretending not to notice the heartless indifference to his Venetian pathos, went up to the barista as if it had been his plan all along to get his hands on some Turkish coffee, which he summarily ordered.

Turning to look at the sudden ruckus, little Aslan threw the rest of the bread overboard. The gulls plummeted after it. Quickly shuffling his comical, muscular legs, the boy ran to his father.

"Dad, get me some ice cream! I want ice cream!"

"Ice cream?" his dad asked, coming to. Then he turned around tautly, as if he were in a saddle, and suspiciously examined the ice cream line, struggling to make sense of it. "Where did they all come from?" He sounded surprised. "Hold on for a minute. I'll get some once they're gone."

"I want it now!" the boy shouted.

"You'll wait," his dad responded. "Here, finish your Pepsi."

"I don't want it," said the boy, but then he unexpectedly brought the cup to his lips and started blowing into it evenly, causing the drink to bubble.

His father, head inclined again under the weight of his glasses, peered over the rim at what his son was doing, as if he were observing an intriguing chemical experiment that could feasibly lead to highly unexpected results. The results never came, and he flared up:

"What kind of equality can there be among people? Man is inimitable! As a boy, I would be training ruthlessly up to five hours a day while he was busy fainting from a wasp sting!"

"Hold on! Hold on!" Andrei yelled. "What do wasps have to do with anything? Who fainted?"

Andrei had been in Moscow for so long that he had clearly never heard the story.

"Oh, that's just . . ." Yura waved it off and then continued academically, keeping an eye on his son, who suddenly decided to run away. "What can be done if people living in Sverdlovsk are furiously envious of people living in Tula, because Tula happens to be much closer to Moscow?"

"They don't envy it anymore," Andrei joked. "Moscow's worse off than Tula and Sverdlovsk now. At any rate, it's not doing any better than them."

"But let's say that people living Sverdlovsk envy that people in Tula live much closer to Moscow. What can calm them down when they're burning up with such envy? Nothing.

"The only person who can console them is whoever explains to them that what's important to them isn't the distance between Sverdlovsk and Moscow, but between Sverdlovsk and Mars. If they believe that, then they'll instantly calm down. They'll understand that Moscow, and Sverdlovsk, and Tula are all equidistant from Mars.

"It is religion that supplies this new orientation, an orientation towards the celestial, towards eternity, that makes equality between men possible."

"But what am I supposed to do if I don't believe in God?" came the unexpected challenge from Andrei. "I don't feel him."

"You can say that about a broad: I don't feel her," Yura reprimanded. "You can't say that about God. It would be like saying that about your mother: I don't feel like she's my mother."

"But why not?" said Andrei stubbornly. "There are plenty of horrible women who are mothers."

"Anything can happen in life," Yura agreed. "But only other people can judge that. The son has no right to do so."

"But why not the son when he's the one that she's horrible to?"

"It's taboo for the son," Yura was adamant. "If somebody's mother is a horrible woman, he has the right to feel like an orphan. But no more than that."

"What, he doesn't even have the right to think about it?"

"Unfortunately, you can't control what somebody thinks," said Yura, after thinking about it. "Thinking is like breathing. But you have no right to say it out loud. It's taboo. A world in which a son raises a hand against his mother, verbally or physically—such a world is doomed to the syphilis of decay. Keep in mind that the atheistic efficiency of the West is founded on the vast momentum brought about by its past religious upbringing . . ."

But it didn't look like Andrei was going to keep anything in mind.

"I don't believe in God," Andrei repeated stubbornly. "What, I can't even say that?"

"Why can't you?" Yura said, raising his head in surprise. "That's all you've been talking about. But why are you saying it so victoriously? I'm not sensing the great mental struggles you should've gone through to arrive at this thought. Even though some of your best paintings show you unabatedly growing close to God."

Yura's compliment meant a lot to Andrei.

"Really?" Andrei asked, his voice suddenly growing warmer. "I feel something like that myself, but I have no idea where it's coming from. How did you like my *Nudes*, the ones that I brought to the exhibit?"

Although he was quite well known in Russia and even Europe, Andrei Tarkilov liked to show off his works in his homeland. Everybody has their quirks.

"I didn't," Yura replied.

"What do you mean?" Andrei was at a loss.

Yura hammered in the last nail in the coffin: "It's bad." He inclined his head, as if forced down by Andrei's failure, and looked at him over his glasses. "There's no aesthetic warmth. There's no room for hope. Your nudes are like graters. You painted them fine earlier, after your wife had ended, but before your lover began . . ."

Andrei's expression darkened before his very eyes. A vein in his forehead looked close to bursting.

"I wanted them to be like graters, if that's how you see it," he said through clenched teeth.

"Graters, graters," Yura repeated mercilessly. "Stumpy Russian graters and leggy European graters. You have to be made of sandpaper to appreciate them, but I'm just a person. . . You know, hags like that can be incredibly cynical. A young woman died on our street. I came to the burial, said my goodbye, and went outside for a smoke. Suddenly a friend of mine comes up to me. She had just been by the coffin. She's making a fuss. She says about the departed: 'She's wearing such a nice sweatshirt. I don't have a sweatshirt like that!' I say to her, 'You don't have a coffin like that either.' She wasn't offended. She just shook her head and said, 'You know, you've always been strange!' But that can't be what you wanted to say with your paintings."

"That too," said Andrei. "To hear you say it, I should become a monk in order to make good paintings."

"That's your problem," Yura replied mercilessly, and then laughed kind-heartedly. "Render unto God the things that are God's and render unto Caesar the Caesarian section that is his."

Andrei wasn't amused. The vein in his forehead kept threatening to burst. I figured that the C-section would be accomplished with the rapier. And for Caesar's wife, not for Caesar himself. Or rather, for both.

"The artist himself must determine how much he'll put into life and how much into his art," Yura continued, growing giddier for some reason. "I think that that's an aspect of 'talent.' But if you decide to paint a cynical bitch, then there's absolutely no need to undress her. How many of the classics have you seen paint a bitch that was naked? If you undress a bitch, you'll never clothe her again. Or she'll run out of the workshop, naked, and streak across town. You go chase her then . . ."

"Waving your rapier about," Andrei interjected unexpectedly.

"Sure, if you'd like," Yura agreed calmly. "But the *Nudes* you painted after your wife ended, but your lover hadn't yet begun . . . those were gorgeous."

This latest compliment did nothing to mollify Andrei. His expression grew even darker.

"Don't you think you're presuming a little too much?" he said angrily, sticking out his lower lip. He looked Yura over. "Here, in your crummy little coffeehouse? A new-age Socrates!"

"It's no crummier than Moscow," Yura responded with the calm voice of a lector, reasonably pointing out the congruent crumminess of both.

"As for Socrates," he went on, "his philosophical identity has no bearing on what we're discussing. Some naïve people are surprised as to why such a great ancient philosopher says nothing about the injustice of slavery. Because it was part of the rules of the game back then, and nobody would have even considered fighting slavery. If two hundred years from now, people will drink artificially created milk, they'll be astounded that we stole milk away from innocent calves and that nobody fought milk-drinkers. It's the same with free people and slaves. Socrates might have been made a slave himself if he had been taken hostage. He fought in the war, after all . . ."

"Waving his rapier about," Andrei said again, but this time, he completely missed the mark.

"His rapier?" Yura sounded surprised. He raised his head high and gazed as the future unfurled before him. "The Greeks didn't know what rapiers were. Haven't you read Homer? Fencing is an Ancient Roman pastime. Julius Caesar began it, but the first rapier was implemented under Nero."

"A crazy weapon for a crazy emperor," Andrei tried to win it in round two, but Yura simply ignored him.

"So it's highly ahistorical of you to accuse Socrates of failing to fight slavery," Yura went on, overlooking the fact that Andrei never really targeted Socrates for failing to uphold the ideals of equality. "It's the typical, foolish mockery of progress. Can you be completely sure that an intelligent Greek slave owner treated his slaves worse than a modern executive treats his employees? I have no such convictions. From the point of view of ontology, freedom and equality are resolved only through the will of people, only through love. Let's take Savelyich from *The Captain's Daughter*.[24] Just try to tell him: 'Petrusha is your owner. I'll help you get rid of him.' He'll kill whatever bastard suggests such a thing! He loves his Petrusha, and Petrusha loves him. Which means they're equal and free with regard to one another. Savelyich's deep love for his owner verges on tyranny. But Petrusha understands that it's the tyranny of love, and loving him in turn, he can't truly punish him. If we think about it, it's unclear who is the owner and who the vassal! For your information, Savelyich enjoys the most freedom and happiness in Russian literature! And yet you're bringing up Socrates!"

But that's when Andrei went on the offensive.

"Here's what I'll say about God," he began, raising his head and seething with restrained passion. "God is the favorite excuse of the unlucky. He represents a chance to try and eke out a second throw of the dice. If you believe in God's plan, then how can you justify the destruction of the *Admiral Nakhimov*?[25] Hundreds of innocent people drowned. The cold, grey, ruthless water consumed children as young as your boy. For what?

"With that image in your mind, if you have an honest brain, how can you not see with all clarity that the catastrophe happened because of the foolishness, negligence, and callousness of people? Coincidence? Sure,

---

24 A Pushkin novel from 1836 on Pugachev's Rebellion.
25 A passenger liner that sank in 1986, resulting in the deaths of hundreds.

negative coincidence. But there was also positive coincidence in it not happening earlier. So the two coincidences cancel each other out. We're left with rudeness and self-adulation! There's no supernatural power affecting it!

"But if there *is* something supernatural at large, then God has clearly become a forgetful and cruel old man who himself doesn't understand what he's doing. Do you truly prefer to believe that the world is run by a senile, cold-hearted God rather than by nature—cold-hearted, frightening in its apathy, but pure?

"And one more thing. If this catastrophe is one of those incomprehensible attempts by God to enlighten the scumbags of the world, then I say: 'I don't accept such a God or such an attempt to enlighten these bastards! I prefer a world without a God, a world in which the ship captain simply pushes the bastards away from the helm. Maybe a world like that is impossible, but I prefer it!'"

As soon as he started talking, Yura grew very serious. His thin, big-nosed face seemed to sink in on itself further. He listened to him, slowly raising his head, struggling now to overcome not only the weight of his large, horn-rimmed glasses, but the weight of the whole planet.

"Oh, my friend," Yura replied, unexpectedly bitterly and softly. "You've hit it right on the head. There are hundreds of books written on the subject, but they don't explain anything. I don't know why God allows innocent children to die, but I know and believe that without God, life would be worse for those still here."

Yura stilled and then, banging the table with his fists, flared up:

"Here's my last formula for you: God isn't omnipotent, God is right! It's an Old Testament tradition to believe that God is omnipotent. That way, you can keep children of a certain age well-behaved with the threat of omnipotent punishment, rather than the beauty of truth. God is omnipotent only within the eternal nature of his loving rightness. The world is full of war, rape, mental breakdowns, ruthlessness, cruelty, betrayal, and it all lasts centuries, millennia! But man suddenly wakes and looks around: while all that was happening here, there, somewhere above, waiting for him was the stable, patient, ineradicable, loving rightness. All things pass, but God's rightness remains! His rightness is constant, and he constantly calls for our involvement. If you think about it, this little detail is soul-rending! God is right, but he doesn't need his rightness—we do. Think about it—he's calling on me to help him save me! As he calls on everyone. But being the stubborn asses we are, we dig in our heels."

"I think I'm tired of this," Andrei muttered, embarrassed by his embarrassment, and repeated: "He calls on me to help him save me . . . You might be on to something . . . That's good . . ."

Yura's face suddenly lit up with the tender, philological smile of a medieval monk who had, at one point, served as a soldier too. And in that moment, he looked devilishly handsome.

Andrei poured the cognac, trying to naturalize the unusual feeling of inspiration with a familiar situation.

"Let's drink to God's being right in the morning," Yura said and then drank without clinking glasses.

* * *

And that, my dear reader, is when something entirely unexpected happened. I fell asleep. I must have felt that the world was in good hands so long as Yura lived. I could safely doze off. I fell asleep to the sounds of Yura's voice, to the droning in the restaurant, to the atonal screams of the insolent gulls that were thankfully abstaining from attacking the children.

It's interesting that you can fall asleep to the sound of human voices for completely contradictory reasons. You can fall asleep in concert with the sound. Children fall asleep that way to the quiet voices of their parents in the other room. But you can also fall asleep to the essentially meaningless sounds of human speech. Our mind demonstrates its aptitude for shielding, walling us off from senselessness.

So you can fall asleep in either mutually contradicting case. But in the first case, the sleep is healthy, while the second case results in a sleep that is sickly. It is as if we sense the wrongfulness of our falling asleep to the sound of human speech, which is partly directed our way.

From what I remember about myself, any meeting that I attended throughout my life saw me wage a heroic, but doomed fight against sleep. Knowing this, I would always try to sit in the farthest possible corner. As strange as it sounds, sleep enjoys a fight, sleep likes it when you struggle. And when we're overcome by sleep in the most inappropriate of places, we experience at the same time horror and the sense of forbidden sweetness.

During my many years as a writer, I never went to meetings and forgot about this. Then, suddenly, I was elected to parliament, and my struggle against sleep took on a horrific character.

On the one hand, they are more comfortable than ordinary meetings: there are a thousand people, and you can easily hide in the crowd. But on the other hand, TV cameramen are constantly roaming and lurking between the rows. And you can never hear them coming.

One time, one of them got a hold of me. It might have even been unintentional, he might have even pitied me somewhat. I then watched the result on *Vremya*.[26] It all seemed civilized enough. It looked like I was trying to peck at something with my nose, which will-wishers could feasibly have framed as follows: his head was bowed by the oppressive alacrity of the orator's speech.

But where can you get well-wishers like that!

I had barely finished watching the segment when I started getting calls from friends and acquaintances that had suddenly developed a feverish interest in my parliamentary activity.

"I was stone-cold sober!" I yelled into the phone every time, loudly enough for whomever was tapping the conversation to hear.

Then the night before another session, you would lie awake for hours, unable to go to sleep with the horrible feeling that you'll fall asleep tomorrow at the session. You start having outlandish fantasies about the session getting cancelled: war, earthquakes, a conspiracy. A conspiracy actually did happen once, but it was during a parliamentary recess, so it was neither here, nor there. That too showed how permanently those mediocrities were doomed to fail. And then, the next day, you go to the session, and the cycle starts anew. And most importantly, you spend the short intervals of sleep arguing tediously with the jackass-provocateur trying to expose your sleeping, and, in your sleep, you try to prove to him with unwavering mendacity that you're not sleeping.

Akhmatova[27] was a genius! She managed to surmise everything without once sitting in the Kremlin. In her poem "There's no need to live in the Kremlin, the Preobrazhensky man is right,"[28] she writes that the Kremlin air has been diseased with microbes of evil, cunning, and betrayal since the times of Ivan the Terrible.

---

26   *Vremya* (literally, "time") was the main evening newscast in the Soviet Union.
27   Anna Akhmatova (1889–1966) was a renowned Russian poet.
28   The Preobrazhensky Regiment was one of the oldest guard regiments of the Russian Army.

Conventional wisdom has known this for a long time. At least in my time, when people in our villages lived through some kind of misfortune, like the death of a child or a suicide, the remaining family members would burn the house and move somewhere else. They knew that they couldn't keep living in that house. Folk wisdom lies in people's endless, expansive experience. The poet's talent manifests itself in the swift and clairvoyant vision of this endlessness.

So not only do you not have to live in the Kremlin, you don't have to attend sessions there either. Even though the Palace used for sessions is a relatively new building, it is already chock full of microbes.

I was at one of these sessions once, flitting between the murky sweetness of sleep and dreamlike wakefulness, and I sensed as waves of betrayal roiled through the air. It smelled like a wine cellar. And many congressmen were simply radiating fetid streams of vanity. To say nothing of the ones that were waiting their turn at the microphone. The fetid streams emanating from them were corporeal enough to smack the backs of people's heads: poof! poof! poof!

Meanwhile, the waves of betrayal are rolling throughout the hall. I nearly suffocated when a particularly strong wave rolled through. That's when I fraternally touched the hand of the person sitting next to me. He was watching the orator without moving a muscle.

"Comrade," I said, searching for solace through solidarity in suffering. "Are you feeling the waves of betrayal?"

"No," he replied, looking at me with very clear eyes, and added: "That's the air conditioner."

After which he shifted his gaze back to the orator and froze again, his posture resembling a breakwater. Air conditioner! These people are all nuts! Where the hell was I? The orator was speaking, the breakwater was frozen again, breaking only God knows what. Not the waves of betrayal, though.

... And I felt the deadly sin of envy. And I yearned to be just as nuts as they were, for my own sanity ...

It's true, you don't have to live in the Kremlin or to attend sessions there. It should be turned into a museum. The custodians should then be paid extra for the hazardous work conditions, and instead of slippers, visitors should be given gas masks. Maybe a century down the line, it'll air out properly.

So, sitting under a tent at the Amra, enjoying a nice, cool breeze, I serenely fell asleep to Yura's voice. The fact that I didn't sleep much that night probably played a part too.

I usually take sleeping pills. I've been doing it for so long that the ritual plays out automatically. The pill goes into your mouth, water washes it down, the glass finds its way back to the table, and suddenly you're in bed.

But sometimes, once you're in bed, you futilely try to remember: did you really take the pill or were you just getting ready to take it? And you find yourself in an inexplicably idiotic situation. Should you try to fall asleep? But if you didn't take the pill, you'll have to wait, and wait, and finally, after coming to terms with the fact that you didn't actually take the pill, you'll take it in the wee hours of the morning and start the day with a heavy head.

In these situations, you don't get why you can't fall asleep—because you didn't take the tablet or because you're concerned about the fact that you didn't take it? Your soul is taken hostage by an egregious form of Hamletism.

Sure, you can take a pill and know for sure that you took at least one. But, first of all, it's a shame to waste a pill unnecessarily—sleeping pills aren't that easy to get in our neck of the woods. And second of all, you don't want your head to feel like an anvil.

After two pills, you start the next day with the feeling that Morpheus himself, armed with his magical forceps, spent the whole night navigating your ear canals and packing your head full of wool, musing at the dubious merit of your head's karstic spaciousness and delighting in the fact that he had decided to get the cheap wool.

Why then, you think, *did I spend so much time sleeping when it wasn't even remotely refreshing? It would have been better to simply lie in bed and think about something pleasant.* But that there is the rub—if you could lie in bed and think about something pleasant, you wouldn't have to deal with insomnia.

It's a difficult question: did I take a sleeping pill or no? If the pills were previously sealed and you had only fished out the first one that night, then clearly you did.

If you had taken the last pill, then that would solve the problem too, because it had been the last pill. Though, at this point, today's insomnia might very well rear its head because you start worrying for *tomorrow* night. The fact that I won't have a pill tomorrow increases my propensity for insomnia today (despite the fact that I've already taken the pill for today), because I decide to worry today about not sleeping tomorrow, which would merit another pill, which I don't have. But if I had a second pill, then I wouldn't need it, and I would stop worrying about tomorrow night. And that's what we call peering into the future.

One of the reasons that I never know whether I took a pill is that I never drink the whole glass of water. I take a few sips and put the glass down. After which I can't remember whether I drank any of it at all.

I decided to implement a strict rule requiring me to finish the whole glass. Then, if I begin to have doubts about whether I took a pill, I can turn on the light, look at the glass, and have everything fall into place. But that plan failed too. If I remember before falling asleep that I have to drink the whole glass after taking a pill, then I remember that I already took the pill anyway. You have to finish the water automatically, but that doesn't happen.

Strange, nobody ever taught us to finish a glass of wine or a shot of vodka, but we finish it anyway. Then again, you can't really wash a pill down with alcohol. Incidentally, as a rule, people of the West don't finish their drinks. They take a few sips and leave the rest. A few sips, and leave it.

They must trust more in the natural flow of life. And we don't trust that somebody won't take it away if we don't finish a drink when we can. Which is why we rush to down the whole thing. There's something in our lives reminiscent of a train station. It always seems like either the snack bar's about to close or the train's about to leave. And in the end, the snack bar closes, and the train leaves anyway. Typical.

Right, so insomnia. True, booze is the best sleeping pill in the world. But even that's not for certain. If you don't have enough, then you're irritated, your night is filled with bad dreams, and in the morning your head is heavy enough that you start thinking you had *too much* to drink. But if you drink too much, your head is heavy in the morning, but your evening is just dandy. Which is why people prefer to over-drink than under-drink.

But there's some kind of boundary, some kind of dosage. There must be some mysterious congruence either with our daily rhythm or with our value to other people or to God when we drink and the whole world seems brighter and happier! We fall asleep just fine, and we wake up full of energy and peppy! Even peppier than when we didn't drink! And it's true. This has happened, though rarely.

And so you have to search, to experiment, which isn't easy. Because nobody knows the exact dosage because of its quicksilver dependence on our daily merits. And it's incredibly difficult to divine how valuable you are on any given day. Sometimes you don't do anything, but God smiles at you anyway: you did good. And sometimes, you spend the whole day toiling away, but you can just *feel* how God just shakes his head in disgust: I don't want to hear a word about you or your work. You dirtbag.

And why are you a dirtbag? That doesn't merit a response. Figure it out yourself. Once you figure it out, you'll clean up your act. Or vice versa. You'll clean up your act, and then you'll figure it out.

But let's get back to what I was saying. I got a glass of water from the kitchen, took out a pill, and got my book to read for half an hour before going to sleep, when suddenly in hit me. You're in bed, holding your book, but for the life of you, you can't remember if you took the pill or not. It seems like nothing, but sometimes all kinds of thoughts race through your head. Like: am I alive or not? I can't remember. If this is life, then why'd it start so soon? It's all wrong! Starting so soon is pointless!

If you were given something to understand, then you should have also been given time to tell about it. Did you rush? Rushing is cheating. Rushing means stealing other people's time or selling unripe fruit. The fruit's not ready yet. What right do I have to rush and pick it? Something's off here.

And then you get up quietly, so as not to wake anyone. You approach the bar, trying to keep the door from squeaking, and dig around in your stash. You make your choice and take a swig. And another. And a bit more. Stop. Not bad.

Most importantly—don't be ashamed. No shame. There is nothing shameful about this. This isn't weakness. True weakness is wheezing through life, pretending to be strong. You need a break, a pick-me-up. You held out your hand and got it mended. What's shameful about that? Bearing the pain is much worse. So, I say, *this* is good, because life becomes warmer and brighter, which is the point of life, after all.

Curious thoughts make their way into your head. Unlike with sleeping pills, after having a drink, you can't really say: I can't remember if I had a drink or not. People might joke about it in order to have some more. But they remember. A drink is simple. Once it's inside you, it doesn't pretend that it isn't. But people who have had a drink sometimes pretend to be sober. And that's funny. But when drunks pretend to be even more drunk, that's not good. That's not good at all.

Strange thoughts flutter through your head. Why do all large birds have horrid voices? Gulls, eagles, crows, peacocks? Why are all pleasantly voiced birds small?

This obviously isn't coincidence. Nature is trying to point something out to us. But what? Maybe large birds are imbued with the drive to command, while small ones strive to charm? It would appear that the drive to command precludes the development of harmonic sounds and facilitates sounds that are dreadful and frightening. After all, given the strength of a nightingale's voice, shouldn't he be able to make a menacing sound too? To mask his weakness, for self-defense. But nope, the braveheart just sings and sings!

It would be fun to apply this theory to people. Pushkin was physically the smallest of all the Russian poets, but he is also the fairest-voiced.

Mayakovsky[29] was physically the largest poet in Russian poetry and has the most commanding voice. There's some literary analysis for you.

Mayakovsky was born that way, and he spent his whole life consciously restructuring poetry and subconsciously strengthening his commanding intonations. Even though from time to time he would plunge into bestial melancholy that was worthy of ten lyricists.

Why does Mayakovsky say so much about his height? With pain, with bitterness, with irony, or with tragic pride? It's unclear. Why was he so intent on making the future arrive as quickly as possible, as if he felt in his gut that the future harbored his motherland, his own people. Interestingly enough, he was quite right in a biological sense. Statistics clearly show that these days, after children grow up, they are larger than their parents. Maybe a century or two from now, his height will seem pretty normal.

But why did this agonize him so? I think he was vexed by the duality of his nature. His enormity corresponded to his commanding voice, while his talent for lyricism opined for softer melodies. There are plenty of accounts when, in a daze or caught unawares, he would whisper the words of a folk song, or lines from Yesenin or Mandelshtam.[30] Love-hate. It would seem that commanding and lyrical voices aren't compatible by their very nature. By giving free rein to his commanding nature, he silenced his lyrical gift, or when he couldn't silence it, he let it through and reached unbelievable levels of ingenuity: a soul-rending lament about a fallen horse or about the solitude of a lovestruck steamliner.

Could this be where children's faith in technology stems from? You can hammer anything together, even two voices. The "Brooklyn Bridge"[31] is a hymn, but is it extolling only technology or the fact that it will finally bridge the two shores? And is that what gives rise to the poet's strange apathy towards nature, or rather his private resentment of it for this tragic duality?

---

29 Vladimir Mayakovsky (1893–1930) was a Russian-Soviet poet.
30 Sergei Yesenin (1895–1925) was a Russian lyric poet. Osip Mandelstam (1891–1938) was a Russian poet and essayist.
31 A poem by Mayakovsky.

And the essence of our country has something in common with this person: its enormity and its eternal, soul-rending attempt to combine a commanding voice with a lyrical one.

However, my discussion of sleeping pills has gotten me off-track. All I wanted to do was say one simple thing. Here at the Amra, sitting at a table under a tent, I fell asleep to Yura's soporific voice. And suddenly I dreamed of my mother. I rarely dream of her. But in my dreams, she is always sorrowful. And I always know that I am the cause of sorrow. And as strange as it is to say, I put on a brave face in my dreams, trying to show her that everything's not as bad as it seems. But she doesn't believe me and keeps grieving.

And suddenly, this time I dreamed of her, she appeared as if she was almost ready to smile. She was standing on the bank of a river, while I was in the river itself, and she was looking at me. I felt with my submerged, bare legs that the current was very strong.

Our storytellers famously have a performative flourish with which they begin their tales: "Oh, the times in which we live . . ." But in a dream, the river is real. The powerful, powerful river swept around my bare legs. And the grains of sand, the many grains of sand swept up by the current clung to my legs, surrounding them, tickling my feet, my toes, my ankles. The grains of sand bumped into my legs, playing, caressing, giggling, and whirling away.

I woke up refreshed, cleansed, and clear-eyed. I must have slept for some fifteen minutes. And the first thing I thought after waking up was: everything will be alright in this country. And as is often the case with someone who has a dream, and not because of any external logic, but because of some deeper understanding, I knew that the grains of sand were children. They'll be alright, and the country will be alright, though maybe not so soon: children are quick, joyous, golden grains of sand.

I think I was woken up by a scream, childlike, but not at all gentle:

"Dad, when are you gonna get me that ice cream?!"

Yura slowly turned around, directing his large, horn-rimmed glasses at the ice cream line. It seemed hopeless once again. He had no desire to get in line, especially since the waitress had left to go to the barber's and had clearly gotten stuck there.

"Wait a little. The line will go away soon."

"Mom's right. All you can do is speculate!"

Yura was clearly taken aback. Hiding his embarrassment, he smiled and said:

"I wasn't entirely sure of that. Give mom my gratitude."

"I won't!" the boy yelled.

"Drink your Pepsi," Yura nodded at the glass. "Then I'll bring you some ice cream."

"I'm sick of your stinking Pepsi! I'm sick of your seagulls!" his son yelled, and, in the heat of passion, smacked the glass of Pepsi off the table.

And that's when I saw the lightning flash of a once-famous fencer! I swear, Yura didn't even look in the direction of the glass. Maybe he glanced at it out of the corner of his glasses—I don't know.

Without turning, he threw out his hand and caught the glass just hairs above the floor. The glass didn't have a chance to flip, and most of the drink stayed inside. Yura made as if to put it back on the table, but then hesitated and for some reason spilled out the rest of the Pepsi, treating is as an unnecessary witness of the little tempest. Only after that did he put it on the table.

Inclining his head, he regarded his son over his glasses, clearly getting ready to say something, but he missed his chance. His son, seeing some boy at the other end of the Amra, dropped everything and ran in his direction. Yura turned to Andrei and continued the conversation which I had slept through:

"It's such a shame that in his famous novel *Das Kapital*, which will certainly be a treasure for philologists of the twenty-first century, Marx said nothing about the spermititude of money. It's so close . . . Here, let's assume that a thousand years from now, housing will no longer be an issue . . ."

"What," Andrei exclaimed. "A whole thousand years from now?"

It was surprising that Andrei was astounded by the end of Yura's sentence but wasn't bothered at all by its beginning.

"And why not?" Yura said calmly. "A thousand years ago, people thought that in a thousand years, housing wouldn't be a problem."

"You're probably right," Andrei agreed.

"And many social issues are no longer issues," Yura went on. "But will there be equality? Of course not. Imagine this: a homely, but intelligent and kind girl goes to her first school dance. And she suddenly sees that not a single boy wants to dance with her. All they're interested in is dance with some pretty little airhead. And a spiteful one, at that. What does it matter to our brainiac that plenty of social issues have been solved when she, trying not to burst out crying in front of the whole school, runs out of the dance? Where's the equality?"

"So what will console her?" Andrei asked, curious.

"The same thing as a thousand years prior—God. In him, she'll find a friend who, through his own struggles ultimately came to the thought that a kind heart is prettier than a pretty waist. She can also be consoled through any selfless deed . . . By the way, Russian literature is full of aunts or grandmas who, not having any family of their own, stuck to their families. They loved and helped raise their kids, without any complexes of their own.

"So, equality is a chimera. Lenin once said a famous phrase during a meeting at Kschessinska's castle . . ."[32]

Yura suddenly stopped, raised his head, and looked at me quizzically. And I understood that he knew whom I was waiting for. His gaze was full of inexplicable humor. He was thinking either: I'm sorry, did I just play your card? Or: are you going to need this card? I shrugged in response, meaning that I myself had no idea.

Yura turned to Andrei, who had noticed with surprise our looking at one another and couldn't grasp what we meant by it.

"So. He was delivering a speech on a balcony," Yura kept going. "And suddenly he saw a passing car. He waved in the direction of the car and shouted to the crowd:

"'See that car?'

"The crowd turned to look.

"'That's *your* car!' Lenin exclaimed.

"And every single person in the crowd thought himself to be the future owner of that car, forgetting that there was only one car and that it would probably belong to Lenin. How could they refuse to follow Lenin after that?

"Equality is legalized envy. Envy can be overcome only with love. You don't envy your loved ones . . ."

"Hold on!" said Andrei. "Why only love? Why can't you overcome it by achieving whatever you envy?"

"Your envy will instantly turn to something else!" Yura exclaimed cheerily, waving the suggestion away, seemingly directing attention to envy's comical persistence. And then he added unexpectedly: "I'm done with the chimera of equality, but the chimera of crassness draws near. Hard work isn't what made mankind, like Engels thought—the first convulsion of squeamishness made mankind mankind. Our distant progenitor first pushed away his girlfriend when she, smacking her lips, slurped up a live worm like spaghetti. She had chowed down worms before, but this worm turned out to be very fat and

---

32 Mathilde Kschessinska (1872–1971) was a Russian ballerina.

far too wormy. This caused an aesthetic explosion—the beginning of the comprehension of beauty."

"Exactly!" the artist agreed heartily and slammed his fist on the table definitively, hammering in the nail of truth. "I always felt that aesthetics are older than ethics."

"Nothing of the sort," Yura said, absentmindedly gazing at Andrei over his glasses. "Ethics already existed, because our progenitor tolerated them. But this enormous worm caused an aesthetic explosion. Generally speaking, aesthetics are a form of comprehending ethics. They were disfigured and severed only later . . ."

He fell silent. It was only then that I noticed where Yura was looking. Andrei turned around too. From the second entrance at the opposite end of the Amra, a mutual acquaintance was drawing near. He was a vogue rising star of a lawyer. He had a round face and a large body and was very cheerful from the excess corporality. He was carrying Yura's son. As it later became clear, the boy complained to him that his father wouldn't buy him ice cream. This lawyer was what Yura called the chimera of crassness.

The lawyer stopped halfway to the table, still holding the boy, and started speaking to someone sitting at another table.

As soon as he stopped, Andrei quickly turned to look at Yura in a hurry to forestall the lawyer and said:

"No, you're wrong! A butterfly flies into the room of a kid who has never seen a butterfly in his life. The kid smiles, reaches for the thing. Without understanding what it is, he already takes joy in its beauty. An understanding of beauty is primal."

"You are naïve, my friend," Andrei responded, continuing to observe the lawyer, who had stopped at another table still holding his son. "Admittedly, an artist probably should be. For a kid, a butterfly is an extension of the sunlight. And sunlight is an extension of his mother's love, which he has already felt. That's why a butterfly seems like a playful manifestation of kindness . . ."

At that point, the lawyer waved something off, turned, and hobbled in our direction, and Yura made a few last lunges.

"A child's ingeniousness lies in the unity of kindness of beauty. If a butterfly had a stinger and stung the kid, the next time he'd see a butterfly through his window, he'd scream in horror and disgust. Man's fall began when he said, 'Yes, this butterfly stings, but it is pretty!'

"We'll discuss the pseudomasculinity of that decision and the acknowledgement of the devil's ingenuity later."

The lawyer was coming closer.

"Is somebody refusing to get little Aslan some ice cream?" he roared jokingly from afar. "Is somebody cluttering up his head with otherworldly nonsense?"

The little boy sat imperiously in his arms like a prince whose royalty had finally been recognized. He was gazing at his father from on high with abashed pride: take *this*, dad!

Without stopping and jestingly refusing to greet his father, the lawyer carried him past Yura and hobbled past the line to the ice cream stand.

"Some ice cream for the orphan," he said loudly so that the line would hear him. "His mother ran off with an American millionaire. His father went crazy. It's terrible!"

The sullenly suspicious line was silent. The lawyer's fleshy surplus was too impressive. But as always, there was one heroic woman.

"You should be ashamed!" she exclaimed but didn't leave the line. "That boy ran up to that man over there and called him dad! And they talked! I heard it with my own ears!"

"Madame," the lawyer turned to look at her after handing little Aslan a bowl of ice cream. "Did I say that he was mute? I said that he was crazy. They say that he was a national fencing champion. But if you ask him what nation he represented, he doesn't know."

And suddenly, the line relaxed, people started shuffling around again and smiling to show their understanding of the joke. The amazing part is that this all happened in the beginning of August, before the Putsch, before the country fell apart. But talks of it splintering were already in the air. And back then, the idea seemed so absurd. It could never happen.

Having gotten his bowl of ice cream, the prince jumped off his throne and ran to his dad's table. The spoon's alpenstock flashed in the sunlight, piercing the alabaster mound. The lawyer, swaying, his steps somehow matching the rhythm of his swaying, came to the table too. He nabbed the closest chair, shoved it under himself, and melted onto it.

Having finally gotten what he wanted, the boy calmed down, but the level of conversation sharply went down. You have to pay for everything. Yura and Andrei easily and even eagerly jumped down to the lawyer's level, demonstrating that they too can appreciate the crevasses of crassness, seeing as these crevasses have their own advantages and are much more inhabitable. For that matter, we are all like that.

In turn, as if to reward their amicable omnivory, the lawyer invited them to a new little restaurant where the food was (for now) simply finger-licking good. To accentuate his point, he brought his fingers to his mouth and loudly smacked his lips. His gesture reminded me of our progenitor's distant girlfriend. But for some reason, no convulsion of squeamishness followed. Everyone got up, trying to match the lawyer's raucous merrymaking, and left the Amra. The boy was holding his hand.

My friends, there is no need to be angry at Yura: the rapier isn't broken. It's resting.

3

The Hunting Hawk

One clear, sunny day on a green hill right by the sea, a local cop and I are catching sparrow-hawks. Or rather, we're trying to catch them.

Here's how it's done. You build a small shelter to hide in, so that the hawk can't see you from above. You hammer a net into the ground next to the shelter and put a shrike—a small, feisty bird—under it. Around these parts, it's been tenderly feminized, and people call it a shrikette. We'll call it that too. The shrikette is tethered to the ground, and it gyrates beneath the net, quickly flapping its wings, gamboling about.

A hawk passing above should notice the gamboling shrikette and nosedive for it. It remains unclear why he shouldn't notice the net. Either he's too fired up, or he just dismisses it as harmless vegetation.

It is my first time doing this. I want to see what it looks like to capture a hunting hawk, but in my heart, for some reason, I'm convinced that nothing will come of it. Who knows why. Maybe I just don't believe that a hawk could be that stupid. Even more so, maybe I don't believe that I'll get lucky and see a live hawk floundering in the net. I'm not even that interested in seeing the hawk stuck in the net as much as I am interested in seeing how the quick-as-lightning predator swoops down and strikes the net. But I don't believe that it can happen. A strange sense of misfortune, foolishness, and tactlessness has been hounding me since yesterday.

I was in town. I met with an old friend, and he told me that one of our mutual acquaintances was very ill, essentially dying from cancer, and that we should visit him.

I knew him well, but we had never been close. But it's a small town, and everybody knows each other. In his day, he was one of those golden youths whom I had nothing to do with. But we would sometimes meet up in a café. I valued his mirth, which crossed into wit, and his inexhaustible supply of anecdotes. Tall, with a beak of a nose, he made an impression on the ladies. Especially the Slavic ladies. On his mother's side, he was a Pontic Greek. But it would obviously be an exaggeration to consider his being a magnet for Russian girls the aftereffects of Ancient Rus' endlessly yearning for Byzantium. Though, on the other hand, even Dostoevsky dreamed of Constantinople.

At any rate, there was always a pretty, well-dressed girl sitting next to him. It was clear that in their world, the two attributes were equally appreciated, and both were mandatory.

For a girl to be either just pretty or just well-dressed—that never happened. And it wasn't that they went out of their way to find a pretty girl, fall in love with her there and then, and take her to some underground safe house to change her wardrobe in accordance with their tastes. Nothing of the sort. They were too young and frivolous for that.

It is more likely that their fathers did that. No, not with their girls, but with their own ladies. Admittedly, one time, amusingly overflowing with pride, one of them told the story of how his father made a move on his girl while he went out to buy cigarettes. The tone of his story made clear how his father was well within the bounds of the natural feudal law that he took advantage of, and how he himself will take advantage of this heritage once his own son brings a girl home and remembers that he forgot to buy cigarettes or drugs or what have you. He probably already *has* taken advantage of it while I am sitting here guessing, considering that it has been an awfully long time since then.

So it is probably fair to say that girls like that swam in their direction of their own volition—or rather in the direction of their cars. In the interest of fairness, I want to note that in those times, cars were much cheaper. But in the interest of that same fairness, I want to note that we are talking about school-age kids.

My God, how long is it going to take me to get to the point? I just want everything that will follow to make sense. In the end, he married one of those girls. By that point, he already made a name for himself in town as an electronic engineer.

Years and years passed by. We rarely met up, maybe no more than once or twice a summer. We would sit in cafes, reminisce, and he would retroactively, maybe even unwillingly include me in his group of friends. Sometimes, it felt like he was a step away from asking: "Listen, what kind of car did you have back then? I don't remember." No, he never did ask me that, but he stopped just short of it.

If I ever did hang out with them a few times, then I've got to say that the main conclusion I came away with (that I would keep to myself, of course) was this: I am *such* a good person for not detesting them. I could easily detest them, but I don't. Their fathers were making careers for themselves, while mine were grubbing away in Magadan and fading into the permafrost. But these guys weren't to blame. No, I don't detest them. My heart is vast. And the more I drank with them, the more I delighted in its vastness. *Everyone should be united*, I thought. *Everyone but the executioners.*

It was strange and naïve of me to not even once consider whether they detested me for having almost no money. I never considered it. Maybe they thought that you didn't need any money for the kind of life I was leading.

Back then, I was a student at the Institute of Literature. But whenever they started having discussions about high literature, as sometimes happened, I listened patiently until I couldn't take it anymore, at which point I subtly herded them in the direction of Yesenin, whom they liked in their own way, even though they mistakenly believed that they understood his verse.

Incidentally, I even remember them inquiring with a degree of naïve practicality about what was currently considered good literature. And their ears pricked up when I replied.

This was one area in which they were thankfully different from our current leaders, who, when asked by journalists what they are reading at the moment, invariably, with comical frankness respond: Pikul.[33] It's too much to ask them to say, oh, I don't know, "I'm reading Faulkner." No, they're reading Pikul—who cares? Who would check? Some might think that I'm trying to land myself a gig as a consultant for these leaders. No. I'm just writing the truth.

There was this one time that I found myself in a boat with this group. Let me say right away that my Pontic, beak-nosed friend wasn't among them. But the others were all there. We swam far from the shore. Then the sea started being unruly. We turned around, but the shore was far, far away. Some of them may have started experiencing small doses of seasickness. At any rate, they definitely experienced some level of discomfort and instantly wished they were back on land.

But the instantly part was rather problematic. The boat was pretty heavy, and, by the way, I alone was rowing. And suddenly, I felt very clearly

---

33 A popular Soviet novelist whose style was marked by an extreme nationalistic tone.

that everybody in that group—all the pretty girls, all the thoroughbred dandies—was steadily giving off a powerful, evenly distributed stench. It was the stench of egoism. Cluttered tightly in the boat as they were, they broke apart and at the same time, came together once and for all in an oppressive nimbus of stench.

There's no doubt that the guys were unfazed by the possibility of the boat capsizing. First of all, living on the Black Sea, they were all pretty athletic, and so there's no question about them worrying about suddenly finding themselves in the balmy, summertime waters.

As for the girls, I can't really attest to their athleticism. They were all out-of-towners, and I was seeing them for the first time. They probably just didn't realize the possibility that the boat might capsize. And it didn't matter a single bit whether they knew how to swim.

What's useful in proving that their knowing or not knowing how to swim had no bearing on the situation was the fact that the stench emanated with equal strength from them all. And if somebody who can swim emanates the same stench as someone who can't, it's clear that the cause of the stench lies elsewhere.

They simply suddenly became uncomfortable in the boat. They wanted to disperse, but there was nowhere to go, given that they were surrounded by the sea. So, sparks started flying, hissing, whining, accusations, insults.

Once the boat hit the shore and they jumped off onto the pebbles, they were suddenly a jovial and pretty group of friends again. The stench instantly dispersed, and I went to tug the boat into port. But even today, many years later, if anyone asks me if the stench was real, I reply calmly and firmly: yes, it was.

Moreover, it even came back under absolutely extraordinary circumstances. My closest friends from school and I were sitting one evening in a café. It was an incredible day that crossed over into an even more incredible night.

That day, they announced that Lavrentiy Pavlovich Beria[34] was arrested. I don't remember if the idiocy about him being an English spy was announced, and even if it was, nobody paid any attention to it.

---

34 Lavrentiy Beria (1899–1953) was the minister of internal affairs and the head of the secret police under Stalin. He played a major role in the Terror.

I was in our local publishing house in the morning, and one of the big-deal, in-house ideologists told us the news in a half-whisper, even though the portrait of Beria that used to hang on the wall opposite his desk had already been taken down. The portrait had been there so long that it left a trace on the wall where it used to hang in the form of a pale square.

While telling me what had happened, the big-deal ideologist would intermittently glance at the wall where the portrait used to hang with comical apprehension, as if the portrait hadn't been taken down, but was hiding behind the wall, listening to what was being said about him, and by whom.

Let's take a clinical detour and talk about our war chiefs. Hopefully for the last time. I was a nine-year-old punk when they took my favorite uncle. He was a radiant sun of a man. My aunt made me write letters addressed to Lavrentiy Pavlovich Beria. My aunt said that he went to an actual school with my uncle here in Mukhus. Lavrentiy Pavlovich couldn't have forgotten him! Everybody loved my uncle! As soon as he finds out what happened to my uncle, Lavrentiy Pavlovich will not only let him go, he'll punish whomever was responsible for the arrest.

Obviously, they made me write these letters to move him.

We even got a response from Beria's office. They promised to look into it. But nobody looked into anything, and when the war started, they took another uncle to boot. Nobody in my family returned home. The front was kinder. Not everyone came back from the war, but many did.

It was under Khrushchev that a leading physicist and (I think) a kind man told me that Beria was very smart. He dealt with him because he worked on the atomic bomb. On the Problem, as they called it to keep it a secret.

"Why do you think that?" I asked.

"There was one time," he said, "that Beria handed off to me the work of a physicist who had been nominated for the Stalin Prize. 'Look it over,' he said, 'I don't think it merits the Prize.'

"I familiarized myself with the work. It was very qualified, but it really didn't merit the Prize. When we next saw each other, I said, 'Lavrentiy Pavlovich, the work really doesn't merit the Prize, although it's quite good. But you're not a physicist, how did you know?'

"He shrugged. 'It wasn't about the Problem, so I figured it wasn't good enough.'

"It was simple and smart, you've got to give it to him. He knew that all the talented physicists were involved with the atomic bomb. And since this physicist wasn't, he couldn't have been talented enough to do work on a level that merited the Stalin Prize."

"Why didn't you think instead," I protested, "that he was rather acutely sensitive towards his own career? Let's assume that the physicist got the prize, but Stalin then found out that he wasn't involved in the Problem and asked: 'Why did you ignore such a talented man?' It's improbable, the risk is barely even there, but he didn't want to deal with a risk that was even that slight."

"That could be true too," the easygoing physicist agreed.

Generally speaking, we're all inclined to perceive reasonableness in influential (my typewriter accidentally first wrote "unhealthy") politicians as a sign of great intellect. Admittedly, sometimes, when we're disillusioned, we hit the opposite extreme. We interpret everything that they have done as the fruits of monstrous foolishness.

But here is something much more interesting. An old journalist once told me this. I can't vouch for its wholesale veracity, but it seems true.

During the Mingrelian Affair,[35] word has it that Malenkov was bringing back to Stalin a list of Party people in Georgia who were slated to be arrested. Representatives of the highest echelon of the government had to approve the list, or they "had the option" to disapprove of it. It was a standard move for criminals—get everyone's hands dirty.

Looking over the list, Stalin noticed that Beria was among those recommended for arrest.

"How did Beria get on here?" he asked Malenkov.

"He added himself, Comrade Stalin," Malenkov responded.

"When the time comes, we'll take him ourselves," Stalin said and crossed Beria's name out.

You can't deny that was a powerful psychological play on Beria's part. He understood that the Mingrelian Affair was in large part designed against him. By intentionally placing himself in danger before his opponent's combination of moves played out, he took a risk, for sure, but he also increased his chances of breaking the combination.

Stalin knew that Beria too was very powerful, and if he was sticking his neck out so brazenly, then he was clearly confident in his power. That meant

---

35 The Mingrelian Affair was a series of fabricated cases in 1951 and 1952 against high-ranking Georgian officials.

the time wasn't right. Stalin had to wait, to come up with a new play. But he didn't. Beria outfoxed him.

I remember how once, during the Doctors' Plot,[36] I was standing next to a booth on some street in Moscow, reading an article in *Pravda* about the heinous crimes being actively committed by doctors everywhere. And then I got to the last paragraph, which was stylistically awkward and strange even in that bizarre article. The author ended the article with: "That's all fine. But where was our law enforcement looking when it was all happening?"

I read and reread that last paragraph with those words, and I just couldn't wrap my head around what the author and the editor of the main newspaper in the country had just done. Even if you managed to accept the light criticism of our security apparatus, what were you supposed to do with: "That's all fine?" What's fine about murderous doctors killing their patients?! I didn't manage to wrap my head around that idiocy then, but I will always remember that ending.

And it was only much later, once word started seeping through that in the last years of his life, Stalin wanted to get rid of Beria—and come to think of it, not only Beria—when I remembered that article. I'm confident that before being published, it was sent to Stalin, who added the ending himself. Obviously, nobody dared change what he wrote. When he wrote "That's all fine," he probably wasn't referring to the sinister events described in the article. They probably never even happened. And even if they did, he organized them himself. He meant the work that the journalist had done—his retelling of the whole story. "This is all true (that's all fine), but it's time to call out our national security, who completely missed these murderous doctors." It was a quiet, but threatening growl aimed at the Lubyanka.[37] By the way, the phrase belies a degree of impatience on Stalin's part. And who knows, maybe that impatience turned out to be fatal for him.

If he had carefully read Osip Mandelstam before dooming him, he might have recalled an appropriately prophetic line:

Do not rush—haste is a luxury.

---

36 The Doctor's Plot was an antisemitic campaign by Stalin designed ostensibly to target fictitious doctors who were ruthlessly murdering their patients. The plot's end goal was the total deportation of all Jews in the USSR to Siberia and the Jewish Autonomous Oblast.

37 The Lubyanka building housed the KGB headquarters.

By the way, I just remembered something that happened right around that time. I was a student at the Library Institute. The anti-cosmopolitanism campaign was in full force.

One time, in the lobby, I saw a Jewish librarian I knew in a crowd of students who were roaring with laughter. He would visit the Institute every now and then. He was an invalid.

He stood in the middle of the crowd, eerily cheerful. He was swaying his truncated legs while leaning on his crutches, as if to demonstrate the absolute freedom and happiness he enjoyed within the confines of the crutches. He was telling a parable about his life.

He worked as a bibliographer in a large library in Moscow. After a vacation, he came back to work and found out that he was laid off under some pretense. And it was clear to him that his boss, the senior bibliographer with whom he had never been on good terms, had played a part in it. He appealed to every department he could, but to no avail. He tried to find a job in another library, but to no avail.

Then he remembered that when he lived in Birobidzhan as a little boy, plagued with a debilitating case of polio, he had written Stalin a letter. The doctors had recommended that he be taken to Crimea for treatment. But his parents didn't have the money. Which is when somebody gave them the brilliant idea to write to Stalin. Which he did.

The storyteller's legs hit an exceptionally high point between the crutches.

And sometime later, the little boy and his mother really were sent to Crimea on the government's dime. So now, desperate to find a job, he wrote to Stalin again. He told him about his hardships and reminded Stalin that he had already helped him once.

"'You've already saved my life once,' I wrote to him," recounted the bibliographer, indefatigably swaying on his squeaky crutches. "Save it one more time!"

The letter reached Stalin. And he saved his life again. Sometime later, our librarian got a call from the director of the library where he had worked before, inviting him for a chat. "Astounded" by the unfairness of what had happened, something he had "failed to notice" when it was happening, the director gave him the opportunity to take the place of the senior librarian the very next day.

"But you already have a senior librarian," said our narrator, surprised.

The swinging stopped.

"What senior librarian?" it was the director's turn to be surprised as he glanced around. "He's already been transferred to your old position!"

The swinging triumphantly resumed! Freedom and happiness between the crutches!

He told the story several times to the friendly laughter of the newly arriving students.

I'm trying to figure out how and why it happened. Stalin received thousands of letters. Obviously, he couldn't and didn't want to read them all. People working for him sifted out the ones that they thought he should absolutely see. I should think they had two filters for choosing which letters the tyrant got to see, which really combine into one.

Let's divide them up à la Stalin. Filter number one: these are letters that, if they don't reach Stalin, might prove to be dangerous for the people picking the letters out. That is, if word somehow reaches Stalin that there is a letter that he would consider important that was kept from him, then that would be very unfortunate for the letter-picker-outers.

Filter number two: these are letters that should please Stalin. Giving a tyrant a pleasant letter is another good way of prolonging your life. Hundreds of thousands of people asked for help, including Jews, who were persecuted as cosmopolites. It is unlikely that they paid any attention to letters like that. But this letter had one line that hit the bullseye: "You've already saved my life once. Save it one more time!"

Even a tyrant like Stalin isn't immune to occasionally succumbing to a particular, panhuman desire: to not ruin his own good deed with a subsequent evil one.

By doing somebody a kindness, we see ourselves in them. They are a mirror that reflects us in a good light. It is unpleasant to have to break a mirror like that. On the contrary, you want to clean it until it shines.

Similarly, if we do someone ill, we begin to despise them. They are a mirror that reflects our hideousness. We want to break a mirror like that. By doing someone ill, we subconsciously strive for their utter annihilation, if not physical, then spiritual.

There are people who are kind and easygoing. They are the ones I pity the most. They do not avoid those who have once already done them ill, believing that lightning is unlikely to strike the same place twice. If you nobly do not wish to take revenge on someone who has done you ill, then at least avoid them, because they will take revenge on you themselves, if only because you do not want to take revenge on them and therefore have already taken your revenge by morally surpassing them.

Good deeds aren't so simple either. Let's put it curtly like this: when doing good, cover your tracks, lest the dark energy of ingratitude hunts you down. And enough about this, or we'll soon drown in distracted musings. Let's get back to our evildoers.

Judging from everything told here, it is clear that Stalin wanted to use the Doctors' Plot against Beria too. But it didn't work out. Beria deftly vaulted over Stalin's corpse, but suddenly faceplanted, tripping over Khrushchev's porky, outstretched leg. And now we finally get back to the day that Beria's arrest was announced.

There were different reactions to be had in our little, southern town. Most people were exuberant, though quietly so. Some people's mood darkened, but silently. At night, though, the exuberant found their voices.

Two of my closest friends and I were sitting in a café. We were sipping wine and reminiscing about the anti-Stalin conversations we had back in school. We talked about him often, but we never lowered ourselves beyond him. Nor did we go higher than him. He was the pole of evil.

And that's when the dandy from the boat sat down next to us. For some reason, his friends called him after the European manner—Serzh. We'll call him the same thing, if we call him anything at all. Strong, wide-shouldered, wearing a fashionable button-up shirt with small shoulder marks, short-cropped hair, fiery and at the same time, glossy eyes. He was loud and acted as if he were constantly issuing challenges to everyone around him.

"Beriaites are all around us," he said passionately, as if he had just been released from a dungeon and was hellbent on revenge. "This town needs to be cleansed of Beriaites. Friends, let's drink!"

He ordered a lot of cognac, and we started drinking. My friends didn't know him. They decided that he was one of us, only much more radical. I didn't expect such political mettle from him myself. "Man is a mystery," Dostoevsky said, "whose desire to own Constantinople is, in turn, a mystery in and of itself."

I knew that Serzh's father was an important physicist who worked at a nuclear facility not far from Mukhus. According to him, his father had met Beria several times, as he oversaw the country's nuclear industry. It turned out that his father had just about had a falling out with Beria, and their being in Abkhazia was essentially exile.

"I can tell you stories that nobody knows about him," he said.

I won't lie, I was overflowing with curiosity: I was going to be a writer, after all. But at the same time, his stream of liberal indignation was getting to be dangerous in the café. People whose moods had darkened after the announcement were already giving us dirty looks, concentrating their darkness on us. Obviously, if there had been a brawl, they would have come up with another excuse.

However, it was precisely because he was demonstrating such liberal bravery that stopping him would have really been right. He finally said:

"Let's go to the motor ship. It's at the wharves right now. I'll tell you everything at the bar there. This place is full of Beriaites."

"They won't let us in," one of my school friends protested.

"They won't let *me* in?!" Serzh was furious. "My father and I used to take that ship to Odesa. The skipper would invite us to dinner every day. He loved me like a son!"

We headed towards the wharves. Mukhusites generally enjoy going to the motorboats docked at the wharves. It was a different world, a floating other. But you couldn't always get on. A lot depended on you knowing someone from the crew or the dock workers.

Nevertheless, sometimes, the watchmen would let everybody onto a ship for some unknown reason. Maybe because of their trading plan. Mukhusites would be very loose with their purse strings in those floating palaces.

Our new, fair-haired rogue of a leader gave off a wild energy, and we submitted to that energy as we came onto the gangway. But the sailor on duty stopped us.

"I urgently need to see the captain," Serzh said and named the captain by name. The sailor was unfazed by this announcement. He may have noticed that we had already had a bit to drink.

"The captain's resting," he said.

"Then call him, wake him up," Serzh insisted irritably. "He invited us."

"Get out of here," the sailor said with disgust. "You're drunk."

Serzh started screaming and called the sailor a Beriaite. I tried to get him to leave, but he pushed me away and kept rabblerousing. After he had roused enough rabble, the sailor called the port police, who promptly evicted us from the wharves.

It's amazing that they didn't take us in. I think that the authorities were still reeling from Beria's arrest. They led us out of the port and were about to let us go when Serzh decided it would be a good time to call them Beriaites too, for good measure.

"Papers and identification!" roared the police captain, laying it all on the line, readying for the possibility that his demand might cause the definitive disintegration of both his authority and the surrounding buildings. But his authority and the surrounding buildings both stood strong. This clearly invigorated him.

None of us had our papers. Only our fair-haired dandy had a pass to the building where he and his family lived. I think he gave him his pass fully expecting the captain to see his father's name, then respectfully tip his hat and let us go. But that's not what happened at all. The captain, invigorated by the sturdiness of his authority and the surrounding buildings, even without Beria's all-seeing guidance, put the pass in his jacket pocket and roared:

"Get out of here! Or I'll take you to the sobering station! You can get your pass back tomorrow with the port police! . . ."

"They won't let me into my building without that pass!" Serzh exclaimed, urgently sobering up. He himself now noticed, too late, that the captain's authority was holding strong.

"You can sleep where you drank," the captain said, after which he and his silent comrade left, stomping energetically with their boots.

The farther they receded, the more our fighting cock grew furious. Once the stomping was consumed by the nocturnal silence of the wharves, he once again began to cast doubt on the authorities' integrity.

"I won't leave this alone," he finally shouted. "They're all Beriaites! We're going to the Cheka right this instant!"

He had apparently decided that with Beria arrested, we could now go back to the noble, idyllic traditions of Dzerzhinsky.

And he took us to a building that we, like all people who lived in our town, typically avoided. What force dragged us after him? It wasn't just the power of hops. Besides, I've never in my life heard of anyone going to the KGB while drunk. So, what was this force? It was the force of what had happened, of course. Beria was arrested! That meant the entire system of repression was condemned! Even so, it was still a bit frightening to go to that frightful building in the middle of the night. And with a complaint against the police that had taken Serzh's pass, no less.

My poor friends went along because I did. And I went so as not to abandon the drunk fool, so as not to betray our drinking companion, who, as it turned out, was far more radical than we were. And to think I considered him just a party animal looking for a good time! Still, I made a few halfhearted attempts to make him change course.

"You can all go!" he barked. "People like that are what held the Beria system together!"

After that outburst, it was impossible not to accompany him. He was drunk, but brimming with a certain, alcoholic vivacity. He didn't waver, he wasn't slurring, and was quite capable of saying more than was necessary. I wanted to back him up at least by inconspicuously nudging him in the right direction once we got there.

We got to Engels Street and came up to the infamous building. The door was wide open. There was no guard. A lamp faintly illuminated the hallway.

Our leader confidently went ahead of us, violently tugging on every door, but they were all locked. There was a feeling that every time he yanked on a door, he felt the lascivious rush of victory.

"Run away, have they?!" he growled, futilely trying to jerk the last door of its hinges. He left it and flew up the stairs to the second floor.

One of the doors turned out to be open, revealing a well-lit room. We went into the room to find a security guard sitting inside. To my pleasant surprise, Serzh calmly started explaining that we were headed for the motor ship, where the captain (whom he named) was expecting us, when we were accosted by representatives of the port authorities, who took away his pass to his place of residence. He asked him to call the port police, order them to return his pass, and punish the men who took it in the first place, especially since they were probably Beriaites (you idiot, why?!). And in general, the whole town was full of Beriaites (you lunatic!)!

Our Serzh had begun so deliberately, so reasonably, so peacefully. He was in exceptionally good form when telling about the captain who was expecting us. Who may have even warned the sailor on duty to let us pass unmolested.

While he was saying that, I imagined the commotion that would have been happening on the ship.

The adoption is aborted.

The guests all leave, embarrassed by having to take back their presents that were intended for the newly adopted. But leaving them would be foolish.

The furious captain bites his pipe in half with the powerful teeth of an old sea wolf.

The sailor on duty is put in the solitary ward.

The captain despondently downs all the whiskey that was intended for the guests.

The captain tumbles into his bunk and sleeps like a corpse.

But unbearable moans can be heard from the sleeping form: "Serzh, where are you?"

Serzh, meanwhile, is demanding his rights be respected with the security guard. Put short, he started out great. And it was only towards the end of his speech, when he brought up rope in the hanged man's house that the guard figured out that he was drunk. Nevertheless, he calmly asked us all to go home.

He explained that he doesn't have the right to give any sort of order to the police (probably since that very morning). Which is why it would probably be best for us, he explained tactfully (somebody with less tact could have just said: for the state you're in), to spend the night at your friends' place, and go to the port police in the morning. Essentially this was the same as what the police captain told us to do, but it was so much more delicate, so much more human. Let's recall the police captain for a moment: "Get out of here! Sobering station! Sleep where you drink!"

This was where we should have, if not nudged, then shoved our friend out of there. But I guess we weren't decisive enough.

Meanwhile, our friend fundamentally rejected the guard's peaceful proposition and kept railing away, skirting painfully close to dangerous territory, insinuating that there were still too many Beriaite benefactors in town.

That's when the guard couldn't take it anymore. He must have decided that even though Beria was arrested, the security apparatus still had some strength to spare. He could risk it. And time proved him right.

He unexpectedly and with unexpected strength slammed his fist on the table. Refreshed by the daylong pause in activity, the fist left a serious impression. For a second, it seemed like the slam singlehandedly sundered the walls of Beria's prison, after which he emerged and immediately set about his duties, not even pausing to shake the dust off his clothes. Speaking of, it later turned out that there actually was an attempt to break him out of prison.

Having introduced his fist to the table, the officer screamed:

"Demagoguery has no place here, young man! Drunks coming in here in the middle of the night, spreading anti-Soviet nonsense! I'm detaining all of you!"

The officer threw us a look that promised no mercy. For several seconds, there was a heavy silence. A bleak curiosity passed through me: will he beat us? Then, as if in slow motion, the officer reached for the phone. It was clear that he wanted to call someone to take us to a holding cell. The lethargy in his movement could be interpreted as his indecision as to the kind of cell in which we were to be held.

"You shouldn't detain me," suddenly clucked our radical warrior. "I'm the son of professor (and he gave his last name) . . . my parents will be worried."

The atomic scientist professor's semi-secret name—*because* of its semi-secrecy—gave off an aura of heightened national importance. Serzh's words had an effect on the officer. But he didn't give up right away. He dug around in his papers, read off a phone number, and asked:

"Is that yours?"

"It is!" Serzh happily replied, as if he and guard were longtime buddies whose friendship was put on temporary hiatus because of a little misunderstanding.

The officer dialed the number and said:

"Hello, comrade professor. Please forgive the late call. I'm calling from the authorities . . . Is your son home? . . . We have him here, if it's really him . . . What is he doing here? He broke in with a group of drunkards and is making some silly claims. Please, speak with him, and if you recognize his voice, I'll let him go out of respect for you . . . With whom? I don't know . . ."

He turned to Serzh.

"Who's this with you?"

"They're just random acquaintances," he said quickly, trying not to strain the officer's attention with unimportant, secondary details. But even these words didn't hold a hint of flattery for the officer's attention—rather, he was probably reminding him that his attention belonged entirely to him. And as he did so, his tone didn't betray a hint of embarrassment with regard to us.

True, in some higher sense, we really were random acquaintances. But he meant something completely different. He meant: let me go and do with them as you please.

"He doesn't know them himself," the officer said triumphantly, handing the phone to the son.

Serzh grabbed the phone, but I just about stopped listening. Every so often, I would pick up with some subconscious, predatory glee moments in the conversation when he backstabbed us. Not even remotely ashamed by what he already said to the officer, he insolently told his father that he forgot his pass at home, but that he shouldn't look for it and instead call the guard to let him enter when he returns.

A scorching feeling of shame before my friends and loathing for this bastard blinded me. The familiar stench that I came to know on the boat was back, only this time it was much more saturated. And having said that, it's worth noting where this was happening—not out in the sea, but an enclosed space much more adept at cordoning itself off.

He left without once looking in our direction. But that doesn't mean that he forgot about us entirely. He blew past us with a certain polemical aloofness, saying on his way out:

"You think that what I'm doing is shameless, but that's exactly why you're the shameless ones, because you don't understand the difficulty of my position as the son of a famous professor."

"Aren't you ashamed? Getting the son of such a professor drunk!" said the officer, as if justifying him, but then he added: "Though that one's a keeper too."

"He's the one that got us drunk!" one of my friends protested. "He joined our table. He dragged us here!"

"Do you have identification?" the officer asked. When we told him no, he added: "I have to detain you . . . An important professor's son and blackmail go hand-in-hand . . . Though this is the first time I've seen him, but we've heard stories . . ."

And that's when I took my chance. The officer spoke flawless Russian, but by his slight accent, I had understood long ago that he was Abkhazian. I spoke to him in Abkhazian.

He was shocked by the unexpectedness. And, what's more important in this situation, he was even embarrassed. But he got a hold of himself. As people in situations like this are wont to, we started talking about where we were from. It turned out that we were almost from the same place. My mom was from Chegem, while his parents were from Dzhgerda, which is nearby. Honoring the cult of communal bread-breaking, he said:

"So he drank with you? You went out together? And now you're just random acquaintances? The pig! *And* he's the son of such an important governmental figure."

"What do you think about what happened?" I carefully asked him in Abkhazian, referring to Beria's arrest.

The situation called for philological nuance. To ask a stranger about this in Russian would have been downright insolent. The language itself is imbued with ideological censorship about certain topics.

Abkhazian wasn't ideologized enough yet, not enough to not be able to discuss facts with someone. Shepherdly traditions still held strong. And if something happened, then why not ask your neighbor: what happened to your shepherd?

The officer was momentarily consternated. As an Abkhazian, he couldn't dodge my question completely, but as an employee of such a terrifying institution, he couldn't respond either. Which is why he anxiously looked over the whole office, as if looking for a spot that wasn't bugged, but any such spot seemed to elude him, and he said constrainedly:

"We're small people. Moscow calls the shots."

Though the officer was assured that we were from neighboring villages, he didn't let us go right away. He apologized in Abkhazian and then asked me in Russian to run home to get my passport while my friends waited for me there. I sprinted home. Not wanting to wake my mom, I quietly came into the house, got my passport, quietly walked out, and set off again.

The officer and I left on fairly amicable terms and by four in the morning, we were outside again. We walked along nighttime Mukhus. My friends didn't needle me at all. We simply agreed that in the lovely school of our youth, we never let people like that close to us.

Lots of people I knew found out about this story, though I never went out of my way to spread it, just like I didn't go out of my way to keep it secret. By the way, many years later, Serzh became a big trade representative in one of the smaller European countries. Well, to hell with him, though this does all relate to the story I'm going to tell.

So, we went to my acquaintance's apartment, the one who was very sick. His wife let us in and took us to his room. It was a warm day. He lay under a light blanket. He had grown horribly thin, and trying to conceal my astonishment, I came up to him and kissed him.

I think he liked that I didn't gasp or wince, and that I just inquired about his health. He said he had an ulcer that he'd been neglecting. I don't know if he even suspected that things were much worse than that.

It seemed like his pains didn't really concern him. He joked and messed around, even told a few fresh anecdotes. His wife came in with two cups of Turkish coffee. When his wife came in, I suddenly noticed that the blanket had slid up to reveal two very skinny legs.

Not knowing why myself, I left the cup of steaming coffee untouched, got up, approached the bed, and tugged the blanket over his bony, yellow-skinned feet. And I realized that I was covering his feet because they seemed dead to me, and it was uncomfortable to have to see them while drinking coffee. Maybe in lieu of coffee, I wouldn't have paid them any attention. It's difficult to say.

I realized why I was doing it while doing it, and I was scared that he might realize it too. I looked at him. Our gazes met. On the outside, his look didn't convey anything beyond a strange degree of attention and slight irony. It seemed like he was looking at me from some cold depths that I forced him into. The look that we exchanged was not a good one. And yet I still hoped that he didn't understand what had happened. But he understood everything and instantly got back at me for my (albeit subconscious) egoism. He always had been quick-witted.

He suddenly started telling me about whom else but Serzh. He said that Serzh had become a highly qualified expert, that any minute now, he was going to be named the country's chief trade representative (I had thought that he'd been chief long ago), that he doesn't leave Europe, but that he characteristically always vacations in Abkhazia. His childhood friends were the single most important thing for him. He had seen everything this world had to offer, but nothing was more important than friendship, than the friends of one's youth. His words.

The little twerp's great, big career didn't upset me. If anything, it only confirmed how his betrayal many years ago wasn't an accident. But my storytelling acquaintance's tone was so lyrical, he imbued his words with such tenderness, that by the end of his monologue, he even shed a tear. That's how much he loved him. And for some reason, that was uncomfortable. Usually what hurts us isn't the subject matter that somebody wants to hurt us with, but the conviction with which they want to hurt us.

Of course, I still can't say with absolute certainty that his loving recollections were revenge for my subconscious and therefore all the more deeply rooted egoism. His feet, you see, look like they belong on a corpse. Let's cover them up so that we don't have to think about the transience of our own (thank God) not-yet-fading life. But what's the person who those feet are attached to supposed to do?

It's true, I *had* sinned, but I didn't do it when I was covering his feet. I did it when had come to see him in the first place, when I had come to see someone who was deathly ill without a hint of earnest love or pity for him. I mean, I did pity him, but it was an abstract pity.

If I had borne him earnest love and even had the same intention while covering his feet, then, even if in passing, my hands would have tenderly patted the blanket around his feet, and maybe even squeezed them in farewell. And I think he would have interpreted my gesture differently.

The poor guy responded to my curtailed gesture with a similarly curtailed act of vengeance. In telling me about his childhood friend's career, he pretended that he didn't remember what had happened forty years ago. And he formally had every right to do so, because I wasn't the one to tell him about it.

But why did he decide to tell about him specifically? And why was his voice so full of affection? His friend's life was passing before his eyes, and his delighting in that life couldn't have been unexpected. If his childhood friend had disappeared from his life for many years and suddenly reappeared with his glorious career, it would be justified. But he brought him up precisely because he had preemptively gotten revenge on me for today's tactlessness almost forty years ago.

None of this can really be proven, but that's exactly how it happened. Generally speaking, lots of things that can't be proven are true. And much that has been proven turns out to be untrue or a mistake, and even though we can't prove that it's a mistake, we're certain of it anyway.

You can't prove that God exists, but our actions that are guided by faith are right. Lenin's existence is quite provable, but our actions that are guided by his teachings are wrong. All things considered, we can say that God can't be proved, but he exists, because that is right. Lenin can be proved, but he doesn't exist, because that is wrong.

Let's ask ourselves a question: does God exist if not a single person in the world believes in him? Obviously, that can't be possible. But if it could, we would be forced to say: man has yet to become man, and that's why nobody believes in God. But God exists. He is preparing to open man's eyes. This situation is clear.

Something else is much more frightening and unclear. Let's say people believe in God, but then, for some reason, mankind in its entirety stops believing in God. Does that mean that humans have stopped being human? But how could God let that happen? It's one thing when humans have yet to become human. God's still ahead of us, then. But when humanity stops believing in God? Then either God is dead or else he's turned away from humanity to make it yearn and reach out for him to remedy its sudden cosmic orphanhood.

Anybody who is sound of mind gets that morality cannot be rationally explained. Let's say that one drizzling, fall evening, somebody is headed home when they suddenly hear a lonely kitten meowing in the bushes. That person feels a stab of pity. But they think, "I'm not pitying this kitten to counterbalance my egoism, so people might not take pity on me when *I'm* helpless. This pity cannot be explained." And there is no substitution, such as likening the kitten to their kid, that can explain the feeling of pity. We clearly understand that the pity piercing us is more primal than our understanding of it. We might bring up morality, conscience, God, but we don't understand what they are, even though we understand that other explanations are wrong.

Let's imagine that we found a piece of shiny metal on the road. One person says: it's gold! Another: it's copper! But a metal expert inspects what we found and says: it's not gold *or* copper, though I don't know what metal it actually is. I've never seen it before.

It's clear that the metal expert is closer to the truth than the others, even though he himself cannot explain just what it is that we found. Similarly, faith in God is partly knowledge, sufficient enough to keep us from many earthly mistakes, but not complete enough to understand ourselves.

I think a powerful, indisputable argument in support of atheism would be the destruction of life on Earth. Yes, if that happens, then right before the Earth dies, the last atheist will be able to say: "We were right. There is no God." But no one will hear him. But enough about that.

. . . Here, by the sea, strolling along the green hills of the Gudauta Region, my mind was either soaring among the heavens or again returning to yesterday's unpleasant experience. But the day was beautiful. Slow, heavy hawks swam in the deep, autumnal sky. Some circled around the hills for a long time, others made directly for the sea. Beneath the hills, you could hear the dull cracks of gunfire. Someone was hunting quail.

Looking at the autumnal hawks that were swimming through the sky, I came up with the following thought. Let's say that one's spiritual life consisted of studying the flight patterns of birds and catching them. In that case, executing that spiritual objective would constitute the best conditions for executing one's material objective.

Unfortunately, only a hunter would buy into the power of faith with such clarity. In reality, that's exactly how things are. Faith is powerful, but its power is available only to those who have faith without seeking power.

All birds of power fly beneath the heavens, but man raises his gaze upwards for the first time to see the sky, and not because the sky is full of birds. That's the only way it's possible to correctly determine the relationship between the scope of the sky and reasonable power.

That's when a person appeared on the trail. By the look of things, he had just been studying the flight patterns of birds, and rather successfully at that. He had a hunting rifle slung over his shoulder and two enormous vultures hanging from either side of his belt, swaying and dragging their feathers along the ground.

In some Abkhazian villages, people eat vultures and even preserve them for the winter. So, if we accept my thoughts on man's material objective, then we can say that he just solved it. And he did so while accounting for his spiritual objective too, as it's impossible to kill a vulture in flight without looking at the sky. For that matter, he himself later told me about his spiritual preferences.

We approached each other. He was a man of middling height, very thickset, and his rustic face was kind and wide. He wore a grey shirt with a hunter's belt strapped across it, jodhpurs, and boots. As I later found out, his name was Ruslan.

I greeted him in Abkhazian, and he eagerly started up a conversation with me. He and I chatted, flitting between Abkhazian and Russian and back to Abkhazian. But before we started chewing the fat, he suddenly stopped, his face clearly signaling that he was waiting for me to engage in the ritual of marveling at his feathery trophies.

And then, adopting the air of someone who's taken aim at a soaring eagle or two himself, I felt one of the immense vultures. The wings were still warm.

I felt the wings with the look of someone who understood every detail of what he was doing. Mm-yes, I've seen a few vultures in my day. Indeed. Though they weren't this big. No, no, truth is truth, they were never this big. I even spread the wings apart, but the wingspan was wider than my own arm span. No, no, I never bagged ones this big. Even that Amazonian condor that one time was probably a bit smaller. Amazonian or Cordilleran? No matter. It's so difficult to keep track of them all. What matters is that he was smaller. I can't lie to you.

He waited with benevolent patience as I felt up his trophy with quiet and experienced admiration. He even spread out the arm under which the vulture was hanging for my groping convenience. Women adopt this same benevolent patience when they let other women feel up a new blouse or a new dress of theirs.

Not knowing what else to do with him, still busily ruffling around with his enormous wings, I brought one of them up to my shirt as if I had long been an admirer of aquiline fabrics. Mm-yes, when *I* go hunting for leather,

I procure only the finest hides for my needs. Yes, yes, we were quite adept with the needle once too, yes.

Seeing his amazement, I leaned in, took in as much breath as I could, and for some ungodly reason started blowing right on the vulture's chest, trying to get to his sinewy body.

Who knows why I did that! Maybe at some point somewhere, maybe in Chegem, I saw somebody do something similar. Yes, that's it, only they did it with hens to test how fatty they were. And if a hen didn't have enough fat, it was released to graze some more. It was probably a little late to let those vultures go out and graze or do anything else for that matter. And if I'm being completely honest, I think they blew on the rump, not on the chest.

This last operation of mine completely blew Ruslan's mind. He had no idea I'd be evaluating his trophies so fastidiously. He anxiously stood still. But once I straightened and looked him in the eyes, he understood that things were alright.

I decided that the ceremony was over, unless I was planning on gliding away from that hill on the back of one of those vultures. But that wasn't about to happen. With touching readiness, Ruslan spread his other arm as if to say: don't offend the other vulture, complete the ceremony in full.

There was nothing left for me to do other than climb under his arm and busy myself with the second vulture. This one was smaller than the first, but I spread his wings anyway, as if hoping to find that my own hunting achievements can match Ruslan's at least here. But it was hopeless—his vultures were still impossibly larger than anything I'd ever brought down.

And despite being smaller than the first (which is where the hope stemmed from), this vulture's wingspan was still wider than the span of my arms. Poor Ruslan kept standing there with his considerably raised elbow, most likely having figured out the source of my private disquiet and even rooting for me, waiting for me to finish my gloomy inspection. I folded the vulture's wings and shook my head slightly: no, I never had a vulture like this.

"You're not going to blow on him?" asked Ruslan.

"Are they from the same flock?" I inquired, the distinguished specialist that I was.

"Yes," Ruslan replied.

I waved his suggestion off, letting him know that if they're from the same flock, there's no need to check. Ruslan appreciated both my ruthless honesty and the lack of hairsplitting in my inspection of the second vulture's constitution, since they were from the same flock. Overcome with magnanimity, he invited me to have lunch with him and one of the vultures, and even made as if to take the bird off his belt.

Now, I must note that his hands moved in the direction of the second vulture, the one that was smaller than the first, but, of course (alas), many times superior to any vulture that I had ever shot out of the sky. I appreciated the gesture, but I decisively stopped his attempt.

Ruslan was surprised. "But you know your stuff about vultures. Are you one of the other Abkhazians who don't eat them?"

"No," I said. "I do! I'm not one of the other Abkhazians who don't eat vultures. Back in Chegem, vulture meat was a favorite dish. Grandpa would sometimes yell to one of his sons: 'Go bag some vultures. I feel a hankering for some nice, juicy vulture.'"

This was unadulterated crap. I was exactly one of those Chegemites who never ate vulture meat and never needed an excuse to make fun of people who did.

"Your grandpa was a wise man," Ruslan said. "But there are Abkhazians who despise vulture meat. But if your pumpkin-headed fool of a wife can't make satsivi[38] with vulture, which is nothing like chicken, then why deal with the poor vulture in the first place? And if you preserve it for the winter, then you'll never need another snack, it's like chocolate."

I decided to leave vultures alone, feeling the topic posed a certain danger to me. I asked him where he works.

"I'm in the police," he said and gestured towards the shoreside vale like a viceroy at the land he presides over. "I work as a security guard at three different health spas . . ."

And though I couldn't see the spas, I knew they were there. Again, the duality of what we can see and what actually exists.

"But that's not the point," he went on. "As a member of the police, I have to fight for fairness. And I do. But I can't stand backward people, even if they're Abkhazian! When I see a backward person, I feel so sick that I can't look at them. I walk by them looking the other way! And it might not be because of the vulture thing. I just generally hate backward people. But especially those who hate vultures. You know, some smart people are saying that things will be very bad soon. There'll be nothing to eat. And meanwhile,

---

38 Satsivi is the walnut sauce base used in a variety of Georgian dishes. It also refers to the dishes themselves.

in the fall, thousands, *thousands* of vultures fly by on their way to Turkey. At no cost. Hey, do Turks eat vultures?"

"I don't know," I said.

"Where do you live?"

"Moscow."

"I've been in Moscow twice," he said importantly. "First time was ten years ago. Second time was last year. And what's interesting is that ten years ago, Moscow was full of pigeons. But I didn't see any last year. What, were they all eaten?"

"I doubt it," I said. "Things aren't that bad yet."

"What do you do?" he asked.

"I write books," I said.

"What do you write about?" he perked up. "Our Abkhazian history or just whatever's at hand?"

"Mostly about our Abkhazian history," I said, and then added in an attempt to lower the pathos: "But sometimes about whatever's at hand."

"Power to you for writing about our Abkhazian history!" he exclaimed. "I could kiss you for that, anywhere you want! But when you have time, don't forget to write about whatever's at hand too. Somebody somewhere probably needs that as well. But power to you for writing about our Abkhazian history!"

He was so pleased with my chiefly writing about Abkhazian history that he once again decided to gift me one of the vultures.

"Listen," he said menacingly. "I swear by my two kids, I'll be offended if you don't take this one!"

His hands made for his belt, but this time towards the enormous vulture. Never before had I received payment in the form of vulture.

"No!" I grabbed his hands. "Thank you, friend. I wouldn't be able to prepare a vulture properly. I'm just visiting with some friends here."

"Listen," he looked me hard in the eyes. "Maybe you just don't want to say that you've never had vulture? I'm not like that. I won't be offended. That doesn't mean that you're a backward person, it just means that you lived in Moscow. Even if you lived in Abkhazia and never ate vultures, I won't be mad. You write about Abkhazian history, that means everything to me! But then you have to write the truth: I lived in a backward village called Chegem, where people didn't eat vultures. And if you find somebody who broadens your horizon to the taste of the vulture, you have to honestly write about him!"

"No," I said. "Thank you! I've been eating vultures since I was a kid. I even roasted it on a spit!"

"What do you mean on a spit?" he asked wonderingly.

Even if I had roasted anything on a spit, it was mostly corn on the cob and chickens. In my grandpa's home, roasting a vulture on a spit would have been the same as roasting a crow. But I had nowhere to retreat.

"I mean on a spit," I repeated, lowering myself into the stream of lies. "Like a turkey."

"A turkey's one thing," he said almost snidely, "but a vulture's completely different. A vulture has tough meat. It needs to be boiled properly."

"And why does wine exist?" I retorted, catapulting myself into French cuisine, which I hoped he knew even less about than I did. "We Chegemites marinate the vulture in wine. For a whole day! And then we roast it on a spit. That's how we used to do it."

"Hold on! Hold on!" he called out and hit me in the shoulder, imploring me to slow down. "What wine specifically? 'Kachich,' 'Isabella,' 'Tsolikauri?'"

"Any!" I exclaimed as any liar would have, covering up my lies with pathos. And then I thought: now I've really stepped in it!

"Can you marinate it in chacha?"[39] he asked, trying to grasp every variant of the new Chegem mindset.

"No," I said strictly. "You can only wash it down with chacha."

"That I could have figured out," he nodded. "But marinating a vulture in wine before roasting it on a spit—I've never heard anybody do that before. It's no wonder that they say that Chegemites are as much underground as they are above it."

In Abkhazian, that proverb refers to great slyness, or even outright, ruthless cunning. I once again tried to steer the conversation away from those damn vultures before I was caught.

I asked him if he knew anyone who caught and trained hawks. And suddenly he smiled such an unexpected, blissful smile. His wide face became a tapestry of boundless geniality. His whole body relaxed as he inclined his head and looked at me silently for a few seconds.

I realized that the ecstasy of vulture hunting had subsided. The ablution of a vulture in wine just before sliding it onto a spit had sweetly gotten the best of him. The poem had ended. Though small fragments would later resurface.

---

39 A kind of Georgian brandy.

"He's standing in front of you," he said quietly and clearly. "I'm on my way to my shelter . . . And here's my shrikette . . ."

Having said that, he unbuttoned his shirt and carefully took out a little shrikette with a cord attached to its foot. The little bird seemed very disconcerted by our talk of vultures. He wrapped the cord around his palm, leaving about half a meter free. He shook his hand. The shrikette took flight and started gyrating above him like a propeller. We set off.

"She's a feisty one," he nodded towards the bird. "I just fed her some grasshoppers."

We reached the shelter. It was covered with dried fern leaves, which also served as its floor. We stooped and went inside. Standing on his knees, Ruslan took off his rifle and put it in the corner. Then he took off his hunter's belt with the two enormous, brown vultures, took it to another corner and carefully put it down.

It was hot. The shelter stank of rotting fern. Ruslan took off his shirt, stuck a hand out of the shelter, shook his shirt, and carefully threw it over the vultures, instantly debilitating their aquiline essence by making them seem like a pair of elderly ladies snoozing under a blanket.

After that, he took out a matchbox out of which he got two pieces of wax. This entire time I was holding the shrikette. He took her out of my hands and unexpectedly deftly placed the pieces of wax over the bird's eyelids. The operation was painless, but rough. The lumps of wax on the bird's eyelids, though lending her an air of pedantic erudition, didn't enhance her attractiveness. Turns out that's done to keep the shrikette from seeing the approaching hawk and hiding from it. Ruslan unwound the cord and let the bird loose under the net. It took a few steps, then flew up and got tangled in it.

It would seem that far from just any bird demonstrates such a fiery desire to live. That's exactly why the shrikette attracts hawks better than other birds. The livelier a living being acts, the more alluring it is for predators.

We sat facing the net, glancing at the ridge of picturesque hills on the other side of the blooming vale. As it always looks when you're standing above something, it looked like towards the left end of the vale, the earth was bulwarked by a great wall that was the sea.

When Ruslan took off his shirt, I noticed an impressive scar on his forearm.

"What's that?" I nodded towards the scar once we sat down.

"Hah!" he smirked. "That was three years ago. I was guarding a spa during a dance. And I see some guy—from *my* village, I might add—constantly badgering a girl that had come in from out of town. She doesn't want to dance with him, but he keeps badgering her. I took him aside and warned him to stop messing around.

"It looked like he had left her alone, but then he was back at it. She doesn't want to dance with him, but he keeps badgering her. Persistently and roughly. I took him aside and warned him that things might get ugly if he doesn't stop pestering her.

"And then? He took another break. Either he thought that I would forget about him or he wanted to prove to his boys that he could forcefully bring the girl to heel. He was back at it. I had a situation on my hands.

"What was I supposed to do? If the spa had a detention cell, I could take him there. But the spa doesn't have a detention cell. If I had a car, I could take him to the police station. But I don't have a car. So, I have to solve the problem with my hands. Which is why I took him outside and gave him a fatherly punch in the face. He never showed his face in the club again. I think I knocked some sense into him. After the dance ended, I headed home, but I live in the village.

"I'm almost home when I see some guys standing outside my house. He's with them. They're standing right on the road, there's no way to get past. I walk up to them. One thing leads to another. And suddenly that bastard takes out a knife and stabs me. Thank God I managed to turn my shoulder."

The minstrel of ancient Abkhazia (that is, me) was distraught by this story.

"How," I said, "could a young Abkhazian guy stab someone from the same village who was twice his age?"

Ruslan froze and looked at me with eyes wide from wonder.

"What, were you born yesterday! They'd beat their own mothers to death! These are the thugs we have to deal with these days!"

But then a thought flickered in my head: it was the shoreline! People here are more quickly corrupted by the allure of resort life. When you want to defend a thought that has always warmed you, you always find a quick explanation. Ruslan went on:

"Blood starts fountaining out of me. I go inside. My wife bandages my arm. The next day, I'm bedridden. An entire delegation of his relatives comes to visit. They promise money. They promise everything in the world just so long as I don't go to the authorities. Attacking a policeman in the line of duty—God knows how much he'd get. And they know this. They beg me. But I tell them:

"'I won't go to the authorities. But when the wound heals, he and I are going to fight. Three witnesses on his side, three on mine. Let him show with his fists what he's capable of.'

"'Why fight,' they say, surprised. 'Just take the money. You have a young wife. A little kid. Money always comes in handy.'

"'No,' I say. 'No money. This is the only way.' And so, we have an honest fight. He's a bull, but he's stupid. Meanwhile, I was a first-rate wrestler in school. In short, I thrashed him. It was such a rush, as if I had shot down a sixteen-kilogram vulture with a single bullet. That's where this scar comes from . . . Quiet! Get down!"

I got down, not understanding what was happening. Ruslan got down too and started jerking the cord. The shrikette started up a flurry of movement, suspended in the air. Looking out of the shelter, I saw that the sky above the net was clear, devoid of vultures.

But he was looking in the direction of the parallel hill, which was about a kilometer away. And he kept nodding at me and pointing at the hill—the vulture's over *there*. I looked as hard as I could, and for a long time, but I couldn't see a thing. Finally, I thought that some bird's silhouette flashed against the backdrop of the green hill.

I thought that even if it was a vulture, it was impossible for him to see our shrikette from so far away. But my companion kept watching the other hill, waiting for something, making his bird flutter around.

"He flew away," he said finally, and stopped tugging on the cord.

"Could he really have seen us from there?" I asked. I had always thought that eagles see far by gazing on the world below from great heights. In this case, if we had really seen the same bird, then the hawk had been next to the other hill at the same height as us.

"Of course," he said confidently. "He sees everything! He just accidentally didn't look here. If he had—boom! . . . Yeah, so," he said, leaving the cord alone and letting his bird calm down. "You're surprised at our thugs. But it's the thieves—there are so many thieves, if you only knew. Essentially one out of every three guys here has done time. Where are the authorities? Where's the Supreme Soviet, what's it blithering about?"

"Why?"

"Let's say a man steals. The court proves it. He does his time. Then he's released. He steals again. The court proves it. He does more time. He's released. And he steals again. What's the point of jailing him? Somebody like that needs to be shot! Somebody like that isn't suited for society. He's good for nothing."

"But Ruslan, that's taking it too far," I said. "Nowhere in the world is there a law like that."

"Is there anywhere in the world where people steal like that?"

"I don't think so."

"And that's why I'm saying," Ruslan continued, "that we need a law like that. But it can't be sprung on us suddenly. That would be unfair. People should be warned. Those that have been in jail three or four times should be left alone too. But new thieves that are caught and put away need to be honestly warned: if we catch you again, fine, but the third time we'll shoot you. That way, after his second time, if he thinks about stealing again, he'll think: no, no. They'll shoot me.

"There's under-the-table stuff that happens in the police too. But I can't do that. My hands are clean. I earn about three hundred. But is that enough to live on these days, especially if you're risking your life? What if that idiot had used a gun instead of knife? Try turning your shoulder then!

"My wife and two kids live in a private apartment in the city. I pay a hundred rubles. In practice, I get by on manual labor. The resorts are next to our village. After guard duty, I come home to my father. I plow, I hoe, I reap the harvest. We live off of that. Who am I—a policeman or a peasant? I don't know."

I must have grown somber, because he suddenly smiled widely and slapped me on the shoulder.

"Don't sweat it," he said. "It's a shame, sure, but we keep up. As you can see, I even get out to hunt. Quail, vultures, when the season's right—all you can eat. I don't miss my relatives' weddings either . . . What do you think, do Turks eat vulture?"

This question really seemed to bother him, and he forgot that he had already asked me.

"I don't think so," I said. "They're doing fine food-wise right now. Why?"

"Things are still okay around here, thank God. But I'm thinking about the future. If there's a famine, the army has to help us."

"What army?" I must have missed something.

"I've thought it over," he said. "If the army gives us thirty or forty helicopters during vulture season, we'll get through it. The helicopters will herd the vultures closer to the shore, so that it takes them longer to get to Turkey. At the same time, everybody who lives here will shoot at them. We'll teach whoever doesn't know how. Fifteen or twenty preserved vultures will let a small family easily make it through the winter. But that's only if the Turks don't eat vulture. If they do, it won't be decent of us. We'll be taking their food away from them."

"I'm sure they don't eat it," I said. "I have an editor I know, I can write him . . ."

"Could you?" he said. "Only don't tell him everything. Tell him that you heard Turks don't eat pork. But what about vulture?"

He grew pensive, gazing up at the sky where vultures, flapping their heavy wings, were slowly and uninhibitedly making their way towards Turkey, not even suspecting about the schemes fermenting in Ruslan's head. Some of them naively circled above the hills and sometimes even sat on trees.

"Do you believe in God, Ruslan?" I asked.

"Of course," he said, sounding surprised. He glanced at me. "Who did all this if not God? The mountains, the sea, forests, man, animals?

"Some say it's nature. But that's silly. That's like a woman saying that she impregnated herself. Or somebody coming into my father's house and saying: 'Ruslan, look at the beautiful corn that grew all on its own!' On its own? I know whose hard work made it grow like that! This is the same."

"What do you think, Ruslan," I asked, "Does God pay attention to our affairs?"

"Never!" exclaimed Ruslan with such force that the shrikette leapt and started flapping about under the net all on its own. "Only backward people think that! He doesn't need us, he's not going to pay attention to us! He has millions of planets like this! Like any good, strict father, he put man and nature on their feet: live, reproduce, be friends! And what did we do? Look at what's going on even here in the Caucasus! If he saw all this, a huge gob of his spit would fly right at the Earth. For now, it's just us humans spitting at one another."

"What is man, Ruslan?" I asked, figuring that I should see our philosophical chat to its logical end.

"He's cunning, like a goat," Ruslan replied simply, as if this was old news.

And suddenly, a tender, wistful smile split his wide face. I realized that he had come up with the ideal person for his story.

"Let me tell you about my son," he looked at me, still smiling. "He's six. He's a tricky little devil, but he doesn't eat very well. Though he devours vultures like a little tiger. He takes after me. But in general, he doesn't like to eat. My wife doesn't know what to do with him.

"Here's what's interesting. Sometimes I come home from work when my wife is making him eat. And he looks me in the eye and understands everything. Everything! Sometimes I come home after guard duty, mad like hell. And then he eats, because I might blow up at him. And he doesn't like that. But if I come home happy, then he starts whining and turning away from the food.

"So I *just* get back from work, haven't even had time to say anything, and he's looking me in the eyes—should he eat or should he whine? And he's *never* been wrong!

"... You'll laugh ... I'll tell you anyway. He and I tell each other riddles. Sometimes I get back from work, lie down on the couch, and he plops down on my stomach, and we start telling each other riddles. We have a blast! One time, he says:

"'Dad, what should you drink to feel good?'

"'Wine,' I say.

"'No,' he says, 'medicine. You lose.' It's a coincidence, but my wife is cackling as if he'd just gotten me good. But he actually saved my life once..."

Ruslan grew thoughtful, gazing off into the distance, chewing on a fern stem. Then he tossed it away, looked at me with his suddenly blazing, brown eyes, and almost yelled:

"Listen, I'll tell you something you won't read in a single book. It's a hoot! But you're one of us, you have to know about it.

"Two years ago, some woman from Moscow came to one of the resorts I guard. A nurse. Full figure, pale skin, she was a beauty. And I fell in love with her. And turned out she liked me too, but I didn't know about it. I lost my mind. I'm in bed next to my wife, I close my eyes, and all I see is her. Plump, pale—and she's laughing. I come to guard duty, and she's there again. But this time in the flesh! Plump, pale, and laughing.

"And I couldn't take it anymore. I finally told her that I can't live without her. And she agreed. And we made plans to marry and then for me to move to Moscow. I rented a room next to the resort, where the personnel works. It would've been awkward to go to her room in the resort. After all, I'm a staff member. So, I rented a room.

"I thought that nobody would notice at home, because the resort I guard is next to my village, and I usually spent the night at my father's. It was fifteen kilometers to the town where my family lived, and I don't have a car. So, I usually spent the night at my father's, especially since I had to work the fields. My father's pretty old.

"But I was a wreck. Sooner or later, I had to tell my wife the truth. But I love her too, and my son, little Timur, is to die for. We didn't have our girl yet. But what was I supposed to tell her? What was she guilty of? Nothing! But I can't live without Lusya either. Her name was Lusya. She was a nurse in an important hospital in Moscow. I was losing it. I'd close my eyes, and she'd be right in front of me: plump and pale and laughing. I'd open them, and there she was.

"While I was torturing myself over how to tell my wife, turned out somebody already told her. Somebody told her, I even know who, but that's not important anymore. Yeah. She knew. But she didn't say a word to me. Apparently when the poor woman found out, she couldn't eat for three days afterwards. Couldn't stomach a single bite. How could I forget something like that? She knew, but didn't say a word to me. I'd come home, she'd put food on the table, clean everything afterwards. But she was silent. I thought she must have felt something, but she just already knew. And I didn't know yet that she knew everything.

"Now then, Timurchik. About half a year beforehand, we went on a trip to town as a family. My friend drove us. He has his own car. And suddenly, his hands slipped off the steering wheel, he lost control of the car. The car drove right into a ditch and flipped over. My family was in the back seat. I barely managed to turn around, like this, and ask them if they were alive.

"'Don't look at me, you pigs!' my wife screamed. Turns out when the car flipped, her skirt flipped up too, and she couldn't cover herself because of the tiny inconvenience posed by the car being flipped over.

"Welp, since she's yelling, I figure, she's alive, and so is Timurchik, his eyes are just a little wide with fear. My friend and I somehow got out of the car. I got the back door open and carried them both out of the car. What's interesting is that nobody had a scratch on them! It was a very successful flip.

"My friend and I started laughing at my wife's reaction. But she wasn't. Timurchik laughed too, though he was four, what could he have understood? But since we were laughing, he got that something was funny, so he laughed along. My friend and I were laughing because of my wife's voice when she called us pigs and told us to turn around—as if we had turned around intentionally to make her skirt flip up. Listen, we were just in an accident, I'm worried for my family's safety, and she's concerned about her skirt. And she just doesn't get why we're laughing, and that makes it all the funnier. And Timur was laughing too, even without understanding what was happening.

"I stopped every car I could, but nobody had a tow cable. Finally, I stopped a truck that had one, we flipped the car over, and got it out of the ditch. We kept going. The back door was slightly dented, but that was the only damage. Ever since, both in Russian and Abkhazian, my son doesn't use the word 'rope.' He only says 'tow cable.' He thinks a rope and a tow cable are called the same thing.

"So, after that happened, my son asked me to tell the story of how it happened several times. He pestered and pestered me: 'The car fell!' I tell him what happens, and he giggles, thinking about how fun the whole thing was.

"Timur and I still play riddles. I read him a children's book, but when I leave or when his mother puts him to bed, he always begs me: 'The car fell!' He listens to the story, but he doesn't laugh like he used to. He lies there all serious and just listens. As if he wants to say something. But what can he say? Of course, he doesn't laugh. Then why recall it at all? But I'm patient with him, because I feel guilty before my own kid.

"And each time I go to tell my wife the truth, I can't. Lots of people have forgotten who they are these days, but I come from a family with principles. Relatives from both our sides would come and ask me: 'Why are you leaving your wife? If she's ugly or useless, where were you when you married her? If she's got a bad attitude, why didn't you tell us? We would have gotten together and told her to stow it, or else we'd send her right to her father!'

"But there was nothing wrong with my wife, and I had nothing to say to them. And so, after torturing myself for days on end, I finally decided to tell my wife the truth, cut ties with my family, and leave for Moscow to be with Lusya. Since they wouldn't let me live a peaceful life here anyway.

"So, I come home for the last time. I'm thinking, either I tell her everything today or that's it—I'm done. I hold myself together. I play with Timur. I figure I'll wait for him to fall asleep, and then tell my wife. She's in the kitchen. He and I are alone. We play, then I read him a book, and then he drags me to the couch. I instantly know what he wants.

"'The car fell,' he says, and lies down, still holding my hand. Great, just what I need. But what can I do? I can't let my kid down. I tell him the story, and he listens and listens, but doesn't laugh. He looks so serious, as if he wants to say something. But what can the kid say to me?! And I'm mentally killing myself over how to tell my wife! And I slowly start to slip, but I'm still holding myself together. When I finish, he gives me the order again: 'The car fell!'

"I tell him again, and he holds me by the hand and listens with such a serious expression, as if he doesn't know what's coming next. He waits. But what is he waiting for?

"I barely made it through that second time. You have to be an adult to understand what was funny about the story. And he's not laughing anyway. The car flipped over, big deal. We all made it, we tugged the car out, hurray. But he hangs on to my every word with such a serious expression. As soon as I finish, he orders me again:

"'The car fell!'

"And that's when I snapped. I threw his hand down and screamed:

"'I'm tired of your car! It's bedtime!'

"'No!' He yells right back and starts to cry so loudly that his mom runs into the room.

"She picks him up. Calms him. But he just weeps, and he's looking at me through his tears, looking at me and saying over and over:

"'The car fell! The car fell!'

"He was having a fit. There's not even a word for that in Abkhazian. I don't remember anything that happened after that. I only remember that I went out of the room and slammed the door as hard as I could. I drank a lot that evening. A hell of a lot. But I never lose my head. I went to Lusya. She knew that I had a difficult conversation with my wife ahead of me that evening. She thought that I had drunk so much because I already had it. And she didn't ask me anything. She figured I'd tell her myself the next day.

"For the first time since we got together, I went to bed alone. I was asleep the minute I hit the bed. And then, in the middle of the night, I wake up as if someone had pushed me. Hard. Angrily, even: wake up!

"I wake up. My head's clear like glass. But I had drunk a lot. And it was a miracle, and I instantly understood what my boy wanted to say to me. And I was even amazed at how long it took me to figure it out!

"My boy wanted to tell me: let everything be as it was before, when the car flipped. Scary at first, but then funny. And the poor kid sensed that something scary was happening in our house, but the funny hadn't come yet. And he, my little boy, kept pushing things in that direction. But I never got him. 'The car fell!'

"I jumped up like a madman. I start getting dressed. Lusya wakes up. She asks in alarm: 'What happened?' 'Sorry, Lusya,' I say. 'I can't live without my son!'

"I walked fifteen kilometers in the night. So many thoughts ran through my head. At five in the morning, I knock on my door. My wife opens it. She doesn't say anything. I don't either. I go right to my son. And I undress and lie down next to him. He senses me and starts moving. He hugs my neck with one arm, and, without waking up, I checked, he says sweetly: 'The car fell . . .'

"He did it. The next night, we planted another seed in our family garden, and we had a daughter. We've been going strong ever since. My son saved our family."

Ruslan fell silent. He was thinking about something. While he was telling the story, he was so inspired, that his simple, wide face transformed before my eyes. At the moment, his face expressed victory, beauty, antiquity. But a minute later, it started fading, like the sky at twilight, and it soon took on its usual expression.

To the right of where we were sitting, a small flock of sheep emerged out from behind a bend in the hill. Huddling together and interweaving among one another, the sheep slowly went along the bend towards the bottom of the hill, the silently undulating ball of fleece gliding along the immobile fleece of the fading grass on the ground.

They started up their familiar bleating. Then more. More. Even more. But much more familiar than the bleating itself was its dolorous echo in the chest. But why? Is it a reminder of childhood? A reminder of life's transience? What if I remember that when I was a kid, it seemed sad to me too?

Maybe we interpret the bleating as the language-less yearning for language? But then it's even less clear why a human would get so sad upon hearing the bleating of sheep or the mooing of cows. Humans actually *have* language. The thing is probably that to one degree or another, every person feels his own ineffability. The chorus of our global bleating serves only to stress man's solitude. And only love, as with Ruslan and his son, sometimes surmounts this ineffability.

That's when something unexpected happened, even though it was exactly what we should have anticipated. I heard some kind of noise coming from the sky. I came to my senses only after the hawk slammed right into the net and started thrashing around in it, flapping its wings and contorting itself. Ruslan jumped up and untangled the hawk from the net. The poor shrikette was petrified in horror and was lying prone under the net.

Ruslan sat under the shelter, holding the hawk in one hand, covering its head with the other. The hawk's yellow eyes blazed with loathing and terror. His talons twitched, trying to bore into the air.

"The hawk's wrong," said Ruslan, looking him over.

"Why?" I asked.

"It's the wrong type. It's dumb. Teach it all you want, but it'll never learn. It never gets accustomed to people."

"Let me hold him," I said and, carefully keeping away from the talons, took the hawk. The hawk's warm, light body shuddered beneath my palm. His blazing, yellow eyes and warm, light body pulsed all over with terror and loathing. Terror and loathing.

"So what should we do with him?" I asked.

"Let him go, we'll catch another."

I exited the shelter and tossed the bundle of terror and loathing up into the air, with a degree of satisfaction, I might add. Panic and joy dictated that hawk's action as he rapidly flapped his wings, and quickly, as if not believing his good fortune, he started gaining height. It lasted maybe five seconds, maybe seven, but no more.

And then it was as if he had forgotten about everything. He soared directly above us as if nothing had happened, just calmly surveying the countryside for some prey. All that was left was for him to nosedive for our shrikette again. But he lazily rode the aerial streams farther and farther away until he hid from view.

His sudden transformation was so unexpected, so comical, and so accurately codified the life of everything that isn't human.

Only mankind runs on memory and imagination. Man's present is the crossroads of memory and imagination. Which is why the more man lives in accordance with his essence, the more constricted are the boundaries of his present.

The more constricted someone is, the more fulfilling is his present, when it's normal. But for the same reason, the more constricted someone is, the quicker does his unfortunate present bring about his spiritual death, because his memory and imagination can't help him. If things are exceptionally good for someone when things are good, then they're exceptionally bad when they're bad. For that matter, people of the Bible already knew that.

I had to go. I had to meet up with some friends. I said goodbye to Ruslan. He told me the days he would be in his shelter and invited me to his village.

"I'll make some vulture à la Chegem for you," he said. "Just give me a day's warning. I'll marinade it in my house 'Isabella.'"

"No," I said, "We'll be your guests. Prepare some Gudauta-style vulture first, then we'll see . . ."

"Done," he said and gave me a firm handshake.

I left. Sadly, we never saw each other again. I had to urgently leave for Mukhus. But I hope that we'll see each other yet, and that I finally try vulture meat, prepared not only Gudauta-style, but Chegem-style too.

In the latter case, I ask that I be considered the brilliant creative mind behind the dish, and if it becomes a staple of global cuisine, I demand that I be appropriately compensated in accordance with all laws of private entrepreneurship, which it seems like we're slowly, ever so slowly, opening up to.

4

The Beauty of Norms, or a
Boy Waits for a Man

Here at the Amra, one of our young historians—one of those who tenaciously digs around in archives rather than tearing his vocal cords at meetings—recently showed me an interesting document. It was a note written by my father. Not the original, obviously, it was a typed-up copy. It was my father's response to the city authorities about what he saw on the wharves. An echo of local events here in 1905.

The wharves became today's Amra. There didn't used to be a restaurant or even a second deck. It's a relatively recent addition. In my youth, at the end of the pier, there was a diving platform, and the boys and I would often swing by here.

Turns out that at the turn of the century, when the tendrils of the revolution[40] had only just crept their way here, my father would, as a young man, hang out at the wharves too. Probably not alone. And one day, a boat moored at the wharves, and a policeman exited along with the passengers. He was immediately arrested and taken away by representatives of the so-called civil police, who had been waiting at the dock. It was something like the current national guard. That's all that was written about in the note, which my father probably wrote after order was restored.

My God, my God, the beginning of the century and the end of the century! And nothing's changed. A note written two empires ago. You can still pick out the subtle, ironic note with regard to the policeman and with regard to the civil police, which the transitive property redirects towards the addressee as well.

---

40 He is referencing the revolution of 1905.

Aside from high school (which I don't think he finished), my father didn't have any formal education. I was surprised by his excellent Russian. That means that that was already possible here on the edge of the empire.

My father's voice, which I haven't heard since my childhood, tenderly flowed from the note like a spiritual caress. What's amazing is that I felt a kinship to my own writing style in his tone. Apples falling close to their trees. It was a strange feeling. I wanted to gently pat the note, as you would a child, on the head, and to kiss it. My father as a child. But I refrained from such a sentimental gesture, probably only because I was holding a reproduction and not the original.

My father never wrote anything, of course, but just like his facial features, his spiritual handwriting was passed on to me too. That's what you call the call of blood, the genetic flourish of the quill.

Later, I put the note somewhere and lost it, like I do with everything in the world. Chalk it up to my prohibitive absentmindedness. Maybe it's for the best. The more things you lose, the cleaner the runway of your inspiration. Or so I'd like to think.

. . . First, they came for my father's brother, Uncle Riza. Then they exiled my father to Iran after remembering that that's where my grandpa was from. Then, during the war, they came after another of my father's brothers, Uncle Samad, who was a bitter drunk.

I've already written everything I remember about my father and Uncle Riza, but I rarely mentioned Uncle Samad. I had my reasons. Now that my mother is no longer among the living, I'd like to think that she and my father are happy together on the other side. But here's what's interesting. When I say "mom!" a hot wave of blood crashes into my heart, and I feel like my essence reflects my exclamation. But when I mentally address my father, I can't say "dad!"—I feel that it's unnatural, because the hot blood wave doesn't crash into anything.

Years and years and years of separation siphoned that blood out of me. Too often in my childhood and youth I would wistfully repeat: dad! Eventually, the word lost any edge it might have had and disappeared. All I was left with was the sorrowful "father." But I don't have the strength to use that either, and so I don't have the right to address him directly at all.

I see a boy. He's running. He's always running somewhere. He intermittently feels either paralyzing pain or explosions of delight. He laughs. He always pays extra attention to anything funny. He commits the funny things to memory, as if amassing a collection of arguments to combat grief. He remembers the funny things as if they were a ripe cherry in someone else's orchard. Funny things, just like the cherry in someone else's orchard, seem larger than anything else.

The instant before he gets into a fight, a wave of calmness washes over him. The shame of worrying foolishly before an exam. What remains of his self-control is used to suppress that shame.

I see a boy. He's running somewhere. Where? Where is this boy? Sometimes you dream about the rough draft of a story, made golden by blood and sunlight, a beautiful story about life and childhood. Even if it's unfinished, childhood is life's most talented rough draft. But, like a mad writer, life rewrites and rewrites it, and hopelessly makes it worse with every rewrite. It must all be restored!

And you see in your dream that sunlit, blood-lit rough draft. At times I read it, at times I feverishly skim it so as not to forget the text, even if only in the dream. At the very least to remember the flow of its sound, the tangibility of its essence. It already exists! All that's left is the sweetest part: wake up and clean it up slightly, like peeling the skin off a fig. When I wake up, I don't remember a thing. But I know it was there. And that's a start.

* * *

The boy sat on the stone steps in front of his house. He did almost nothing but stare at the end of the street, which led to the market. He waited and worried. He felt like he had never worried so hard before in his life. He'd been sitting and waiting like that for two hours. Somebody was supposed to appear at the end of the street, but he didn't. What if he doesn't come? *If he doesn't come today*, the boy thought, *he'll never come again.*

His favorite dog, Belka, had stuck her face in his belly, and he was petting her. Belka felt that he wasn't happy, so she didn't leave his side.

He petted her, and it made him feel better that she was next to him, that he could touch her, that they loved each other, and that there wasn't a force in the world that could separate them. Sometimes the dog nudged him in the stomach, which meant: don't lose heart! Everything will be alright!

Sometimes he stopped petting her, and then she'd nudge him again: pet me! You'll feel better, and I'll be enjoying myself. The boy always knew that she was the smartest dog in the world. But at that moment, his thoughts were elsewhere.

To the left of where he sat, across the street, on the bank of a nameless river, which, for some reason, the locals hurtfully called the ravine, there grew an enormous poplar tree. The boy had never seen a poplar like it in his life. According to the boy's observations, it was the largest tree of all those he'd seen in town.

The boy loved that poplar for its enormity and its straightness. He took pride in the poplar, as if the tree belonged to him. He felt that way partly because the poplar belonged to nobody.

If it were growing in his neighbor's yard, then it would belong to his neighbor. If it were growing in the middle of the street, then it could be considered the government's poplar. But it stood on the bank of the river, which was much lower than the surrounding houses and streets, and it didn't obey or belong to anybody.

The boy thought that the tree was so enormous because it was growing on the very riverbank and its roots were drinking the river's water nonstop.

He loved the poplar and took pride in its enormity. But he noticed that the other guys didn't pay any attention to the poplar, simply because it didn't bear any fruit. But the boy loved the poplar for its straightness and its enormity, for its might, sturdiness, and reliability.

And now, when he diverted his gaze away from the end of the street, he reflexively turned to look at the great tree and admired its mountainous, green crown, which was wreathed in sunlight, its millions of leaves sifting the wind, which couldn't be felt out on the street. Sometimes flocks of sparrows would flutter out of its roots, as if someone were shaking them out of there.

Having admired the poplar in full, though not really thinking about it, the boy turned his attention with renewed hope to the end of the street, where he expected to see the person appear. Will he come or won't he?

Sometimes the stadium two blocks away from his house would be bustling with noise. The local team would be playing against the Tbilisi Dynamo. The stadium would at times erupt with overjoyed roaring and at other times just be buzzing angrily. The former meant that our boys had scored. The latter meant that Dynamo had scored. Alas, as always, the stadium was buzzing angrily rather than erupting with joy. Piercing whistles would occasionally cut through the air, which meant that the spectators weren't happy with the referee or with a player's behavior. The boy heard everything, but he was too busy to think about his favorite game or to root for his team. He was waiting for somebody. But that somebody wasn't showing.

Five steps to the boy's right, his buddies Anesti and Bocho were playing Coins. They called him over to play with them, but he was already waiting for somebody, so playing Coins right then would be foolish and uninteresting.

The boy turned them down so sharply that they stopped trying to get him involved and started playing by themselves. It was a throwing game. A tower of coins was erected on a flat stone. The players stood a specified distance away from the tower, usually about ten steps away, and then each tossed an ancient and heavy coin called a breaker at it. The player whose breaker lands closer to the tower of coins goes first. He wins however many coins flip from heads to tails. The first player goes as many times as coins his throw flipped. If he doesn't flip a single coin, the second player goes. The first throw at the tower was usually the most bountiful.

The boy would occasionally throw an absentminded glance at the players, then look again at the end of the street. Even though he wasn't thinking about the game, he could tell by the boys' exclamations and shouts who was winning and who was losing—and judging by Bocho's especially heated ones, he was losing. He could also tell that the game was imperceptibly unfair, which was why Bocho was slowly losing. But he didn't want to let some trifle distract him. All of that was small potatoes in comparison with what was currently happening to him.

The boy was waiting for somebody named Grandpa Vartan. He was a tall, beautiful old man from the village Esher. His auntie said that he was a beautiful old man. But the boy knew that himself. And it wasn't just because of his carefully trimmed beard, his curly, grey hair, or his gentle, clear eyes.

The boy likely found beauty in something less external. The old man had an air of rightness, precision. Almost everybody the boy had met the last several years had been imprecise. They would all mumble, tone themselves down, or soften around the edges in order to squeeze out of harm's way. Grandpa Vartan was always the same. And the boy knew that he didn't even think about how he should behave. And the boy found that beautiful.

Whenever Grandpa Vartan came, sat down, drank tea, got up, smiled, or spoke, he was always precise. And even though he usually spoke with his auntie in Turkish and the boy didn't understand that much, he knew by his quiet, steady voice that Grandpa Vartan was still precise and right.

His auntie quickly befriended people—she deafened them with her noisy brand of love and her generous candor, and people opened up to her in turn, surprised by her love and her finding personal worth in each and every one of them, worth that they themselves suspected nothing about.

But after a time, these people began to get on his auntie's nerves, after which she would grow rather cold towards them, and the poor people simply couldn't figure out what they did to make her stop loving them and what happened to their worth, which she herself had discovered. But such was her nature, she couldn't even control it. And the boy understood that.

Over the many years of Grandpa Vartan's visits, the boy noticed that his auntie, as she was wont to, tried several times to rope him into the same familial relationship that she did everyone else. But precise Grandpa Vartan softly, but decisively evaded that relationship every time.

And to the boy's great pleasure, his auntie finally got used to having an even, healthy friendship with Grandpa Vartan. And she even liked it. He was probably the only person in the world with whom she had such a relationship.

The boy knew that if Grandpa Vartan met her unfettered openness halfway, he would inevitably start to bore her. And one day, she would look out the second-story window and see him coming to visit, and she would inevitably say:

"God, I'm so sick of that bum! Can't get a minute to rest in your own home, and then there's *this* creep with his basket!"

The boy didn't remember when Grandpa Vartan started coming to their house. He began visiting before the revolution. About once a month or rarer, on his way home from the market, he would stop by, bringing handpicked fruits that he carried in an angular, woven basket strapped to his back. The fruits varied based on the season.

Auntie said that during the revolution, when nobody had any idea who was in power, he still came by with his fruits, possibly in that same, sturdy, woven basket. The Bolsheviks would occupy the town and everybody would be too scared to stick their nose out the door, but he'd still drop by. The Mensheviks would occupy the town and everybody would again be too scared to stick their noses out the door, but he'd still be dropping by.

Naturally, auntie gave him what presents she could when he left. Kerchiefs for his family, socks for his granddaughters, or candy, or cookies, or halva— whatever was at hand. Auntie was generous, and the boy loved her for it. And forgave her a lot of things.

The thing is that many, many years ago, his uncle was a lawyer. And in some unjust trial, he managed to successfully defend Vartan. Others couldn't, but he did. This was before the revolution. The boy asked his auntie what the trial was about, the one where Uncle Samad mounted a successful defense. But it was so long ago, she herself couldn't recall.

"He defended him against some wrongdoers. What's it to you!" she responded irritably when he asked. The boy understood that she was angry precisely because she couldn't remember what sort of trial it was. And it would have been a bit weird to ask Grandpa Vartan. He had been stopping by for so many years with his fruits and everything always went so smoothly, as if everyone remembered everything. The boy understood that if he asked Grandpa Vartan, it would become clear that nobody in the house remembered what the trial was about.

But that's exactly how it was. Nobody in the house remembered what had happened before the revolution and why his uncle defended Grandpa Vartan. And it was sad and pretty funny that the uncle because of whom Grandpa Vartan brought the fruits was almost never home when he did. The uncle came home much later and was always drunk. He had long ago become a quiet alcoholic, and that's how the boy always remembered him.

The house version of things has it that the uncle's young and pretty wife left him on a steamliner headed for Istanbul. He didn't want to leave his homeland, but she left him, and with his friend to boot. This broke him. He began to drink. He did try to marry one more time and to stop drinking. But nothing came of it. He couldn't forget about his first wife. And he couldn't live with the second one, especially without drinking. And he decided that it was better to be alone and drink than live with a new wife and not drink. And they went their separate ways.

The boy thought that if his first beautiful wife simply ran away to Istanbul, he could have still trooped through. But she didn't just run away, she ran away with his friend. And this broke him. For a long time, the boy couldn't understand how a friend could marry his friend's wife. He didn't understand it to such an extent that when he was younger, he thought that his uncle's friend simply went with his wife to guard her on her way to Istanbul.

And it was much later, when his auntie was telling the story to her friends in his hearing that he understood that "she left for Istanbul with his friend" also meant that the friend married his uncle's wife. If you're so in love with Abkhazia, you can stay in your Abkhazia, and I'll go to Istanbul with your wife. For some reason, the boy was also intrigued by the other side of the marriage. He knew that they left in a hurry and couldn't figure out where exactly they married—while they were still on the ship or once they got to Istanbul.

The boy remembered that one time, Grandpa Vartan stayed a while longer at their house and was still there when Uncle Samad came home.

As usual, his uncle came home a little tipsy. He politely greeted Grandpa Vartan, but didn't recognize him, of course. The boy's auntie sat him down to drink some tea and explained to him at great length how he, Uncle Samad, defended this man in court from some nasty people before the revolution.

The boy hoped that someone would suddenly remember what his uncle represented the man for, but that never happened. The only thing that got through his uncle's head was that one time, he defended the man in court. But who he was and what the trial was about, he had no idea. The boy was ashamed that his uncle didn't manage to recall who Grandpa Vartan was.

"We *were* racehorses once," he said in Russian, and then added something in another language. It was a Latin proverb, but the boy found that out much later, when he was a student.

But back then, it was clear that his uncle was apathetic towards every topic that was brought up at the table. Especially since there was nothing to drink on the table. His uncle halfheartedly drank his tea.

The boy thought that if there were vodka or wine on the table, his uncle maybe would liven up and successfully recall the trial. But there was nothing to drink, and he didn't recall anything, and he just halfheartedly sipped his tea.

Grandpa Vartan behaved correctly and precisely in this situation too. He didn't show his disappointment or hurt. For that matter, he probably wasn't even hurt. Uncle Samad had probably stopped recognizing Grandpa Vartan long, long ago. He had been drinking and coming home after Grandpa Vartan had already left for so many years. When the boy's uncle went to bed, Grandpa Vartan glanced at the door that slammed behind him and said:

"Oh, this world . . ."

He said it in Turkish, but the boy understood him. He then added something in Turkish, and the boy vaguely understood what he meant: there was a time when clients would be nipping at his uncle's heels, but now . . . His auntie mercilessly said something in Turkish, and the boy figured out the meaning of her response too: those clients are the ones who made him drink.

How can that be, the boy thought indignantly. His auntie was the one that said so many times that he drank because of his beautiful wife. She herself had drawn the parallel between those two things. Just before the last ship left for Istanbul, his friend burst into the house and said to the boy's uncle, shamelessly pointing at his wife:

"Tell her to come with me. The last ship leaves tomorrow."

"Let her choose for herself," the uncle responded. "But I don't advise anyone to leave. This new government won't last longer than two or three years."

The conversation was happening in the uncle's room, but they were speaking so loudly, that everyone in the house heard. And though it didn't happen right away, the uncle's wife made up her mind and left with his friend for Istanbul the next day. Where *did* they end up marrying? They wouldn't have had the time to do it in town before they left. They only had one day. Too much ruckus. Besides, a wedding needs to be planned. On the ship that was overflowing with refugees? Or in Istanbul? But then how did he introduce her to the other people on the ship?

In telling this story, the boy's auntie would fly into a rage.

"Instead of killing the bastard on the spot, he was giving him advice!" she seethed, and then snidely added: "Two, three years . . . they all said that then . . . Intellectuals! To hell with their education if the rabble turned out smarter than you! They'll still be in power a thousand years from now!"

And now she was saying that the boy's uncle started drinking because of his clients. He had caught her in similar contradictions many times and never ceased being amazed. But he shared in his auntie's fury towards that bastard. He would kill him himself, even if he were still just a kid! He'd smack him in the head with something heavy and kill him. The gall he must have had to come into their house and say to his uncle:

"Tell her to come with me! The last ship leaves tomorrow!"

Slimeball, slimeball, thought the boy when thinking about that man. But why didn't his uncle stand up for himself? The boy agonized about this many times. No, he wasn't a coward. The boy knew that for sure. He would still sometimes say such things about the government that the adults in the room would grow uncomfortable. They would look around anxiously. They explained it away by saying he was a drunk and that he himself didn't know what he was saying.

But why then didn't he stand up for himself in front of that bastard? The boy agonized about this many times. Maybe because he used to be his friend? No, the boy thought, if he said what he said, then right at that instant, he stopped being his friend and had every right to deal with him differently.

The boy agonized about this many times and finally came to the following conclusion. Lawyers in their town were called defenders. And if his uncle was such a good defender that clients would be clamoring to hire him, and if he defended Grandpa Vartan when nobody else managed to do so, that meant that all of his strength was spent defending others, leaving nothing for his own defense. He simply wasn't used to defending himself. He was used to defending others.

That's the problem! He still looked so skinny, fragile, and defenseless. And no matter how little he looked like himself in his prerevolutionary photos, where he seemed so proud, so handsome, so dashing wearing ties that nobody wore anymore. And there were photos of him at the beach with his beautiful wife, who really seemed beautiful to him, even though her bathing suit looked pretty odd, looking more like a dress. And they were smiling in that photo and were hugging each other so closely that it seemed like they'd never leave each other. Though, the boy noticed, that even then, his uncle's muscular frame was already fading.

But on the other hand, the boy knew from many books, that muscles weren't in fashion at that time. Nobody was big on physical exercise back then. It was only in our time that muscles became fashionable. And the boy liked that. And he sometimes thought that if his uncle had bigger muscles, he could've let even his former friend have it and he could've hung on to his wife. But he rarely had such thoughts, and after coming around, he himself understood that everything was much more complicated than that, and with a heavy sigh, he rejected his own thought.

The boy's crazy uncle came out of the yard with empty buckets in his hands and, singing some meaningless tune of his own creation, went off in the direction in which the boy was looking, waiting for Grandpa Vartan. His uncle's little tunes were meaningless, but they clearly demonstrated that he was happy.

Two blocks from their house, there was a yard with a water pump, which allowed locals to get their hands on especially cold and delicious water called Souk-Su.

His uncle would be sent to get this water, and he took pride in the fact that he was given such an important assignment. On top of that, his auntie wouldn't give his uncle just ten kopeks, which is how much two buckets of water cost, but whatever coins she had lying around. And, of course, never asked him to return the change. So, his uncle left the change for himself, and after amassing a bit of money, went to the store, bought a bottle of lemonade, and proceeded to have a good time. He loved lemonade. And even though he was crazy, he understood how profit worked. The boy pondered that many times and came to the conclusion that brains aren't really necessary in order to understand how profit works.

Looking at the receding figure of his uncle with the buckets, he suddenly had the piercingly rueful thought that his crazy Uncle Kolya was now the only man left in their house.

The prewar years brought so much suffering to their family: his favorite Uncle Riza was arrested, his father was exiled to Iran. The boy's grandfather on his father's side was from there but had come to Russia back in the nineteenth century. His grandpa had died long ago, back in the twenties, before the boy was born. And then they suddenly remembered about his father: go back where your father came from in the nineteenth century. It was absurd, malicious hogwash! His father was born here and never had another homeland.

But then the Great Patriotic War began with Germany, and almost all of the men in the family left for the front. The boy's older brother left home, as did his auntie's husband. Only crazy Uncle Kolya was left, along with the useless alcoholic, Uncle Samad. Every morning, he would, as usual, head off to the café that was in the bazaar, where, in return for drinks and some food, he would write pleas for the local peasants.

The boy thought that the war brought about an end to the arrests. There were too many other things to do, the most important thing was to defend the fatherland. And then, one day, they took Uncle Samad right in the café. Two men in grey overcoats came and arrested him. So said a man who knew his uncle well and happened to be in the café at the same time.

"Things are really bad," he said, "if they're here in our café. That means the Germans will be here. That's for sure."

He left, and the boy considered his words for a long time. It must have meant that our government didn't want to surrender towns where there were alcoholics. Maybe they wanted to show our enemies that the Soviet Union doesn't have drunks? No, that's idiotic!

The boy was upset over losing his beloved father and his beloved uncle (this is recounted elsewhere), even though he never stopped believing that sooner or later, they'll come back.

What may have been even more sorrowful was that his uncle and father's friends gradually stopped visiting. Before the war, his auntie's husband was still there, so it was impossible to say (the boy thought about this too) that there were no men left at the house and that it was strange to go into it.

The boy knew for sure that they stopped visiting out of fear. He knew that none of them believed that his uncle or his father were enemies of the state, but he knew that they were all scared of visiting them.

Although, the boy did hear that a few of them were arrested too. But others the boy would sometimes meet on the street. Some would even stop and pat him on the head. They would ask him about his father and uncle: what are they writing, how are they doing?

The boy's responses were strictly dependent on how long the person asking kept visiting after his father and uncle were taken away. Nobody kept visiting indefinitely, but the boy remembered well who stopped visiting sooner and who eventually gave up, but still kept visiting for a while.

He was never rude, of course, as that's no different from intruding. But he felt that the dryness of his responses and the impatience with which he wanted to walk away from them should have let them know how base and pitiful they were as humans.

Some of them, though, would ludicrously turn away from him any time they saw him (cowards! cowards! Grown men turning away from some kid!), and if they didn't manage to turn away in time, they would smile guiltily and sidle on past. In his childhood, he used to sit on many of their knees and draw pictures of war. And how his pictures would make them laugh! And how ashamed he was now to even remember that! And how cheerless their once populous and joyful and merry house now seemed!

And only Grandpa Vartan kept dropping by with his sharp-cornered basket, filled with fresh fruit. The boy thought it was so strange that he had never before compared them to each other. Friends of the house with Grandpa Vartan. His visits were always causes for celebration, which began before the boy was born and would last forever. And he had never before felt any heroism or bravery in the fact that Grandpa Vartan kept dropping by. He was sure that Grandpa Vartan himself had never thought about it. He was from another world, and the boy would have been surprised if Grandpa Vartan thought he was demonstrating courage by visiting them. It would have been no different than if the moon, the trees, or the sea suddenly developed a fear of being arrested.

But Grandpa Vartan hadn't come for more than a month. And a nagging concern had started lurking inside the boy. If they hadn't taken Uncle Samad in that time, he wouldn't have even thought of worrying. Nobody ever knew when exactly Grandpa Vartan would visit. He usually stopped by whenever he went to the bazaar.

The boy's worry grew stronger with every passing day. But he didn't tell anyone about it. What if he never came again? What if he decided that since they had arrested the person in whose name he brought them fruit all those years, there was no point in him coming anymore? But how could he know that the boy's uncle was arrested?

The boy suddenly realized—it must have been that same café. He was at the same bazaar. *But no*, he pepped himself up, *that can't be it*. That can't be it. What if those men in grey overcoats had approached him at the bazaar and said: if you ever go to that house again, we'll arrest you too! And then he decided to stop coming.

But, the boy kept thinking anxiously, *if those men, the ones in grey overcoats, were keeping an eye on their house, then somebody would have told him about that after Uncle Riza's arrest or his father's exile. Why didn't anybody tell him?*

The boy kept thinking anxiously, and suddenly he grew cold as realization dawned on him. They all know. And that's why they knew that he kept coming not for his father or for Uncle Riza, but for the sake of his drunk Uncle Samad, who had once helped him in some case before the revolution. But now that they took that uncle too, they warned Grandpa Vartan to stop dropping by.

And suddenly, an unexpected thought flickered through his head: if they knew, that meant they knew how specifically his uncle had helped Grandpa Vartan that one time. What if he asked? The boy shuddered in disgust at himself: how could he even have the thought! They don't know a damn thing, and nobody was keeping tabs on their house! If anyone had been watching their house, he'd have noticed long ago. It was all crap. Crap. Crap.

Ever since they took Uncle Riza, exiled his father, and the flock of friends that had once horded in their house stopped coming, the adult world had become very unreliable, but he couldn't let foolish suspicions into his head.

The boy grew tired of looking at the end of the street and shifted his gaze to the mighty poplar again. The sun was setting and wreathing the tree's enormous, breathing crown in a golden halo.

The sound of coins could be heard to his right, where Anesti and Bocho were playing their game. It sounded like two indefatigable blacksmiths were forging coins. They erected another silvery tower of coins on the flat stone, retreated to the agreed-upon distance, and had at it one more time.

The boy glanced absentmindedly at the players again and realized why Bocho kept losing the long and arduous game. His breaker was smaller and lighter than Anesti's.

When the players tossed the breaker onto the tower of money, it usually bounced off to the side or behind it. But sometimes, if it hit the ground at the right angle, then it could just stay in place. In which case the accuracy of the throw was the deciding factor. But that happened very rarely, as the breaker usually bounced from the ground, skid a distance, and stopped. The heavier the breaker, the less it bounces and skids. It brings no advantage in a short game, but in a long game, a heavier breaker offers greater utility. It usually lands more accurately, which is why Anesti had the privilege of smashing the coins first more often than Bocho. The first throw was usually the most bountiful.

"Bocho," the boy said, "can't you see that his breaker is heavier? That's cheating. Either play with the same breaker or play heads or tails."

Bocho, inflamed by the thrill of the game, tried to calm down enough to understand him. Anesti turned around sharply and blurted:

"What are you getting involved in other people's game for? You sit there and keep your Belka warm in your stomach. Or you'll get this breaker right in the teeth!"

The boy's hands, which were petting his dog, froze. He didn't suspect that the spiteful pain of vengeance for everything that had happened in his home had suddenly concentrated on Anesti. He himself didn't know what he was going to do, but Anesti could tell by his eyes that the fight would start immediately and that it would be merciless.

And he retreated, even though he got into fights often. He sensed the boy's fury and couldn't figure out what its cause was. Playing with a heavier breaker wasn't even really cheating. Some guys grew so accustomed to their own breakers that they themselves didn't even want to use another one, even if it was heavier.

"Alright, let's just use mine," Anesti said and then added: "You're like your Uncky—nuts."

And they started taking turns using Anesti's breaker. And they started putting Bocho's breaker wherever the other one landed to tell who got closer to the tower of coins. The game became more even, but the boy stopped looking their way. He went back to looking at the end of the street. He was waiting.

Everything will be decided today, he thought. Today. The thing is that earlier in the day, his auntie had sent him to the bazaar for groceries, and he accidentally saw Grandpa Vartan. He was selling fruits.

The boy froze. His heart hammered so hard that his chest began to hurt. He didn't approach him. No, anything but that! The boy mechanically retreated, afraid that Grandpa Vartan would notice him and thereby be forced to come visit them. He retreated without taking his eyes off him, afraid that Grandpa Vartan might recognize him from his back and figure out that the boy had already seen him and thereby be forced to come visit them. He retreated into the crowd. Grandpa Vartan never noticed him.

And now he sat on the front steps and waited. Looking at the end of the street where Grandpa Vartan was supposed to come from.

The sun had almost set. When a car drove by on their unpaved street, the dust it raised hung in the air long afterwards, shimmering in the sunlight. Shortly afterwards, a crowd of people appeared at the end of the street, and the boy figured that soccer had ended and they were coming back from the stadium. And it was clear why the game had ended so quietly.

The people were coming back, loudly discussing all the chances our team had missed as they lost once again to the Tbilisi Dynamo. They all seemed so foolish and boring to the boy. How long can you keep talking about the same thing! How long can you hope that it was an accident that your team lost! And how can they possibly win when every year, our best players are lured over to the other side?

When one of the soccer fans, a friend of the first uncle who was arrested, walked by their house, he suddenly looked at the second floor, where the uncle used to live. And something wistful flickered in his gaze. The boy remembered that he had held out longer than everybody else, that he conceded last.

The boy sighed and looked at the end of the street again. Uncle Kolya appeared with buckets full of water. The boy thought that Grandpa Vartan would turn onto their street at the end of the block. But he could appear from where his uncle just came too. He would appear most often, however, out from behind the corner. No, that wasn't him either. His uncle was walking with overflowing buckets, and even from afar, the boy could see how he fiercely looked every which way to make sure that not a single cat or dog dared to be anywhere next to his buckets. He was very finicky and could fly into an incredible rage if a dog ran by his buckets.

That's why he preemptively called loudly to scare away any quadruped that dared show its face on the street or leap out of an alley.

Admittedly, his rage could descend on a person too, if they passed too close by his buckets or if by some infernally foolish curiosity, they tried to take a look at what was in it. The boy knew this character trait of his uncle's and thought that excess physical fastidiousness didn't reflect an exceptional mind either.

"Dogs!" he growled fiercely as he approached the gate and noticed Belka on the boy's knees. He looked at it with such cautionary belligerence, it was as if Belka was getting ready to jump right from the boy's knees into the buckets.

In reality, when Belka heard the uncle's voice, she not only didn't demonstrate a strange desire to jump into the buckets with water, she even pressed closer to the boy. The uncle disappeared behind the gate.

The boy remembered how his crazy uncle talked with the portraits of his brothers that hung at home. Sometimes, his grandmother stood in front of those portraits, begging God at great length to return her sons.

But his crazy uncle didn't understand that his brothers were arrested and exiled. He only understood that they had gone somewhere and weren't coming back, while his grandma wanted very much for them to come back. He understood that.

And he sometimes approached the portraits and spoke to them, asking them to come back as soon as possible, to stop making the boy's grandmother sad. He usually spoke to them in a very tender voice. He probably thought that the more tenderly he spoke to them, the sooner they would return. But sometimes he lost his patience and began chastising them for not taking pity on the boy's grandmother, for not having returned yet. He even brought up old grievances of his own. And the boy's grandmother would have to chase him away from the portraits and get him to quiet down. But it was impossible to try to explain to him what happened to his brothers.

The boy looked at the end of the street again. The soccer fans had caused their ruckus and left. He couldn't see anyone. The boy started thinking about the government. That had become habit. A rather unshakeable habit. The only things that saved him from it were long games, swimming in the sea, or the nonstop reading of books.

But there was no clarity here, and he liked clarity. He couldn't stand anything vacillating, blurring, or winding. And he thought and thought incessantly to make things make sense.

The boy loved revolutionary songs. He like all songs, but he loved revolutionary ones. He got a warm feeling when he listened to them. In those moments, he was ready to die so that other people could be happy, joyful, and healthy. So that everyone could laugh and joke and endlessly have guests over and treat them generously.

But his deepest wish was the following. What would happen when the revolution finally won out? Here's what would happen: the wharves, where the guys swam in the sea and sometimes unloaded watermelons from the ships. A whole mountain of freckled watermelons would sometimes tower above the wharves. They were then taken to the bazaar. Sometimes, they were sold right on the wharves. And he was sure that when the global revolution finally won out, grown men would toss watermelons to the boys swimming in the sea. They'd toss them and laugh merrily. And the boys would swim up to the watermelons from every which direction. Whoever would get there first would get the first watermelon. A cannonade of watermelons would fly at the sea, unfurling the water. Blam! Blam! Blam!

And after the boys would get tired of playing with the watermelons and after cooling them enough in the water, they would finally swim towards the shore, headbutting the watermelons ahead of themselves. Once on the shore, they would break the watermelons open with rocks and bite into their sweet flesh, their faces covered in red juice.

And the boy found his dream pleasant, though a bit sad too, because he envisioned himself as one of the adults throwing the watermelons into the sea, rather than a boy fishing for them in the water. Though, sometimes, he forgot that it wouldn't be so soon, and he saw himself among the kids fishing for the watermelons. In his dreams, the color of the revolution turned into the color of juicy, sweet watermelon flesh.

The boy was confident that since revolutionary songs were so beautiful, it meant that the revolution was correct and necessary for everybody in the world. It was so obvious. If that weren't the case, the songs couldn't be so delightful. The revolution was magnificent. It's just that after it started, a few mistakes were made, spies and saboteurs cropped up, and the government became confused and foolish.

For example, everybody in his native village hated the kolkhoz.[41] Sometimes they laughed at it, other times they cursed it.

They didn't call the revolution a revolution either, and that was pretty hurtful. They forgot or pretended that they forgot what it was called.

"When the time of the kolkhoz came," they said when they meant when the time of the revolution and the new government came. And the boy surmised that they all believed in their hearts that the new government didn't have anything planned other than kolkhozes, and if they didn't implement them right away, it was only to lull people into a stupor, gather their strength, and then chase everyone into kolkhozes. The boy was offended on the

---

41 In Russian, *kolkhoz* is a portmanteau for "collective farm."

revolution's behalf, but he liked clarity and wanted to understand what happened.

And in observing village life, the boy tried to understand why everybody cursed the kolkhoz. He knew that the peasants kept plowing the ground on bulls, as they had before the revolution. They kept swinging their hoes as they did before the revolution. In theory, if the peasants were swinging their hoes on a common field owned by the kolkhoz, then they should have been working more efficiently. But why? He saw with his own eyes that the opposite was true. Even if they eagerly swung their hoes on their own land, what they did out in the common field could more accurately be called lazy flourishing.

True, before the revolution, there was no school in Chegem. And the new government built a school, and children learned in it. And the boy thought that was very good. But why didn't the government say honestly and clearly: you get a school, we get a kolkhoz. Deal?

Once, he was with his grandpa above the Sabida Basin, standing in some hazel brush. His grandpa was chopping young hazel to later make rods for propping up beanstalks, and the boy was chipping off the excess. His grandpa suddenly straightened, held out the hand holding the beaklike axe, and gestured in the direction of the sea, where Kengursk could be seen through the lavender fog.

"Before the Great Snow, your Stalin robbed a steam liner."

"Before the Great Snow" meant before the first World War. "Your Stalin" meant he was urbanized, not from the countryside.

"How's that, grandpa?" the boy was surprised.

"Just like that," said his grandpa and chopped down a young hazel tree with a single swing of the axe. "He robbed a steam ship with his band of cutthroats. And then he shot them all and went off on the Lower Chegem Road."

The boy didn't believe his grandpa, even though he knew that his grandpa never lied. The boy decided that his grandpa's hatred for Stalin made him confuse him with some band of mountain robbers. In Chegem, everyone despised Stalin, believing that he cornered them into a kolkhoz.

And since the boy loved the revolution, and the wonderful revolutionary songs made it clear as day that it was done for the sake of the people, he had to sacrifice Stalin. He didn't like him anyway. He saw and heard him in newsreels, and he thought it pretty obvious that Stalin didn't resemble the revolutionary songs at all. Looks like he had to be shunned from the ranks of the war chiefs. But he knew that he couldn't talk about that out loud in town yet.

Who else was left? Voroshilov.[42] He saw him in the newsreels too. He probably resembled the revolutionary songs, especially when rode his horse across the Red Square to inspect the troops. Everyone else was so negligible that they didn't even merit consideration. How could you compare the goat-bearded Kalinin[43] to the revolutionary songs? It was laughable.

The boy loved revolutionary songs. But he wanted everything to be fair. Stalin had to be sacrificed. The kolkhozes, at least the mountain ones, had to be sacrificed.

There were obviously spies and saboteurs. They were the reason that innocent people like his uncle were arrested. But where was Stalin during all that?

No, he couldn't be a war chief. He didn't even speak Russian all that well. Even here in Mukhus, people speak Russian better than him. And he lives in the Kremlin! You can speak Russian that poorly in some hut in the mountains. But in the Kremlin . . . the boy didn't know then that everyone in the Kremlin spoke Russian poorly, because he had only heard Stalin.

But what else did the revolution achieve besides beautiful songs and mighty power plants? Free school, which he attended along with all the other kids. Even breakfast was free. Though it was just a piece of bread with jam. One bite and it was gone. But they *were* in the middle of a war. And because of the free breakfast, few kids missed classes.

As for capitalist countries? Droves of people without jobs. And people *with* jobs, to say nothing of black people, can't afford to put their kids through school. They don't have the money. And they've never even heard of free breakfasts. Want a snack? Nibble on a napkin or something.

The boy's auntie sang wonderfully. He loved her for it and forgave her a lot of things. She sang in Russian, in Abkhazian, and even in Turkish. Mostly, she sang in Russian. They were usually romantic songs.

But revolutionary songs sometimes found their way into her repertoire too. And what's amusing is that she was always going on about how the revolution was bad, though she mostly did so at home among her own. But

---

42 Kliment Voroshilov (1881–1969) was a military officer and politician very close to Stalin.
43 Mikhail Kalinin (1875–1946) was a Bolshevik and a member of the original politburo.

she sang the revolutionary songs in such a heartfelt manner that it was as if she was ready to give her life for the revolution.

But the boy knew for sure that his auntie wasn't ready to give her life for the revolution. Hell, she wouldn't give a brick from his grandfather's brick factory for the revolution willingly. She could probably lob the brick at some casual revolutionary's head, if, that is, there *were* any casual revolutionaries back then. She herself wasn't greedy, but she didn't acknowledge the revolution and didn't want to give anything up for it.

So, the revolution had to take away his grandpa's brick factory along with all of its bricks. His mom used to say that his father's eyelids were damaged (even though the boy never noticed it), because he would stand day and night next to scalding hot furnaces. When his father returned, whenever that may be, it would be interesting to ask him what happened to his eyelids.

No, the boy wasn't sad about his grandpa's brick factory, which the revolution took away from them. He would even have given up a candy factory if he had one. His grandpa's brick factory wasn't too far from town. The boy was so fundamentally not sad about giving it up to the revolution that he had never been curious enough to look at it even once. But he heard people say that the factory had long ago been abandoned and that nobody worked there anymore. But then why did they take it away? More lack of clarity.

Long ago, even before the war, the boy had noticed that Stalin liked to equivocate, thereby diminishing the revolutionary songs' integrity. With agonizing zeal, he would catch the government in boldfaced lies.

When the war with Finland ended, he didn't believe for a second that the Finns had attacked the Soviet Union. Finland was so small, and the Soviet Union was so large, and he knew for sure that Finland couldn't have attacked our country. The revolutionary songs made it clear that all peoples are equal, that the revolution protects the weak from the strong.

He pitied Finland, and one night, he suddenly recalled a map in school depicting an enormous Soviet Union next to a tiny Finland, and he started crying. Nobody could ever find out about those tears, but he himself never forgot them. Even though he didn't know it yet, those tears may have been not just for Finland, but for his father and uncle too, whom he had already lost by that point. He saw in his head a tiny Finland and started crying because of his helplessness when faced with ignobility.

When the Great Patriotic War began and the Germans began rabidly marauding across our lands, the boy listened to Stalin on the radio. And the boy noted with surprise that Stalin spoke much better Russian than he did in the earlier newsreels. Many people noticed. Some adults spitefully said to each other in hushed tones: "It because he's scared."

And when the papers started describing the Germans' brutality in occupied territories, the boy believed them. But he also noticed more equivocation. The papers should have first written that the Germans had occupied our land, and only then should they have brought up their brutality. But they skipped right to the brutality so that they could use the brutality to distract the masses and keep them from thinking about the occupied land. Even though before the war began, they had promised that the war would take place only in other countries. No, he didn't let himself be fooled this time. Later, he once heard two adults talking about the war. One of them said to the other:

"What brutality could there be? It's all lies. Propaganda. Germany is a cultured nation."

The boy was taken aback. Was he wrong in believing the papers? He liked the antifascist songs. They were a lot like the revolutionary ones. He once again had to deal with that damned lack of clarity. But then, to his good fortune, he saw for the first time a brave soldier return from the front with his arm deftly bandaged over. He was sitting on a bridge's cement parapet, smoking and joking with the girls that were walking by, and they were rewarding him with wide smiles.

The boy talked with him about it. The soldier confidently said that the papers were right about the Germans' brutality—he had seen it with his own eyes. And then he added without rhyme or reason:

"The Germans are brave. I was there when they executed an SS soldier. They're shooting at him, and he just goes on smoking."

The boy didn't like hearing this, but he intuitively understood that the soldier was telling the truth. But could fascists really be brave? They shouldn't be, but it turns out they can be. It's unpleasant, but true.

The boy came back from his thoughts. Grandpa Vartan was still nowhere to be seen. A few men came out of the neighboring house, made themselves comfortable on the porch, and started playing Backgammon. Two men played, and the rest stood around them, smoking and talking. The boy could hear the measured rattle of dice on the board and the clacking of pieces being moved. Sometimes the measured rattle was replaced by sharp smacks. That meant that the dice throw was lucky and whoever threw them victoriously smacked them on the board: take that! Take that! Take that! Then again, those smacks may have been cunning dissembling designed to throw the opponent off his game: you might think that I had a bad throw, but that's all part of my genius plan. The boy knew how to play Backgammon, but he wasn't interested in that just then. His ears just automatically picked up the clatter of the pieces and the ebb and flow of good luck, or what the players tried to pass off as good luck, from one player to the other.

The sun had sunk even lower, and the incredible poplar, glittering in sun's dying rays, was relishing the warmth. But there was nobody at the end of the street.

The boy suddenly remembered something that had happened long ago. He thought that he had forgotten it, but everything that had happened suddenly came rushing back.

His auntie was having everyone over for a feast. Everyone was sitting at the table, and the air was full of noise and cheer. Then suddenly came Uncle Samad, drunk as usual. Since he was always drunk, nobody who knew him took him very seriously. As if they were much smarter than him. Though the boy knew even then that that wasn't quite true. But he, like everyone else, didn't much enjoy his uncle always being boozed up, especially in front of everyone.

They invited his uncle to join the table. His auntie gave him a plate full of appetizers. She even put a shot glass next to his plate and went to the kitchen. His uncle got up to wash his hands. And then one of the guests, cheerful Uncle Mitya, looked at the boy and nodded towards the pitcher of water so that he poured his uncle water instead of vodka. The boy liked the joke. It even seemed beneficial. His uncle wouldn't notice and would only sober up a bit, and the guests would enjoy him drinking water without realizing that it wasn't vodka.

The boy even felt proud that he was the one that Uncle Mitya gave the mission to. It looked like he too, a little punk still, was counted among the adults who considered themselves smarter than his uncle.

The pitcher of water was right next to him. The boy took it carefully and quickly, got his uncle's shot glass, and filled it with water. While he was doing this, he was thinking proudly that the adults had given him this assignment, and that he had to prove himself worthy of such a mission. And he gave it his all, careful not to spill the water by inclining the heavy pitcher too far, gingerly making sure not to accidentally hit the glass off the table and break it. His mission turned out successfully. He himself even put the glass back next to his uncle's plate. Being given a part in this grownup prank filled him with such pride that when he sat back down, his posture and every movement implied to the adults in the room that he would sometimes pull off pranks like that all on his own, even though he never pulled off anything quite like this.

Having washed his hands, his uncle came back and sat down. Everyone paid a little more attention to his uncle now, waiting for the prank to pay off. Usually, people were dismissive towards him. Even his auntie didn't always let his uncle sit at the table when there were guests over.

She let him join them today because she noticed that he was only tipsy. No, he never made a scene, though he sometimes started arguing when others reproached him a wee bit too much about him drinking too much and shaming his family. The boy noticed that his uncle felt everybody paying more attention to him than usual and that he liked it.

He raised his glass and said a toast. He said something important about the fate of humanity and dark times. At that time, the boy didn't understand anything his uncle was talking about. But he already understood that there were dangerous conversations that strangers shouldn't be privy to.

This was happening on the second-floor patio. There were no strangers there. But when his uncle began his speech, one of the guests shut the window, as if there were a team of secret agents eavesdropping below. But nobody could hear him from below, especially since his uncle never spoke too loudly.

The guests' eyes were all full of laughter as his uncle spoke: go ahead, the floor's all yours, buddy! Some jokingly grabbed their heads in mock terror, as if his speeches would land them all in jail.

His uncle finally threw his head back, took the drink, and put the glass back on the table. The first instant, it seemed like his uncle didn't get what happened. He even took his fork to start following up on the drink. But then, his thin, long face grew grey, and he slowly surveyed everyone at the table. The fork fell out of his hand on its own and clanged to the table. The boy grew cold from fear. Everyone at the table shut up and felt that the prank didn't work.

"You wanted to degrade me with this water," my uncle said quietly, peering at the guests. "But you can't degrade me. Life has already degraded me so much that further degradation isn't possible . . . You're trampling the already trampled . . . What did I do to you? Why?"

Thankfully, the boy's auntie was in the kitchen throughout all this. She didn't even notice anything. Although she herself gnawed away at his uncle for drinking and shaming the family, she might not have forgiven her guests for something like this. And then God knows what could have happened!

She could have jerked the tablecloth off the table, thrown everything to the ground, and chased everyone out.

But she was in the kitchen. After saying the words that shook the boy to his core, his uncle quietly surveyed the room, quietly stood up, pushed in his chair, and went to his room.

The boy was petrified. No, he wasn't scared that his uncle would find out that he was the one to pour water into his shot glass. Nobody would tell him. He was horrified of what he had done. And he couldn't grasp why something that seemed like such an innocent prank turned out so abhorrently ignoble.

And now, recalling all this, he directed his furious hatred at Uncle Mitya, who had hitherto always seemed so cheerful and the most pleasant of all the guests that came to their house. Bastard! Bastard! Bastard! All he wants is a cheap laugh! *And* he was one of the first, if not *the* first, to stop coming over their house.

And what the boy previously liked about him—the fact that he was always the instigator of any and all merriment—now seemed like nothing more than gluttony, slobbering and repugnant gluttony. How hadn't he seen it before? Uncle Mitya was always a glutton for cheer and even now, he was probably guzzling down cheer somewhere safe in another home.

Nobody loved his uncle, the boy thought sadly. Nobody except for his grandmother. *I didn't love him either*, he thought to himself. Only sometimes, when he coughed at night, he would pity him. At night, his coughing fits would go on for so long, so unbearably long! And in the morning, he got up and headed off for the café as if nothing happened.

When Uncle Riza was being arrested, his auntie rented out Uncle Samad's room and moved his bed to the room where the arrested uncle used to live. It was the largest room in the house. The boy's grandmother slept there, along with Uncle Kolya, and the boy himself slept on his favorite uncle's bed whenever he spent the night. That's where they moved Uncle Samad's bed when the boy's auntie rented out his room.

His uncle didn't say a word about being left without a room. That's when, sleeping in his favorite uncle's bed, he began listening to his uncle's long, unbearable fits of coughing at night. But his auntie didn't stop there. Sometime later, his uncle's bed was moved to the top floor reachable by the central set of stairs.

Ever since his favorite uncle was arrested, nobody used the central stairs, and the central door was shut tight. In the boy's mind, the center of anything was celebration, so a center and a celebration were essentially the same thing.

That meant that the central stairs and the central door were celebratory stairs and a celebratory door. But what celebration could there be if his favorite uncle was arrested? The central door was shut forever, and nobody used the central stairs.

And so, the boy's indefatigable auntie dragged Uncle Kolya, along with Uncle Samad's bed, up to the top floor. His auntie said that the whole house stank of alcohol because of him. The boy didn't notice, but maybe his uncle's coughing could be heard in her room and irritated her. Even then, his uncle didn't say anything to anyone. He didn't care, especially since they heated only the kitchen during the winter, leaving all the other rooms equally cold.

Everybody was so tired of him drinking that nobody loved him. Only the boy's grandmother loved him, even though she berated him the most. But she alone got him to put on something warm when it was cold out and tried to get him to eat something when he came home in the evening. She thought that he just drank and never ate anything. And that was probably exactly true. He was so thin that he looked more dead than alive.

The sun was setting. Looking out their windows or standing by their fence gates, the neighbors were calling their kids back home. The boy remembered that his mom and her sister had left for the village to trade for groceries. They had left for a few days. *Will Grandpa Vartan really not come?* the boy thought, staring at the end of the street with hopeless obstinacy.

Suddenly, Uncle Alikhan, who lived nearby, emerged out from behind the corner. He was rolling a portable stall before him that was full of eastern sweets that he sold at the bazaar. The boy's heart sank. *It's over.*

Uncle Alikhan came back from the bazaar only after it closed. If he was selling at the bazaar and not on Portov Street. But the boy knew for sure that if Uncle Alikhan sold on Portov Street, he came back from the opposite end of the block.

This time, he was coming back from this side, which meant that the bazaar was closed and there was nothing left for the boy to wait for. Pushing his stall in front of him, he came closer, like a harbinger of the end. Having reached the fence gate, he stopped to take a breather and angle the stall towards the gate. The boy could make out golden brittle, sticky with honey, under the stall's glass cover. Uncle Alikhan sensed something.

"Want some brittle?" Uncle Alikhan gave a tired smile and, without waiting for a response, opened his stall.

"No, no!" the boy responded hastily. At that moment, he wanted nothing to do with the sticky brittle that he wouldn't even enjoy.

"You don't want any?" Uncle Alikhan sounded surprised. "It's good brittle. With Tsebeldinian honey."

"Uncle Alikhan," the boy asked suddenly, trying with all his might not to give himself away. "You didn't happen to see Grandpa Vartan, did you?"

"Of course I did," Uncle Alikhan raised his eyebrows in surprise. "He's coming."

"Where is he coming?" the boy almost yelled out, forgetting that he was trying to give himself away.

"He's coming here. Where else would he come?" Uncle Alikhan smiled in understanding, figuring that the boy had missed the taste of fresh fruit.

And before Uncle Alikhan could even get his stall through the narrow gate, Grandpa Vartan rounded the corner at the end of the street. The boy instantly recognized his tall figure, hunched slightly from the basket on his shoulders, his breeches tucked into the unchanging, woolen, white socks that he wore at any given time of the year, the measured pace of somebody bearing a heavy load.

The boy looked and looked at the approaching figure, sensing how his whole body was filling with delight, and then, as if he were afraid—which he was—that his delight would tear him apart, he ran off into the yard. His dog, quickly recovering from being sent flying from his knees, raced off after him, barking happily. She understood that he was better now and that him darting off was an invitation to play.

He ran across the yard, scooted up the stairs to the second floor, ran along a long hallway that turned off to the left and expanded into the patio. His auntie was sitting next to the window, observing as always life out in the yard, and sometimes imperiously making changes to that life as she saw fit.

"Auntie!" the boy yelled. "He's coming!"

Belka, who had caught up to him back in the hallway, started barking joyfully. His auntie gave a start at the unexpected news, and, in keeping with her artistic habit of exaggerating the consequences of his unexpected intrusion, asked him frightfully:

"Who's coming?!"

"What do you mean, who?!" the boy yelled, stunned by her imperceptiveness. "Grandpa Vartan!"

His auntie looked at him, her face expressing a mournful submission to fate: here comes another crazy. You can't hide from fate.

"So what?" she said, submitting to fate's will, but trying to speak clearly. "It's not like you're seeing him for the first time."

"But..."

The boy fell silent. He knew she wouldn't understand him. He suddenly understood that it was shameful to doubt like he had. He lowered his head, trying to catch his breath and calm down. His auntie felt his embarrassment and figured that he was atoning for his loud and unexpected intrusion. Her expression softened, showing that not all was lost of her nephew's mental presence.

"You read too much," she finally said instructively. "You could lose your mind. You spend the whole day either reading or running around like mad... Belochka, shut up right now!"

And Belochka stopped barking. Having easily quelled the small uprising, the boy's auntie regained her composure and looked out the window.

"And here's Grandpa Vartan," she said as if nobody had said anything of the sort to her and she was the one to notice him first. "Tea's ready just in time!"

She jumped up and rapidly strode off to greet Grandpa Vartan. She sang as she walked:

"And in that moment of sweet reunion,
Only the moon looked on through the glass."
She cheerfully greeted Grandpa Vartan.
"*Hoşgeldin!*"
"*Sefa geldin!*"
Turkish speech flowed forth. Grandpa Vartan approached the patio table, turned his back to it, bent over, poking it with the corner of his angular basket, and, supporting it, unclipped it from his back. He then carefully put the basket on its side and started emptying it with the boy's auntie's help.

Even though their overgrown garden had some fruit-bearing plants, the season was already past anyway, and nothing could compare with this.

At the top were tender, dark figs, so ripe with juicy, red flesh that they had cracked. Just under them were brushes of yellow grapes, so translucent that their seeds were visible. Under the grapes were large, honey-colored Duchesse pears (how did the tree branches not break beneath the weight?). And the pears lay on top of firm apples, made swarthy by the sun. As always, the fruits were arranged from top to bottom in ascending order of firmness. The fruits were arranged the right way.

As soon as the boy's auntie sat Grandpa Vartan down in the coveted spot by the window, his grandma and Uncle Kolya came to the patio. They came out of the house. They must have been sitting on the balcony, so they saw when Grandpa Vartan had showed up.

"Pappy Vartan, Pappy Vartan," jabbered Uncle Kolya like a little kid, even though he himself was getting up in his years. He eyed the fruits greedily, but didn't dare touch them, because the boy's auntie hadn't allowed it yet.

His auntie filled a large vase with the fruits, not paying any heed to their firmness. And the boy knew that she was right to do so: with him and Uncle Kolya there, they wouldn't be in the vase for long. She placed the rest of the fruits in the cupboard.

She then got out some fruit wine that was stashed away and poured Grandpa Vartan a glass. She had a drink herself, as did the boy's grandma, muttering a prayer for God to bring her sons home. Then they had tea with bread, jam, and syrup. They poured syrup instead of sugar into their tea. The boy didn't even touch the jam that he had gotten sick of. He ate bread with figs, washing it down with tea. The figs' rich sweetness was better than any prewar marmalade. He chowed down with appetite that he hadn't felt in a long time.

Everything had changed, and he was ashamed to think that he had refused the brittle offered to him by Uncle Alikhan. Maybe he would remind him tomorrow? Remind him that he himself had offered it, rather than ask for some. There's a difference. It's one thing to remind someone and another entirely to ask.

During dinner, it turned out that Grandpa Vartan did find out about Uncle Samad's arrest at the café, just like the boy thought. And it had happened that very day. The boy was sure that everything would be alright now. He was confident that everyone would return from their prisons and the war. He was almost drunk off the food and his joy at Grandpa Vartan's arrival, even though he had none of the wine.

The thought suddenly flickered through his head that prison life would make Uncle Samad stop drinking. He knew that nobody got wine or vodka in prison. He would come back a non-drinking man. And the entire family would be proud of his willpower. And everyone would love him like they probably loved him back when he was very young. And he would finally remember how and from whom he defended Grandpa Vartan. And they would come together as a big family again and would sit at the same table, and Grandpa Vartan would visit them from time to time. And it would last forever.

The boy thought how the previous year, he and Grandpa Vartan once visited many different ironmongers. Grandpa Vartan wanted to buy some nails and couldn't find the right ones.

"Look at that house," said Grandpa Vartan suddenly and pointed at an ordinary two-story house, the likes of which were common in town.

"What about it, Uncle Vartan?" asked the boy after looking the house over and failing to find anything extraordinary.

"You'll find out later, just remember it for now," said Grandpa Vartan importantly, and they kept going. The boy didn't get what the big deal was. They then went to several different ironmongers on several different streets, and Grandpa Vartan would intermittently say: look at that house.

The boy looked and didn't get it. They were ordinary, old two-story and three-story houses. The boy didn't get what Grandpa Vartan meant. He must have meant *something*. They would go into a store, and the nails they needed would invariably not be there, after which Grandpa Vartan would examine and evaluate various other goods, and it would seem like he had forgotten about the houses he was pointing out and whatever he wanted to say to the boy. But then they would leave the store, wander the streets in search of another store, and Grandpa Vartan would suddenly say once again:

"Now look at this house."

And the boy looked and still didn't get it, because it was once again another ordinary, old house. But the boy understood that though the houses Grandpa Vartan pointed out were quite ordinary, they evidently had some feature that Grandpa Vartan found unique. But what was it?

"All of these houses are made from your grandfather's brick," he finally explained with an air of significance. "And there are forty houses like that in town, not including yours. You should be proud of your grandfather."

A beautiful, revolutionary idea suddenly warmed the boy's heart. "Grandpa gave out bricks for free?"

"Why for free?" Grandpa Vartan calmly corrected him. "People bought the bricks and built houses for themselves. The bricks will last for centuries more. These bricks rang like water in the mountains. They were so good, you wanted to eat them. Remember this!"

But the boy's interest faded as soon as Grandpa Vartan said that he sold the bricks. What was there to be proud of? No, there was nothing to be proud of—in fact, there was more likely something to be ashamed of. It was nothing like the revolutionary songs. You can't make a revolutionary song out of bricks that were sold. It would be absurd.

But on the other hand, the boy liked that Grandpa Vartan was admiring his grandfather. There was some kind of duality in his head, but he didn't let it persist. No, there was nothing to be proud of. Grandpa Vartan was an old man, a kind man. And him admiring his grandfather was nothing more than the ancient joy of an old man. Let the old man express his ancient joy. The boy made an exception for Grandpa Vartan, like he did in grammar lessons in school.

Now, remembering all this, he suddenly thought that the fact that Grandpa Vartan kept visiting them was a kind of ancient loyalty. Which meant that something ancient could be good too. What to make of that? He knew that at some point in the future, he would think more on it, but he didn't want to for the time being. He was too full. The boy and Uncle Kolya had emptied the vase almost entirely on their own.

Grandpa Vartan bid everyone farewell, strapped on his basket, and left to spend the night with his relatives.

The boy's grandmother then went to bed after first praying a little. Uncle Kolya went to bed too. Full after dinner, he was humming songs of his own composition. They were meaningless, but happy.

The boy undressed too and got in his favorite uncle's bed. Belka lay down on a bull hide next his head. Though his uncle hummed his carefree songs, he sometimes raised his head in the dim light that fell through the window and looked at Belka, vigilantly ready to remind her that she'd be in for a world of trouble if she went up to his bed and started tugging on his blanket or whatever else her cunning canine mind could think up. Little Belka, of course, had nothing of the sort in mind and didn't even come close to his bed. But that was something that couldn't be explained to Uncle Kolya.

"Dogs!" he growled about Belka, after which he resumed his sweet humming.

Finally, after a particularly frightful growl, Belochka's nerves couldn't take it anymore, and she decided to play it safe by jumping into the boy's bed. He covered her with his blanket and hugged her close. And the boy was happy next to the beloved, warm, slumbering dog. Half-asleep, he could already see all of his family returned from prison and from the war, and he could see Grandpa Vartan visiting them, while the wharves overflowed with mountains of watermelons that adults would throw into the water. And the boys, trying to outpace each other, would hammer away at the water with their feet, surrounding the watermelons from all sides: stroke! Stroke! Stroke! The boy fell asleep.

... Years passed. The war proved kinder than the prisons. By no means everybody, but many returned from the war. Nobody returned from the prisons. Including his father.

As for Grandpa Vartan, he kept coming over their house until his very death, his angular basket strapped to his back, full of choice fruits. But the boy wasn't in town any longer. He was a student in Moscow. But he remembered Grandpa Vartan his entire life. And in the worst and haziest times, when he would put his hand on a friend's shoulder and the shoulder would suddenly go limp or, even worse, elusively slip out of his grasp, he thought about Grandpa Vartan, and the strength to live and endure rose up on its own.

The right of someone who has done a kindness to forget about it. The obligation of someone warmed by kindness to remember it. The world crumbles anywhere that this connection is severed, where someone who has done kindness importunately remembers it, and someone who was warmed by kindness experiences a bout of forgetfulness.

A world in which you've seen even one person remember the warmth of a kindness even when the person who did the kindness forgot about it and disappeared without a trace, giving up his light body to the eternal frost—that world isn't yet fully lost and deserves our courage to live and to be human.

5

The Light of the Twilight Youth

Saida was Habug's daughter. Zaur was Saida's only son. In the summer of 1927, old Habug's wife fell very ill, and he brought to Mukhus from Chegem a doctor who had been treating her for thirty years. She had double pneumonia. Saida helped the doctor take care of her sick mother. When her mother began improving, the grateful daughter fell in love with the doctor. Fortunately, the love turned out to be mutual.

A year later, she married Zaur's future father and moved to Mukhus, where he worked in the hospital. By all accounts, they lived quite well, even though Zaur had distant memories of his mother complaining that his father would be stuck at the hospital for days at a time.

1936. Lakoba's[44] funeral. Here's what stayed in the seven-year-old Zaur's memory: the blackened town streets are filled with crowds of people. And kids are shouting: "They're burying Lakoba!" "Where?" "In Botanicheskoe!" "Guys! To the magnolia! You can see everything from there!"

Zaur knew nothing about the real cause of Lakoba's death, but these streets, blackened by the crowds of people, were alarming—either something big just happened or something big was about to begin. The undulating darkness of the crowd spent many long years undulating in his memory.

Twenty years later, Zaur found out certain details about the somber affair. The local authorities got a telegram from Tbilisi about Nestor Lakoba's sudden death from angina. Government officials came to his house and

---

44 Nestor Lakoba (1893–1936) was a Communist leader in Abkhazia who helped consolidate Bolshevik power after the revolution. He feuded with Beria, who eventually poisoned him.

knocked on the door. Sarya, Nestor's wife, opened it. When she was told about the telegram's contents, she screamed fearlessly right there in the doorway:

"He didn't die! Beria killed him!"

And indeed, when Lakoba's corpse arrived from Tbilisi, the house doctor determined it was poisoning and was secretly sent to bear this news to Moscow. However, he was waylaid in Sochi and killed. Sarya came to Moscow with one of Lakoba's notebooks that would have exposed Beria. She didn't get to see Stalin, but Molotov saw her and took the notebook away. The poor woman didn't get that everything had already been decided.

Yes, it had all been decided. Sometime after his funeral, they declared Nestor Lakoba an enemy of the state, clawed his corpse out of his grave, and threw it out somewhere. The bacchanalia commenced. The trial of Lakoba's companions was a bit tainted by the absence of the accusation's chief witness—his wife, Sarya. Though, like all trials, it too went off mostly without a hitch.

Sarya refused to confirm her husband's false charges. Her fellow inmates from the prison she was thrown in after being tortured survived. Her son was beaten in front of his mother, and his mother was beaten in front of her son. The torture drove her to insanity, and she died in the prison infirmary. Having never been educated in the dialectic, she knew for sure that only a monster would betray her husband and opted for death instead. Her only son, Rouf, who had obediently waited to come of age, was shot as well.

In those distant times, little Zaur didn't know any of this, but sensed something peculiar about 1937 after listening to the whispering adults throughout the town. He understood that something frightening was happening in the country. Judging by the conversations he heard at home, it sounded like Stalin—who was openly despised in Chegem, where Zaur went every summer—was behind it all.

One time, Uncle Makhaz came from Chegem and spent the whole evening convincing Zaur's father to leave for the mountains and wait it out there until better times came. His father joked it off, saying that he didn't eat garlic to have to hide from people. Zaur struggled, but understood that the garlic was allegorical.

One early morning a few days after Uncle Makhaz's visit, Zaur woke up with a bitter taste in his mouth. He had felt it even in his sleep. Zaur slept in the same room as his parents, and he now heard his father and mother arguing angrily.

Zaur didn't understand much of what they were saying, but he understood that his mom wanted his dad to leave for the mountains and hide there, while his dad thought it foolish and advised his mom not to get involved in the affairs of men.

His mom's voice was hard and stubborn, and she accused his father of cowardice for not wanting to leave. Zaur was shocked by the rudeness and unfairness of such an accusation. Just the opposite was true! Only cowards hide! How could his mom not understand that?

After that morning, he woke up many more times from those same voices, and they were always arguing about the same thing and growing more and more bitter. And nothing in Zaur's life was more miserable than waking up like that. And, lying in his bed, he curled up tighter and tighter into a ball, as if his whole body was listening to their voices and by curling up, he could lessen his vulnerability, as if by assuming a fetal position he could transport himself from this world into the dark and warm world of a mother's womb, where it was impossible to hear the voices that were tearing at his soul.

And one day, he woke up and heard his parents quietly discussing something irrelevant. Their serenely fatigued voices were marked by tender friendliness. They were reminiscing about different times from their lives, going farther and farther into the depths of time and thereby coming closer and closer to each other. And Zaur had never been so happy in his childhood as he was that morning when he listened to the lengthy, watery murmur of his parents' voices, and, as if he were standing in that warm, murmuring stream, he stretched his limbs and relaxed to its sweet sound.

Three days later, his father didn't come back from work, and Zaur found out that they had taken him. Taken. He had been hearing that detestable word for about a year now. It was as if people had suddenly been transforming into mindless pieces of wood and taken for that reason. In Zaur's memory, his father was always large, loud, and cheerful, and try as he might, he couldn't imagine him as a *thing* that could simply be taken away. He feared that word more than any Siberian prison.

His mother made a lot of fuss about it, but nothing came of it. They received two letters from his father in Magadan, after which their correspondence came to a definitive end. Everyone at home believed his father to have been transferred to a camp where writing was forbidden.

A few months before his arrest, his father took a vacation and went to get Zaur in Chegem. They stayed at his grandpa's, but went over someone's house almost every day, either Aunt Masha's, or Uncle Sandro's, or the hunter

Isa's. Later, thinking about that trip, Zaur felt like his father was bidding farewell to the close people in his life in anticipation of their long separation.

One moonlit night, sitting with a group of farmers in his grandpa's yard, his father listened to one of them tell a tale about how he searched for treasure in the ruins of an old fortress. Zaur had heard similar tales of hidden treasure more than once, treasure that, for some reason, always turned out to be looted as soon as they found the place where it was hidden.

Now, Zaur was curiously observing the attentive and serious expression on his father's face, and he couldn't understand his usually cheerful father paying such close attention to the joker telling the tale, as if it wasn't obvious where the tale was going. Little Zaur listened attentively to the farmer as well, but he knew how it would all end. But his beloved, intelligent, adult father seemed to have no idea. When the storyteller, after many trials, finally made it to the place where the treasure was hidden, he found that somebody had already dug everything up, leaving behind mere fragments of the treasure urn. Foiled again!

"The ground was still fresh," he exclaimed, bringing his tale to a close. "I was just a day too late, just a day!"

But after everything that happened, Zaur most often recalled that particular night, the receding hairline on his father's head, turned slightly blue in the moonlight, benevolently inclined towards the storyteller, and especially the expression on his face: agreement, peace, and a sort of strange serenity uncharacteristic of his father. Even then, Zaur knew that it all meant something, but what exactly it meant he didn't know.

And it was only when he was an adult, after the Twentieth Congress, after he knew for sure that his father had perished, that he felt like he understood the significance of the expression on his father's face that night.

In the bloody chaos of 1937, his father was basking in the naïve harmony of that tale, the unparalleled stubbornness of man's pursuit of fortune, knowing full well why the harried farmer fantasized up such a tale of missed opportunity. It seemed like all the opportunities that accompany an ordinary flow of life had been missed, and his father was getting used to the tale's version of events. What a man! And how long ago it had happened!

. . . The town was peppered with portraits of Stalin, people sang songs about him, people talked about him on the radio. The contradiction between what people said about him and what he saw in the streets dampened Zaur's spirit.

He very early on began suspecting the surrounding world of dissembling and himself of abnormality, because he couldn't earnestly take part in all the communal bonfires, poetry declamation sessions, all the military games. He didn't buy into the widespread oath of eternal loyalty to the person that his grandpa despised so much.

Sometimes, Zaur felt like everybody knew that Stalin was evil and only pretended that they loved him out of fear for their own skin.

But sometimes, he felt like his peers, who sang their songs around the communal bonfires, who played their war games and lived in a state of excited, celebratory anticipation of a global revolution were quite earnest. He felt it in their eyes and their smiles, in the heartfelt way they listened to adults when they read them books about brave pioneers[45] or German fascists.

And that's when Zaur's young heart was filled with extraordinary bitterness, with an acute sense of his own abnormality, the sense that he was not like everybody else on the inside. And he knew that he had to hide his abnormality not only because it was dangerous, but because it was generally abnormal, and that it was shameful to let others see it.

Zaur spent every summer in his grandpa's house in the mountains. Every summer, he would gather his strength out in the fresh mountain air, eating simple, healthy food, and his rejuvenated physical strength would be accompanied by a sense of self-worth and an understanding that he wasn't the one who was somehow wrong on the inside, but that the city folk and their children were constructed wrong, and that they were forcing their malformation on him.

The first days of school after the summer vacation, it was as if he was always rushing to confirm his self-worth, which most often led to scuffles and brawls with his peers. And at first, he always won, but he never knew when to stop, and as soon as one fight ended, he picked a fight with another boy, investing in it a fury that the other kids didn't understand, and sometimes he even won several times in a row, but in the end, deathly tired, he wound up losing.

And then in class, he would lie motionless on his desk, biting his fingers in despair and slowly recovering from his draining fatigue.

---

45 The pioneers were the Soviet analogue of the Boy Scouts, but inundated with Communist ideology.

When he was fifteen, Zaur despised Stalin with the most furious and romantic hatred that a youth can muster towards a tyrant. He believed that the revolution, which required so much sacrifice, was nevertheless necessary and therefore beautiful. But the tyrant took power and warped everything. Or so he believed back then.

For a time, Zaur even wanted to become a pilot just so that he could nosedive at the Kremlin where Stalin lived.

Once, leafing through Stalin's book, *Concerning Questions of Leninism*, he found an interesting spot. Stalin polemicized against one of Bukharin's[46] supporters with regard to the issue of government. Stalin pointed out that Bukharin always held to the wrong views on the government and that in his time, Lenin argued against him.

In response to this, Bukharin's supporter said that Lenin did argue with Bukharin about the government, but the very first time they saw each other after their argument, the first words out of Lenin's mouth were that he was now of the same mind as Bukharin regarding to the government. In order to convince Stalin of the veracity of his claim, the Bukharin supporter called up Krupskaya, who had been there, as a witness.

Without casting doubt on the fact that Lenin ultimately agreed with Bukharin, Stalin added that Lenin, assuming that Bukharin had considered his argument, changed his mind, which meant that of course they now agreed with one another. The directness and simplicity of such deceitful logic astounded Zaur. He couldn't believe that it was printed on paper, plain as day. He shut the book and threw it aside in disgust, as if saying: and who's the real abomination? You or me?

Zaur was naturally athletic, though he never really took up a sport. When he was sixteen, he went to the town gym to try boxing. In his very first sparring match, it became apparent that Zaur had a very powerful right punch. His trainer was delighted.

Nearly every sparring match resulted in a knockdown, and the trainer's delight began to take on an unseemly character. When his opponent fell after a successful hit, Zaur ran to him to help him up, while his trainer ran to *him* to hug him triumphantly, and it looked quite comical.

---

46 Nikolai Bukharin (1888–1938) was a Bolshevik who originally helped Stalin against Trotsky, but later began disagreeing with his former partner and was executed during the Terror.

"Ten years I've been waiting for you," his trainer said to him, and Zaur tried with all his might to hide how pleased he was to hear that.

If his trainer really had been waiting for him for ten years, he should have waited for at least another year before letting Zaur take part in the town-wide youth championship. But he let him have at it.

For his very first match, Zaur got paired with a fighter who was experienced for his years, a fan favorite who was brimming with a certain combative beauty.

When he stepped into the ring, the crowd went wild. The fight began. Zaur's opponent took the lead without once leaving his open stance, lithely dancing around him, and Zaur felt the crowd grow still in anticipation of a beatdown.

"Don't kill him right away, Vitek!" someone called out, and the crowd laughed. The voice betrayed the crowd's desire for a long and meticulous thumping.

Zaur felt this and understood what was going on with some sixth sense. He let a few light and quick hits through and realized that that's how he had to wage the fight—in a state of halfhearted uncertainty—in order to capitalize on his only chance, his powerful right arm. A cross or a hook. He needed his opponent to keep boxing in a semi-open stance.

After he let in a few of his opponent's hits, the crowd couldn't take it anymore, with many yelling out:

"Vitek, let him have it!"

His opponent did a one-two punch, then hesitated slightly, leaning towards Zaur, and Zaur, sensing that he could get him, threw out his right arm with all his might.

The next instant, his opponent was on the floor, and the crowd gasped in a state of contradictory bewilderment. Everyone was still in love with their old idol, but they suddenly felt that a new idol might be about to rise up, and they were torn by this contradiction.

However, a second later, his opponent jumped up and assumed his stance, showing his readiness to keep the fight going. The referee counted down the necessary seconds and continued the fight.

The crowd was howling with contradictory sentiments, and Zaur, listening closely to the yelling, felt a loathing for the crowd.

Zaur's opponent stopped dancing around him and began defending himself better, but he had shown no fear or desire to hide behind a defense. Despite the knockdown, he was still confident in his superiority and thought that he had simply walked into an aberrant, though powerful cross.

He couldn't wait to restore the atmosphere of his superiority, and he launched several new attacks, and Zaur let in a few significant punches. The crowd had shaken its bewilderment and was once again shouting in support its favorite. Their idol launched another attack, and Zaur threw a counterpunch. His stinging hook caught his opponent right on the jaw.

His opponent sprawled on the floor. The uncontrollable crowd bowed before the new favorite. Beneath the crowd's tireless roar, his opponent was still sitting on the ground, trying to come to his senses.

Zaur was absolutely sure that he would not only stay sitting for the full count, but that he couldn't even hear the ref counting. But on the seventh second, he got up, assumed his stance, and showed he was ready to keep fighting.

The ref, at a bit of a loss, looked at the judges, and allowed the fight to go on. Zaur's trainer indignantly shouted something. Zaur himself saw that his opponent hadn't yet fully recovered completely and that he was very unsteady on his feet, but he saw in his grey eyes a clear lack of fear and a desire to keep the fight going.

Although the crowd didn't see it, Zaur's opponent was clearly half-conscious, and the judge shouldn't have allowed the fight to continue. His attacks were exceedingly straightforward, and Zaur could have knocked him out with a single calculated punch. And the crowd, sensing this and somehow having learned Zaur's name, was screaming:

"Let him have it, Zaur!"

But Zaur simply deflected the attacks, allowing his opponent to come to his senses. Zaur's feelings were more complicated than simply not wanting to hit somebody who was incapable of defending himself. His resistance to hitting his opponent was augmented by the screaming crowd—it was a subconscious attempt to go against the crowd's wishes. The bell finally sounded.

"Why didn't you hit him?" his trainer said, fanning him with a towel. "Couldn't you see that he was barely standing on his feet!"

"That's why I didn't hit him," Zaur responded, trying to breathe as deeply as possible.

The next round began, with the crowd roaring:

"Zaur, let him have it!"

But his opponent had collected himself, and his defense was now on point. His fearless grey eyes peered at Zaur out from under his gloves. For half the round, Zaur couldn't break through his defenses, and in the second half, having completely recovered from Zaur's earlier punch, he went on the attack.

A series of blows followed one after the other, like a cadre of bombardiers carpeting a town. Zaur's desperate attempts to regain control of the situation were fruitless. His opponent, having realized that he had a devastating right hook that had floored him twice, kept his head, and rather than mounting a permanent defense, he continued the fight with even greater fury, while paying significantly greater heed to his right arm.

Zaur's hooks flew over his head, while his crosses were met only with his opponent's gloves. The second half of the round was dictated entirely by Zaur's opponent, who had definitively regained the upper hand. The crowd had fled back to its previous favorite and was now deafeningly shouting in support of him, as if to make up for their earlier betrayal and simultaneously thanking him for prolonging their carnal pleasure with his seeming defeat in the first round.

Zaur was too inexperienced to defend himself properly. Just about every flurry of attacks delivered by his opponent saw at least one punch make it to its target. And Zaur, shaken by the attacks, sometimes felt like his opponent had three pairs of arms.

A round and half turned into a nightmarish, dark carousel, accentuated by the roar of the crowd, with flickering lights and blurry specks that were human faces zooming past him.

After the fight ended, Zaur's opponent hugged him tightly and said over the thundering applause:

"I get it, buddy. You took pity on me in the first round . . . I won today, but you'll do work just as good as mine . . ."

Any other time, a confession like that from Mukhus's most popular young boxer would have been flattering to Zaur. But not then. In that moment, he felt only a deathly fatigue and a loathing for the crowd, whose roar had doubled in strength when their favorite hugged his thoroughly crushed opponent.

After the fight, Zaur couldn't go to school for a whole week because of how badly his face was beat up. He never showed up in the gym again. If boxing matches were like court proceedings and could be held in privacy without an audience, Zaur wouldn't have left boxing alone. But since that was impossible and since he couldn't come to terms with the crowd, he left it behind.

What is a first love? Why can humans feel love for the first time? Why does such a powerful emotion come to a youth who is absolutely unprepared to deal with it? There's a certain paradox to it. It's as if somebody who can't swim is taken to a stormy sea and then told: "Well, here we are. Let's learn to swim, shall we!"

Zaur didn't learn how to swim, but he didn't sink either, though he did get a mouthful of salty water. It may have been his tenebrous, though restrained passion that frightened that charming schoolgirl who was so surrounded by admirers. And it was only at a party one night when her hand (they turned the happiness on and then immediately turned it back off) tenderly swept aside his topknot, and Zaur, like a horse that feels its reins loosening and reaches for the nearest strand of juicy grass, felt his reins loosen and followed her hand, at which the girl laughed and hid her hand behind her back. He came to, as if somebody yanked on his reins, while somebody invited her to dance.

That was in ninth grade. For a long time, Zaur thought that when people looked at him, they thought he was hopelessly in love, as if he had one of Cupid's arrows—probably golden, certainly stainless—perpetually embedded in his chest. Zaur came to Moscow with that very arrow dangling out of his chest and became a history major.

His very first month in Moscow, Zaur was seduced by a thirty-year-old woman, the daughter of his apartment's landlady. Barely grasping what was happening, bitterly surprised at the fact that it was possible to love one woman and sleep with another, Zaur heard through his window a romantic song being played over the radio, which mysteriously coincided with his own state of being:

No, the fire of my love isn't for you,
And I myself am blind to your own beauty . . .

For a whole week, something got in their way—probably the stem of the arrow jutting out at such an awkward angle. But the experienced seductress eventually broke it at the very arrowhead, and the love boat rammed into the sandy shore after a unanimous swing of the oars.

Though the young woman's mother had to work the night shift every other day and nobody was there to get in their way, Zaur quickly moved to another apartment. He was ashamed to meet her mother's eye, as he was afraid that she would figure out his connection with her daughter. In reality, she knew everything: the traces of their sleepless nights rather effectively explained the bags under their eyes.

Two years later, their romance died peacefully, as his beloved married a second time, and Zaur parted with her with a sense of relief and gratitude. The point of that golden arrow was still stuck in his heart, but he hoped that it was no longer noticeable. Little did he know that he was destined to love only the kind of woman he fell in love with the first time, the kind of woman that had been imprinted in his brain long before his first love.

. . . Once, during a parade, he saw Stalin standing on the Mausoleum from afar, one hand raised halfheartedly. Without feeling anything out of the ordinary, he and the rest of the student column got in line parallel to the Mausoleum, and then suddenly the whole group broke out in a delighted howl. It was so unexpected that Zaur broke out yelling along with everybody else, feeling a powerful electric shock to his insides. When everyone had their fill of yelling and started moving again, he felt how he was barely able to walk, suddenly feeling like his legs had turned to wool and he himself was about to faint.

It was only later, in his dorm after they all had a few shots that he finally came to, though he still didn't fully understand what had come over him.

Here's what happened. All of his old pains that he bore wherever he went, the ones tied to his father, to his destitute grandpa, the country, the explosive unconformity lurking inside him, the pains that he not only hid from everyone else, but that he now hid from himself too—all of these pains collided with the delighted roar of the crowd and his own traitorous yell, at which point an extraordinarily powerful explosion went off inside him, and he felt how the shards of his disintegrated soul hit him right in the chest.

Caught up in the murky wave of other people's delight, he yelled right along with them, even though he already felt horror and shame at his yell, which transformed into a monstrous howl of grief for his father, his mother, for everything. And if back then people could have discerned his individual voice from the crowd and deciphered his yell, it wouldn't have boded well for him, of course. But that wasn't an ability that people possessed back then, separating voices from the crowd, and he himself—probably thanks to his youth and natural constitution—recovered from the shock. If, that is, he really did recover, and there weren't any lasting consequences.

During the next parade, he had a grip on himself, and the column he was marching with didn't lose its mind like that again. Back during the first time, they were just a little too close to the Mausoleum.

After getting his degree, Zaur came home and got a job at the Republican Institute of History and Ethnography. Those were the years of Khrushchev's heroic rejection of Stalin's cult of personality, as well as his confused reforms and blinding hopes.

Zaur believed that history was mankind's judgment over itself. But at the end of the day, we're only interested in history in order to understand today. There is no and cannot be any other reason. But that's exactly why historical research must be flawlessly precise and not merely a way of validating the present.

If somebody is interested in history only to hide from the present, then that means that's how he understood the present. Zaur didn't consider such a path to be entirely fruitless, but he did believe it to be spiritually cowardly and therefore shameful for himself.

He wanted to study Abkhazian history from the beginning of our era, before the fall of the Byzantine Empire. He was interested not only in the empire's multifaceted relationships with the little people, but also wanted to understand a history of bright spots in history. Were the times when people led fairly fortunate lives destroyed accidentally, or were those times themselves accidents?

Is the crystallization of society within ethical boundaries possible, or is any crystallization always partial, and its doom is predetermined by the chronic anemia of human nature?

Zaur was so hurt by civilization's cleansing of the cultural layer of society's ethical traditions that it was as if he was being flogged alive. *We live in an era*, he thought, *of societies that are bald or rapidly going bald.*

What did modern life substitute for the charm of the patriarchal hearth? The allure of a hearth, the center of a home, which Zaur managed to experience in his life, the hearth with its many layers of relationships (elder, younger, daughter-in-law, neighbor, guest) and utter freedom within those layers, where everybody knew his part, like in an orchestra, and began playing only where he was supposed to and fell quiet when his voice was unnecessary for the orchestra to go on, where there was a mutually warming understanding of everybody's individual role, an unspoken acknowledgement of each person's value, where the person who appropriately fell silent was as valuable as the person who appropriately started up a conversation, where the silent's dedication didn't go unnoticed—what did modernity exchange all this for?

The intelligentsia? Disorganized babbling borne of vanity.

Simple folk? Glossy eyes boring into the glassy television screen.

Has there *ever* been in the history of people a critical mass of morality? No, no, and no. Only culture, healthy culture was and is the mighty repository for mankind's ethical experience. But here, we come to a dead end.

Those who need it most use it least. Civilization, while stripping away different societies' ethical experience with conquistador-like crudeness—experience that was accumulated over millennia—promised to return that experience to them through culture, enriched by the knowledge of other societies' experience. But that didn't happen and could not happen. Culture entered society as nothing more than literacy, which isn't what the people need, but what civilization itself needs to facilitate the dissemination of ideas and advertising for various goods. And that dissemination distances people even more from culture and from their own ethical roots.

In creating the illusion of universal integration, sources of information imbue people with an erroneous shame for the uniqueness of their own inimitable traditions: if everybody lives differently than you, you shouldn't lag too far behind.

... Zaur developed a strange and unclear relationship with the local, left intelligentsia. He despised them, but didn't really want to deal with anybody else, as everyone else was worse. He noticed the same thing both here and back in Moscow in student circles. The people who talked the most about the country's need for freedom were themselves not free.

The people who commanded respect weren't the most astute or the most perceptive, but the most radical. They were the little tyrants in their circles, because they said the bravest things, and it was assumed that they took on the greatest risk under certain circumstances. But the certain circumstances never came, and as Zaur thought, never would come. And in the meantime, these people profited off of interest from nonexistent capital. And vigilantly defended their authority, forcing people far more astute and perceptive than them to bow down!

People, thought Zaur, *most often obey strength of temperament, rather than strength of intellect. The Hitler effect.* Zaur was only irritated by that temperament. But many others slavishly surrendered to it.

People, thought Zaur, *are always wistful for somebody with confidence, for a war chief.* What is that called? A subconscious desire to delegate one's conscience. Conscience tires a person out. A few of Zaur's outbursts against this thralldom were ruthlessly put down, and Zaur retreated into himself.

What is freedom? The person who enjoys freedom isn't the one who's free—the person who allows others to enjoy it is. If I converse with someone, then I am free in that conversation insofar as I allow my interlocutor to freely express his thoughts on people and life in large. And my interlocutor is free insofar as he grants me the freedom to express my thoughts on people and life at large.

Freedom isn't what I take—it's what I give. The freer a person is, the less limited is his desire to bring about his freedom—that is, to grant freedom to others.

But the more freedom a person enjoys, the less chance there is that he'll meet somebody as equally willing to grant him freedom as he is willing to grant them. That's the drama of a free person. Somebody who is free is always at least partially subjugated to other people's lack of freedom. But he accepts this drama and this subjugation in the name of some higher internal nature—to be equal to himself and his conscience in the name of opulence.

If freedom consisted entirely of being in possession of yourself, then a tyrant would be the freest person in the world. *But when we closely examine the tyrant's life*, thought Zaur, *we're astounded by his constant, cowardly caution, his extraordinary dependence on his own fear.* He kills out of fear of being killed, but, in killing, he finds another reason to be killed and then attempts to balance the new portion of fear by killing anew.

After mulling over in his mighty brain all the utopias of social and philosophical teachings, Tolstoy reached the sole conclusion: cleanse your souls of your own impurities, and then society at large will in turn be cleansed. There is no other way.

Our intelligentsia found this path to be too long and boring. You want to show off in front of the public, but how can you when you're too busy cleaning out your soul? The intelligentsia ignored Tolstoy.

Although the revolutionary intelligentsia had enough honest idealists, thought Zaur, *it's time to say in all honesty that for the most part, it consisted of lazy, luckless careerists and cunning charlatans.* That's the only way it could have been. Now, just like then, the most irresponsible people opt for the most dynamic path.

Inside every person, there is an indomitable desire to stand straight, a desire to stretch out your limbs in every direction of justice! The feeling is organic and natural. By expanding his soul in every which direction of justice, a person might very well ram into the solid wall of governability, in which case he has the moral right to begin a discussion with the government. And *only* in this case!

But, as a rule, revolutionaries stretch out the feeling of justice in their souls only in the direction of the government. Their morality is such: since I have the courage to criticize the government, I have the right to bully others.

The most irresponsible of people mendaciously take on themselves the responsibility for others. Tomorrow's promises are the indulgences of today's amorality. Therein lies the unholy allure of leftism. He believed that the intelligentsia's job was to correct, soften, and humanize the government's relationship with the people. But what if the government disdainfully turns away from its counsel? What do you do then? Drown yourself?!

No! You have to be honest within the confines of your own life, which isn't easy either, but it is possible. And in so doing, you can preserve the courageous flame of your soul, which is also unable to bring light to the whole country, but it *does* conquer the idea that darkness is absolute! *Yes, yes,* Zaur thought, *what's most important right now is defeating the idea that darkness is absolute.*

* * *

Having worked in the institute for more than three years, Zaur often left town to go to archeological dig sites to collect ethnographic material.

Because of his constant trips, the institute couldn't get Zaur to take part in more or less consistent social work. But that's exactly why when the department he worked in was offered to send one canvasser to work at a polling station and nobody in the department wanted to do it, all eyes turned to Zaur, and everyone immediately remembered that he had always shirked from doing any such thing.

And so, he had to agree and not long after, at seven in the evening, as was required, he made his way to his polling station. Even though the station was in the most picturesque, suburban part of town, Zaur wasn't happy about it.

It was a damp, occasionally drizzling, early spring evening. Zaur stepped out of the bus, wrapped his coat tightly around himself, and turned onto the green street. Cherry plum and apple trees grew on the local yards he passed by, blooming tenderly, as mulberry trees were covered with the curly wisps of their first leaves. Even the trees that weren't yet in bloom were coming to life, springtime juices flowing through them, and it was evident by the soft and elastic bend of the branches beneath the gusts of wind, so unlike the sclerotic shudders of trees in winter.

The polling station was in a suburban school building. During the day, there were classes, but when the sun set, the light mysteriously (for the unenlightened) stayed on in the faculty room, as canvassers and activists got together and pored through lists of voters and had pre-electoral strategy sessions.

During one of these gatherings, Zaur ran into a fellow Chegemite—Tendel, an old hunter. His son worked in the local agricultural management, and you could surmise when Tendel the hunter was in town. But how did he come to be at the polling station, looking around with his hawkish eyes, his legs in gaiters, holding a staff that he was leaning on importantly, arms crossed?

Zaur approached the old man, whom he often ran across in his childhood in Chegem. The old man didn't recognize him, though he brightened up when he heard Zaur speaking Abkhazian. In response to Zaur's question as to what he was doing there, the old man said that he was representing his son's house, because every house had to send a representative. Zaur asked him how he came to be in town for such a long time. He recalled that the old man hated large towns and couldn't stand to spend more than a night in one.

"The rhoomatism's killing me," he said, pointing at his legs. He then added with a sly look on his face: "Maybe they'll send me to the healing waters."

"Who will?" Zaur didn't get it.

"Whoever I vote for," said Tendel and looked Zaur right in the eyes with his own crazy, hawkish eyes.

"But why will he send you there?" Zaur began to be amused.

"If I, an almost hundred-year-old man, go here and am ready to give him a vote, then why wouldn't he honor my request?"

"He's not in charge of that," said Zaur, feeling that he was disappointing the old man. "So don't waste time."

"Don't worry," the old man said conciliatorily, "he might not be in charge, but they sometimes send one or two valuable people to the waters . . . Last time, a nice girl got me some leemonade here . . . Pretty . . . I think she had some Chegemite in her, even though she was chirping away in Russian . . . Oh, here she is."

Zaur turned around. A young woman came out of the director's office, and she stunned him with her youthful aura and a pale face and lips so bright it was as if they had siphoned all the blood out of the rest of her face.

She noticed the old man's gaze and smiled at him tenderly, as if thanking him for acknowledging her charm from his venerable, aged vantage point.

The old man caught the smile and happily started nodding, his round, hawkish eyes flashing. How *couldn't* he notice her!

At the same time, she couldn't fail to sense that Zaur couldn't tear his eyes away from her, and she tensed up, which was evident beneath her yellow, tight-fitting dress. She held a light coat in her hands as she walked across the narrow space between the red-cloth-covered table and the faculty room wall. Tendel, leaning on his staff, sat at the very end of the table, while Zaur stood next to him. In passing by them, it was as if she was carefully transporting her explosive (in light of how narrow the space was) aura of charm.

And suddenly Zaur remembered what seemed like a long-forgotten instance from childhood. He remembered himself on top of a wild pear tree, overgrown with lianas and grapevines. He reached his hand out through the tangle of thorny branches and dry twigs and closed his fingers on a large bunch of grapes. Using the nails on his thumb and index finger, he gnawed through the sprig holding it to the tree. The huge bunch of grapes didn't quite fit into his hand, which he couldn't quite squeeze all the way for fear of squashing the grapes, but which he couldn't retract directly through the thorny branches, vines, lianas, and twigs. He had to constantly make minute adjustments to his extended arm: lower, so as not to hit a branch, then higher to circumvent the liana, then twist his arm to keep the dry twigs from lacerating the ripe and juicy berries, then . . .

"Ho boy! If I could lose some seventy years, you'd never see her here again!" cried Tendel, and Zaur came out of his memories. "That's right, what a catch!" he added. "If you'd saw how she poured me the leemonade, you couldn't have thought straight for a week."

"She's pretty," Zaur guardedly agreed, trying to steer the conversation about the girl into another direction, knowing well the sharp tongue of Chegemites and afraid that he might offend her with an errant word, almost as if he had already decided that the girl was to be his bride. Something suddenly hit Zaur. "Hang on, how are you sitting here when you don't understand a word of Russian?"

"And good thing, too!" Tendel explained eagerly. "I don't know what I'd do with myself otherwise with all their babbling . . ."

Zaur walked away from the old man, feeling that the space instantly grew lighter, as if somebody at the power plant generously decided to flood the town with an extra dose of light.

Zaur found out from a student he knew who walked out of the office that the girl was also a student at the same institute from the philology department.

Her name was Vika. She was here on social assignment, comparing the voter lists with the number of actual voters, overseeing the addition of new voters' information, as well as accounting for "dead souls," that is voters who left for other districts without absentee ballots.

The student told him all this with a sad half-smile, letting him know that he understood Zaur's extracurricular interest in the young woman, his voice making it clear that she, unfortunately, was out of his own league, or else he wouldn't get out of Zaur's way. But Zaur, it seemed, was in the proper league.

"Got a smoke?" he asked Zaur. As if in compensation for the honest information, he took out a cigarette from the pack Zaur offered, brought it up to his mouth, and left.

That day, Zaur was supposed to deliver a lecture to the electoral body. The lecture had nothing to do with the elections in general or with the person the district's voters had to vote for in particular.

This was happening right when the corn craze[47] was starting, and Zaur's lecture was called "What We Expect from the Queen Crop of the Fields." Zaur's higher-ups approved how it was to be called, and there was nothing left for Zaur to do other than shrug and agree to the silly-sounding title.

Zaur wasn't a stranger to the biological qualities of corn and considered widespread adoption into the nation's agricultural landscape to be a great boon. This is exactly why he was worried about the overestimated limits of its geographic dissemination and the farcical fanfare surrounding its adoption.

Here in the suburbs, where everybody had their own yards, he didn't think that his lecture was altogether a waste of time. Though, judging by the voters' faces, they either didn't expect anything good from the queen of the fields or themselves had no idea what they expected from it and didn't want to expect anything more.

At the same time, he felt like he was speaking much more livelily about corn than usual and that, for some reason, he constantly wanted to smile. He felt like it was Tendel's attentive, hawk-eyed face that was forcing his involuntary smiles, along with his gaiter-clad legs, his prophet-like staff, his utter incomprehension of what was going on, and his thorough lack

---

47 After returning from a trip to the United States in 1955, where he saw Iowa's corn fields, Khrushchev launched an agricultural campaign to create an analogous corn belt in the Soviet Union, making it the primary Soviet crop. However, the campaign was not very successful, as the corn failed to acclimate to many Soviet regions.

of embarrassment with regard to the fact that he had no idea what was going on.

The editor of the local newspaper, Avtandil Avtandilovich, came out of the director's office. He gestured calmingly to the audience, imploring everybody to refrain from loudly interrupting the lecture in order to greet him, though nobody was planning on greeting him in the first place, and passed through the faculty room into the hallway.

"What about bay?" one of the audience members suddenly asked when he finished the lecture and asked whether there were any questions. He meant bay leaves.

"What do you mean?" asked Zaur.

"Two years ago, they took a hundred and fifty kilograms, but last year, they took a hundred, what about this year?"

Zaur honestly replied that he had no idea how much they would accept this year, because it depended on the bay leaf harvest in other districts in the republic too. At any rate, he suggested refraining from planting more bay laurels.

Ever since the government began accepting bay leaves (and for a decent sum too), many suburban and collective farmers planted so many extra bay laurels that it became more and more difficult every year to export it to the north.

"Okay," said the man who asked the question. "So, now word is throw out the bay and replace it with corn?"

"Or let a goatibex into the garden,"[48] said another, whom Zaur had noticed in the beginning of the lecture sitting in the back row, his eyes sparkling expressively. Everybody laughed. Zaur waved the thought away, took his coat from the closet, and went outside.

While he was walking back to the bus, an idiotic melody from an idiotic song was on loop in his head, which began with the words, "I met a girl with a crescent brow." Thinking about Vika, he didn't remember at all whether she even had a brow, let alone if it was crescent or straight. Still, he got a happy and warm feeling when he thought of her in the half-empty bus headed for town.

---

48 *The Goatibex Constellation* is another of Iskander's works, which features a hybrid animal—a cross between a goat and a Caucasian tur.

Two days later, they were formally introduced to each other in the campaign center, and it was as if there were magnets between the two of them. Zaur had previously noticed that places like that heightened people's senses, either because of the large amount of red cloths and banners or because human nature generally heightens one's senses in an attempt to balance the frigidity of social rhetoric. Zaur also noticed that in his many business trips. He sometimes had to sit in a district chief's office and listen to him drone on and on about the district's achievements in the spheres of culture and education, as well as with regard to Party indoctrination. Zaur's mind would slowly start coating with a soporific film, but the guy would just keep babbling and babbling . . . And Zaur, feeling his mind slowly shutting down, also felt his senses heightening.

Zaur understood, of course, that this was completely different, but the surroundings still accelerated the process.

For three evenings, with a day or two in between each, he accompanied her as she canvassed voters' houses, sometimes following her into a house, other times standing outside and smoking.

She told him about her girlfriends, about one of her teachers, who, whenever he enters the classroom, searches for her with his eyes, while she tries to hide, about movies that she managed to see in her free time, and about various nonsense whose existence he either couldn't even imagine or had forgotten about long ago.

And though he thought most of what she told him was empty prattle, he liked the prattle, because he liked her lively expression, which sometimes unexpectedly lit up as she confidingly looked at him. He liked that sometimes, in the middle of her heated speech, she noticed that he wasn't so much listening to her as much as enjoying looking at her, at which point she simultaneously grew angry at him for not listening and pleased that he liked her so much that it got in the way of his listening skills. Sometimes, her quick hand flitted to his face and closed in on his eyes, lightly pushing them away—his eyes, not his face, though his face got caught in the push too. The gesture meant: "Stop staring at me already!"

The simple, or maybe childish gesture (he didn't really know how to classify it) always amused him. It was so full of spontaneity and belied a need for affection, for another's touch—a need that maybe she herself didn't even realize.

Once, Zaur saw her outside a movie theater with a swarthy guy and unexpectedly felt a sharp pang of jealousy. They met up the next day, and he, trying to maintain a joking tone, told her about it. She flared up, carelessly waved it away, and said:

"Oh, that was just the movies..."

He still accompanied her as she canvassed voters' houses. Once, shutting the gate behind her, she came out onto the sidewalk and scrunched up her face, trying hard not to laugh and waving him away, telling him that she'd tell him what the matter was only after they put some distance between them and the house.

An elderly widow lived in the house, and Vika made such an impression on her that she wanted to marry her to her son, an engineer from a tool engineering plant.

She made her tea, showed her the house, and the whole time, her son, who, to hear Vika tell it, was a sweetie, stood nearby and listened. Meanwhile, the woman showed Vika their new furniture, their new beds, and the rooms where they would live. And all the while, her son stood there, listening, and it was clear that the woman had such strength of character that she kept her son in hand and did whatever she wanted with him. That day, as he accompanied her to the porch, the groom's mother looked around at the garden and sighed:

"Forty-five tangerine roots..."

"Not counting two persimmons," the son put in unexpectedly. Those were the first words he had uttered.

According to Vika, when she heard his two cents, she started laughing so hard on the inside that she nearly fell off the porch. The mother must have sensed something, shot a glare at her son, and muttered:

"*You're* a persimmon..."

"And that's how I met my husband," Vika said, laughing. She glanced at Zaur with her quick, fiery eyes, as if asking whether she was doing the right thing in laughing about it. Zaur smiled back in response—of course it was the right thing.

* * *

The next day, he was sent on a four-week-long trip for work. He tried to protest, claiming that his presence was indispensable at the polling station, but his department chair shut him down, saying that at the end of the day, he got paid not at the polling station, but at work.

The three days that Zaur spent in the region's capital, he missed Vika very much. He was surprised that he was even capable of missing someone so much. He was twenty-six, he hadn't been truly interested in anyone for two years, and he thought that that had ended, and he wasn't sad about it. Or rather, he kept telling himself that he wasn't sad about it.

Having come back to town a day early and hastily having taken a shower and changed his clothes, he flew to his polling station in the same elated manner with which a conscientious citizen comes there on election day. True, despite his elation, he hid in the bus behind a newspaper, fearing to accidentally run into anyone from work.

When he entered the faculty room, she was sitting at the table, comparing the official list of voters with the handwritten list in her notebook.

Even before she lifted her head, Zaur turned his attention to the infinitely sad expression on her face as she gazed at her list, as if the voter registration list actually contained the names of her dead friends.

She raised her head and noticed him, at which she gave a start and barely nodded in his direction, which made him think that maybe something had happened that now made her ashamed of their acquaintance.

His mood fell, but he managed to get a grip. He took off his coat and greeted everyone in the room. The well-known artist Andrei Tarkilov was hunched over in the corner, drawing a poster. Two canvassers were also comparing lists. There was really nothing for Zaur to do. He came up to the artist and parked himself behind him, watching him make sweeping strokes on the poster, his cigarette not leaving his mouth for a second.

A few minutes later, he came up to her again and parked himself behind her, like he did with the artist. Like the artist, she didn't turn around, and he eventually began to get angry.

And then he noticed that her gaze wasn't leaving her notebook to the list, and her finger was pointing to the same last name it had been pointing to for a few minutes now. *She knows I'm here.*

"Did something happen?" he asked quietly and bent over.

She silently shook her head. No, nothing had happened. She bent even closer to her list. Somewhat mollified by the sad, but cold gesture, as well as the smell of her hair and the delicate sight of the back of her head, he asked:

"You check everyone?"

Translation: we should get out of here and talk about things.

"Two more at home," she said, sighing. He understood that she was willing to step out. So as not to loom over here or cause suspicions about his interest in the young woman (though everyone already knew about it), he went to the artist again.

The large poster now had a person on it, happily lowering his ballot into the voting urn. Zaur thought that the happily smiling man kind of resembled someone he knew. *Oh god, that's the candidate himself*, thought Zaur. *What, he's just voting for himself?*

Then, he heard her chair scoot back. She got up and took the list to the director's office, where the elections commissioner or his deputy could usually be found. She then walked out of the office, approached her chair, put her notebook in her bag, got her coat from the coat hanger, slung her purse over her shoulder, and left.

Nobody paid any attention to her, and Zaur kept looking at how the candidate voted for himself, though he wasn't seeing anything anymore, as the artist, still on his knees, kept adding more to his poster, his expression becoming somewhat Spanish, as with all artists in the middle of a painting.

A couple minutes later, which seemed like an eternity, Zaur got his coat and went outside. He barely made out her light coat in the darkness, and only because he knew which direction she must have been going in.

It was about eight in the evening. A wet March wind was blowing in from the sea. The newly reborn leaves on the young sycamores lining the streets were rustling silkily in the darkness, sometimes crescendoing to a loud, blundering, slapping noise. The star-dotted, springtime sky glittered through breaks in the clouds.

She turned the corner, and he caught up to her. They stopped. She was silent, her head bowed. They were right outside somebody's suburban garden. Young bay laurels were lined up along the fence, their crowns carefully barbered. Each gust of wind sent another wave of dry rustling through the eternally green leaves. And every time an especially strong burst of wind came along, the dry, self-indulgent, worldly-wise rustling was interrupted with the slapping of the young sycamores. And after roiling through the trees, each powerful burst of wind playfully stirred the bottom of her light coat as an afterthought. He could make out her downturned face through the darkness, and her black eyes.

"What's wrong?" asked Zaur.

She was silent. Her head was cast down. Then, she slowly raised it and at the same time, grabbing the fence as if for better support, she said quietly:

"I became a pessimist . . ."

Zaur was flabbergasted. He immediately understood that these naïve words were a confession of love. Many years later, he would still carry with him memories of that wet springtime wind, gusts coming in from the sea that picked up the scent of blooming wisterias three houses away and playfully tugged on the bottom of Vika's unbuttoned coat, beneath which the outline of her body flitted between being well-defined and lost beneath the veil of clothes. The intermittent, flap-eared sputtering of the young sycamores, the twilight of her lowered eyelashes, the bashful transience of her figure, so instilling in him a desire to lend her his steadiness when only an embrace was capable of granting her that steadiness, and the long, supple, swaying steadiness, and her willow-like arm, finally lacing around his neck.

Not that evening, nor any that followed did they make it to her last two houses. So if the people living in those houses were displeased with their candidate and wanted to spite him, they could quietly go to another district without absentee ballots, and their absence would only have been noticed on election day.

. . . They usually walked down the suburban road that led to the beach. Cypresses lined the road prettily, their dense crowns casting shade on just about the entire road.

When it rained, they stopped beneath one of the cypresses, where it was always dry, and stood there, tightly embracing each other. They kissed, listening to the patter of the rain, reveling in the dryness of the foot of the cypress and in the smell of the tree trunk, which safeguarded the warmth of the summer days.

The kisses would sometimes drag on, and Zaur lost all track of time and space, as did she. When this happened, they would be called back to reality by a ray of sunlight suddenly smacking them in the face or the squelching sound of car wheels zooming past them at great speeds.

If they had to stop beneath a cypress, he tried to pick out the thickest possible tree trunk to better hide from the cars on the road. Still, a few times, a car did stop and they had to listen to various obscenities thrown their way. In these instances, they went farther away from the car. The car would then zoom off, as if the people sitting in it had fulfilled their civic duty by making them relocate. Though the obscenities were demeaning, they didn't really faze them. Zaur believed that there was an ethical discount related to moving at different speeds. If a pedestrian hurled those obscenities at them, that would have been much more hurtful.

Sometimes, they went to the deserted beach and sat on a round bench beneath a superfluous sun umbrella. It was superfluous not only because there was no sun, but because if it started raining, it did nothing to protect them, as it was too high up to do anything against the wind-tossed drops of rain.

They sometimes waited the rain out beneath the canopy of a summertime kiosk, which was stuffed to its roof in other seasons. Despite the piercing, wet wind, they were happy, because they loved each other, and that warmed them. But as closely as they pressed against each other, the storm eventually defeated them, as indifference always defeats passion. Tired and chilled to the bone, they left the beach, hitchhiked a car or waited for the bus, and returned to town. In these cases, Zaur always felt responsible, as if he shouldn't have given up, but did anyway.

Once, when they were hiding from the tireless rain beneath the awning of a kiosk and Zaur's disquiet was refusing to go away too, it suddenly dawned on him where they could hide.

Next to the kiosk, there was a storage building for beach chairs. The building was a huge iron cage covered with a plastic, red, pyramid-shaped roof. Behind the iron bars, there were rows upon rows of wooden chairs, stacked right up to the very roof.

Zaur sprinted through the rain to the building, and she followed suit. They got a bit wet before they made it to the roof. The stopped next to the iron door, which had an enormous granary lock on it that made you want to quietly, without uttering a single word, move to another planet.

"What, are you going to break the lock?" she asked, curious more than judgmental.

He looked at her in the dim light of the mooring lights and saw again how beautiful she was in the plastic, indigo coat and hood, which had flown off her head while she ran, but which she had pulled back on. Drops of rain glistened in her hair beneath the transparent hood like jewels beneath a magnifying glass.

"No," Zaur said. He approached the corner of the cage, still protected by the roof, and examined the side wall. At the top, the fence became a sparse palisade of iron rods. Near the middle of the palisade, he thought that the rods were more spread out.

He burst from under the cover into the rain, grabbed the cold, wet iron, and quickly clambered up. Peering inside, he saw the plastic roof's red light reflected onto the chairs, the dry, comfortable chairs hidden from the outside world.

He felt a desperate surge of energy, pressed his left side against the iron wiring, and pushed with his right hand on one that already seemed bent. The finger-thick rod slowly bent further. Then he turned, pressed his side into the bent rod, and pushed on the one next to it. He made a hole wide enough to clamber through, which he wasted no time in doing, as he had gotten quite wet in the meantime. His body was shivering slightly from exertion, and the spot on his palm he used to push the rods apart was burning up. On the flip side, the rain couldn't get him anymore, and now merely seemed like a pleasant, pattering accompaniment on the roof to an otherwise cozy situation.

"Zaur, where are you?" he suddenly heard her quiet voice. He had gotten so caught up in searching for a safe haven, he slightly forgot about the woman he was doing it for. He looked out and saw her peeking out from the corner. Her head, wrapped in the hood, reminded him of something pleasant he once saw, but then forgot about for some reason.

"Come here," Zaur said quietly and waved her over. She adjusted her hood and rounded the corner. Coming level with Zaur, she stopped and hesitantly looked up. He got down next to her and showed her where to put her feet to climb up. Then, hugging her from behind, he started helping her. When her hood slid off, he couldn't help himself and kissed her confused, wet face, and when she fumbled at the hole he had made, he quickly climbed inside and tugged her in after him.

When she stood up, rubbing one slightly bruised knee, he got a burning desire to pull the rods back together and close the passage.

She stood in the semi-darkness, rubbing her knee, and she looked around, listening to the patter of the rain, gazing as intermittent headlights from passing cars illuminated the roof.

He took her hand and led her away from the entrance. She stepped carefully, not trusting the unsteady mass of stacked chairs.

"Won't they fall?" she asked, pushing him slightly, staring around the whole time like a kid in a stranger's house.

"Where would they fall?" he replied. "See how they—"

He wanted to say that they were too densely stacked, but instead slid a hand beneath her wet coat, and embraced her warm body in a hug, which surged with life at his touch. He hugged her awakening body all the more tightly, and she, having slid her hands beneath his coat, hugged him back with bashful strength. Not tearing his lips from hers, he unzipped her coat, and his hands slid to her legs to warm them. She was shifting from one foot to the other, and he felt that they were freezing from the frosty touch of her coat.

And he saw with eyes that had acclimated to the semidarkness the soft, defenseless outline of her legs, and, stunned by the tenderness, he wrapped his arms around them, hid them, clenched them in his embrace, and unable to maintain her balance, she knelt into his embrace. His shivering, disobedient hands dragged her out of the wet and crackling coat and threw it aside. The same disobedient hands removed his own coat, laid it out on the ground, and carefully, as if afraid of waking her, laid her on it.

"You think there are mice here?" she whispered suddenly, raising her head as if trying to break free from the darkness. But there was nowhere and no need to break free.

They lay next to each other for a long time listening to the rustling of the rain, the beating of the waves, the cars passing by on the road, headlights momentarily illuminating the semitransparent roof of the storage room. She caressed his head, and, surprised by the tirelessness of her affection, thought how it was probably the manifestation of some subconscious pity at the bittersweet pain that he felt in the last instant when her fingers grabbed his hair as if making a last-ditch effort to clamber out of the stream that was sweeping them away.

Their springy sanctuary was comfortable and smelled of the sea and the remnants of all the scents of summer. They began to find humor in its constant inconstancy. A single, tiny movement, especially a repetitive one, caused the whole system to come to life and begin emitting a variety of creaks, as if the specters of the summer's sunbathers were either sorrowfully or slightly enviously reminding them about their existence.

As time went on, they grew used to the sea's damp sighs, to the dry, envious rustle of the specters, and even began distinguishing their creaks and rustles, growing surprise when one familiar creak or another mysteriously disappeared or reappeared, sounding in the most unexpected place.

The second time they came here, he installed a slight improvement into their secret sanctuary. He removed a few chairs from the place they had settled down, thereby creating a comfortable hollow. They spent five or six evenings there, and those evenings were beautiful and unmarred. They were happy there, but nowhere does happiness last very long.

Once, when they came there and he started clambering up the iron lattice and peered inside, he saw somebody lying in their spot. Zaur recalled an apprehension he had: sooner or later, something like this had to happen.

He peered intently into the semidarkness with the gaze of somebody who was expecting to find the worst. All things considered, without such an intent gaze, he would never have been able to make out the person lying in that semidarkness, which now seemed so maliciously crimson-stained. The man must have been sleeping—Zaur could make out a bodywarmer, the remains of an unfinished dinner, and an empty vodka bottle that stood next to his makeshift headboard. Zaur felt like the man was demonstrating his claim to the sanctuary. Why else would he have settled himself in their exact spot?

"Well, did you get stuck?" she asked from below, and he quickly climbed down, quietly took her aside, and said that their spot was taken. He thought she would be horrified at that thought that they might have climbed inside and only then have discovered the newcomer. But to his surprise, she wasn't horrified, but very disappointed. He even thought that she was upset with him for giving up their sanctuary to some tramp without so much as a fight. She was sullen the whole evening. And when they were parting ways and he kissed her a few times, he felt that she wasn't responding to his kisses. He understood that it wasn't feminine moodiness, but profound disappointment.

But it would have been awkward, he thought, *to wake the tramp up and lay claim to the storage building.* Especially since Zaur was certain that the guy had claimed it before they did. The slightly bent iron rod he had noticed when climbing up the first time and the fact that the entrance was shut the second time they came (meaning that the iron lattice was perfectly unbent—he had thought that it was the work of a beach worker) indicated that somebody had been there without them and before them. He figured that the tramp didn't spend every night there, and it was simply their good fortune that they had never run into each other before.

Later, he was remembering how upset Vika had gotten, and he suddenly thought about how his mom must have been similarly upset with him, as he had yet to sue their neighbor, who had swiped a piece of their land.

A few years back, when that bastard began expanding his house, he asked Zaur to allow him to encroach a meter and a half into his land at a width of eight meters.

Despite his mother's protests, the popular lawyer begged Zaur so obsequiously to allow him to expand his home, Zaur gave him the green light.

His mother said that the lawyer wouldn't be satisfied and would appropriate the entire width of their plot. Zaur was astounded at how boundless a woman's fears could be, though he had seen quite a bit in his life.

And what happened? After one of his work trips, Zaur walked through his fence gate and discovered a new stone barricade that their neighbor had built. The barricade, which had been put up with the speed of the Berlin Wall, spanned the entire width of their land—not just the eight meters they had agreed on.

"So, sonny, who turned out to be right?" asked his mother, her voice full of funereal gravity. Zaur was once again astounded at how the poorly educated woman was often infinitely more perceptive than him.

"Don't worry, mom," he said. "He won't get away with this."

"Please let it go," his mother replied, and he himself realized how hollow his threat was. The lawyer's baseness was so shameless and overwhelming that Zaur simply lowered his hands and couldn't—and knew that he wouldn't—have the strength to fight the lawyer.

All the same, he went to the city council, where one of his former schoolmates worked, and told him what happened. His old buddy replied that the lawyer was a man with a lot of connections and that it would be very difficult legally to win back the piece of land, especially since Zaur himself allowed him to expand into his land. He said that he should never have allowed him to do that and that he would use any argument to defend himself, even something like the trivial fact that their plot of land (he checked in the blueprints) somewhat exceeded the area permitted to an urban home, and so on.

Nevertheless, he advised him to write a formal complaint, gave him a pen and paper, and sat him down in his own chair. Zaur sat and sat over that piece of paper, and, unable to come up with anything other than an address to the city council chairman and acutely sensing the foolishness and hopelessness of his endeavor, tore the paper up and stood up, which infused his old school buddy with a wave of energy.

"See, here, where we work," he said, "nobody will ever believe that you allowed him to expand onto your land for free. Especially since domestic expansion is permitted in very rare cases. . . Obviously, he must have bought off someone in the city council, and now they're invested in you losing your case."

"I don't care," said Zaur. "But it sucks for my mother—she can't come to terms with it."

"Tell your mother that your land was larger than allowed," he gave him one last bit of advice.

Obviously, that meager argument never satisfied his mother, and any time her gaze shifted to the prospering lawyer's house, it filled with unremitting loathing. Zaur simply stopped saying hello to him, never having discussed what he had done.

The first time they saw each other after the wall had been built, he sheepishly looked away after throwing Zaur a lewd glance. Zaur thought then that the lawyer *must* have been experiencing some degree of discomfort at least, but every time they saw each other afterwards, he simply lowered his gaze, and Zaur felt and understood that he himself was much more discomforted by the whole thing than the lawyer.

Then, one fine day, after coming home from work, his mother nodded resignedly at the lawyer's house:

"Take a look!"

Zaur saw the new drainpipe attached to the corner of the lawyer's house. The end of the pipe was facing their property.

"He said," continued his mother, "that his land is too level, but ours makes a great drain."

Zaur finally felt the rage welling up inside.

"Explain to her, Zaur," suddenly called out the lawyer, who was looking out his window and must have understood what they were talking about, "that there's nothing in this . . . There's no need to be offended."

"Give me a second," replied Zaur, still feeling the rare power of rage building up in him. He headed off for the storeroom beneath their house, where they kept an axe.

His mother sighed, glancing loathingly at the lawyer. "It's because there's no man in this house . . . But there is God . . ."

Meanwhile, Zaur, armed with an axe, exited their basement and headed straight for the stone wall.

"Zaur, what are you doing?" his mother asked him in alarm.

He didn't respond.

"Zaur, have you lost your mind?!" cried the lawyer.

"Zaur, wait!" yelled his mother and ran downstairs.

But Zair had already reached the stone wall. He put the axe on the wall and clambered over it in a swift movement. He picked up the axe and walked to the house along the wall. Seeing Zaur approaching, the lawyer bleated madly:

"Bloody murder!" and he shut the window.

"Zaur, I'm begging you!" his mother shouted. But Zaur, angry at both of them for misunderstanding him, quickly approached the corner of the house where the pipe was sticking out. He swung the axe back, having quickly steadied himself, and struck the end of the pipe with the axe haft. The first hit left a dent in it. At the second hit, the end of the pipe loudly clattered to the ground. Zaur jumped down from the wall, picked up the pipe end, and tossed it over the wall onto the lawyer's property.

"You should've explained," said his mother, having finally calmed down. She was beaming with pride for her son, who had finally shown that he was able to stand up for himself. The lawyer didn't file any complaints and simply made a drain beneath his own house.

In recalling this anecdote, Zaur felt a surge of warmth at the thought that his girlfriend had demonstrated a primal similarity to his mother, which made him happy and simultaneously upset, because their similarity manifested itself in an analogous condemnation of his lack of will to stand up for himself.

And since his girlfriend, who had never heard of Chegem, thought exactly like his mom, who had grown up in a village in the mountains and who had inherited from her ancestors the indomitable energy of the early pioneers, it meant that they were probably right.

And suddenly, thinking about how she stood beneath the cover of that beach storeroom, dressed in her hooded, plastic, light blue coat beneath which drops of rain glistened in her hair like precious stones, thinking about the agonizing sweetness with which he tried then to recall who she reminded him of, he clearly realized now what he couldn't realize then.

It was in Chegem in his early childhood, living in his grandpa's house, when he was digging around in a desk full of tax statements, that he discovered an old card with the head of a beautiful young woman covered by a hood and slightly fell in love with that head at the ripe young age of ten.

The mesmerizing beauty of that head, peering out from under the hood stayed with him for his entire life. That expression that managed to be both fragile and teasing, the combination of monastic timidity and a mischievous half-smile that seemed to be parodying the monastic timidity. And he discerned all of this and loved to stare at that card for long periods of time, simultaneously scared that other kids and especially adults might discover his hobby.

How strange, he thought, *that I didn't try to filch and hide that card. And how strange*, he kept thinking, *that my whole life, I was attracted to girls who* looked good in hoods and who always turned out to own a coat with a hood. And if they didn't, then he mentally pulled a hood over them anyway. The point is that they always had the kind of face that looked good wearing a hood.

How strange, he thought, *that such a small coincidence could determine my taste in women for such a long time, maybe forever.* But most surprising was that despite his fear of being found out, he never wanted to filch and hide that card away and then look at it as long as he wanted.

That may have been his tragic character flaw: he never ameliorated the rules of the game that he was forced to play with life.

It was never a secret pride or anything, but it was almost always a subconscious desire to test the *truth* of whatever it was he was trying to achieve.

And he didn't steal away that card in his childhood only because he saw it as the universal truth of beauty that had suddenly opened up to him. And since the truth had suddenly opened itself up to him, how could he have stolen it or hid it away? The truth is the truth because it's for everyone. It would have been the same thing as trying to hide the beauty of a blooming summer day that had suddenly dawned. He might have been ashamed at feeling such overwhelming joy at the sight of such a day, but then again, it wasn't his fault. And how can you hide a fresh, glistening, beautiful day with its endless sky anyway?!

And so, each time finding the opportune moment, he would dig around in the desk where the card lay amidst terrible photos made by a Kengurian photographer who came to town once a year, as well as no less terrible photos that Chegemites brought back from Mukhus, where they went to sell corn, cheese, meat, nuts, and where they were photographed by a crazy, red-bearded chiromancer who worked at the bazaar until a federal photo studio drove him out of business and he was forced to abandon the semi-mystical art of photography and devote himself fully to the thoroughly mystical art of chiromancy.

Back then, in his childhood, while gazing at the photo of the young woman on the thick, prerevolutionary paper, he didn't notice how the photo was glued on to a piece of cardboard. And all other prerevolutionary photographs also seemed to be produced on thick, unbending paper with the studio's brand on the flip side, and conversely, all new photos were made on thin paper that distorted and bent easily.

And there was some secret consistency in all this: in the sad density of the sturdy, yellowed paper, where the faces maintained a trace of the gravity and monumentality of what was happening, in all the photos of someone's ancestors with their hands on pistols and daggers, in all the women holding up babies in their tiny white shirts, in their husbands, unwaveringly standing behind them with intermittent expressions of bestial hubris. All of these people bore on their faces a trace of understanding that they were tangentially involved with eternity. Entire families went to town to get their picture taken with an air of importance that made it seem as if they were going there to write their last wills or, more specifically, to leave an imprint of their faces as a kind of macular confession.

It seemed like all those people had their pictures taken knowing full well that they and their way of life would soon disappear, and it seemed like they made their peace with that inevitability and were concerned only with transmitting their likeness to future generations.

And vice versa—the faces on the new photos seemed smudged, undependable, as if the people understood that the whole thing was just self-indulgent, rather than the act of securing one's likeness in eternity, especially since in their heart of hearts, they sensed that there wasn't all that much to secure anyway.

And so, the faces that look out from these photos are the faces of those who have forgotten their beginning, stupefied in their incessant waiting for a future that never comes. They are the faces of people who have been denied their own destinies. Yes, denied their own destinies, for their souls have been carelessly tossed into the communal cauldron of political alchemy, and after the great experiment, whose conclusion keeps being delayed, the lid of the cauldron will be opened and everybody's soul will be returned, enriched by the golden alloy of universal good fortune.

Which leads all these smudged and undependable faces to look out of their photos, as if saying, "Oh, we just thought it would be cool to get our pictures taken, since we don't have what's most important to us. Now, when they'll give us back our destinies, we'll get our pictures taken and acknowledge the full weight of what we're doing, enriched by the most golden of all alloys." But their smudged and undependable faces also belied expressions of disoriented fatigue: on the one hand, you feel sad for yourself for having to live so long without your own soul, which you gave away to the communal cauldron—though, it really was *taken* away more than given away—and on the other hand, it would be a shame to get it back without the promised golden alloy, even though it *is* taking quite a long time—maybe it *would* be better to get it back now, golden alloy or no . . .

And Zaur would look at those faces for long periods of time. He recognized almost all of them from Chegem—almost all of them were neighbors or relatives, and he knew them and pitied them, though back then he did so subconsciously as sorrow welled up in him. And when he shifted his gaze to the beautiful young woman, the sorrow didn't go away, but was instead infused with tenderness directed towards the young woman and transformed into the sweet desire to one day meet a girl like that and eventually see all of those faces happy and joyful, maybe even bearing concealed gratitude to Zaur for helping them break out of the cheerless stagnation of fruitless anticipation.

Oh, how high into the clouds did his daydreams take him! And yet, despite time dulling their youthful vividness, forcing them to change in concordance with the poison of life experience, their essence stayed with him. He hung on to the hope to one day meet a girl like that and the hope to one day do something for all those people.

Zaur had known for a long time that the country's agriculture had hit a dead end and would spend the next years making itself more and more comfortable in that dead end, unless something changed in the relationship between the farmer and the government in the form of a modern collective farm.

He was confident that over the course of millennia of existence, mankind in general and the farmer in particular was created as a private initiator, and that collectivism was thoroughly incongruous and harmful not only for agriculture's development, but for the idea of collectivism itself. Zaur believed that the idea of collectivism lay hidden in mankind's psyche, where it had been rooted since the time of primitive societies, and that under normal conditions, this reflex activated only in times of unfathomable calamity, catastrophe, or simply misfortune that beset another man.

And he believed that this reflex should not be roused and activated for an everyday activity like manual labor, because like any reflex that is activated without need, it will gradually weaken and will eventually only halfheartedly activate when faced with signals of calamity that call for a collective effort.

At the moment, thanks to a certain liberalization of public life, communal farms had essentially begun to play host to lease relationships. Unproductive plots of land or small plots that were unsuited for mechanical development or too far away from the farmers' residences were given away under private leases to collective farm families, usually on equal terms: half of the harvest goes to the collective farm, half to the farmer.

Zaur didn't have the chance to investigate how this relationship came to exist in the collective farms and semi-regularly continued to exist. It most likely came about naturally, thanks to the liberalization. Some farmer could have one day nodded at an abandoned plot of land and said to the farm chair:

"Let me plant some corn here. Otherwise the land's just wasting away."

"Go ahead! Half goes to the farm, half to you . . . Sound good?"

"Sounds good!"

A dialogue like this could have been quite conceivable given the liberalization. People's responsibility for common sense lessened. (Zaur, thinking about this in these terms exactly didn't pay attention to their paradoxical nature, seeing as it so permeated the very air of that time.) The communal farm chair could have easily said something like that, confident that nobody would accuse him of "counterrevolutionary sentiments" anymore.

People were doing this in lots of places, and Zaur did everything in his power, directly or otherwise, to check the profitability of these micro-islands of private initiative. He had spent two years gathering grains of such information to have undisputable facts at his disposal. Judging by the data gleaned from the farmers, these plots of land yielded on average three times greater harvest than the collective fields. He knew that there was no way this data could be overestimating—if anything, it may have been undershooting the truth. The collective farm chairs and the farmers themselves weren't really loose-lipped with this information among strangers. But, as was occasionally the case, if they found that Zaur was interested in their affairs not for any higher-ups, but for himself, then they opened up quite willingly. Once, he went to talk to an old farmer who happened to be a distant relative of his. Zaur asked:

"What if the government said that whoever wanted to could leave the collective farm? Would you do it?"

The old man thought it over and unexpectedly breathed out:

"No."

Zaur was astounded, but the response he had gotten was so decisive that he didn't inquire about the reasons. The collective farm where his relative lived wasn't one of the best ones, but it wasn't too weak either. He must have gotten used to his way of life and didn't want to change anything in his twilight years. *Things aren't so simple*, thought Zaur.

Another old man from another village told him about a curious run-in he once had with Stalin. It happened in the early 30s. Stalin was vacationing in Abkhazia and decided to have a kind of "breakfast on the grass" in the company of a local farmer. Nestor Lakoba, who accompanied Stalin, found such a farmer. The farmer decided, just in case, to hide the fact that he didn't understand Russian.

It took place in a forest glen. A campfire, kebab, wine—the works. The "representative of the people" did notice security guards flickering through the brush. Plus, there were guards sitting right next to them.

As they were having their idyllic breakfast, a wasp suddenly appeared out of nowhere. It tried to land either on the war chief's plate or on his hand. In short, its intent wasn't too clear, but it was obviously insidious. The war chief waved it away a couple of times, but it remained resolute and steadfastly hovered over his plate. Whatever he did, it wouldn't fly away.

Everyone around was up in arms, some wanting to smack it with a towel, others considering demonstrating their marksmanship and shooting it out of the air with their pistols. But comrade Stalin lightly gestured with his hand in rejection of such crude methods of dealing with the wasp, picked up a fork, and froze. The wasp spent a long time circling above his hand and plate, capriciously unable to decide on the perfect landing platform. Comrade Stalin waited patiently until it finally set down on the plate, slowly reached out, and squashed it with his fork. Then, he lifted it up with the same fork, tossed it aside, and said:

"It wasn't aware of my main advantage. I'm very patient."

Towards the end of the prolonged breakfast, Stalin asked the farmer:

"How do you feel about collective farms?"

Lakoba translated the question, which was perfectly clear anyway. Collective farms were only being introduced in Abkhazia at the time.

"Let's try them out in two or three towns. And we'll see. If they work good, we'll join up," answered the farmer with a certain wily air about him.

Lakoba translated the response.

"No time, no time," said Stalin, furrowing his brow.

But the beautiful fall day, the kebab, the fire, the good wine, and the scintillating forest sprinkled with guards must have put the war chief in a good mood, and he forgave the farmer his not quite tactful response. When saying goodbye, Stalin even said to Lakoba:

"Let him ask for whatever he wants."

Lakoba translated the war chief's benevolence.

"We could really use some nails," the farmer asked carefully.

"Ask for a school," Lakoba whispered to him in Abkhazian.

"We could really use some nails and a school," implored the farmer.

Lakoba translated the request.

"You'll have your nails and a school," Stalin promised and left.

And the village really did soon after get its nails and a brand new school, but they also implemented a collective farm.

Gently laughing while telling Zaur about this, the old man added:

"Maybe I shouldn't have asked for the nails? But how could I not when someone like that commands you to make a request?"

Another old farmer that talked to Zaur about collective farms irritably waved him away, as if Zaur were inquiring about the health of someone whose health was long ago hopelessly compromised. He yelled out suddenly: "In 1937, they took eighty-five people from our village! That's two hundred homes! And *who* they took! Blood and milk! They were all between twenty and forty! The strongest among us!"

"Why?" asked Zaur. He had never heard of such a thing. He had always thought that 1937 primarily concerned cities, and he now felt ashamed of his ignorance.

"I don't know," responded the old man. But he grabbed a hold of himself and added: "Or rather, I do. The Myussera resort isn't far from here. Stalin vacationed there. They were afraid of an assassination attempt. But what attempt could there have been! They didn't let anyone close. The guards! A bird couldn't have gotten through! A *mouse* would have been hard-pressed!"

He said this with such passion and even bitterness that Zaur could suddenly clearly imagine both sides admitting that an attempt on Stalin's life could have been quite possible. He imagined that the tyrant, waking up in the morning, looking around, and realizing that he was still alive, would think to himself: *Aha, they didn't get me this time. Now it's my turn . . .*

During his trips, Zaur grew confident that the collectivization of Abkhazia's lowlands had been much bloodier than he imagined. Before, he used his native Chegem as a point of reference, where they took all the livestock, but didn't harm the people *Apparently*, thought Zaur, *they must have thought that those who lived in the mountains had more of a chance to defend themselves.* There was no other explanation. The madness of that time was also fraught with carefulness. After all, the founder of the Assyrian government—that's what Zaur sometimes called him—had a criminal-like intuition that allowed him to discern which individuals and even entire peoples could stand up to him.

Yes, during this time, people have grown quite unruly, varied, even wild. In the villages of Abkhazia, where farmers spent millennia producing wine, there suddenly appeared alcoholics.

In Zaur's opinion, small, hidden islands of lease relationships not only improved the national agriculture but improved the farmers too. Soulless work where a person doesn't give it his all does not and cannot result in a spiritually healthy person. Zaur was confident of this. This was especially true for the farmer whose fruits of labor are in his sight all year round either plunging him into the depths of ennui with dwarfish sighs or lifting him to the heights of inspiration with the delightful rustling of strong, healthy corn stalks. If the farmers are once again given the gift of plenty and fecundity, then they themselves will grow healthier and blossom.

He wrote an article on all of this and a lot more that had to do with the deep, hidden psychology of the farmer. In the article, he called for a careful and gradual transition towards lease relationships, where it would be beneficial (this was a subtle move, as he believed that it would be beneficial everywhere). He thoroughly edited his work, then typed it up, put it in an envelope, and sent it to Moscow to the Party's Central Committee.

He believed that either his work would be taken into account, which would gradually lead to a new era in the nation's agriculture, or he would be punished as a disseminator of foreign views. He was ready for such a turn of events too, and he gave the away his letter at the post office with a steady hand. Half a year passed, but still no response. He quashed his impatience and stubbornly waited and believed that sooner or later, he'd get a response. A letter like that couldn't go unanswered. The higher-ups must have been seeking the advice of many experts before responding. *Let them seek advice,* he thought, *let them come at the problem from every angle.*

Here's the idea that had fueled him the last few years, though if we're being honest, he had spent his whole life unwittingly preparing for it.

Zaur had been in Vika's home many times. She had a well-off family that Zaur thought was outright wealthy and happy. Her father was a professor, one of the leading workers of a large scientific research institute. Her mother worked in the same institute, though she was a rank below him.

Vika's father often went abroad on business trips, and he would bring back to his women (Vika also had a sister who was still in school) various pretty clothes and film strips showing what life was like in far-off lands.

The first night that Vika brought Zaur home, before her father had even gotten a chance to get properly acquainted, he immediately started getting out his film stuff and showing one of his films about American towns, suburban villas, and beaches. He had just returned from a business trip to America.

Zaur found the film to be naïve, uninteresting, and foreign. And he was especially surprised that Vika's father was clearly enjoying watching the same film and enjoying talking about it. In the darkness, Zaur sipped on some cognac that Vika's mother had put on the table as an aperitif and quietly listened to the professor's delighted exclamations about the film.

Zaur knew from working in his own institute how business trips were alluring not only to the young, but to many white-haired scientists too. Zaur never demonstrated an interest in going abroad, though. In this regard, as in many others, his thought process was simple and unequivocal: when someone's sick in your home, don't go gallivanting around other homes. Zaur believed that in the home that was his nation, the nation itself was sick. He was amused by the comical paradox that was embedded in these trips. People whom the higher-ups considered to be exemplary workers were sent abroad. Which meant that as a reward for being a distinguished servant of socialism, you got a free trip to the realm of capitalism. But wouldn't a true servant of capitalism view this as a punishment?

Zaur was greeted with great cheer in the professor's house, as if he were Vika's groom or groom-to-be. *Do they suspect about our relationship?* thought Zaur on occasion. But he didn't have an answer.

Once, Vika's father suggested that Zaur should apply to the doctoral program in the pedagogical institute, intimating that he was on friendly terms with the provost. Zaur gently brushed the suggestion aside. The professor's implication seemed naïve to him. Another time, the professor amazed him with an even greater burst of naiveté.

That evening, there was a party in their house primarily intended for local youths. Vika's father was there too, though he wasn't a drag on the party at all. When everyone was dancing, he leaned in to Zaur, indicated one of the girls with his eyes, and suggested that maybe they should dance together. Zaur replied that he didn't really want to.

"She's the daughter of the secretary of the city committee," Vika's father whispered to him.

"So?" Replied Zaur in confusion.

"What do you mean, 'so?'" Replied Vika's father, equally confused.

By the way, Vika's father had a hobby—he collected ancient Russian furniture. This innocent pastime irritated Zaur for some reason. In his opinion, too often was the house filled with conversations about trips to consignment shops.

"How do you like my Russian Empire?" he once asked Zaur, indicating the style of the furniture.

"I prefer the Russian shire," Zaur responded jestingly.

"Clever," nodded the professor, smiling halfheartedly. For the first time, the thought crossed his mind: could this young man be a danger to his daughter?

However, he did like Vika's parents for their hospitality and kindness. But he felt that there was and will always be a barrier between them. Zaur didn't know what to call it, but the barrier was their inexplicable mental simplicity.

Actually, it was pretty explicable. Zaur felt that the essence of their simplicity was that they were fully in charge of their lives—they didn't know the horrors of 1937, had never suffered major losses. It was as if they didn't suspect that aside from the official explanation on life, there were other explanations that didn't even remotely resemble the government's version.

On top of that, Zaur thought, they were rich. But they weren't as rich as his neighbor, the popular lawyer, or others who profited off of one form of fraud or another. Their riches were the lawful reward from the government for their work. And this made them both very unlike the families of local fat cats and unlike families like Zaur's.

His earnings and his mother's pension were barely enough to make ends meet. Zaur was undemanding with regard to food, clothing, and everyday life in general. But poverty still denigrated him. He felt demeaned by their furniture with the awful dresser, cases, cupboards, and rickety stools. From his father's house they only managed to hold on to one room and the veranda—everything else had been sold after his arrest.

His mother hung on the walls dozens of photos of relatives—mainly dead ones. And this patriarchic cult of the dead that he couldn't forbid her augmented the discomfort of their home. It was why Zaur rarely had friends over his house and never women he may have been interested in.

Zaur was ashamed of his poverty, but in some odd way, his shame convivially got along with the clear understanding that he found and would always find it uninteresting to deal with pretty things or clothes. Even if he had the money and time.

His ambition soared in higher spheres of imagination. He felt that he was blessed with a certain something that definitively placed him above such lowly mercantile interests.

But when living in conditions when everyone around you, like the neighboring lawyer, was trying to squeeze as much as they could from life—a goal for which they didn't shy away from thievery or bribery—it was difficult to maintain a loathing for life's material comforts. Too many people lived exclusively to satisfy this insatiable desire to get their hands on as much as possible. In their eyes, his poverty, the poverty of a young man, full of energy, seemed like the result of his mediocrity and even worthlessness.

And Zaur, as sad as it may be, was ashamed of being poor and was simultaneously ashamed of his shame.

. . . After the beach that he had given up without a fight, Zaur felt like he had doubled down on his position in the park of the closed resort. It was located about halfway between the beach and the school with the electoral office.

It was a beautiful park, built before the Revolution by the Russian millionaire Smitsky for his most likely beloved, tuberculous wife. He had saturated the park with different kinds of flora from all over the world.

As far as Zaur knew, after the Revolution, the former millionaire continued to live next to his park, where he now worked as a gardener. Smitsky's wife outlived him and kept living there in the 30s, earning a wage by making private dinners for more or less well-to-do vacationers.

Towards the end of the 30s, a hidden or even super hidden resort was built in the park, because the heads of the country, even Stalin himself, would sometimes vacation there. That must have been why the resort had its own backup power plant, in case the town's stopped working.

After Stalin's death, the private resort became semi-private. It became open not only to the Party elites, but the scientific elites too. For that matter, the Party elites fastidiously dispersed among other resorts that still maintained a respectable air of privacy.

The previous year and the one before that, a well-known academic chose to vacation there. He was a student of Vavilov's[49] who had miraculously

---

49 Nikolai Vavilov (1887–1943) was a Russian-Soviet botanist and geneticist. When he expressed criticism of Trofim Lysenko's (a biologist-ideologist who had Stalin's favor) ideas on genes, Stalin had him arrested. He died of starvation in prison.

survived on some God-forsaken research station. Lysenko had probably forgotten about it too.

Zaur became acquainted with him at a banquet and made a good impression on him. He then showed him around Abkhazia and even visited him there a few times. All you had to do for the watchman to let you in was show him a passport, which he would use to confirm that you were on the list of invited individuals.

The first year, the academic was confidently disposed and said that any day now, the park would be given to the Academy of Sciences to be used as a perfect center for crop research. He said that the problem would be fixed in no time. But the problem wasn't fixed that year, or the next one, or at all.

Zaur concluded from this that the liberalization had been carefully halted. If smaller partitions within the larger partition had been torn down— that is, if a greater amount of people was now being allowed to experience greater goods and benefits—that didn't mean that the larger one would be entirely torn down, which would necessitate the law to apply universally, rather than privately, as was the case. Once, while walking with the scientist in the park, Zaur noticed in the top corner of the fence a large hole—it was an obvious, though quite illegal, passage. He also noticed how a dozen women who were loudly talking and teasing each other were headed directly towards it. Some of those women were holding scythes. And for a brief moment, Zaur forgot where he was. He felt like he was on a nineteenth-century estate and the group of women were field workers headed home after a day in the fields.

Having lost his haven on the beach, Zaur remembered that hole in the park fence and came there with his girlfriend. The spot where the year before there had been a gaping hole now had two unpainted boards nailed over it. Zaur came up to the fence and tugged on one of the freshly nailed-in boards. The bottom nail turned out to be loose, and the board easily let itself be pushed aside. The bottom of the second board was equally untethered. He moved aside these two golden rays and led her into the park.

"Oh!" she exclaimed in a whisper. "It's so cool here!"

Right next to the fence, there was an asphalt pathway. It circled around the whole park. Behind the path, there was a tangerine plantation.

Zaur took Vika's hand, and they carefully passed under the tangerines and entered the park, which was full of sequoias, cedars, and palms.

"A baobab!" she exclaimed and ran up to the silvery trunk of the closest palm. She threw her arms around the mighty tree's trunk like a little kid who tries with all his strength to lift an adult, failing to understand that he'll never be able to accomplish that, but doing so to express his boundless joy nonetheless.

"That's not a baobab," he said, smiling. "That's a palm tree."

"No, it's a baobab," she replied, pressing close to the trunk and hugging it, as if she were defending the trunk from an attempt on its life, her strict gaze clearly relaying the message: Don't you come near us . . .

And Zaur reached out to her in response to the seemingly protective, though in reality enticing gesture, and suddenly once again got a good look of her well-defined lips and kissed her for a long time, feeling with his lips the youthful fortitude of her own lips, made cold by the weather.

Three days later, when they were lying on Zaur's coat under a tangerine bush and he was feeling with his side the unevenness of the damp, bumpy ground, surprised that she wasn't feeling any of it, he suddenly saw a security guard and his dog patrolling in the moonlight.

They were walking along the asphalt path. Growing cold with horror, Zaur realized that the guard with the dog probably wasn't just out for a relaxing stroll—they must have been searching for them. They were walking from up top, probably from that same hole in the fence.

Still lying on the ground and afraid that she might suddenly say something, he quietly put his hand over her mouth, raised his head, and observed the path. He heard the guard's footsteps and intermittently saw the dog's shadowy silhouette as it occasionally slid into view behind the tangerine grove. He felt like he could hear the dog sniffing with predatorial glee the scent of their tracks.

They drew level with them and kept walking. Zaur sighed as if a great weight had been lifted off his shoulders. Any old mutt could have probably sensed their presence, but for some reason, this duty-engrossed security hound had failed to do so. Zaur was now confident that the dog was searching for them specifically, because after some thirty more paces, the dog turned off to follow their tracks, rather than continue along the asphalt path.

That was where they had turned off the path today and, before they came to the tangerine bush where they made their ramshackle camp, where they had gone to the palm tree she had hugged the first evening. It was quite a ways away from where they were lying now.

"My baobab saved us," she said, ducking into the hole in the fence and running out onto the road.

* * *

A few days later, Zaur got the audacious thought to get together in the school director's office, which served as their polling station. He cooked up a brilliant plan: once all the canvassers left, they could get into the building through the gym window, then easily get to the faculty room, and then to the director's office. Inside the office was a magnificent couch. Zaur knew that only the school's outside doors were locked. The key would stay with either Avtandil Avtandilovich or his deputy.

In the evening, when all the canvassers got together, he snuck into the gym and just slightly opened the window so that it still seemed closed to someone looking from the inside. The same night at eleven, he and Vika went into the schoolyard, circled around the building, and stopped outside the window. It was impossible to reach the window while standing. He jumped up and opened the window mid-jump. On his next jump, he grabbed the ledge and with all his might dragged himself onto it. After descending, he reached out over the ledge and caught his girlfriend's hands. He started tugging her up with all his strength until she was lying on the ledge facedown. At this point, he took her beneath the arms and swept her inside.

Three nights in a row they reveled in the sweet solitude of the director's office, but when they were preparing to leave after their fourth night, he suddenly heard a knocking sound at the other end of the building.

"Quiet!" he told her and froze. They were sitting on the couch. They heard the front door slam shut and then the sound of footsteps. The footsteps were coming closer and closer. Someone came into the faculty room. He heard a man's footsteps accompanied by the clacking of heels and the whispering tones of a woman. The next moment, the office door swung open and two silhouettes, one male and one female, stopped in the doorway. The man reached out, felt around for the light switch, and turned on the light. It was Avtandil Avtandilovich with some tall, dirty blonde. Zaur had never seen her before in Mukhus—she was clearly from out of town.

When Avtandil Avtandilovich saw them, his face first took on a frightened expression, and his jaw slowly started to drop. Zaur felt like time had stopped for it to drop so slowly and never quite manage to drop all the way. The director's companion's quiet, cooing laughter suddenly cut through the silence.

"What are you doing here?!" asked Avtandil Avtandilovich so indignantly as if he had caught them in his own home. The woman's cooing laughter brought Zaur out of his stupor.

"The same thing you are," calmly replied Zaur.

"What thing?!" quietly erupted Avtandil Avtandilovich, for as a responsible professional, he couldn't admit their equality even in this matter.

"This thing," replied Zaur, took his girlfriend by the hand, and walked by Avtandil Avtandilovich and his companion, who was still laughing her quiet, cooing laugh. They had clearly come here after a prolonged sit-down, and his companion was slightly drunk.

Zaur thought that Avtandil Avtandilovich hadn't closed the front door, which is why he bravely set off for the front entrance with his girlfriend in tow. The door did turn out to be open.

After plunging into the nocturnal frigidity and crossing the schoolyard, they went out into the street, at which point they burst into a fit of laughter. They spent a few minutes convulsing in mirth, leaning on each other for support, thinking about the expression on the director's face and occasionally glancing at the school building, where the lights in the director's office were still on. The lights suddenly went out.

"That's better," said Zaur, indicating the dark windows.

But what were they to do now? They had lost their last sanctuary. They kept getting together in town, going to movies, and then kissing pitifully in the approach to her house.

Zaur renewed his acquaintance with an old buddy who lived alone in a three-room apartment, and they once spent a night at his place. She told her parents that she was going to her friend's birthday party and that she would spend the night. Zaur's buddy turned out to be so kind that he told them to drop in and spend the night whenever they wanted to. But then something happened that didn't allow Zaur to take advantage of his hospitality.

* * *

That day, the phone rang in the room where he worked, and a colleague who was passing by the phone picked up the receiver.

"It's for you, Zaur," she said.

Zaur went to the table.

"Hello?" he said, listening intently to the phone and trying to ward himself from the noise in the room.

"This is Inspector Grigoriev," said the voice in the phone. "Would you be so kind as to stop by the local police station, room ten?"

"When?" asked Zaur, his breath catching in his throat. He thought he was being called in because of his letter to the Central Committee. But his anxiety quieted down a few seconds later when he realized that he was being called in for an entirely different reason.

"Right now, if you're free," said the voice.

"Alright, I'll stop by," responded Zaur calmly and put down the phone.

Zaur wasn't afraid of meeting with the investigator, but a sense of caution had stirred in him. He went outside onto the sunlit street, breathing in the fresh May air and thinking about what had happened a week ago.

It all began with a similar phone call to his office. He had picked up the phone that time. He had been waiting for a call. It was for him. It was Vika. They were supposed to make plans about their evening rendezvous. Zaur tried to give monosyllabic responses so that his colleagues didn't understand what he was talking about and whom he was talking to.

He especially didn't want Aleksei, who worked in the same department, to hear him. He had recently found out that Aleksei had once tried to hit on Vika. But they didn't get any farther than a few trips to the movies.

Zaur would forever remember the sight of Aleksei stopping dead in the middle of the street when he first saw them together. She later told him about her fling with Aleksei, and he didn't give it much thought.

Admittedly, Zaur later gave him a half-explanation in which he said too much about how close he was with Vika, though he didn't reveal everything. But what he already said was unnecessary, which he regretted and was ashamed of to this day. But he could do nothing about it. It happened because Zaur held on too tightly to the image of Aleksei stopping dead, and Aleksei himself oddly turned the conversation to say that they still had an equal shot and that it wasn't clear yet who she'd prefer to be friends with in the future. Zaur didn't do it to boast—he just wanted to explain to Aleksei, to dispel his illusions, and so he told him what he couldn't have told him without demeaning his relationship with Vika.

They never spoke on the subject again. Or rather, Zaur evaded any such attempts, though he occasionally felt Aleksei's nagging curiosity trying to worm its way into the conversation. He had a stubborn side that Zaur considered to be the result of his ethical boorishness. Once, in a restaurant, he invited some girl to dance. She refused, but Aleksei, instead of letting it go like any other would have done, spent the next twenty minutes trying to talk her into it and finally got her to dance with him. He might have been relying on his tenacity here as well.

And so, during Zaur's phone conversation with Vika, Aleksei came up to the table where Zaur was standing with the phone to his ear and started rifling through papers, as if he was looking for something he suddenly realized he desperately needed. In reality, of course, he was listening with all his might to the voice coming out of the phone, trying to determine who the girl that Zaur was talking to was.

"You got a date?" he asked when Zaur put the phone down.

"Yes," said Zaur, surprising himself. "With Vika ... We're going over Yura Vasiliev's."

Zaur himself probably couldn't have said why he told the truth. In part, the truth was mystical compensation for the fact that Zaur achieved a relationship with a girl with whom Aleksei only experienced failure. In part, it was in his nature, his reluctance to equivocate or resort to falsehood or trickery.

"Ahhh, Yura," drawled Aleksei. "I might stop by too ..."

Zaur shrugged, as if to say "I'm just a guest, if you want to stop by, talk to the host." They were both pretty well acquainted with the master of the house, but obviously, Zaur wouldn't be coming over if he hadn't been invited. Zaur knew that Aleksei might have the audacity to show up even if nobody had invited him.

That evening, Zaur successfully met up with Vika, and they went to a store and got a bottle of cognac and a box of chocolates. Yura Vasiliev, a young architect, lived in an excellent three-room apartment in the center of town. A year earlier, his parents left to go on a multi-year business trip abroad, and he inherited the universally comfortable apartment. At least once a week, the apartment was flooded with a horde of youths partying vociferously.

When Zaur and Vika came inside, they saw a lot of familiar and semi-familiar young men accompanied by wives and girlfriends. Women were setting the table and preparing some fabulous salad in the kitchen, while the men helped them or walked around smoking in festive anticipation of the meal. Everyone was healthy, happy, and kind, because they were young, full of energy, and liked each other and themselves.

The party was hitting its stride when the doorbell rang. The host went to let whomever it was in, and a few minutes later Aleksei appeared in the doorway, accompanied by a painter who was their mutual acquaintance and a distinguished drunkard.

They sat not far away from Zaur, and it seemed like they acclimated to the general, uplifted mood. But then, Zaur noticed that they had both drunk quite a bit, and Aleksei started throwing out suggestive comments about Zaur and Vika's relationship.

One of the comments was so crude that everyone at the table suddenly fell silent. Zaur didn't get the chance to respond, because the host got up and called Aleksei out to the anteroom. His drunkard painter friend followed on his heels.

A minute later, the front door could be heard slamming shut, and the radiantly smiling host came back into the room. He had simply thrown them out. The interruption had been dealt with, and the party was back in full force. For a time, Zaur felt awkward that it was the host and not him who had dealt with the offender. But he soon took his mind off of it, especially since Vika touched his hand under the table, showing with the tender caress that she wasn't mad about Aleksei's foolish comment and was calling on him to follow her lead.

Around midnight, the guests started trickling out. Zaur and the host, giddy, somewhat drunk, saw all the dear people with whom they had spent such a lovely time today out. Only the architect's wife and Vika were left inside.

After seeing the guests to their buses and taxis, Zaur and the host returned. They entered the yard and laid their eyes on something extraordinary.

Two police cars stood in the yard, and a few policemen were crowding around the entryway into which they were about to go. One of them had a dog on a leash. Zaur felt like the policeman wanted the dog to smell them over. Cautiously eyeing the dog, Zaur and Yura went into the entryway and rang the apartment. It was on the first floor.

The frightened women opened the door. Apparently, after they left, Aleksei and his drunkard artist friend rang the apartment, but the women refused to open the door, saying that no one was home, that the host was seeing the guests off.

Not believing them in full, Aleksei and his friend left, and sometime later, the sound of a broken window and a wild shriek could be heard from the neighboring apartment, which just happened to be the apartment of the city council chairman. The women quite sensibly figured that Aleksei and his little friend had done it, having mixed up whom the window belonged to.

The voices of the neighbor and the policemen could be heard for a long time behind the wall. Footsteps could also be heard from outside the windows. They must have been leading the dog close to the building in an attempt to sic it on the perps' tracks.

The following morning, when Zaur and Vika were having breakfast with their hosts, the doorbell rang. The architect went outside and led Aleksei and the drunkard artist into the room. They looked pitiful and lost. They had come to apologize for their actions the previous night and promised to bring a glasscutter to put in a new window.

"Our window wasn't the one you broke," said their host, unable to hide a smile. "Take your glasscutter to the city council chair."

He nodded at the neighboring apartment. The color drained from Aleksei's face. He looked at the windows to make sure that they were all intact.

"By the way, what'd you smash the window with?" asked Yura.

"A brick," sighed Aleksei. "If he finds out, we're done . . ."

"They were here with a dog looking for you last night," said Yura.

Aleksei and his little friend stood there, shifting from one foot to the other, and they looked quite pitiful. They were begging the others with their posture not to rat them out, though they didn't have the courage to ask that out loud. The drunkard painter also managed to sneak peeks at the bottle with the remains of yesterday's vodka, but nobody offered it to him.

As soon as they left, the doorbell rang, and Yura let in the town mayor himself. He was a tall man with attractive silver wings in his hair. Looking at his authoritative figure, it was difficult to imagine that it was him last night swearing like a sailor.

"Listen," he said, "judging by the noise, you had guests over last night . . . Did any of them have any . . . disagreements?"

It was evident now that he had been very frightened the previous night.

"No," said the host. "It happened when my friend and I went to see the guests off . . ."

The town mayor looked sideways at Vika and Zaur, as if sensing that their presence here in the morning bore witness to the disorder that may have been part of a chain of events that led to the window being broken. He must have sensed that last night's events were somehow connected to this apartment, but couldn't get his hands on a single straw of evidence. He slowly turned around and exited the apartment, and the host closed the door behind him.

A few days later, Zaur's buddy was summoned to the police office, where, in an attempt to track down the perpetrator, an investigator interrogated him. Judging by things, the case had become a local priority, with rumors of an assassination attempt on the city council's chairman's life making their rounds. The chairman himself breathed life into the theory. The event had even piqued the interest of the regional committee, and the investigator was trying to press the architect for *anything*. However, his efforts were met with failure.

Yura told Zaur about all this, and a few days later, Zaur got the phone call from the investigator. Somewhat on edge, but in full control of himself, he headed off for the police building. On his way there, he met an old actor he was acquainted with. He was a good actor, but on account of his age, he was rarely on the stage anymore. He would instead tramp around town with his lion's mane flourishing in the wind, stopping in one place to chat up some locals, stopping in another to have a cup of coffee . . .

"Where are you rushing off to?" he asked, stopping Zaur.

"An investigator called me," Zaur replied.

"An investigator," the actor sounded surprised. "What's the matter?"

Zaur gave him a short account of what happened, without giving away the identities of those actually responsible. The actor took out a box of candy from his pocket (he had stopped smoking), took a candy himself, and offered one to Zaur.

"You look like you're in a rush to buy a present," said the actor, plopping a candy into his mouth.

"Clear conscience will do that to you," said Zaur in jest and put his candy into his mouth as well.

"Time," said the actor mysteriously. "The times have changed."

He wished him luck and went his own way. *It's true, though*, thought Zaur. *The times really have changed.* Behind Zaur, the Party's Twentieth Congress was taking place, filling him with confidence. He was so brimming with it that once he found the room he was looking for, he wanted to swallow his candy, but then he thought, *To hell with it!* and opened the door, still relishing the candy.

"May I?"

"Please, come in," said an elderly man, getting up from the table and reaching out to shake his hand.

The investigator was a short man with a squashed, tired-looking face. *Unlikely*, thought Zaur, *that investigators would previously greet suspected criminals like this.*

Zaur sat opposite him. The investigator started puffing away on a thin, filter-less "Belomor" cigarette. Zaur acutely sensed the antiquity of the investigator's habit of smoking Belomors when these days, most people smoked regular cigarettes. *Let's see you try to fish out the truth*, thought Zaur, confident that he would be better at this game than the small investigator with his squashed and tired-looking face.

"You probably don't know why I called you in here?" asked the investigator.

"No," said Zaur.

"Do you remember a week ago, when you were at your friend's place, somebody broke a window nearby?"

"Yeah, I remember," said Zaur.

"Do you have anything to say in this regard?" asked the investigator, inhaled deeply, and deposited his cigarette in an ashtray.

"Nothing," said Zaur. "I have no idea who did it."

"None of the guests could've done it?" asked the investigator, picked up his cigarette from the ashtray, and inhaled deeply.

"No," said Zaur. "It happened when we were seeing everyone off."

"So, you weren't even in the building when it happened?"

"No," said Zaur.

"Do try your best to remember—maybe one of your friends was jealous of another's lady friend?"

"No," said Zaur, thinking about how close the investigator was to the truth. "There was nothing like that."

"Alright, and what do you think about what happened? Do you have any guesses on the matter?"

"I think someone who was drunk did it," said Zaur.

"Between you and me, I think so too," agreed the investigator.

Zaur thought he winked at him.

"But some see this as a political move," the investigator continued. "But I think that's nonsense . . . Some drunken troublemaker probably just thought he'd have a laugh . . . But some do see this as a political move, and we have to carefully consider all possibilities . . ."

Zaur was shocked by the investigator's candor. A happy thought came to him: *that's how the times have changed! They tell the investigator that it's a political move, but he sees through it and believes that it's simply roughhousing! And has the bravery to say it to me directly.* The Zaur felt such a rush of respect and even gratitude to the investigator that he even swallowed what was left of the candy in his mouth.

"Politics have nothing to do with it," said Zaur in support of the investigator.

"That's the thing," sighed the investigator. "You spent the night at the place, didn't you?"

"Yes," said Zaur, now thinking that the investigator knew unpleasantly too much. When they were interviewing Yura, they let him know as well that they knew about how his friend and the friend's girlfriend spent the night. Zaur was afraid that the investigator would bring Vika into the picture, and that would be terribly unpleasant.

"Nothing to be worried about," said the investigator, as if trying to smooth over the awkwardness. "It's a young case . . . Did you hear anything else suspicious during the night?"

"No," said Zaur, again feeling a surge of gratitude that the investigator didn't start asking him questions about his girlfriend.

"Right, of course, it was some drunken idiot," said the investigator thoughtfully.

Zaur was feeling something almost akin to tenderness towards the investigator.

"He broke the window for a laugh," the investigator went on, equally thoughtfully. "Only what could he have used to break it . . ."

"I mean . . ." said Zaur, and wanted to add: a brick, obviously.

Suddenly Zaur felt an electric shock course through his whole body and glue the last word to the tip of his tongue. Without yet understanding why, he knew that under no circumstances could he utter that last word.

". . . He probably used a stick or something," he finished his thought after a momentary pause.

"Yes, of course," the investigator agreed, but Zaur could tell by his expression that he had lost any and all interest in him. Zaur realized that the whole conversation up to this point was simply an overture to this trap in which he almost got caught.

"You're free to go," said the investigator, removing the blank papers from the table and putting away his pen into his jacket pocket. "We'll keep searching for the perpetrator."

"Goodbye," said Zaur, standing up.

"Goodbye," replied the investigator. His expression no longer seemed so squashed or tired. Zaur felt as though he was now impatiently waiting for him to leave in order to get up and leave himself. Suddenly Zaur realized that the investigator was from another department entirely, and that this wasn't his office. Could've reasoned that one out earlier.

He went outside, feeling as if his legs had a mind of their own. *Obviously,* he thought anxiously, *I couldn't know what the random drunk used to break the window . . . It was Aleksei who said it was a brick.*

Zaur thought he had heard the trap clamp its metallic teeth shut, just barely missing him. It was a beautiful, sunny day in May. He set off at a brisk pace towards his institute. He was astounded by a new, hitherto unknown feeling. He felt like the times, which he thought had changed irrevocably, were merely hidden, lying in wait . . .

* * *

Some ten days later, the phone rang in Zaur's office again: he was being invited to have a little chat with the secretary of the Party's regional committee. Zaur knew that his time had come.

Truly worried, he made his way towards the regional committee building, which was on the seashore. After showing his passport to gain entry, he entered the regional committee headquarters.

There were a few people waiting for their turn in the second-floor waiting area outside the secretary's office. The office assistant greeted him, looked at him in a peculiar fashion, and quietly went into Abesolomon Nartovich's office. Zaur figured that she went to report his arrival. And indeed, when she came back out of the office, she nodded at him and said:

"You'll be next . . ."

Zaur felt uncomfortable that he was cutting in line, but the way she said it dispelled any desire he had to argue. The people waiting their turn were even less likely to argue with her.

Zaur was very worried but felt that there was more joy than alarm in his worry. He had spent a long time pondering the fate of his memo and had decided that if things had been truly bad, he would have been called in to see the KGB. But now after receiving a summons from the regional committee, he couldn't and didn't restrain himself from having a hunch that things wouldn't be all that bad.

When the visitor before him left the office, the assistant nodded at Zaur and looked at him in that peculiar fashion again. Her look expressed a non-occupational curiosity.

Zaur opened the door and entered the office. After a brief surge of agoraphobia, he crossed the expansive office and approached Abesolomon Nartovich's desk. The regional committee secretary extended his hand, and Zaur clasped it, subduing the preemptive rush of warm gratitude. Abesolomon Nartovich gestured towards the chair, and Zaur took a seat.

Abesolomon Nartovich asked who his parents were. Zaur told him. After learning that Zaur's father had done time, but was recently rehabilitated, he nodded kindly in understanding, like somebody who was directly involved in the new times that saw his father freed. He then asked whether Zaur had been working at the institute for long. Zaur told him. He then asked whether Zaur read lectures to the community at large with the intent of disseminating scientific findings. Yes, Zaur said. He did.

This whole time, sitting in his chair, Abesolomon Nartovich was caressing the first page of Zaur's message. During Zaur's responses, he nodded, as if giving permission, as if he had expected nothing else.

Having climbed up the ladder to be among the top Party officials during Khrushchev's reforms, Abesolomon Nartovich liked to meet and converse with the intelligentsia. Furthermore, he liked to meet and converse with the intelligentsia not in his own office, but in banquet halls in restaurants and private resorts. He would have presently also preferred to be speaking with the young man over a bottle of good "Isabella," but the issue raised by him was too important to risk meeting with him in less official circumstances. Even before he had read Zaur's message, which had been forwarded from Moscow, Abesolomon Nartovich knew how to react, because he had received a phone call from Moscow.

"Call him in, chat with him," sounded the suggestion from Moscow, which meant that any repressive means of dealing with the author had to be shelved. This corresponded to both the spirit of the time and Abesolomon Nartovich's personal disposition.

"I have read your note to the government carefully," said Abesolomon Nartovich, finally getting down to business. "Do you know what this is?"

He looked at Zaur with an expression of well-wishing slyness. Zaur had no idea how to interpret his question and shrugged slightly.

"These are the views of contemporary social democrats," he added regretfully, lifting Zaur's message and tossing it aside. It landed on the table with a smack. Abesolomon Nartovich tracked its flight path and then glanced at Zaur, as if he had been testing and allowing Zaur to observe whether his manuscript could stay airborne to his satisfaction. Clearly, it was thoroughly devoid of any aeronautical capacity.

"Social democrats," asked Zaur involuntarily, inadvertently revealing his unpreparedness for dealing with attacks like this.

"Yes, social democrats," repeated Abesolomon Nartovich, plainly displaying his delight in Zaur's confusion. Then, as if increasing the dose of delight, he added: "And if we dig a little deeper in history, this is a typical Bukharinite outcry..."

"Why Bukharinite?" asked Zaur, his mouth dry.

"Because Bukharin expressed similar views," said Abesolomon Nartovich.

Zaur got a grip on himself.

"I don't know what views Bukharin may have espoused," he said, "but I'm convinced that all farmers that rent land from collective farms reap three times the harvest than that from collective farmland..."

"Creeping empiricism," happily explained Abesolomon Nartovich, "but we Bolsheviks have always fought against creeping empiricism."

"I don't know what it's called," said Zaur, "but I'm confident in one thing—that it's beneficial to our farmers, our farms, and therefore the government."

"Today, it might be beneficial, but tomorrow, the leasers might grow into rabid opponents of our way of life."

"But why?!" Zaur cried out.

"The logic of class consciousness," smiled Abesolomon Nartovich in response to his exclamation.

Zaur could neither understand, nor accept this.

"But why is the consciousness of people who work poorly on collective farmland more elevated than the consciousness of people who work well on leased land?! Aren't we shouting from the rooftops about the high productivity of labor?..."

"We have always fought for that and will eventually achieve it, but not like this," Abesolomon Nartovich interrupted him, and his tone involuntarily took on a hard, metallic note. But he quickly recalled that such an approach hadn't been recommended by Moscow, and he purged it from his voice.

They spoke for half an hour, and every time the discussion's logic reached a point that Zaur felt left his opponent only room enough to agree with his findings, Abesolomon Nartovich whipped out an ironclad formula that definitively halted the flow of the conversation. A few times, Abesolomon Nartovich inquired why Zaur, a historian by profession, was concerning himself with issues of agriculture. He identified this, in part, as the source of Zaur's confusion.

At the end of their chat, Abesolomon Nartovich jokingly noted that he was only criticizing Zaur's fallacious views, whereas in his time, people would disappear to Siberia for suggesting something similar. It was when Zaur shook his extended hand over the table that Abesolomon Nartovich remembered something.

"By the way," he said, "is it true that your neighbor occupied part of your property?"

"Yes," said Zaur, amazed at Abesolomon Nartovich's degree of knowledge and struggling to understand the transition to the new topic.

"Be assured," happily said Abesolomon Nartovich, "he'll be returning your stolen property and will be rapped on the knuckles for doing so in the first place."

"But, please . . . It's not even . . ." Zaur was at a loss, struggling to get over the transition to such a specific topic from such a general one.

"The rascal needs to be taught a lesson," Abesolomon Nartovich accentuated the thought by wagging his finger, "and we'll be the ones to teach him . . ."

He looked at Zaur significantly, as if letting him know that the issue wasn't as general as Zaur may have thought, and that by helping him, he was simply defending justice and fairness, as in any situation, even if that weren't always readily evident.

Zaur left the regional committee building. He returned to work feeling completely empty. If he had been threatened with exile or arrest, he probably involuntarily wouldn't have felt as disappointed as he did now.

He thought that his views would be either combated mercilessly or adopted. In both cases, at least their value would have been recognized. But this way, the data that he diligently collected and analyzed, which he imbued with such significance, couldn't influence anything or anyone . . . It was just a distraction . . . Didn't warrant anything but a brief chat . . .

A couple of hours later, once he returned home from work, he noticed with sorrowful surprise how a few workers were standing next to the lawyer's stone wall, demolishing it with crowbars. Zaur's mother had gone out onto the porch and was listening with palpable glee to the sound of the crowbars on the other side of the wall. He glanced at the open window in the lawyer's house and locked eyes with the owner. There was no indication in his gaze that he felt any ill will towards Zaur—on the contrary, he even greeted him ingratiatingly for the first time. His imposing figure, adorned in a set of striped pajamas, was radiating amiability and a readiness to serve, and he even waved at the crowbar-armed workers, as if to say, "You boys go ahead, don't worry, I don't mind." Zaur realized that he must have been grateful to him that at least his house would remain untouched. *Strength. That's the only thing that people respect and believe in in this country*, thought Zaur sadly.

That evening, after meeting up with Vika, they strolled along the crepuscular streets, after which they went to a park, picked out the remotest corner, and sat themselves down on a bench. Zaur told her for the first time about his idea, about his meeting with the regional committee chairman, and about everything that had been getting him down throughout his entire adult life.

Vika sighed in sympathy, looked at Zaur with her big eyes, caressed his hand, and Zaur understood that for the first time in her life, she had come face to face with all those damned questions that she had never thought about.

They were sitting like that, not paying attention to how much time had passed, when a policeman suddenly emerged out from the boxwoods that grew next to the bench and came up to them. At the sight of him, Zaur didn't give him any great significance—he looked at his watch, barely saw in the dim light that it was eleven, and that the policeman was probably going to kick them out.

The policeman approached them and asked to see their papers. Zaur said they didn't have any papers. Then the policeman demanded that they accompany him to the station.

"Why?" calmly asked Zaur, not moving. "What have we done?"

"Don't make excuses," said the policeman. "I saw what you were doing..."

Zaur realized that the policeman was blackmailing them. He had heard that policemen sometimes caught couples out at night in secluded corners of the park and shook them down for money.

"We weren't doing anything," repeated Zaur, overcoming his revulsion at himself for trying to explain their behavior. "We were just sitting and talking."

"I saw how you were talking," said the policeman mockingly. "Come with me."

"We're not going anywhere," said Zaur firmly. "We weren't doing anything, and you know it..."

"If you weren't doing anything, why are you afraid of going to the police station?" asked the policeman.

"We're not afraid," said Zaur. "There's nothing for us to do there."

Looking at the policeman's big-lipped, wide-nosed faced, Zaur suddenly felt like this was cosmic vengeance for the happiness of all their unmarred nighttime get-togethers.

"If you won't go willingly, I'll use force," said the policeman, looking at Zaur, then at his companion, as if trying to evaluate which one will bend first.

Judging by his tone and hard eyes, Zaur understood that he wouldn't let them go easily. Zaur decided to buy him off but didn't know how to do that. He thought it would be terrible if they were taken to the police station. He imagined the insolent and demeaning questions they would have to field, and he couldn't allow Vika to explain that there was nothing between them to those savages. No! Anything but that!

"If we're in the park after hours . . . then fine us," said Zaur, overcoming the disgust he felt towards his own voice and words.

The policeman was expectantly silent.

"I'm ready to pay," Zaur managed to get out. He reached into his pocket. Silence.

Zaur took out all of his money. He had seven rubles—all singles. He took out of his pocket the fistful of paper money and offered it to the policeman. They hands met, and as Zaur was putting the money into his hand, he tried to do it carefully, so that the papers didn't fall out of the policeman's grip.

There was something revolting about his trying to carefully fit his money into the policeman's hand. After taking the money, the policeman started sorting through the bills, bringing each one into the light to determine its value.

Knowing full well that each bill was just a single, Zaur felt a rush of panic. He felt the policeman's disappointment growing with every bill he inspected.

The policeman really was disappointed. Of course, if he knew that Zaur didn't have any more money, he would have been satisfied. But Zaur had stuck his hand too carelessly in his pocket and had too carelessly withdrawn the money. He had consciously done it carelessly, because he was ashamed of what he was about to do and thought the policeman was embarrassed that he was about to hand him the money. Hence his seeming carelessness, which seemed to signify that there was nothing special in what they were about to do, in him reaching into his pocket and, having separated a small, careless fistful of money from a larger sum, offered it to the policeman. Which is why in thinking about the carelessness, the policeman decided that he must have more money than he was offering him.

"No," said the policeman, handing Zaur back his money. "We're going to the police station."

"But I don't have any more money," said Zaur, correctly understanding the policeman. He stood up.

"I don't want to hear it," said the policeman, not believing Zaur. "Let's go to the station, we'll figure things out there . . ."

And then, Zaur made a choice. He remembered his boxing days. He had a strong right hook. He just had to land the hit through the shroud of worry.

"But we didn't do anything!" repeated Zaur, without understanding why he was saying it again. Maybe he was trying to appeal to the policeman's conscience, maybe he was trying to mollify his vigilance.

"We'll figure things out at the station," said the policeman, thinking that Zaur was bargaining and offering him back the money.

Without preparation, Zaur hit him in the chin. But his body and arm were too tight, and the hit wasn't sharp enough.

The policeman fell, but he didn't lose consciousness, as Zaur hoped. He immediately sat up and started shaking his head, trying to shake off the black spots dancing in his vision. Zaur hesitated: should he attack before he reached for his gun or should they run? When he hit the policeman, Vika had jumped up and grabbed on to him. And Zaur felt that attacking the policeman would mean blood and crime, and, understanding that they couldn't tarry any longer, he grabbed his girlfriend and ran for it.

They had put some forty meters between themselves and the policeman when they heard: "Stop! Stop!"

The exclamation was followed by a gunshot. Still holding Vika's hand, Zaur changed their direction and took off with all his might. They made it out of the park, ran down several dark streets, and finally stopped, sure that they weren't being followed.

Vika's home came into view. They ducked into the entryway and ran up to the fourth floor, where her apartment was. Zaur felt a surge of joy when the door shut behind her (there was nothing to be afraid of anymore, even if the policeman caught him later), but the surge of joy was instantly marred by a dull sense of umbrage, the source of which he couldn't immediately identify.

It was only sometime later, when he was outside and then later, at home, in bed, that he nailed down what it was that hurt him dully.

He remembered the way she shut the door. She shut it in such a way, it was as if she wasn't only happy that she was rid of the vile policeman, but of him too, of both of them, and that was rather unpleasant.

He tried to tell himself that he had imagined it, but the sharpness of her action left no doubt in his mind that she was very happy to be rid of him along with the policeman. She closed the door with a haste that the situation no longer called for. Tossing in bed, he could for some reason most clearly envision not the meaning behind her action, but its external, physical form, the vulgarity of the form: she tugged the door closed as soon as she had the opportunity, as if afraid that he would try to open it from the other side! The move reminded him of a gypsy stuffing beneath her clothes something she stole or was foolishly given: quickly, quickly, before anyone notices!

Some ten days after that night, afraid of running into the policeman, Zaur still hadn't seen Vika and went to work with a cap pulled low over his eyes. They finally ran into each other, but it wasn't a happy reunion.

That fateful night had apparently made Vika very frightened, and she thought hard about her relationship with Zaur. She told her father about his meeting with the regional committee chairman, and her father became very worried and told her to tell Zaur to immediately write the secretary a letter in which he realized the error of his ways and views. He said that if he didn't do that, Zaur would be denied any further paths for career growth.

He wanted to meet with Zaur in person, but Vika dissuaded him from doing that, afraid that a spontaneous talk between them could be offensive to Zaur. But Zaur was deathly offended by her merely relaying her father's advice. He was offended that she had told her father and, most importantly, that he was now being advised to do something he considered extremely demeaning.

"How can I write him a letter when he failed to prove anything?" said Zaur with a grin, trying to hide his irritation.

"So what, Zaur, big deal," she said, but gave it up and kissed him on the cheek. Hiding his irritation, Zaur took a step back. For the first time ever, he wanted to push her away.

They didn't speak of it again, and Zaur, out of patriarchal respect for her father, tried not to show how offended he was by the suggestion. *He's just afraid for his own career, for his trips abroad*, thought Zaur viciously, *he's just pretending to be concerned about me.*

Vika's father really was thinking that it they married, such a stubborn son-in-law, such a homegrown reformer would be a lot of trouble. But, of course, Vika father was also concerned for Zaur and about his potential son-in-law's immediate future.

A week later, Zaur called her to get her out of the house and go for a walk. He figured that enough time had passed and that even if the policeman saw them again, he would be unlikely to recognize them.

"Did you write the letter?" she asked him.

So, she's setting conditions for me seeing her, is she? Zaur thought, and he nearly choked from the grievous indignation.

"No, I didn't, and I won't," said Zaur firmly and firmly hung up. The phone rang several times after that, but every time, Zaur picked up the phone and pressed down on the lever to kill the line.

A couple of weeks later, he unexpectedly saw her outside the movie theater standing next to a swarthy guy he had once seen her with. Devoid of any feeling of jealousy, instead filled with tenderness, he thought: *Never, never will I believe that you replaced me with him.* He recalled her funny explanation of her relationship with the guy: he's just for movies.

A day later, Zaur got a phone call at work from his cousin, who worked as an editor in the local newspaper, which was headed by Avtandil Avtandilovich. Zaur loved his cousin but wasn't close to him. The liberal insinuations in his articles slightly annoyed Zaur. He thought that his cousin was too immersed in local politics. He wanted to see something greater from him. His brother knew about his message to the Central Committee, but was skeptical of it originally and, alas, was right to be so. He also knew about his being summoned to the regional committee.

"Listen, Zaur," he said over the phone, "my editor is strongly against your institute. He said at a meeting that a lot of institute workers aren't doing what they're supposed to. He even mentioned you by name. What'd you keep from him?"

"A couch," said Zaur.

"What couch?" his cousin sounded confused.

"An ordinary couch," said Zaur.

"I don't get it," said his cousin. "Care to explain?"

"Sure, some other time," said Zaur.

"By the way, do you know why the regional committee chairman ordered the lawyer's wall demolished? I just found out today . . ."

"I have no idea," replied Zaur. "I thought he did it just to show that he knows everything and has the power to clean house."

"It's way more complicated," said his cousin. "He's in a secret war with the assistant secretary. He has Moscow's support, but the assistant secretary is the shadow capitalists' favorite. That makes their strength just about equal. Your neighbor is connected to the shadow capitalists too. Get it now?"

"No," said Zaur.

"Destroying the lawyer's wall was a strategic move. Self-affirmation. Now they're waiting for a countermove."

"You mean they might rebuild the wall?"

"Doubt it," his cousin gave a laugh. "Hopefully the other side will find another proxy for their war. But you be careful . . . He's got the police and the doctors at his disposal."

"What do you mean?" asked Zaur.

"Who knows," replied his cousin. "These people are unpredictable. But we're still alive, along with Abesolomon Nartovich. Here, I got a story for you from his life. Turns out that during his vacation in Pitsunda, Khrushchev suddenly asked him: 'How many cars drive up to Lake Ritsa every day?' 'About 1,200 cars,' said Abesolomon Nartovich without a second's thought, and Nikita Sergeevich liked the specificity. Another would have started bleating something like, 'Oh, we haven't counted. Should we count, Nikita Sergeevich?' Nope, everything has already been counted, which means that the question wasn't random. He's a fascinating guy. Alright, see you. I'll give you a call if I hear anything."

The most surprising thing was that a week after this conversation, he was at a party and ran into a psychiatrist he knew. Zaur had only seen him three or four times, but he liked him and knew that the feeling was mutual. Such mutual appreciation occurs pretty quickly when people identify in each other a spiritual closeness. Even if spiritual closeness doesn't necessarily correlate with the uses separate spiritual energies are put to. That's something else entirely.

Zaur noticed that a few times during the party, the psychiatrist threw him a sad, but inspective glance. As if he knew something. Or wanted to express his sympathy about something. Zaur caught these glances a few times and when he finally couldn't take it anymore, he blurted:

"Is it true that our politicians are sometimes put into the madhouse?"

There were rumors that said so. But Zaur didn't know anything for sure.

"The worst psychiatric ward is better than a labor camp, trust me," the psychiatrist replied, a bit evasively and hospitably.

"Sure, but someone sent to a labor camp at least knows that he's being punished for his views," said Zaur, "while someone sent to a psych ward is morally demeaned."

"When camps are a possibility," firmly replied the psychiatrist, looking into Zaur's eyes with an expression of fierce hospitality, "beggars can't be choosers."

"Besides, there are rumors about the methods used at the wards," added Zaur. "They try to drive people insane . . ."

"They're rumors," the psychiatrist shook his head. "Trust me, if we could make a normal person schizophrenic, we'd be able to cure schizophrenia too."

"But you can't?" asked Zaur.

"Psychiatry has made an enormous leap," he explained. "There's new medicine available. We can make a patient's condition more tolerable than ever before . . . But why are you so interested in this? Got a new, ground-breaking idea?"

He started laughed, then suddenly reached across the table, grabbed Zaur just beneath the shoulders, and shook him in a friendly manner. Prompted by his kindhearted laughter, Zaur sighed in relief, but simultane-ously felt like the man had some unknown clinical motivation for pawing at his arms. When grasped around his upper arms, the psychiatrist's fingers momentarily bore into his skin with imperious strength, as if checking something in his muscles. But what?

He suddenly felt like the action was somehow related to the hit he had landed on the policeman's face. But again, it was unclear whether the psychiatrist was thinking, "Nice, solid hit!" or "Hm, yes, he could've taken him down."

Who knows, thought Zaur. You could lose your mind just thinking about it. The psychiatrist was gazing at him with satisfaction. He was either pleased that Zaur didn't manage to shake him off, or he was pleased with the result of his little procedure, if that's what it was.

The party continued. Still, Zaur thought it strange that such a member of the intelligentsia like that could defend the psych wards. Maybe he saved someone's life with the help of a psych ward. Or was the placement of political actors in psych wards such a trade secret that he wasn't permitted to discuss it even with the closest of friends? *Then again,* thought Zaur, *both could be true.* This thought calmed him.

This whole time, he was actively missing Vika, though he didn't admit it to himself. One evening, he was walking around town down the darkest, least trafficked streets, when he suddenly saw two people in the semidarkness walking in his direction. The woman stopped, but her companion tactically walked a bit further and stopped off to the side.

They greeted each other. But what could he say to her? What could she say to him? What was most important was off-limits in light of the guy waiting for her off to the side. It was the same guy, by the way, but this time, Zaur felt that he had broadened his occupational commitments beyond accompanying Vika to the movies. They exchanged a few meaningless phrases and went their separate ways. Only now did Zaur realize that he had been walking along the dark streets in the hopes of accidentally running into her.

A few days later, he left on a month-long trip to Moscow. Once, he saw a young woman standing on the opposite side of the street next to a newspaper stand. It was her! She was wearing the light coat she had worn all throughout their spring together. Her father must have been on a business trip, and she must have come along.

His breath caught with excitement. As soon as the light turned green, he ran across the street and, feeling that here in Moscow, their separation had become distant and meaningless, intended to sneak up from behind and cover her eyes, but then decided that their meeting should probably begin more calmly. He stepped up to her and as if he were in a nightmare, realized that the woman was a complete stranger.

For a time after returning from his trip, he didn't see her anywhere. Once, at the Amra, he ran into the student that he had once met at the electoral center, when he told him about her for the first time.

"Did you hear that Vika got married?" asked the student, having greeted Zaur.

"No," replied Zaur, feeling that everything inside him stopped: his heart, his blood, his breath.

"Oh yeah," he said, sipping his coffee and nodding his head. "And I thought you guys were a thing . . . Lots of people thought that . . ."

"No," said Zaur, trying with all his might not to give away that his insides had collectively gone on strike. "There was nothing between us . . ."

"I ran into them not long ago on the beach," the student went on. "Man, she is *such* a looker! To think that such a lout could have gotten his hands on such a girl . . . And I thought that you guys were a thing . . ."

"No," said Zaur, restraining himself with all his might. "Let's have a cognac."

"But I don't have any money on me," said the student.

"My treat," said Zaur, giving him some money. "Get two, hundred and fifty grams each."

The student got two glasses of cognac, two cups of coffee, and handed Zaur back the change. They drank the cognac, finished their coffee, and went their separate ways.

On his way home, Zaur couldn't wrap his head around why the beautiful, sunny day had grown dimmer, even though the sky was completely cloud-free. After the cognac, everything that had hardened inside him had grown softer, and it was easier to breathe now, which made it even odder that the beautiful, sunny day had grown dimmer. It became somewhat strange and uncomfortable having to live in such a dim day.

6

A Sea of Charisma

"You've got it good," said one of my Moscow colleagues. "You write about the little guys. But we've got it way harder. Just try to write about a multimillion-person nation."

"Aren't you from the Smolensk region?" I said. "Why don't *you* write about it, as if Smolensk is the alpha and omega of everything."

"It won't work," he said. Then he thought about it and added breathily, "You've got it good, yes you do . . . Mountains, childhood, Chegem . . . And the editors love you . . . 'This is all distant, off on the edge somewhere, sure, he can write about it.'"

They *love* me?! Better we leave that alone. But how to explain that I face my own set of difficulties? Especially because of my unfortunate penchant for satire. The little guys . . . Everybody knows one another, everybody tracks one another: who'd he write about this time? And they always either guess or make someone up. And then there's a world of complaints, threats, and so on.

I've developed an entire system of camouflaging character prototypes. Regional actors get a makeover—I change their hair color, grow out facial hair or, less often, shave them clean. Bigger fish, though—they get full-blown plastic surgery!

I conduct a thorough reshuffling of our official functionaries. Party bureaucrats become agricultural bureaucrats, which somewhat lessens the character's quality, but ensures my own staying power.

They still figure everything out, or even worse, convince someone that they've got it all figured out and that my work is a temple of slander with grains of truth scattered throughout. My Endurites[50] are misunderstood too.

---

50 The Endurites are people from another village created by Iskander in his work *Sandro from Chegem.*

They're not a specific people or inhabitants of a particular place—we can all be Endurites. Sometimes for a long time. For example, I was a pure Endurite when I chose the path of a writer.

What if I try to write about Moscow? Let's put in a trial run—I'll write about something that happened once, and then we'll see how we make out.

I was invited to a literary soiree. I tried to get out of it, but the director of the student club told me several times:

"You're the one they're most excited about."

And I shuddered: man is weak, vain. They always lure you in like this, but then you see that there are more than enough writers, and nobody was all that excited to see you after all.

I put some of my verse in a leather folder, closed it, and went outside. It was a warm day in August, and the sun was on its way down. Women—elevator operators, looked like—were sitting on a bench next to our house, chatting peacefully, occasionally looking at their entryways in bewilderment. Shepherds would give looks like that at their herds every now and then: everyone still here? Good.

Our elevator operator noticed me. She looked askance at me: will you be back late? I waved at her with my hat, showing that with a hat like that, I wasn't likely to be gone long.

I went out of our entryway and came out onto our narrow, but bustling street. I didn't get lucky with a car right away. All the taxis were full, and everyone else refused to pick me up too. Some twenty paces away from me, there was a group of four. They were hitchhiking too, but nobody was picking them up either.

Then I locked eyes with a man who was walking towards me along the edge of the sidewalk. His congenial gaze was so familiar, so demanding of immediate conversation, that I was at a loss. I couldn't remember who he was. A writer I saw at one of our retreats? A poet? Or did he dabble in prose? There was nothing for it but to respond in kind, and I beamed at him, at the same time trying to hide the fact that I couldn't remember who he was.

I could tell by his glowing look and enthusiasm, which became more evident as he approached, that things wouldn't end with a handshake. I was right. We exchanged kisses, and I did my part passionately so as to cover up my shameful irrecognition. After smacking his lips away from my cheek, he threw back his head and took me in with a look of overflowing happiness. Here, I figured that he must have just read my published short story and was about to share his impressions with me. I was ready to accept his praise with wise modesty.

"Did you see?" he asked. "They published Grisha in *Izvestiya*."

"Oh yeah?" I asked, weakly imitating a look of surprise. "How nice."

Grisha? What Grisha? Who was Grisha? His son! Most likely his son. They must be one of our popular, contemporary writing dynasties. He got his son off the ground and was happy for him.

"Can you believe it!" he exclaimed. "They published him, and for such a large audience!"

"How old is he?" I asked, reasoning that I had every right not to know a family detail like that.

"Grisha?" he sounded surprised. "Forty-seven!"

My face must have given something away, but he misunderstood whatever it was.

"What, you think Grisha is still drinking?!" he exclaimed triumphantly. "He stopped! Stopped! Hasn't been on the bottle in two years—and look at what he's done! I'm so happy for him, so happy! I'm on my way to help out Djuna right now, Djuna's a bit sick . . ."

"So, you're a psychic!" I said, apparently thoroughly recalling who he was.

"Why a psychic?" he sounded surprised. He then added, smiling, "A psychic healing another psychic would be the same thing as a fortune teller predicting another fortune teller's future. I'm a simple doctor . . . What, did you forget? We were at Grisha's ten years ago. He put out his paintings on display in his apartment. And today, four reproductions were printed in *Izvestiya*. I'm so happy for him, so happy!"

Finally, I remembered everything. Yes, that really did happen. Ten years ago, I really did visit that darling of a painter, and this doctor was there too. I was suffused in a warm glow. How great that there were people in the world who were capable of feeling such joy at others' success! We finally said our goodbyes, and he left.

My mood brightened significantly. I decided that us running into each other was a portent of good things. However, still nobody picked me up. Afraid of being late, I decided to get ahead of the group standing in front of me—thankfully there was no official stop there. Easily overcoming the light pricks of my conscience, I went around them, crossed the block, and almost managed to stop an empty taxi right on the corner.

The driver agreed to pick me up but showed me with a nod of his head that he had to cross the street. The light changed to green, the taxi driver crossed the street, and stopped. He was now much closer to the guys standing ahead of me. One of them made for the taxi.

I moved towards the taxi too, I was hit with the difficulty of my situation. On the one hand, I already had an agreement with the taxi driver, but on the other hand, I cut ahead of the guys standing ahead of me. But on the third hand, this wasn't an official taxi stop, and I could have been ahead of them if only my house had been a block over. If only . . .

I decided to cede the way: they *were* ahead of me, after all. But then why did I keep walking? Maybe I hoped that the driver wouldn't take them if he wasn't willing to take them where they needed to go. That happens sometimes. Or maybe I subconsciously wanted to bask in the modest altruism of my decision.

When I reached the taxi, a large, wide-faced guy from the group had leaned in to speak with the driver and was saying something. Apparently, the driver told him that the car was taken.

"No big deal, the hat will wait," said the beefy one loudly, clearly meaning me, even though I wasn't wearing a hat and never had.

Something flared up inside me, which rarely happens. My getting ready to altruistically cede the taxi must have had an effect. I said that being a jackass could lead to one's face being pummeled. The guy quietly walked around the car and sat down next to the driver without even glancing at the source of the threat, which the source of the threat found quite hurtful.

The taxi set off, and the guy rode up to his friends. I once again crossed the street and began waiting for a car on the corner of the next block. But no car came, and I set off. I was afraid of being late. Some thirty meters away, on the edge of the street, some guy was hitchhiking. Taxis full of passengers kept driving by. Unmarked cars kept stopping by him, but he couldn't strike a deal with any of them, and they all drove off without him. They stopped next to me too but didn't take me either. Who knows where they were headed!

I realized that I was running late and decided to walk a bit further down. It was unlikely that the guy was in as much of a rush as I was. And again, what kind of queue could there have been if there wasn't even an official stop? But cutting ahead of someone would still be unpleasant. But what can you do if you're in a rush?

One way or another, I cut ahead of him and decided to stop farther away from him so that he couldn't see me. But I didn't make it twenty paces when a driver with an empty car showed up. I couldn't resist and stopped him. The driver stopped, but after hearing where I was going, he refused to pick me up. He drove away, and suddenly I heard a woman's voice next to me:

"That's not a very nice thing you just did! That man was waiting ahead of you, but you cut in front! That's not very nice!"

"I'm in a hurry!" I retorted and set off again.

The woman kept walking on the sidewalk, continuing to grumble. Seeing that her disgruntlement wasn't about to abate, I sped up. But she sped up too, trying to synchronize her grumbling to my footsteps. If I stopped to hitchhike, she stopped too, waiting for me to fail and continuing to condemn me. It was like I had entered some kind of nightmare. I considered making a run for it, but that would have been shameful too. Especially running from her.

And then, a Zhiguli unexpectedly stopped right by me. I wasn't even hitchhiking. I peered into the window. An old pal of mine from the institute was in the car, the famous Boris Borzov.

"Where you going?" he asked, his dazzling brown eyes sparkling.

I told him.

"Get in, I'm headed in the same direction," he said.

I looked back at the woman, unsure of what she would do next. But she just looked at me, silently transferred her bag to her right hand, which she had previously been using to chastise me, and walked by me.

I opened the door. A bottle of champagne and a cake were on the front seat. He picked both up and put them on the back seat, careful to place the bottle so that it didn't roll off.

"Visiting someone?" I asked, taking a seat.

"Visiting my lover," he said, blinding me with a pearly white smile and trying to discern the effect that bit of information had on me. Having discerned it, or more likely not, he added, "You can congratulate me. I defended my dissertation."

Over the previous twenty years, we met up a few times at the café Nationale, where he would go with his friends. I knew that he was in the biology department and was working at some research institute.

"But you've been a graduate for a long time," I said.

"Doctorate, you twit, doctorate!" he exclaimed, his eyes flaring in my direction, as they would in our youth. "If people hadn't been out to get me, I'd have long been an academician!"

"What was your dissertation on?" I asked.

"I'll tell you," he said. "By the way, before I forget. Could you get me a permanent pass to the Central Writers' House?"

"No," I said. "I can't even get you a temporary one."

"What about the Central Film House?" he asked.

"Definitely not," I said. "I have nothing to do with them."

"Fine," he shook his well-coiffed head. "I'll find someone without your help!"

"So what was your dissertation on?" I asked again.

"'Shell-less Eggs—A Revolution in Egg-Laying Productivity.' Our lab's experiments have immense agricultural significance!"

He shot me one of his significant smiles, inviting me to be pleased with his success and simultaneously implying that his achievements are a consequence of some hidden, panhuman foolishness that he personally shed light on. He was calling on me to be overjoyed with him on both counts and trying to divine whether I properly grasped the miracle of their union.

"What do you mean—shell-less eggs?" I asked and thought with a sense of disquiet that the Goatibex subject would haunt me my whole life.

"See, you're soaring among the clouds," he said, glancing first at me, then at the road. He was beginning to get fired up, as he would during our student years. "But we're doing work, real work! Here's the short version in terms that are accessible to you. Currently, a good laying hen gives about two hundred and fifty eggs a year. If she hits three hundred—bravo! Bravo! When we finish our experiments, hens will start laying three times more eggs than now, albeit shell-less ones! We'll flood the country with shell-less eggs, and then the windfall will finally blow my way. And woe befall whosoever tries to build a wall around me when that happens! What's the bottom line? The egg-laying process needs to be beholden to a strict rhythm. The egg travels through the ovarian tube for no less than twenty-one hours, and ovulation doesn't begin until an egg is laid. Being the barbarian that you are, you have no idea what ovulation is. Write this down: it's when an egg cell leaves an ovary! But is it possible to speed up the formation of an egg and therefore reduce the delay between eggs being laid? That's the question posed by our lab, or rather by your intractable servant. And we partly already have an answer. Let me remind you of something you never knew—the egg's path through the oviduct. The egg is quickly funneled in (and Borzov has no objections on this point) and quickly passes the magnum and the isthmus, but is delayed, tragically delayed in the vagina. Nineteen hours! Why? Because here, right here is where the complex process of shell formation takes place."

. . . As I listened, I recalled when we were first acquainted. We were in different departments at the institute, and we lived in different parts of the dorm. We weren't acquainted yet, but I, along with the whole institute, already knew of him: Borzov the party animal, Borzov the show-off, Borzov the joker.

In the summer, I ran into him in my hometown under fairly unusual circumstances. I was taking a walk along the shore late in the evening. And suddenly, I see a crowd of teens surround some man with clearly unkind intentions. It was pretty dark. Abruptly, a familiar voice tore through the air:

"Borzov doesn't know the meaning of retreat! Have at me, you jackals!"

I ran up, squeezed my way through the crowd, and saw Borzov, fists raised. His eyes were glassed over, his expression wild. The youths, having recognized me as a local, reluctantly stepped aside. I led him out of the crowd. They would have torn him apart, of course.

Borzov was absolutely smashed. It was the first and last time I saw him like that. He usually never got drunk. A crying girl came up to us. Turns out he was with her. She said that Borzov was the one who started getting rowdy with the group of teens.

I took him and the girl to the Ritsa hotel, amazed at the fact that he managed to get a room there during the summer season. With time, I stopped being surprised by such things: he could get away with anything.

Afterwards, I accompanied the girl. She was from out of town and lived in a private apartment. She told me that Borzov had gotten a bottle of chacha at the bazaar, and that set everything off. The girl was good-looking and was so upset about what had happened! I assured her that he must have gotten sick, because I had never seen him like that. I thought she calmed a bit after that.

The next day, after freshening up, showering, and dressing properly, he accompanied me and my friends on a stroll along the shore. He didn't remember anything from yesterday—not the girl, not the drink, not the teens. He was regaling us with tales of his athletic achievements. By the way, he said, he was a professional swimmer.

"What stroke do you do?" I asked.

"All of them," he said after a moment's hesitation.

"And what stroke are you pro in?"

"All of them!" he responded happily.

I thought it strange. But we were planning to go to the beach the next day! There was no way he didn't know that anybody who lived on the Black Sea would quickly figure out how good a swimmer he really was.

The next day, we went to the beach, and I was first in the water, swimming out a bit, waiting for him to join me in the sea. Strong, fit, wearing fashionable swim trunks, he entered the water and swam up to me, paddling his way through the water. There was no stroke to speak of.

"How are you a professional, then?" I asked when he swam up.

In the sea, it's easier to disregard commonplace niceties and delicateness. The sea washes away earthly conventions.

"Ahhh!" he exclaimed, his eyes flashing at me. He smacked the water so carelessly with his hand that I forgave him on the spot.

A fun guy to have around, armed with many fantastic stories to tell, he charmed all of my friends and acquaintances over the course of four days. During get-togethers, he would usually observe enviously whether anyone was resisting his charm. If someone was, he would work exclusively on that person until they gave in. Speaking of, during that time, he picked up twenty-thirty Georgian and Abkhazian words, which, to general delight, he used quite appropriately. While my friends discussed where they should take him to submit him to more prolonged tableside questioning, he suddenly disappeared. As it turned out, he had charmed the captain of the steamship "Georgia," and he invited him on a trip to Odesa.

Next year, we lived in one large room in the dorm, and I could examine him more closely. Naturally, he was a brazen liar. But the most fantastical part about his fantastical stories was that they were sometimes proven true.

He was two years older than us and looked like he was even older than that. To hear him say it, he spent those two years as a cabin boy sailing the northern seas. Maybe that was where he learned to "hunt," if he didn't make that part of his biography up.

He once said that he is a master of hypnosis and that he can hypnotize anybody.

"Hypnotize me," I told the master of hypnosis.

"Lie down," he said.

This was in the dorm. I lay in my bed. All the guys gathered around us. He ordered everyone to shut up and began executing his sorcery above me, proclaiming calming words in a deep voice. I lay with my eyes closed, trying with all my strength to resist the incoming waves of laughter. Finally, I began breathing evenly, pretending that I was sleeping.

"He's ready!" he told the crowd and commanded me to stand up.

I stood up, as if I was obediently pliable to his every whim.

"You lost a letter from your beloved," he said in a sensual voice. "She will never forgive you for that. Climb under every bed to find it, or else you're a goner!"

Accompanied by everyone's muted laughter, as well as mine own, I climbed under all the beds, trying to memorize what he was saying through-out the whole thing so that I could bring them up as evidence later, after I proved him a fraud.

The next task was more difficult. At somebody's suggestion, he com-manded me to drink the unearthly swill that one of the students brewed himself. There was a general suspicion that he made the concoction so that nobody wanted to steal any of it.

"You're hungry," exclaimed Borzov. "You haven't eaten anything in three days. A glorious bowl of kharcho[51] is before you! Eat it! But blow on the spoon, blow on it! It's hot!"

There was nothing for it but sit at the table, blow on the spoon, and lap up the cold gruel, smacking my lips from the over-boiled carrot and crunching on the under-boiled potatoes. Even now when I think about it, I shudder. Accompanied by universal laughter, choking, I ate half a pot's worth of that swill, but he then took pity on me and once again commanded me to lie in bed. I lay down, listening to the effect that gruel was having on my stomach.

He ordered two students to set up two chairs so that I could push on the edge of one chair with my feet and lean on the edge of the other with my head, thereby lying perfectly straight between them without falling.

He then ordered those same students to wedge me between the chairs. They did, and I felt an extraordinary pain in my head and stomach. Not from the gruel, but from the pressure of that horrible pose. But I decided to play my part through to the end and waited through the monstrous pressure mounting in my body. I was only afraid of one thing: that he would sit on my stomach in order to demonstrate the hypnosis's power. But, thankfully, that didn't happen, and, slapping me on the forehead, he finally proclaimed:

"Awaken, you're among friends!"

I happily crumpled through the chairs and hopped up to laughter and applause.

---

51 Kharcho is a traditional Georgian soup made with beef, rice, plums, and walnuts.

Borzov threw out his arms and took everything in with his flaring eyes, standing in the middle of the room as if he were a ringmaster in a circus.

"Your hypnosis is bull," I exclaimed, "I did everything on purpose!"

"Well," said Borzov, not even remotely flustered. His eyes flared even more brightly. "Then stretch yourself out between those chairs on your own!"

I set up the chairs approximately how they were previously. I put my feet on one and, holding on with my hands, situated my head on the other, and immediately crashed to the floor. What the hell! An unbearable pain erupted in my head and waist, and I couldn't hang on for more than a few seconds. I tried to hang on for longer but crashed to the floor every time.

Everyone was laughing.

"If he wasn't hypnotized," some were yelling, "he should finish Kuznetsov's gruel!"

But I wasn't, I wasn't hypnotized! I know that for sure! Then why couldn't I repeat the experiment? To hell with it! Maybe I drained all my strength trying to play into Borzov's hand.

Speaking of hypnosis. A student once told an amusing story. He and Borzov were in the trolley, holding on to the handrail. Suddenly, Borzov sneezed, and he did it so powerfully that it got all over the back of the head of the man holding on to the handrail in front of him.

The guy began cursing Borzov and all of the day's youth, none of whom knew how to behave themselves in public places. Usually sharp-tongued, Borzov stayed silent. The man kept on and on about it, but Borzov just stayed silent.

And suddenly, he leaned in close to the man and started whispering something in his ear. The man instantly fell silent, and his face took on an expression of mild curiosity. A moment ago, he was burning with rage—now mild curiosity.

Surprised by such a metamorphosis, the student leaned in from the side to get a better look at the whispering Borzov. The horror! Borzov wasn't whispering at all—he was standing with the man's ear clamped between his teeth! Five, maybe ten long seconds passed. Borzov released the man's ear and began staring out the window contemplatively. The man, meanwhile, just stood there, the expression of mild curiosity frozen on his face. He stood like that, without once looking at his assailant, right up until Borzov and the student exited the trolley. Apparently, no one had noticed anything.

"Are you nuts?!" shouted the student, convulsing with laughter, once they were on the ground.

"I knew he wouldn't shut up otherwise," calmly replied Borzov.

"And what if he made a scene? What if someone saw?"

"Never!" replied Borzov, smiling. "Borzov knows his people."

Borzov said that his father was a renowned lawyer in Kazan. It must have been true. He must have inherited his ironic eloquence from him. When he was *on*, he would regale us with lectures on societal topics, filled with quotes from newspapers with extraordinary comedic deftness. We would die of laughter. He would make fun of himself too, but he suffered from a minor weakness in that he hated it terribly if anyone were to support that particular direction of mockery.

In the dorm, Borzov acted as the patron to two students—Steinberg and Suchkov. Before exams, Steinborg would supply him with all the info he needed on history and literature. And Suchkov, who was a fledgling poet, would ghost write for him poems intended for another student for whom Borzov had the hots. Borzov would rewrite the poems in his handwriting, loudly read them to us, and then present them as gifts to his beauty. I was amazed that he wasn't afraid that she would find out the true source of the verse. But she never did! Later, he married her.

He did fine on his exams, sometimes even spectacularly, even though he barely touched his textbooks. His knowledge banks were enormous. Back then, he amazed me. I thought that all he had to do was push some internal button, focus his vast energy stores, and he could become . . . Who? I had no idea.

However, he hit an unexpected snag during the winter session.

The western literature teacher told him that he did not know nearly enough about the original literary masterpieces and commanded him to retake the exam.

Borzov spent a few days grimly sitting on his bed, once again listening to Steinberg's expanded lecture, which was pierced by notes of panic.

"Don't you forget, boys," said Borzov, "these things don't fly with Borzov. My counterpunch will sunder this citadel of obscurantism."

He passed the exam on his retake, and we forgot all about it. But one fine day, like lightning in a clear sky, a youth newspaper suddenly published his article on the ideological work being done in our institute. The article was acerbic and utterly demagogic. Its point boiled down to: our institute paid too much attention to western literature and not enough to social sciences.

The institute shuddered. Committee after committee reviewed each department individually, all while he strolled along the hallways, his pretty head cocked, an expression of ideological superiority over all departments etched into his featured. For some reason, it really evoked a desire to smack him upside the head and then check to see if that charming expression of charlatanic, ideological superiority were still there.

One committee kept up its work (lightning struck during the spring semester), while Borzov passed his exams with the help of cheat sheets with which he would stuff himself in the dorm right before our eyes.

The director of the institute taught history, and at times, he would do so vivaciously, captivatingly. At any rate, I liked his lessons. And I pitied him for having gotten into such a mess. And yet, I, like most students, was on Borzov's side. He snowed all of us. Sure, loyalty to our fellow student was also to blame: let the teachers be under pressure for a change. But there was something more at work.

At the time, the campaign against the insidious West was in full force, which we students quite reasonably thought to be ridiculous. That's when the joke was born that Russia was full of elephants.

Obviously, the West wasn't exerting any serious influence over us. Enthusiasts of foreign clothes did hunt down various eclectic rags, but it's the same today! And since Borzov was the institute's prime show-off, we interpreted his article as an act of parodic vengeance for the foolish campaign being run by the adults. We might not have realized that, but we felt it.

A year later, we both transferred to other educational institutions, and I lost sight of him for a long time. He went to the biology department at the Moscow University. And suddenly, many years later, I have it from some writer, a genetics propagandist, that a young, talented scientist named Boris Borzov had bravely delivered a speech against the Lysenkoists, but that the forces were unevenly matched. The young man was facing a lot of resistance. The propagandist suggested that I should write a collective letter of protest to the Academy of Sciences if Borzov was kicked out of the institute. Oh, if only I hadn't known Borzov! Admittedly, given how things went down, there was no need for any such letter. Borzov held his own in his institute.

And so, he and I were in the same car, and he was telling me about the unparalleled superiority of shell-less eggs over regular ones. It was amusing that, while telling me all this, he managed to steal a glance at every store we passed, sometimes mumbling something on the subject.

In one place, we saw a large queue stretching out of a store.

"What's in there?" yelled Borzov, stopping the car and looking out the window.

"Hare hats," someone in line replied grimly.

"Hare," muttered Borzov, thought it over for a second, then drove away.

Another time in an alley, his gaze was drawn by the tiger-like ripple of watermelons in an iron cage. He stopped the car again.

"I'll buy a watermelon and call my lover," he told me, easily transitioning from shell-less eggs to hard-rind Astrakhanian watermelons.

He exited the car, well-built, youthful, in a gorgeous, blue button-up shirt and black corduroy pants. He shambled over to the phone booth, taking small steps, as if reining in the excess jubilation, as if performing the mating ritual of extramarital union.

After dialing, he turned towards the street and spoke while winking happily to some invisible audience. The glass of the phone booth was broken, and I managed to pick up some of what he was saying. He repeated a mysterious phrase a few times:

"I'm calling you from home!"

What did he mean by it? He and I once met up in the Nationale café and spent a wonderful evening together. He was mild-mannered, courteous, hospitable. How to convey it visually? Imagine a painting from the 30s called "The War Chief Covers with His Overcoat the Famous Pilot Who Trustingly Fell Asleep on the Couch. Hello from Sochi!" No, it needs to be more modest. Something like: "The Patriarch of Ideological Battles Personally Cuts up Cucumbers and Offers the Best Pieces of Meat to his Childhood Friend." By the way, I asked him then if he truly was able to hypnotize people.

"Of course not," said Borzov, cocking his head with a disarming smile. "I just believed that you'd play into my hands, and you came through."

"But why couldn't I stretch out between the chairs?"

"Easy," replied Borzov, excited at the prospect of imparting a bit of wisdom on someone. "When I was placing you between the chairs, you were afraid of letting Borzov down, and so you bore it. But when you tried to do it yourself, you didn't feel any accountability to Borzov, and so you crashed."

We cracked up at the same time. In denying that he was a master of scientific hypnosis, he was seemingly asserting that he was master of a deeper, personality-based hypnosis.

We spent a great evening together and agreed to meet up again in a week next to the statue of Pushkin and go somewhere for a drink.

"If I don't show up," he said quietly, "that means that Borzov died. Come to my funeral."

When the agreed-upon time came, I spent some forty minutes next to the statue waiting for him. It was very chilly. When my limbs became too numb, I went into the closest café to recharge. Obviously, I didn't think that Borzov had died, but I would never have guessed that I'd meet him in that very café. When I saw him, I felt a strange sense of embarrassment, as if he caught me skipping his funeral.

He was sitting with a large group of people and was actively rhapsodizing. He noticed me and gave me a curt, lacerating nod, demonstrating that the circumstances had changed sharply, that my very presence was the height of tactlessness, and that it would have been exceedingly tasteless to confront him about what had happened.

He most likely simply forgot about our agreement, but I realized how dangerous it was to give in to bouts of sentimental reminiscing. You had to pay for them.

… Borzov left the phone booth and sharply changed his gait: he fearlessly stepped into the tiger cage right in front of the queue's eyes, picked out an enormous watermelon, weighed it, paid the tamer-saleswoman for it, and quickly brought it to the car, as if afraid that the watermelon might disappear.

Only then did the line of people, which he had turned into an audience, come to its senses, and a few lone voices began protesting. But it was too late. Borzov put the watermelon on the floor of the back seat. He sat in the driver's seat and began assiduously wiping off his hands with a handkerchief.

"That one will take you two a long time," I said.

"You mean my lover?" he asked, sounding surprised. "The watermelon's going home! The family is the foundation of society! Never forget: a true gentleman marries only once!"

He threw me a watermelon-rinsed smile. It was odd that despite all of his masculine qualities, when he smiled like that, his guise changed, and you got the impression that a woman was sitting next to you. The magic of delusion.

The engine roared to life, and the lecture on shell-less eggs picked up where it left off.

"On its own, a shell is great. It's a brilliant evolutionary move on the part of reptiles and birds in their quest to reproduce on land. The shell is a fortress, it defends the egg from the harmful external environment. But is it so necessary for an egg intended as a foodstuff? … Damn it, woman, I will run you over! You tired of living?! No! The entire egg is edible aside from the shell—or do you eat it with the shell? The shell should be treated exclusively as a receptacle for its contents. The shell makes up only ten percent of a hen's egg's mass, but its formation takes up four fifths of the time in the oviduct. We have to overcome this physiological bureaucracy, and we already are! Do you know how many minerals and how much energy a laying hen uses? We could fuel our agriculture on those minerals alone.

"But that's in the future! Everybody is writing about the acceleration, the Perestroika! But I've been working with the spirit of the times even before our time! And so, I asked a question: what if we make hens lay shell-less eggs, as was the case with the ancestors of birds, with scaly reptiles? You and I know that I alone must carry the burden of the knowledge that evolution often leads to a regression of a species' entire organ systems. For example, whales! They are, for your information, the descendants of land mammals, but they long ago returned to the sea, which is why their hind limbs disappeared. Why not turn back the evolution of laying hens by eliminating the process of shell formation? To hell with calcium! There's the slogan you can hang above your desk. It'll be highly relevant in the near future. In some two-three years, our hard-working hens will lay nearly a thousand eggs per season!"

. . . I remembered how one summer, he and I ran into each other in the Leningrad metro. He looked like a noble foreigner in his imported white coat and his imported sunglasses, holding a briefcase in his hands, which was quite rare at the time.

"I'm going to give a lecture on genetics," he declared triumphantly, his eyes managing to sparkle even through his sunglasses. "I alone pushed these lectures through in the entire country! Leningrad's intelligentsia needs to be jolted awake, it's grown far too vegetative!"

I complained that I was beset with difficulties in obtaining a ticket for the Moscow-Leningrad train.

"Come with me," he said. "Borzov has access to tickets."

He headed in the direction of the office of the train station chief, slicing through the resistance of the turgid environment. I followed him, though I lagged a bit outside the office. He didn't notice, tore the door open, and disappeared inside. Twenty minutes later, we walked out onto the platform and then made ourselves comfortable in the train.

Borzov threw off his coat, carefully hung it up, took off his glasses, and sat down. I sat across from him, sensing that our static poses were unsatisfactory to him.

"What, are we just going to sit like this?" he asked, gazing at me sternly.

Meanwhile, the hostess came in to get our tickets. Borzov took out a kerchief, wiped the tabletop with it, and, showing the hostess that the kerchief had become sullied, declared:

"Young lady, I am Borzov. I'm going to get some champagne. When I come back, this compartment had best be in shipshape. Wash the glasses with baking soda!"

He had on a snow white suit and had clearly assumed the role of an admiral. The young hostess froze. He silently slid past her, then turned his head and winked at me.

"What an interesting man, and so stern," uttered the impressed hostess. "Who is he?"

"A great man," I said.

The compartment was worked on until it was in moist, sparkling shipshape. Borzov soon came back with a young black man, whom he scooped up somewhere on his way. Both were packed with champagne bottles.

"He's a graduate student from Lumumba University," said Borzov, softly placing the bottles on the table.

I hadn't expected such a grand gesture in honor of the awakening jolt that was in store for Leningrad's intelligentsia.

The African sat on the edge of the seat, clearly hung up on something and not quite understanding what this Soviet, but still white, gentleman wanted from him. Borzov opened a bottle, and we drank a glass to his upcoming lecture in Leningrad. The African drank his glass with us, but he was very reserved, controlling his every minute movement. Borzov took out of his briefcase a plastic bag of sandwiches with black caviar and generously spread them out on a plate.

While pouring a second round, he suddenly asked the African:

"Is Bulamuto alive?"

The African started, as if hearing the familiar cry of his native savannahs.

"Alive! Alive!" he exclaimed. "Bulamuto underground! Know Bulamuto?"

"Who doesn't know Bulamuto?" calmly replied Borzov, letting the foam subside and pouring a bit more. "Let's drink to Bulamuto. When Bulamuto assumes power," he added, placing his empty glass on the table, "he should be warned not to trust the chiefs of the Takamaka Clan . . . They're corrupted by American gifts . . ."

"Bulamuto know!" the African interrupted him enthusiastically. "Takamaka cunning!"

After establishing that the young African specialized in medicine, Borzov began telling him about his great battle with the Lysenkoists in his own institute. The champagne flowed and flowed, the tale went on and on, time and space became mixed up, and eventually the young African may have thought that Borzov was the last Vavilovite[52] in the world after miraculously surviving the famous session at the VASKhNIL.[53]

Having thoroughly charmed the African, Borzov went to get the hostess and brought her to our compartment. At first, she was a bit shy, but after a glass of champagne, she relaxed and kept her adoring eyes glued to Borzov.

Under the influence of her gaze, the theme of the intractable warrior transitioned into an adagio of the warrior's loneliness, the lack of understanding in his own home, the impossibility of relaxing, of mitigating his fate with a woman's caress. He spoke slowly, leaning inexorably towards the hostess, who was frozen in the pose of a hypnotized chicken, even though Borzov may not have been dealing with laying hens yet.

I didn't know how the scene would end, as imbued as it was with such covert comicality, when suddenly the African began laughing. He reached out his unfathomably long arm, easily leaned through the entire compartment, slapped Borzov on the shoulder, and exclaimed:

"You a jester!"

I gasped. Borzov stared at the African with eyes glazing over with fury. I felt that the African clearly wanted to say something different and, heading off Borzov's rage, I explained:

"He wanted to say joker!"

"Joker! Joker!" the African smiled lightheartedly, clearly not understanding the difference between the two words.

"They're letting themselves go, with Bulamuto underground," muttered Borzov, looking at the African and trying to discern in his expression the slightest trace of irony. But there was no hidden irony, none! Or was there?

Peace was restored, but the adagio had concluded, and Borzov was no longer leaning towards the hostess. Sometime later, he got up, opened the door, and glanced out into the corridor, searching, it seemed to me, for new prey. But it was late at night, and the corridor was empty.

---

52 A follower of Vavilov (see footnote 48).
53 VASKhNIL stands for the All-Union Academy of Agricultural Sciences of the Soviet Union.

Suddenly, Borzov turned around. His expression cold and supercilious.

"Get rid of the bottles," he told the hostess with the tone of an admiral who had grown tired of conversing with the local tribes.

The hostess began quickly clearing the table, and the African helped her out, though his expression took on a sorrowful note.

"It happens, it happens," I nodded in Borzov's direction as I was bidding the African farewell, implying that the sudden worsening of the great individual's mood wasn't at all related to the company he was in when said worsening occurred. But the African didn't hear me and carried his hurt expression away with the bottles. They left. I closed the compartment door.

"They've got a long way to go to European standards," Borzov inclined his head in the direction of the departed, bemoaning his attempts at civilizing. And it was unclear whether he meant the representatives of both cultures or of just one.

"What about Bulamuto?" I asked.

"What about him?" sighed Borzov, then added unexpectedly: "Bulamuto is alone, just like me."

But he didn't devote much time to his melancholy. We began undressing, and he was carefully folding his pants when he suddenly came to life—the engine of civilization roared awake, and he began regaling me with details of his fight with the Lysenkoists, details that had been intentionally kept from the ears of the foreigner out of higher considerations. I got the sudden desire to imitate Bulamuto and go deep underground, but I could only go deep under my blanket. I listened to him, fruitlessly fantasizing about smacking him on the head with one of the champagne bottles—if only he hadn't been the one to pay for them and if only they were still here . . . And suddenly, in the middle of his scientific opponents' most perfidious move, Borzov fell asleep, and I myself fell into the depths of Tartarus.

"Get up, lazybones, you'll sleep through Leningrad" I heard his voice above me.

He was shaking me, like my brother did in my childhood. I lifted my leaden eyelids. Borzov was standing over me, cute, freshened up, elegant, shaven, and clearly ready to jolt awake Leningrad's wilted intelligentsia.

. . . "Good," I said, interrupting his lecture. "Say your experiments are resoundingly successful. In that case, we, the citizens of this country, will all receive a hen that we'll have to squeeze over a frying pan every morning? How else would we deal with shell-less eggs?"

"How? How?" he smiled rewardingly, throwing a quick glance my way. "Squeeze the hen out over a frying pan? Not bad. I'll have to tell my boss about that. True, true, our opponents did have similar doubts, but we dispelled their disbelief. The most important thing is to create hens capable of laying shell-less eggs—the technology for storing those eggs comes later . . . Where is that dunce racing off to? Get back in your lane . . . Imagine a poultry farm where hens lay shell-less eggs. They're in cages. The cage floor is soft, but with an incline towards the egg-collecting transporter. The lain eggs roll into it, but not onto a conveyor belt, which is what dilettantes what you might think, but into water—water! Remember how we splashed around the Black Sea when I came there for the first time? Golden years! Vasya Svanidze—great guy! Did he ever become the port chief? You don't know? By the way, did our Suchok ever become a real poet? Don't know either. You don't know anything! How do you just write!? Ok, so, the water into which the eggs drop will be ozonized and will contain a solution of antibiotics that disinfects their surface. The ability of shell-less eggs to absorb water-based solutions will allow us to enrich them with vitamins and other thing that enhance the eggs' taste. Then, the water flow—swim, my eggs!—will take them to the packaging plant, where they'll be put in synthetic packages."

"Your shell-less eggs," I said, "aren't making me particularly hungry. Anyway, how are you going to get the hens to forget about shells?"

"We're developing hormones that will affect the birds' nervous system," he replied, glancing at me, then at the road, and back. "We're developing strong diastalsis in the part of the oviduct where the shell is formed, which will cause the egg to fly through it quicker than the time it takes for the shell to form. There's a hen in my group whose every third egg is already shell-less. And in my boss's group, the best hen lays about every fifth egg without a shell. There's a fight looming with my boss."

"Why?" I asked.

"He took the American approach," said Borzov. "He uses sulfimide agents. *I* use less harmful hormonal agents in what I feed the hens . . . The fight will determine who'll run the lab . . ."

"Are Americans really doing this too?" I asked, losing my last hope.

"At my suggestion!" laughed Borzov. His eyes flared up with such intensity that people in America may have thought something glinted powerfully nearby. "At the Amsterdam conference! I seduced the Yankees! Now, they send me endless letters and invites! I'm going to the States soon!"

I suddenly felt a keen sense of pity for the hens. To lay nutritional phlegm instead of gorgeous, sharp-sided eggs . . . I felt that the sulfimide agents were having a harmful effect on me too—I had taken them mistakenly a few times. But I got a grip and recalled the source of my bitter optimism: the Goatibexes had all dropped through the face of the earth? Yes, they had!

"I pity the hens," I told Borzov. "But I'm confident that you ultimately won't be successful."

We had just driven up to the club where I was to perform, which, of course, doesn't mean that that's what caused my audacious assertion. I figured he would be offended or argue with me. Nope, he blithely let go of the steering wheel and smiled one of his most cheerful smiles.

"The result isn't important—the process is," he said, giving me an impish wink. "If the night at the Writers' House gets interesting, give me a call."

"Alright," I said, and we parted.

If nothing else is possible, then at least there's this, at least Borzov will be happy, I mollified myself, walking into the club.

. . . The director led me onto the stage. Turns out the evening had already started. But a popular singer was currently onstage. The gnashing ruckus of rock music pierced me like a thousand rusty arrows. The shell-less eggs had somehow combined with this musical shell, which was devoid of any melodic substance, and things got pretty unenviable for me.

You could see half the stage from backstage. The singer occasionally ran out into the open, slammed down to his knees with the microphone in his hands, lay on his back, kicked out with his legs, and kept singing. The music roared on, and the crowd loved it. *Dear god*, I thought, *let me live through this, and I will never, ever again cut ahead of people waiting for a taxi before me.*

About a dozen poets were sitting backstage around a small table that was full of coffee cups and bottles of mineral water. They were glancing at me with dull dislike. I'd have liked to think that I personally wasn't the target of their displeasure, but rather the threatening number of other performers was. I joined them. The host of the evening, also a poet, glanced in passing at my folder (also with dislike) and said:

"Guys, there are a lot of foreign students. Be smart about what you read."

And then he stared at my folder with a doleful look, as if trying to pierce its contents and have a mitigating effect on them. It was very uncomfortable—he just kept staring and staring.

Finally, under the influence of his glare, I intuitively opened the folder, as if to demonstrate that no cobra would slither out and assault the foreign students, seeing as no such cobra was in there. And he leaned in (insolently) and looked inside, as if he could judge a manuscript's capacity for venom just by looking at it. And he and I froze for a few seconds in an unspoken dialogue.

"Cobra?"

"It's a water snake."

"So, a cobra?"

"A water—it's a water snake!"

"A water snake?!"

"Yes!"

"Well, it might not have been . . ."

And he relaxed. It was as if we made a deal: since I opened the folder and he looked into it, that meant that everything would be fine.

Still, the whole thing wasn't right. He and I had been on friendly terms, strolling occasionally through the House's gardens where I would, for some inexplicable reason, collect his cascades of aphorisms, which were actually quite unique in their boorishness.

One time, I was leaving the club, and he called out to me. He was sitting in a taxi. I decided to approach the car and greet him. I was in a good mood and thought he might drop a good quote during our few seconds of conversation.

I came up to the taxi. Sitting in the passenger seat, he reached his hand out the window, but just as I was about to shake it, he jerked it back in horror.

"You don't greet each other over a threshold," he said, exited the taxi, and greeted me then.

I'd never have publicized that moment if he hadn't looked into my folder. This is what happens when you look in other people's folders.

The poets and I agreed to read no more than three poems each, applause notwithstanding. We likewise agreed not to read anything epic and claim that it was just a single poem. Only the miniaturist was allowed to read more than three, though we didn't specify how many was acceptable. And we paid for our liberal negligence. He took advantage of our oversight and read about a hundred of his mini-poems, damn him! Everything needs to be agreed upon.

The singer was still singing. He finally flipped in the air, landed in the open half of the stage, threw his microphone to someone, and left, chased by a sea of applause.

We came out onto the stage. The youths greeted us well. Even the miniaturist. After reading yet another miniature, he would look back at us, reminding us with his glances that he wasn't breaking any agreement, that we hadn't specified a number of miniatures.

Our host was also greeted pretty well. If I say that unlike the singer, who gloriously compensated for his weak voice with an abundance of movement, the host brilliantly compensated for his lack of thought with strength of voice, then the reader will think that I'm continuing to wreak my vengeance. So I'll say nothing on the matter.

After reading his share and having his fill of applause, he looked the audience over and suddenly said:

"I see that our wonderful Spanish poet Manuel Rodriguez is in the audience today! Let's ask him to read something of his!"

There was a veritable storm of applause! The familiar, wizened figure, a smile on his face, was already standing up. I remembered that I had performed with him a few times and that he was called up to the stage each time after seemingly accidentally finding him in the audience. A powerful technique.

After the evening, it just so happened that the Spanish poet and I were going to the metro together. He was happily complaining about one of our editors, who offered to publish him in his almanac:

"He thinks that he speaks to me in Spanish. I speak to him: 'That is no Spanish! That is Italiano! Speak to me Ruso! I don't want to publish in your almanac! Too much poems on death! Death! Death! I don't want to publish there!'"

We parted at the metro. I went home, musing about the power of our literary propaganda, which caused the famous Manuel Rodriguez to indignantly refuse to participate in a collection of poetry that dealt with such a traditional theme for Spanish verse.

7

Palermo—New York

Sad little newspaper articles, sad little tales about fresh, new journals. My mood's shabby enough without them. I *want* to work, but given the general mood of the public, all you can do is add one more melancholy to the universal melancholy—your own. But what for? There's too much of it anyway—I don't need it, and neither do others.

I get up from my typewriter, walk around the room, go into the kitchen for some reason. Nobody. A small flame is flickering in the gas stove burner. I'm out of matches, so it's been burning all day. Or rather, I'm saving my last matches. In the middle of Moscow, we're saving every match as if we were lost in the middle of the taiga.

I look at the flame and remember something similar, but really completely different. I remember how in my native Chegem, the fire in the hearth would be put out every night, but the pulsing, amaranthine coals would be buried in the ash. The fire went to sleep until morning.

And in the morning, the coals were dug out of the ash, fed with firewood, and gave birth to a new hearth fire. In my childhood, it always seemed like an inexplicable and joy-bringing miracle—how can it be that those waning coals were capable of maintaining their heat until morning? I thought they must warm each other all night, guarding their warmth—or maybe it's the ash that saves them from the cold, like a blanket?

I'm not any better-prepared today to say what law made those coals hang on to their heat until morning, but I know for a fact that they did. I also know, even though I never tested this, that if the coals weren't dug out and fanned into flames, they wouldn't have made it to the next morning.

For some reason, the clarity of my knowledge lightened my mood too. It's possible to survive through a normal night, though not necessarily a polar night. The people that live up north can tell you how to live through a polar night. As for me, I'll tell you about a trip I went on in the beginning of the

Perestroika. I can feel things lightening not only in my head, but in my chest too. Such is the power of thinking about Chegem!

So, do you know the land where lemon blossoms grow? Finally, after many years, I can respond to Goethe's textbook question in the affirmative.

I received an invitation to a world congress dedicated to our Perestroika in the city of Palermo, Sicily. Almost at the same time, I was invited to America (I had no money, and here was a golden opportunity), where I was supposed to be going with a delegation of writers.

But before that, something else happened. One fine day, I decided to write a letter to Gorbachev. At the time, I had no idea what would come of it. I think that when he began the Perestroika, he himself couldn't imagine how far it would go. But even then, I could make out through his depressingly banal Party vocabulary that he was genuinely striving towards a softening of our government's convictions. I thought that the soporific banality of his familiar combinations of words was intended to lull the war chiefs into a false sense of security. That's what I thought, and that may have been the case.

I decided to suggest a way to weaken the censorship, but seemingly do it in a way deemed acceptable by the system. Knowing that the critical spirit of the reforms would encounter resistance everywhere, I suggested that the regional newspapers be subjugated to the Party's oblast committees, freeing them from the oversight of the regional committees. Likewise, the oblast-wide newspapers should report to the republican Central Committee, and the republican newspaper should report to the Party's Central Committee. I stopped there, as the logical train of thought would have taken me to suggest that the central *Pravda* newspaper should report to God.

I also wanted to tell him that he should create a personal guard that answered only to him. I felt that freedom might make some of the idiots out there go berserk and get violent. But I wheezed and grunted at my typewriter for a bit, and decided against it. I had a vague understanding of who would be taking advantage of the idiots' savageness. Which is why I decided against it. It would have been too daring and even dangerous. I didn't know who would read the letter. Which is how I modestly proposed modestly outfoxing the Party to its General Secretary.

After putting my short message in the postbox, I nearly forgot about it. About a month later, when I was out of town, my mother-in-law called and told me, tears streaming down her face, that the Central Committee called—they were discussing some letter of mine. I urgently had to return and call the number they gave. I came home. My mother-in-law, wailing that my underage son was going to be left an orphan, gave me the number.

I called. The man who picked up the phone told me that the letter had reached its addressee. He assured me that at the upcoming congress, there would be a discussion about restructuring the hierarchy of regional newspapers. I tried to expand the discussion beyond only regional ones, but the person at the other end focused only on them.

I felt that he halted the conversation on them out of fear that we were being bugged. Possibly out of concern for me. And, maybe, if he was thinking about the complex move combinations of a political career, then he was worried about himself too. His voice sounded very well-intentioned. It was as if the voice was glancing at the wailing mother-in-law and mollifying her.

A few days later, I heard how during the weather report, the television announcer said my name and read a few humorous lines from my short story about how Muscovites listen to the weather report with bated breath, as if they were imminently readying themselves to go hunting or do field work.

It was strange and very nice to listen to that. Usually, when I felt the government's gaze on me, it was always tenebrous and suspicious. But suddenly, the government smiled at me in the guise of a woman.

It was a sign, even though I didn't immediately believe it. We were still living in a system of signs. Soon, the editorial boards of newspapers and journals, musing out loud that I had stopped sending them my works (I *stopped!!!*), began asking me to give them something. Then I began receiving invitations to various international conferences. Such invitations had probably been sent out previously too, but they never reached me. The government must have finally thought: he won't run off, he won't slander us. I started going to them. This time, I told my higher-ups directly about my desire to go to America, but they told me that the issue had been decided: I had to stop by Palermo, then get to America on my own.

Maybe part of my higher-ups' plan was to test me against the Sicilian mafia, and only then, if I survived, the wiser for it, send me to America. But right when we were supposed to go there, they arrested and sentenced part of the mafia, possibly the part that I was supposed to be tested against, because I didn't run into a single mafioso on the streets of Palermo.

On the other hand, that beautiful city almost choked me to death with exhaust fumes. There are too many cars in Palermo, and the city's geography evidently can't handle the degree of contamination. I barely made it out of the city center, especially since our hotel was on the seashore, where the climate was Mediterranean heaven.

. . . And so, the general—a member of our delegation—and I were strolling along the sloped hotel yard next to a cliff that led to the sea. The whole slope was covered in orange trees, which were generously saturated with bright buds.

For a few days, I was wary of picking any of the oranges, because carabinieri would wander along the garden. Eventually, apparently weary of my furtive glances at the trees, one of them nodded to me: go for it. I picked a pair of oranges when it hit me: the carabinieri weren't defending the oranges—they were there to defend us, the members of the congress. It was taking place in the building next to the hotel.

When you come from a country where people aren't valued as highly as oranges, mistakes like this are natural. While strolling with the general, a pleasant man in all senses, I made another mistake, which, in turn, turned out not to be my last.

The thing is, I had seen him in Moscow in uniform, but here, he wore a suit, which, admittedly, sat on him beautifully and tightly, like a military uniform. I felt that such a change of clothes was a fairly dangerous exercise, but the general just strolled along, unabashedly wearing civilian clothing.

Somewhat sensing my tactlessness, but justifying it with my exclusive concern for the general's wellbeing, I couldn't take it anymore and asked him:

"Do they know that you're a general?"

"Of course," laughed the general.

I instantly relaxed. As long as everything was by the rules. As we strolled along the slope of the orange garden, I turned my attention to the lone figure of a waiter from our restaurant who was standing on the cliff, throwing a fishing line into the sea. The fish wasn't playing along, and the waiter looked so lonely and significant, that I eventually picked him up mentally and dropped him into one of Hemingway's short stories. *It's for the best*, I thought. *Everyone should have a place of their own to stand in.*

The general began telling me about the nuclear missiles that we were destroying in accord with America. By the by, he explained that in every missile there were some ten kilograms of gold. I knew that Uncle Sandro would never forgive me if I didn't at least try to find out where exactly the missiles were being destroyed. To think—each one had ten kilograms' worth of gold! Even if just five survived the explosion, it would be an unfathomable treasure!

"Are they blowing them up close to Moscow?" I asked with the note of ecological concern for the Muscovites entering my tone.

"Far away," he assured me, but didn't go into specifics.

I thought about where it could be taking place and figured that the most likely candidates were the Ural or Kazakhstan.

"Curious, did they blow them up in the mountains?" I asked, seemingly concerned by the fate of the surrounding ridges.

"No," he said, trying to get back to his tale. But I didn't let him.

"Then it must be the steppe. The biggest and most long-suffering steppe in the Soviet Union?" I noted, a tone of sentimentality entering my voice, clearly brought on by the thought of great, defenseless expanses.

"Could be the steppe," he said drily. "What's it to you?"

"I just want to know how it all happened. I'd like to have a concrete place in mind."

"That's how they showed it on TV," he admitted.

"And I missed it?" I sighed. "So the place isn't top secret?"

"What's it to you?" he asked, suddenly alert.

"You know," I said, bulging with a pacifist's pathos, "it would be nice to look into the hole where they discarded war."

"They usually guard places like that," he said, apparently approving of my pathos, but forced to mollify it.

I decided to cease my attempts at specification and resolved not to tell Uncle Sandro about it at all.

I suddenly got the thought that maybe contemporary gold mines were merely the traces of vanished civilizations that blew up their own missiles and then disappeared, and after many thousands of years, new civilizations discovered gold veins to use them in new missiles and then blow *them* up too—thank God not over people's heads yet.

I told the general a story that I heard in Chernobyl from a journalist. We had gone there half a year after the catastrophe.

When he was a simple soldier in the army, he and some captain were in a train, transporting atomic bombs. At some station next to a town with a population of more than a million (he didn't identify the city—evidently, it was a military secret), their train sped out of control.

A railroad worker was supposed to put brake units under their car's wheels so that it could slow down. However, the worker turned out to be drunk and did nothing of the sort.

Their car rammed into the rest of the train at a ludicrous speed. This set off a chain reaction in one of the bombs. In a minute or two, the entire town with all of its people was going to fly up into the air and disintegrate. The captain jumped out of the car so that before their communal death, he could execute the railroad worker, who was lolling about drunk not far from the train. The captain shot him.

But the solider kept his calm. He began extinguishing the chain reaction in the bomb with liquid graphite. Evidently, they planned for the possibility that certain situations might set off a chain reaction. And he succeeded.

Afterwards, he lay in a hospital for a few months. He received a blood transfusion three times, and he lived through it. To hear him say it, he received a very strong dose of radiation, but it didn't last long, and that's what saved him. Turns out it's better to get a powerful blast of radiation all at once than suffer through smaller doses over a long period of time. So, if you ever get a choice, choose the big dose and run to the hospital.

When he got better, the top brass called him in. They thanked him for his skillful and courageous actions and told him that they wanted to give him a medal, but alas, the captain executed the railroad worker, and that somewhat dampened the heroic story.

"It's been more than fifteen years since then," the former soldier cheerfully finished his tale. "I'm married. I have two kids. The radiation didn't leave a single trace."

The general kindly heard me out, but said that that couldn't have happened, because atomic bombs weren't transported under such conditions. For some reason, I immediately believed the journalist's tale, but the general didn't, even thought this was after Chernobyl. Maybe because of his high rank, he should have known about this incident, but nobody told him. Maybe he knew, but it was still considered a military secret. Either way, everyone should judge what happened to the extent of their knowledge on the subject. I accurately retold what I heard.

At that point, participants in our congress began exiting the restaurant into the garden. To my surprise, not a single one of them grabbed hold of a tree branch to pick an orange. Maybe they still incorrectly believed that the carabinieri were guarding the oranges, rather than us?

Since I found out that the carabinieri were guarding us, rather than the oranges, every time I passed by the trees, I picked a few oranges and ate them, ignoring the numbness spreading through my mouth. The congress had clearly been scheduled some ten days earlier than it should have been.

I took one last look at the sea, the cliff, peppered with conference-goers and orange trees, presenting a quiet symbolism of a world in which people and orange trees were acceptably interchangeable. And if the good ideas of the former induced something of a torpor with their tautology, the vivifying acidity of the oranges, despite numbing the mouth, had an energizing effect. It would be another thing entirely if the congress had been scheduled some ten days later. The presentations would've had the opportunity to mature, and the oranges wouldn't have been so unripe. But such is the world. When a congress is organized in a country where oranges aren't valued so highly, the organizers can't possibly understand how patriotic and symbolic it would be to schedule the congress in accordance with the ripening of these mighty fruit.

I went to the hotel to gather my things. I had a trip to America before me. I was a bit nervous, because I was going to America for the first time, alone, with no money, and with no knowledge of the language. True, our group's translator assured me that he had already called Moscow, and they confirmed that they already called New York, and that someone was supposed to meet me.

Back in Moscow, I had grabbed a self-help English textbook so that I could learn English while flying over the Atlantic. Which isn't to say that I didn't know it at all—I did know a bit.

Some ten years ago, when things were really bad, I bought the self-help book and began secretly learning English in case they began chasing people out of the country. A few months later, while sitting at in a writers' restaurant, I heard with my own ears a random conversation from which I could clearly tell that the Writers' Union knew about my English studies. *No*, I said to myself, *let's not force the hand that will strong-arm my future into the direction that it wants*, and I stopped studying English. I'll admit that my vigilance may have been wholeheartedly supported by my laziness.

A few more months later, I learned from a particularly cheeky writer who constantly hung out in the hallways of the Writers' Union that I stopped with English and began studying Turkish. Here, I could do nothing. I wasn't studying Turkish. I could only recall that during a grand banquet, I dropped a Turkish phrase in honor of an excellent Turkish humorist that I had heard many times in my childhood in the Abkhazo-Greek fields:

"Eşek gibi çalişiyor, ama para yok," (I work like a mule, but have no money).

That's the story of how I studied English. When the plane took off, I took out the self-help book, put on my glasses, and leisurely began making my way through it. For an hour and a half, I studied in earnest, but then my Italian neighbor nudged me and pointed at a bottle of whiskey. I decided to accept the offer and simultaneously practice my English with the Italian, who, as I understood, didn't make it much farther than I did.

In a conversation with someone who doesn't know a language very well, people who do know the language quite well are, for some reason, always tactless. No, it's too much to ask them to simplify their language to the level of their ill-prepared interlocutor—they rattle off a mile a minute with no cares for the world. So what if your conversation partner is politely nodding his head, don't you get that he doesn't understand a single damn word? But someone who doesn't know a language well is oh so delicate. Almost every word is underscored by gestures that can be understood nonverbally.

The Italian—or rather, the Sicilian—twice offered me a drink, and, after instantly understanding his meaning both times, I acquiesced to his proposal. He explained that he had been living in New York for five years, that he worked as a taxi driver, that he made good money.

He was returning home from spending some time in the Sicilian village where he was from. He remarked melancholically that Italy was exploiting Sicily. But if it didn't end, he added, Sicily would secede from Italy and join the United States of America. It sounded as if that wasn't particularly desirable, but worth it to spite Italy. I tried to joke about how much manpower would be necessary to tow the island of Sicily off to the shores of America if that were to happen, but then realized that I won't be able to tow my heavyweight pithiness into English.

Speaking of, I'd heard such threats back in Sicily. I asked him, "How are they exploiting it?" He thought about it, thought about it a little more, and then said, "In Sicily, gas is more expensive than in Italy."

In Palermo, I told one Italian about the complaints and threats of the Sicilians. He laughed: "They're dependent on us, as is the whole south. They won't go anywhere."

Finished with his native Sicily, my travel companion asked me about the Perestroika. Struggling to find the right words, I told him about what was going on. He attentively heard me out and then asked:

"If I'm a Russian farmer, can I sell my land and move somewhere?"

"Right now, no," I said, sensing that my lecture was crashing and burning.

"Ehhh," said the ex-farmer and waved it off. As an ex-farmer, he wanted to know the most important thing—whether farmers were free. Now he knew.

At this point, a beautiful young woman in fashionably torn jeans approached us and, to my utter amazement, sat on the taxi driver's lap. Looking the girl in the face, the Sicilian smiled rewardingly and then, to dispel any misunderstandings, said:

"Daughter."

Still, this was a wee bit too brave for the former Sicilians. The daughter asked for a drink, and her father poured her some whiskey, though very little. We drank together, then began smoking. I asked her what she did. Her Sicilian eyes flashing at me, she took off in good English, which I struggled to keep up with. I only understood that she was preparing to apply to graduate school to study political science and then, in the future, she wanted to run a revolution.

"In the United States?" I asked her, not very confident that I understood her. It turned out I understood her just fine.

"No," she said, "there's no proletariat there."

"In Italy?" I asked.

"No," she said, "Italy doesn't have a proletariat either."

"In Cuba, then?" I asked.

She smiled blindingly and tenderly touched the back of my head.

"Humor," she said.

"Then where are you going to do your revolution?"

"In South America," she explained, "but time is of the essence. I'm afraid that by the time I finish my studies, there won't be a proletariat left."

"There will be," I assured her, as if I were an elderly sociologist with a world of experience behind him.

Soon after, they turned on the movie, and the young woman went to her own seat. The movie was about two tireless cosmonauts. A very evil and ruthless Soviet cosmonaut and a very brave and kind American cosmonaut. When they met, sparks coursed through the universe. Their clash left small, comfortable planets in shambles.

Sometimes, in the heat of battle, they flew to our planet too. And if the kind cosmonaut let our cosmonaut out of his sight for a single minute, ours would let out a demonic laugh and manage to blow up some flowering village. But he would never be able to blow it up entirely, because the kind American cosmonaut would catch up to him, and after a short battle, he would cast him off into space.

The surviving villagers, who would watch, immobile, as the clash raged on, heartily applauded their cosmonaut savior. The villagers' applause was vigorously supported by the passengers on the plane. Watching their faces was rather entertaining. They were carefully following the narrative. They celebrated and grieved together with their beloved hero. I didn't see a single ironic smile. Everyone was having a ball.

Democracy gives people a lot, but unfortunately, it doesn't give them brains. Democracy gives people the opportunity to grow in any direction they wish, but for the most part, a free person prefers to grow in the direction of asininity, as that makes life easier. (Not a lot of brains—you don't have to strain. Brain's too small—no worries at all. There's the universal principle laid out by folk sayings).

When people on the whole eat better than us, live in better apartments, and make more than we do, then according to the organic logic of things, we feel like they should enjoy a higher quality of art. Naturally, their world has fine art too, but the vast majority opts for something else.

For us, bad art was called "ideology," but for them, bad art is called "the market," as if it were a popular good. However, I have to say, there has always been a difference in attitude towards human thought. Free thought, thought that freely evaluates the surrounding flow of life quite possibly won't be rewarded under a bureaucratic democracy, but it won't be persecuted either. In an ideological government, free thought is the enemy. It is always persecuted.

We had dinner after the movie. My neighbor fell asleep, and let's leave him be until we get to New York. I got out my self-help book and grinded English words for two more hours. When you're in a plane, time clearly drags out. In a train or car, time isn't what it is in a plane. Evidently, the greater speeds of airplanes are harmful to our nature, and by stretching out our sense of time, it creates for itself the illusion of more time passing as we travel long distances.

By the way, I noticed a long time ago that the more dynamic and goal-oriented our lifestyle, the more relative our moral adequacy becomes. The more quickly someone walks down the street, the more reluctant he is to offer someone a light. It would be a scene right out of a Chaplin movie if we suddenly asked for a light from someone with a cigarette in their mouth, zooming down the street in an open car. They would be indignant, maybe even hitting the brakes a bit to express their indignation.

The velocity of one's approach to their goal becomes an argument for the goal's validity. Imagine the following scene. A group of people is sitting together and drinking, having a good time. Let's assume our Russian circumstances. As is known, our people don't drink until a certain condition is met—they drink as long as there is something to drink. But the vodka ends, and the people still want to drink. When possible, the host is obliged to go and get more.

Let's imagine that the host is having some doubts: *Should I go get more? Won't it be too much?* If he walks to the wine store, then these doubts continue to bother him. Additionally, if he is worried that the store might close at any moment, he hastens his step, and his doubts weaken. But if he gets into his car to go get some vodka, then his doubts evaporate entirely. His velocity as he approaches his goal becomes the main argument for the goal's validity.

A person can, of course, speed up his life, but up to a certain point. A person's speed can be considered normal so long as other people's features don't become blurred, so long as we can make out individual people and say about them: *this* one.

At life speeds that are too great, a person has no time to be a person. Then why the speed? Doesn't therein lie the secret of why individuals or societies that are overly goal-oriented degenerate? Nature takes revenge on speedsters who ignore the organic rhythms of life.

The fanatic's true fault isn't that he squashed or discarded another human while living life at great speeds. That's more his misfortune, because he really no longer saw the other person and couldn't stop. His true fault is that he opted for the speed in the first place.

If he were a morally adequate person, he would have instantly disliked the speed at which he chose to pursue his goals as soon as he stopped being able to discern individual people's faces. And he would have become disillusioned with his goal: there's no good mechanism for achieving it.

The fanatic's crime is that his need for anthropological warmth was too lessened, his need to feel another living soul's touch. This is what allowed him to green-light his pursuing of the goal. Love has a many-branching nature.

This is all highly relevant to art. Regardless of the world's speed and direction, art, like a good doctor or priest, shouldn't rush. This is why I dislike the "innovative," fringe baboonery that people claim is trying to keep up with the spirit of the century. They lose sight of what is most important.

And, as I think, the most important thing in art, regardless of what art itself says, is the details of the Unwillingness to Part. And the more significant what art is recounting is, the more acutely hidden within this eternal passion of a loving soul is the Unwillingness to Part. The significance of the content itself is a result, it is the mysterious eloquence of the Unwillingness to Part. When we read a good book, we feel this, we feel it as stylistic charisma, feeling it even though we don't immediately understand what this Unwillingness to Part has to do with us. *Hey, we're not so bad ourselves*, we think gratefully, *since the author isn't in a rush to part with us.* And it's true—we're not so bad.

. . . New York. The plane lands. The passengers applaud the pilots or their own successful landing, but, I noticed, they did so rather wanly. When we landed in Italy from Moscow, there was an eruption of applause the likes of which I'd never heard. I decided then that it must be the result of Italian joie de vivre.

But here, those same Italians, after a much longer flight, applaud only halfheartedly. Must that mean that they were more excited to arrive in their home country? Or maybe our flight was too long, and they didn't have enough strength for gratitude?

The conditions for success in life, alas, resemble the conditions for the success of a performance in a variety show: it has to be short and expressive. If you want applause, you had best speed things up. You should speed up even heroic struggles, even kind deeds, even the writing of a good book. Especially the latter. But if you truly do not thirst for applause, then you can take your time with heroic struggles and kind deeds and the writing of an excellent book.

I said goodbye to my Sicilian American and his lovely daughter in the hope—no, not hope—fully confident that on her path to revolution, she would be waylaid by an impassioned admirer, by which point maybe even the South American proletariat would dissolve.

"Are you carrying more than five thousand dollars?" the customs officer asked me.

"Not a cent," I replied, trying to delight him with the utter impossibility of sabotaging American business. But he remained unfazed.

It was true, I had no money. Though I did still have some quantity of Italian liras. At the baggage pick-up, I caught my suitcase, which was crawling along the conveyor belt. Or to be more exact, I interrupted its awkward attempt to hide from me. I think I understood its feeling as the feeling that arose in any Soviet citizen who found himself in a bourgeois world. It's the same feeling that would arise in a decrepit boa constrictor that was being forced to swallow a small water buffalo instead of a hare. And would ultimately have the buffalo forced inside.

After retrieving my suitcase, I joined the crowd flowing towards the exit and found myself in a strange hall where I saw many people adorned with posters. At first, I thought that it was a political demonstration, but after reading a few of the posters, I realized that on them were emblazoned the names of people who were being met there. I feverishly began reading the posters, searching for my name, but I didn't find it. And clearly nobody was intent on recognizing me, even though as I was gazing at the people I was passing by, I was radiating a powerful and even imposing desire to be recognized. But my yearning went unanswered. Or rather, one person perked up momentarily when he met my provocative gaze, but he quickly came to and for a long time, didn't forgive me his lapse in judgment. What to do?

Worried, I lit up and smoked the whole cigarette in a few deep breaths. I noticed something that seemed like a cylindrical trash can and wanted to throw the butt away, but suddenly, someone gripped my arm. The person had an expression of horror on his face, as if the trash might explode.

"But then where?" I asked despairingly in Russian.

He threw an expressive glance at the floor and stamped into dust the imaginary cigarette butt. Only then did I notice that the floor was littered with cigarette butts. I thanked him and capitalized on his advice, amazed at the simplicity of local norms.

About an hour passed, but nobody picked me up. During that time, a soft-spoken black man came up to me and asked if I had any money. I said that I had liras, but no dollars. He nodded and disappeared in the crowd.

What to do? I got out a notebook with the address and phone number of the place I was supposed to get to. I looked for my glasses but couldn't find them. I upended everything—still no glasses. I must have put them in the seat pocket when I closed the self-help book and left them there. Now I couldn't even read the address. Then again, what good would that do when I don't even have any money to make a phone call?

I'm listing all of my difficulties to justify the feeling of despair that washed over me: I was half-mute because I didn't know the language, half-blind because I lost my glasses, and entirely destitute because I had no dollars.

What to do? I had to look for help among the Americans waiting to pick people up. I threw a predatory gaze over the meet-and-greeters, trying to pick out someone who seemed appropriately kind-hearted. My gaze stopped on a tall, youthful American with what I perceived to be a kind face. I approached him and held out the paper with the address, looking like I was an illiterate, fresh from backwoods country.

"I broke my glasses on the plane," I said helplessly. "Make call."

Why did I say that I broke my glasses on the plane when I left them there? Only now do I realize that it was a subconscious nod at the difficulty of my situation. Evidently, I was implying that I lived through a small catastrophe that resulted in my glasses being broken and, as would become clear, all of my money being lost. He took the paper with the phone number and went to the phone booth. I lugged my suitcase after him. He approached the phone and turned to look at me, or rather at my hand, to take a coin for the machine. Your attention please! This was the most important part.

"I have not money," I said, a note of class-based umbrage entering my voice as I nodded off somewhere into space, either at wherever my catastrophe took place or at Wall Street.

He paused for a second, then nodded.

"Okay!"

He took out a coin from his wallet, inserted it into the slot, dialed the number, and handed me the receiver like a victory trophy.

A woman's voice answered. I leapt at the sound of a friendly voice. Feverish declarations of love on both sides. This is followed by a tale of incessant calls to Moscow and Palermo, persistent, though unsuccessful attempts to find out where I was—in the air, on the ground, or in the ocean. With greater and greater vitality, my voice responded to her, yearning for face-to-face communication. Aside from the woman's voice, sounds of glasses clinking and people having a good time were bubbling through the phone.

"Stay put, a young woman who speaks Russian will come get you!"

So said the voice in distinctly clear Russian. I hung up, and the room instantly lit up with the light of hope and cheer. My savior was demurely retreating. I didn't even get the chance to thank him. I wanted to chase him down, grab him by the arm, and let him drag me along, like in childhood.

Then, the black man to whom I hazily explained my situation came up to me. Turns out he found a currency exchange and was suggesting that I go there. Although after my phone conversation, I could make do without dollars, I was in such a leavened state that I felt that I had to exchange my liras and reward the kind man for his troubles.

I cheerfully tugged my suitcase after him. But the crowd of people receded farther and farther, and we were left in some dark hallway without a single living soul, and the man's intentions began to seem malicious. He, meanwhile, was speeding up in order to lure me farther. And every now and then, he would raise his hand, obviously pretending to look at his watch. Intrigue and love![54]

---

54 *Intrigue and Love* is a play by Friedrich Schiller.

I decided to put a high price on my life and maybe even my dignity as a Russian writer. I decided not to retreat, but instead come up with a plan of active defense, and I did. In case he reached for a knife or some gas pistol, I would fling up my suitcase, catch it with both hands, and bring it crashing down on the scoundrel's head. To make it especially unexpected (he sometimes looked behind at me), I pretended that I was barely dragging it along. Even though my suitcase wasn't very heavy, my heart was pumping so hard that it felt light as a feather.

Suddenly, my guide stopped, nodded at the wall, and said dejectedly: "We're too late."

I took a few steps and saw the closed window of the exchange counter. I realized that the poor guy was simply unlucky, like me. We headed back. The suitcase instantly grew heavier. Through the ruckus of the approaching crowd, I thought that I heard my last name over loudspeaker. Audio hallucinations? Delusions of grandeur? No! No! It wasn't a mistake! America knows about me!

Forgetting entirely about my companion, I rushed towards the crowd. I don't know how much time passed. Everything flew out of my head. Suddenly, a girl separated from the crowd and yelled:

"Where were you? I was calling for you over the loudspeaker!"

I mumbled something as the sad black man who had finally caught up for some reason stood next to me and waited for something. The girl got out a five-dollar (as I found out later) bill and handed it to him. She led me out of the hall, but the man was mysteriously still with us, and his eyes were frozen in an expression of millennia-old sorrow.

We got into a car, but he was still with us, now standing next to the car and waiting for something. But what? Maybe he figured that I should give him my liras, which I wouldn't need now anyway?

"What does he want?" I asked the girl.

"He's an underground taxi driver," she said, and we set off.

The nighttime New York was flitting by through the window. The young girl was trying to bring to my attention various important buildings, but I was always apathetic to that. Though later, when I saw the charming American suburbs and small towns, I fell in love forever. That's where the hearth is, where the lifeblood of the nation is!

"You speak excellent Russian," I told the girl gratefully in order to mitigate by apathy towards the skyscrapers. For an American, she spoke Russian very well. A light accent only enriched her speech.

"That's because I'm Russian," she smiled.

The car stopped outside some house. We got out and went inside. The elevator took us up. One doorbell later, and we found ourselves in an enormous room. Tiny little tables stood in different corners of the room. Our writers were sitting at some of them, some of whom I knew not even by their speeches, but by their books. Loud voices and bouts of laughter bore testament that the mood was on the upswing. They sat me down at a table that was already populated by two men and a woman.

The girl disappeared somewhere and was replaced by a lean woman with the face of a mildly aging schoolgirl, and she handed me a large plate full of potato slabs and an enormous chunk of meat that lay there proudly like a turtle—a respectable reward for my struggles. *Can one person really eat all that?* I picked up my fork and knife and began the experiment.

Suddenly, one of the men sitting at my table, whose large size I thought made him an American, reached out, picked up a smoking cut of potato from my plate, and sent it into his cavernous mouth. I understood that he was one of us. It was a sign of brotherhood.

The juicy meat, washed down with gin and tonic, went down easy, and I suddenly realized that I could quite handily manage the gargantuan portions. The conversation gradually took on an all-inclusive character that involved all the tables at once. It was about the future of the Perestroika. The Americans were demonstrating careful and not-so-careful disbelief and perceived our fairly critical optimism as an attempt to outfox them with a new wave of propaganda. But there was no propaganda—it truly was our last hope.

US. Look at how many blacklisted books have been published.

THEM. So what. They gave back to the people what they stole from the people.

US. Different people did the stealing than are doing the returning.

THEM. Democracy is pluralism. Where's your pluralism?

US. One thing at a time. We'll get pluralism.

THEM. Your Glasnost isn't supported by a law on free press and property. Freedom like that can be stamped out overnight.

US. They're writing laws like that.

THEM. The apparatus won't let it happen. You'll be deceived.

The Americans' distrust had more than a leg to stand on, but it was unpleasant all the same. It was a little like if people living in comfortable apartments observed through the windows of a prison a group of inmates, armed only with toilet seats, trying to break the bars in the windows. And meanwhile, the people in the comfortable apartments wave their arms and say: "Nothing will come of this! You might as well stop trying!"

A few times, the unpleasantness and the alcohol in my veins made me want to get up, politely pay for the food, and leave to go who knows where. But then I remembered that I didn't have any dollars yet, and it would have been somewhat awkward to drag the neutral Italian liras into the conflict. Shutting down the noble impulse, I furiously lay into the food and drink: if I was going down, then I'd do it on an irreversibly full stomach! The meat was wondrously tender, and what had seemed like an enormous turtle soon turned into a small tadpole that, admittedly, I had no intention of sparing.

The American woman sitting next to me reached out with her glass, we clinked and drank. Then she asked me:

"How do you feel about the feminist movement?"

I glanced at my enormous tablemate. I had ascertained by this point that he spoke Russian and English equally well. He nodded, meaning, "Go ahead, I'll translate."

"We have a completely different problem," I said. "If I had my way, I'd send all the working women home to their kids. But, unfortunately, we're not able to do that. Poverty."

As the translation went on, the woman's expression grew icy. She stopped clinking glasses with me or even looking in my direction. Turns out you're not supposed to talk to a feminist there in a joking tone. But I didn't know that yet. Their small ideology, as any ideology, doesn't tolerate humor.

The offended woman didn't bother me for long. They kept serving gin and tonic. Many of western civilization's sins can be forgiven for the creation of that wondrous drink. I said many, but not all. Don't put words in my mouth.

Suddenly, a cry went up from several tables:

"Jazz! Jazz! Jazz!"

Some people jumped up. Everyone decided to go listen to jazz somewhere. Back in the good old days in Russia, after dinner, the scene would often look quite similar, when, after much libation and political discussions, someone would say: "Let's go to the gypsies!" and everyone went.

Together with the hosts, we flocked outside, got into our cars, and set out. At moments like that, you always have the impression that this one thing is that only thing that's missing.

We arrived at some club, took our seats, and were soon listening to jazz. It was loud. It was very loud. It was extraordinarily loud. Which made it all the more surprising that when I turned to my neighbor to ask him something relatively quietly (considering the loudness), everyone threw me dirty looks as if I had begun to speak loudly at a Bach concert. How they heard me over the ruckus to this day remains a mystery.

In the morning, I woke up in an American hotel room and was immediately surprised at the clarity in my head. That's what you call a clean drink! I spent a long time reveling in the clarity, and only much later did I realize that I was exaggerating said clarity, as it was an imperfect clarity.

I jumped out of bed and went to wash up. Splashing water on my face, I felt my bare feet getting wet. My faith in American technology was so great that as I kept washing up, I interpreted the feeling of wet feet as something hangover-related, a consequence of the new drink, and I somewhat lowered my assessment of gin and tonic.

However, after I leisurely freshened up, once I began drying myself, I suddenly noticed that the bathroom was filled with water and that my bare feet really were getting wet. I turned on the faucet and crouched to get a better view under the sink: the pipe was leaking. Just like back home! Oh, dear America, you should display more little weaknesses—you'll seem more familiar to us!

But my joy didn't last long. I turned off the faucet and recalled a few choice horror-inspiring scenes associated with my own bathroom. Clogs, leaks like this one, personal carelessness.

With that running through my mind, I quickly got dressed, got my room key, and went out without locking my room (utter lack of faith in technology) in search of housekeeping. I soon found a maid. She was a stout, elderly black lady. Letting her see what happened in my bathroom, I jabbed my finger at the floor, pointing in the direction of the administrator who was sitting on the first floor:

"Call. Repair!"

"You call him!" she jabbed her finger at me.

"No, you call!" I jabbed my finger at her.

We kept jabbing our fingers at one another for a while, until she finally left. I figured that I had verbally out-sparred her and that she left to personally fetch a plumber. Soon, she came back, but instead of a plumber, she brought a South American maid who started raining Spanish down on me before she even entered my room. Evidently, the first maid thought that I was Hispanic and that that was the only reason we couldn't find common ground. I didn't understand the newcomer at all, so I steered the conversation back to the more appropriate English waters.

"Call down. Repair!" I said in English.

"You call!" she responded furiously in English, and resentfully added something in Spanish, clearly offended on national grounds that I didn't want to speak Spanish with her.

We bickered like that for a while, when I heard a knock on the door and an old acquaintance of mine—a famous Odesan writer—walked into the room. He and I once worked together in *Nedelya*,[55] expanding its circulation. He lives in New York now. When he heard that a delegation of Soviet writers had arrived, he decided to come see me. We hugged, and I explained to him my insignificant, bathroom-related woes. He instantly appraised the situation, puffed out his lower lip in a typical American manner, and said a few curt and precise words. Both maids diffidently quieted down.

"They'll take care of it," he said and led me downstairs.

"How did you get so good at speaking English?" I asked.

"If you spent fourteen hours a day practicing, you'd be no worse at it," he replied simply.

Oh, the mighty, inspired stubbornness of the sons of Israel! When will we learn from them? Or when will they teach us? After all, we taught them how to drink.

Turns out, ten years ago, besieged on all sides in his native Odesa, he tore off to America. He was incredibly poor here, but stubbornly kept writing. And he was finally recognized for it. It took ten years. But his recognition was significant. He currently had several contracts going for several books.

He ordered me a pair of glasses in the closest pharmacy, then took me for lunch to a Chinese restaurant, where we talked about everything like fellow children of the Black Sea. We're unlikely to ever have another.

It was after lunch when I was in the pharmacy trying out the new glasses—which were giving America a whole new clarity—that I said:

"It's a shame that we already had lunch in the Chinese restaurant. In these glasses, I would've been able to make out all the particularities of the elaborate Chinese dishes."

"Are you implying that we should get dinner in a Chinese restaurant too?" he asked.

"Your words," I joked, hinting at his Odesan woes, which started when he audaciously (as it was seen at the time) began exploring the Bible.

---

55 *Nedelya* (literally, "week") was a weekly periodical that began to be published in 1960.

"No problem," he agreed. We got into his car, and he took to showing me around New York. From time to time, he carpet-bombed the poor or careless other drivers with progressively worsening Russian curse words.

His American short stories were written with similar youthful ruthlessness. In them, everybody got some—from rigid bureaucrats to Jewish fat cats who were stingy with money and generous with advice. I never read them, this is just how he writes about them.

I'll tell about my further stay in America some other time. You—wait, and try to create the proper, calm conditions for it, and remember that the words about the Unwillingness to Part hold true.

. . . I typed out the last sentence on my typewriter and tried to light a cigarette, but it turns out my lighter is out of fuel. I had just enough to finish this story, so that I wouldn't have to run to the kitchen when I took my breaks. I got lucky. My mood has been restored. I can smoke up in the kitchen too.

Taking a leaf from the books of those mysterious fat cats, I'll give some advice. If you're in a bad mood, come up with a job for yourself and do it. Even if you have to write a short story or go fishing, like that waiter whom I wrongly derided. That's what's most important.

I went into the kitchen and lit my cigarette on the gas stove like I would with a brand from a Chegem hearth. The "Persian Song" performed by Shaliapin was on the radio. That was a balm for my soul.

I remembered my grandfather's house, and I remembered how Uncle Kazym used to light up with the help of the hearth. Sometimes, he would shove his cigarette right into the hearth, but more often, he would take out a fiery brand, straighten—he was tall, handsome, brooding—puff the fire into the cigarette, and carelessly toss the brand back into the flaring, sparking fire in the hearth.

And this gesture belied either the calm precision of a farmer sowing or the sudden, tired derision of everything that undercut the farm, the house, and all of its inhabitants. Meanwhile, Shaliapin is singing the "Persian Song." And it seems like everyone is alive, because everyone lived, yelled, laughed, cried around that hearth . . . Oh, if only that lasted forever . . . And why not, why not?

8

The Old Men's Bender on the Sea

While I was succumbing to my memories, the people in line for ice cream finally dispersed. Either all the vacationers were finally sated, or else a rejoicing rumor had made its rounds, spreading word that the ice cream stores weren't inexhaustible; indeed, they would be reinforced by snow from Elbrus that had to be processed in American machines, having been previously powdered with Argentinean sugar from helicopters—sugar that had previously been dissolved in milk from Holland. The Kremlin once again shamefully ignored Fidel Castro's protests with regard to Argentinean sugar. Amidst all the other fantastic rumors, this one could have felt right at home.

The furor over the ice cream ended. But then the Amra got a delivery of Zhigulevskoye beer. Bottles of beer began popping up in front of the patrons. Another line formed up, though oddly, it wasn't as long as it was for ice cream.

These were also strangers who had heard that beer was sold here. Many of them were bathers who were sunbathing on the footwalks of the wharf's first tier. They had to get dressed in order to enter the restaurant. You couldn't enter in nothing but a bathing suit.

But some bathers—and this was part of our secret relationship with the government—still only in bathing suits, crowded around the restaurant entrance, obstinately searching for a familiar face within the restaurant (dressed, of course) to hand them some beer money. Then, still at the entrance, without crossing over the invisible line (citizens playing games with the law in response to the law playing games with the citizens), they receive their perfectly legitimate bottles of beer, but this was after they outfoxed the law, making their victory all the sweeter. Furthermore, standing in line almost in the nude, without interrupting the sunbathing process, is a rare pleasure for our people.

"No clothes, no service, you parasites!" every now and then the waitress serving the closest tables would yell. She yelled without looking, confident that the undressed were standing and waiting.

But there was no absolute in this case either. She would suddenly accept everybody's money and come back with a tray of beers. This was most often because she saw somebody in the crowd that she knew, and then she was forced to serve everyone else too.

"No clothes, no service! Last time, you parasites!" she shouted, handing out bottles and looking out past the crowd's front line to check how many were lining the lower steps of the stairs.

But sometimes, even if she didn't recognize anyone, her will broken by the meek patience of the crowd, she furiously grabbed everyone's money, brought out the beer, and forcefully handed out the bottles to the eager, outstretched hands.

It's like when a drunk person, fully intent on hitting you, suddenly changes his mind at the last second and kisses you instead, imbuing the kiss with the baleful energy of the aborted punch.

A large, stocky German was sitting near the entrance with two women. Probably his wife and a translator. The table had on it cups of coffee, glasses, and a bottle of champagne. The German was smoking a pipe and observing the restaurant. His large body was clothed in a fresh button-up shirt, and glasses with a golden frame sparkled on his nose.

An elderly bather in satin swimming briefs, with the small, grey-haired head of a boy who had suddenly grown old, was standing at the entrance, when a thought came to his head. He quickly approached the German's table, leaned in close, and said:

"Brother, order some beer, and I'll get it from you. But don't tell her who you're ordering for!"

He then held out some money, but when the German turned around as soon as he heard the new voice, he fixed his gaze on his close face and didn't notice the offered money.

"Aye-*ja, ja*," replied the German with good-natured curiosity, looking at the close face of the bather with the grey-haired, boyish head.

"No, not you, me!" the bather explained nervously. He threw a furtive glance deep into the restaurant, worried that the waitress serving the nearby tables might notice. She had just left with her orders towards the buffet.

"You'll order the beer, then I'll take it," he repeated, pronouncing each separate word distinctly.

"Aye-*ja*," repeated the German even more distinctly, examining the man's close face with growing curiosity, as if surprised that it wasn't yet showing signs of realized brotherhood.

"No, not you, me!" repeated the bather, his eyes darting back to the depths of the restaurant. "Here, take the money, order some beer, then I take it!"

"Aye-*ja*," said the German again without moving, examining the bather's face with even greater curiosity, still not noticing the money and becoming more and more amazed that the face wasn't expressing a sliver of brotherly understanding.

The translator reached her hand towards the German as if to say something, but stopped herself. She must have gotten scared that the German would understand him, take the beer money, and then they would get in trouble with the management. Her fears were groundless, as it later turned out.

"Not you, me!" squealed the bather, losing all semblance of patience.

The German, again immediately catching on to the heightened intonation, instantly raised his own voice.

"Gorbi vivat!" he said furiously, playing his last trump card of brotherhood.

Something finally clicked in the bather's head, and he waved the money right under the German's nose. At the same time, the translator leaned in and said something. He heard her out without shifting his gaze, as if certain that the bather wasn't someone he could let out of his sight for a single moment.

"*Bier?*" he asked in surprise, continuing to gaze into the bather's close face with fearless curiosity, like the people who stare through an aquarium's walls at an exotic, deep-sea fish. Especially if the fish suddenly spoke in a human voice, asking for beer.

"Yes, yes, *bier!*" nodded the bather vigorously, recognizing the word and feeling himself becoming understood. "We say beer! *Bier!*"

"*Verboten!*" said the German loudly and strictly. And even though he finally shifted, it seemed like he shouted it out not only for the bather, but for the whole country. Which, actually, might not have been such a bad idea.

He continued gazing into the man's face with ever-growing curiosity and fearlessness, maybe even with readiness, maybe even with desire for the aquarium glass to finally shatter, assuming that it would help the people of this country understand the meaning of the great word *verboten*.

The man couldn't handle such fearlessness any longer and abruptly moved back to his previous position. This greatly pleased the German. He allowed himself to turn his great head slightly and look at the man with an expression of primal (or maybe even greater) magnanimity.

Catching his gaze, he livened up, began radiating benevolence, and even began gesturing with his hands that the situation was very simple: all he had to do was dress himself and enter. As soon as you understand what's forbidden, you'll instantly understand what's permitted.

"We won the war, but *they* get to relax on *our* territory," grumbled the man loudly.

"Sure thing," eagerly agreed another, who had observed the man's interaction with the German with some degree of envy. "There is no justice."

The German benevolently exchanged a few whispered words with his wife and translator, took a gulp of champagne, lit his pipe, puffed on it a few times, and suddenly stared forward, furrowing his brow in concentration, as if searching for a second word that he had to say to this country in order to definitively put everything in its rightful place. But the second word was proving rather elusive, and the German's mood clearly dampened.

... Which can't be said about the old men celebrating to my right. The noise emanating from their table had grown out of control. There were eight of them. They had arrived two hours back. The younger ones carried bags with food and wine. Restaurant staff brought out a table and put it together with another table beneath one of the tents.

The old men took their seats. Looked like on top of plates and water they also brought fried chickens, walnut satsivi, greens, cheese. They even brought flour for mămăligă.[56] None of that was offered in the restaurant, and where it *was* offered, the price was astronomic. The old men, probably out of respect for their age, were allowed to come with their own food. I didn't manage to find out what was the reason for the festivities, as I missed the first few toasts, and once I did turn my attention to them, they themselves evidently forgot why they had gathered there.

Facing me beneath the tent were two of the most colorful old men: Timur Aslanovich and Mikhail Arkadievich.

Timur Aslanovich had been a famous romantic actor at the local theater. Now he was a thickset old man with a mane that was yellowing from old age, or rather, "lioning." There was a time when he played a brilliant Othello!

---

56 A southeastern European dish, analogous to polenta.

When he flew onto the stage, letting lose the fire within, wreathed in the flame of his cloak, the audience applauded ceaselessly! Why? Passion. He played passion.

In those times, exposing the people to art, the theater often brought in audience members from the villages. They say that when one shepherd—no less passionate than our Othello—saw the scene where Othello chokes Desdemona, possibly even believing that it was an attempt at rape, he whipped out his dagger and raced onto the stage. Disaster was narrowly averted.

Out of the most humane of motivations, the Party regional committee forbade performing that scene, but during the summer season, when the troupe toured the villages and gave in to its dissident spirit, the actors performed it anyway. Admittedly, when the play neared the tragic scene, the kolkhoz chairmen who sat in the front rows typically stood up and looked over the audience in order to head off any impressionable spectators who may have confused art with life.

Furthermore, in accordance with their own peaceful temperaments, some of them made calming, conductor-like gestures: *piano, piano.*

More often, though, in accordance with the more wide-spread temperament of the chairmen, they raised a fist to the audience to let them know that they should relax. Thanks to their vigilance, flares of mindless sympathy for Desdemona were prevented outright, and the troupe continued its dissident activity in the villages.

After Stalin's death and Beria's arrest, the temporarily weakened regional committee was forced to allow the scene even in the city, though they ordered the firemen present at the performances to be more vigilant.

That's the actor that Timur Aslanovich once was. But now, old age. Long walks on the beach. Coffee. The rare bender. The dormant volcano rumbles quietly at the table. But I don't recommend sneaking a peak into the crater—it might singe.

Mikhail Arkadievich was a tall, straight-backed old man. A small, ruffle-haired head on a long neck. The rolled-up sleeves of his bright button-up shirt revealed the powerful arms of a worker, even though *he* was actually descended from aristocrats.

Some ten years ago, he and I were fishing in the sea. He was filling the expanse of the bay with a mighty rendition of the brigand song "Ataman Kudeyar." I can't say that the dolphins were crowding around our boat to listen, but some passers-by on the beach did stop and look out at the sea.

That day, he out-fished me in the sea and out-drank me on the beach. True, I did out-eat him (fresh striped mullet, a treat), but that's little consolation. When our discussion touched on literature, he said suddenly that, while in the Lubyanka, he read Aragon's novel, *The Communists*, and liked it. We won't get into Aragon's novel, but let's agree that the situation seems pretty spectacular—to relish *The Communists* while locked away in a communist prison.

"I knew them during the French Resistance," he said in response to my bewilderment. "They were exactly how he described them."

He's about a hundred now, but—knock on wood!—he's still in fantastic health. The fate of the surviving Russian aristocrats has something in common with the fate of African-Americans. Both went through a grueling survival process, and only the strongest survived.

But the holds of the ships that were transporting inmates to Magadan were scarier than the holds of the schooners bringing the Africans to America. And the crackling flame of the frost in the Siberian mines burned more truly than the southern sun of America's plantations. And even though the strongest among the aristocrats survived, too few of them were left. And it's a bitter thought that the Russian aristocracy, which spent half a century leading its people to the crest of global culture, will never again be capable of creating Pushkin or Lev Tolstoy.

Mikhail Arkadievich was nicknamed "White Bandit." That's what an investigator called him once. His father was in the entourage of Prince Alexander Petrovich Oldenburg. They lived beneath Gagra in their own lands.

During the civil war, he left the Moscow Conservatory before finishing his studies, joined with Kolchak,[57] and experienced the long odyssey of immigration. After the war, drunk with the glory of his homeland's weaponry, he asked to be let in back to his native country, but then, like other, similar enthusiasts, he was arrested and sent to Magadan.

After the Twentieth Congress he returned to Abkhazia from exile. Now he lives in a small town not far from Mukhus. Until recently, he was an auto mechanic and made a decent wage. It was so decent that he bought a horse

---

57 Alexander Kolchak (1874–1920) was a Russian admiral who, in the civil war (1917–1922), led an anti-communist government in Siberia.

and a miraculously preserved phaeton. He gives rides to kids and relishes his own childhood memories.

At the turn of the century, while zooming along in the first car of the Black Seaboard, he brought universal attention to himself. And now, at the end of the century, to general surprise, driving around on some unearthed phaeton, he is first once again!

Also present was a famous local soccer player from the end of the thirties and beginning of the forties. What can be said when you suddenly see your favorite childhood striker as a desiccated old man, drinking coffee or fiddling with beads? Nothing should be said. Especially since it's not coffee that he drinks these days. A few more words about another old man. He spent his whole life as a director—the director of the printing office, the music school, the tobacco factory, the agriculture expo, the bookstore. Forever a director. We were introduced to one another many times, but I could never commit his name to memory. I forgot his name before it was even said aloud. So let's just call him the Glittering Party Worker.

What's most entertaining is that I knew him since childhood, and he seemed like a completely different person then. His entire life narrative passed before my eyes. Such careful attention is possible only in childhood and only in small towns, where you see everything, but no one sees you because you're small and nobody takes you seriously.

He was walking along our street with his young wife. They must have lived somewhere nearby—I often saw a similar scene unfold. So they're walking along our block. It looks like they're arguing about something.

And suddenly, she tears off forward! Her heels click-clock along the road as she zooms by me, and I see her face red from loathing and fury. But he just keeps walking, without increasing his speed, maintaining masculine restraint. But I see his dried-out face contorted in pain, and I pity him. Where are they going? If they're going over someone's house, then they can't arrive separately, can they? Maybe they're going to the movies? But then who has the tickets? Or do they divide their tickets as soon as they start arguing, knowing full well how the argument will end? Or do they do that at home, knowing full well that they'll begin arguing on their way?

I'm astonished at the indefatigability of her fury and feel that the engine for it is inside of her, and the guy is just an excuse for it. I already know that she's a bitch, but I don't know that that's what it's called.

Then she disappears, and he takes to walking down the street on his own. And then one day another woman starts accompanying him, and they happily walk down the street together, and she never takes off anywhere. The funniest part is that she looks a lot like the previous one. Back then, I thought that he had mistook one for the other and then made his way to this one.

They strolled together so amicably that soon, a little boy started strolling with them. And then another kid, and a third.

But after the third kid, he began to assertively walk a little ahead of them, while she walked with the kids a bit farther behind. Sometimes, he held the smallest one in his arms, but still marching triumphantly ahead of the others. Sometimes he led the oldest one by the hand, but still ahead of everyone, though, of course, not even remotely trying to run away from them or to leave them behind.

Then they disappeared. They must have gotten a better apartment. And then, many years later, I would meet with him as the director of a great many things, but I had long ago grasped his true life, which he, of course, never suspected. He could never arouse my interest in his phantom life as a chess piece that some mysterious hand would intermittently move on the board, never asking its consent, but never sacrificing it, creating newer and newer, unforeseen combinations. And possibly in remembrance of this man's old, true life, I could never remember his name as a director in this life.

. . . When I turned my attention to the old men, they were all worked up.

"Sveta from Odesa, you say?" exclaimed an old man who was hard of hearing. He was sitting with his back to me, and he was cupping his right ear with his hand.

"A fresh new paper, you Old Coot!" boomed Aslanych. "Your Sveta from Odesa went bye-bye to Odesa fifty years ago! And you're still droning on about her!"

"I misheard," said the old man with touching meekness.

"Let me tell you a story," boomed Aslanych again." I had a relative in Achandary. Grew wine his whole life. He was renowned everywhere in Abkhazia. So after the war, when Stalin was vacationing here, General Vlasik—the head of Stalin's personal guard—comes to visit my relative. Stalin had heard about the famous winemaker. And so, Vlasik puts in an order for wine for the Boss. Six percent strong, though I don't remember the sugar content. I remember it was high.

"'Can you do it?'

"'I can.'

"'Round up a barrel of wine. I'll come for it in two weeks.'

"And he leaves. My poor relative loses his mind. There's no way to do this naturally in two weeks. But he gave his word. It's too late to confess: Vlasik has gone. And he risks it. What will be will be!

"He dumped a bunch of sugar into the wine and artificially achieved what they wanted. Vlasik arrives, takes the wine, leaves. My relative has no idea what'll happen: will they arrest him or won't they?

"And suddenly, Vlasik returns. My relative is scared to death. But Vlasik says, 'Comrade Stalin liked the wine. Prepare the same wine for next year.'

"Well, now he has time, and my relative makes the wine that they wanted, but naturally, without sugar.

"Vlasik arrives, takes the barrel of wine, and leaves. Meanwhile, Stalin is vacationing in Abkhazia. A week later, Vlasik comes back to pick up another barrel of wine. He's in a good mood.

"He agrees to have lunch. They sit, eat, drink.

"'How did Comrade Stalin like my wine?' asks my relative.

"'Good wine,' Vlasik says. 'But Comrade Stalin liked the one you made the first time more.'

"'What can be done?' sighs my relative. 'We can't control everything. The weather has its say too.'

"Vlasik leaves happy. We all knew that he came for wine. But what my relative did the first time, he told us only after the Twentieth Congress."

"'You weren't afraid of tricking the Big Mustache?' I ask him.

"And he just laughs.

"'What was I supposed to do?' he says. 'I decided to risk it. I figured since they don't understand anything about agriculture, they won't know anything about wine either. Turned out to be true!'"

"Ho! Ho! Ho! Ho!" the old men began ho-ing, amazed at the Achandarsky winemaker's daring.

"Listen, Mikhail Arkadievich," the old actor buzzed in his direction, "you met with the Prince of Oldenburg, the one that ruled in Gagra. You could say you grew up at his feet. Did he know wine well?"

"Brilliantly, brilliantly," boomed Mikhail Arkadievich. "He knew everything well."

"Tell us more about him. Especially since not everyone here knows you."

"I saw Alexander Petrovich close, like I see you now," he began, pushing away a plate with walnut sauce and chicken leg, clearly believing them to be inappropriate witnesses for his impending tale. "My father had land close to Gagra. Horses at first, then a 'Laurin and Klement' automobile. That was a brand back then. When I was seventeen, I rode it on all of the roads along the Black Sea. What happened to my golden youth?

"The Oldenburg Prince organized the first ever auto race in the Caucasus. From Novorossiysk to Gagra. I remember it like it was yesterday—September 21, 1911, twenty-nine cars left Novorossiysk. The drivers, what drivers they were! Count Shakhovsky in a Mercedes! Baron Osten-Saken in an Opel! Meller in a Benz!"

"And all noblemen!" exclaimed the Old Coot.

"It's as if they knew that one day, they'd be Parisian taxi drivers," snidely put in the Glimmering Party Worker.

"Yes! Yes! Gentlemen!" enthusiastically wheezed on Mikhail Arkadievich. "It's a tragedy! But back then, in Gagra—military music. La-la-la-la! His Majesty the Prince of Oldenburg greets us with his train, which my father was in . . . Daddy, is that you smiling at me?! Forgive me, friends, forgive me . . ."

He got out a handkerchief, dabbed at his face and eyes, and put it in front of himself in case lyrical necessity struck again. He calmed down and continued his tale, now in a more stirring tone:

"You'll never guess who came in first! You think it was yours truly? First place went to the car being driven by the Lady Staroselskaya! Yes, there were indeed women in Russian settlements! I came in fifth, but that's not the point.

"The Prince of Oldenburg organized a dinner in the town skating rink in honor of the racers. The table could seat two hundred. That's what you call Russian expanse!

"Present at the dinner was the Black Sea governor, the vice president of the imperial, pan-Russian automobile society—Svechin . . . I don't remember his name or patronymic, God forgive me! There were representatives from the press, *Novoye vremya*.

"And the dinner itself! Cold sturgeon with Provençal sauce! Culotte de boeuf with Madeira sauce! Cold ham with Cumberland sauce! . . . Where's Cumberland sauce now?! What was wrong with Cumberland sauce? . . . Fruits, wines, music!"

"Now that's the life!" boomed the old actor. "And you're going on about Sveta from Odesa!"

"How old *are* you?!" furiously exclaimed the Old Coot, sensing that he would never catch up.

"Ninety-eight," responded Mikhail Arkadievich dignifiedly, as if taking pride in his extensive and faithful marriage with life. "But there's still powder in the keg. I set the goal for myself to outlive the Soviets, and I've almost succeeded. But, gentlemen, here's the most surprising thing, whether you believe it or not! When I became ninety, I suddenly felt that I was growing used to the Bolsheviks. You know, some of them are getting to be well-bred, and they've even begun respecting my own ancestry . . ."

"They gorge themselves better than we do! That's all the breeding they have!" the old actor flared up.

"True, true," agreed Mikhail Arkadievich after a moment's thought. "But now, it looks like the democrats are rearing their heads. I've almost gotten used to the Bolsheviks, but I've forgotten about the democrats. It's tough. They're shortening my life."

"If you aristocrats were so tough," yelled the Old Coot, "why did you give away power to the Bolsheviks?!"

"War, Rasputin, fate," wheezed Mikhail Arkadievich. "I was with Kolchak. But I didn't fire a single round . . . I was a musician. After the rout, we made for Harbin. From there, we made it to Japan. No money. No work. But I had my voice! I settled down in a restaurant. Once, I even sang before the Mikado. Afterwards, your Cheka—no, the NKVD—never forgave me for that. It's baffling how they even found out about it! But they did!"

"Ho! Ho! Ho! Ho!" ho'd the old men in delighted horror at the thought of the all-seeing eye.

"Did you really sing for the Mikado himself?" asked the Shimmering Party Worker, astounded that a person could still be alive after taking such a fall.

"I did, I did, I had to," said Mikhail Arkadievich, but at that moment, his voice was drowned out by a border copter that was flying right above us. He lifted his head, looked at it, and it became evident from his long, wrinkled neck that it had borne his light head for a very long time. "Interesting," he said after silence fell. "Who among you knows when the first airplane flew over Mukhus?"

He raised his head again and pointed at the sky. The old men followed his finger with their gazes, looked up at the sky, but didn't see anything and shook their heads in denial.

"1911 again! November 27! I remember it like it was yesterday! I seem to recall that that's the year the twentieth century began for real! The 'Blerio' airplane. A famous aviator of the time, Kuzminsky, got it into the air. He was, by the way, the son of the presiding senator and the nephew of Lev Nikolayevich Tolstoy, a renowned foe of the technological civilization.

"The plane flew up from the field where there is now a park in the front of the House of Government. Buffalo and horses would always graze there. They chased them off to the periphery, and Kuzminsky took flight. The plane gave an unpleasant shudder in midair, everyone gasped, but Kuzminsky straightened it out and flew towards the sea. He disappeared. We thought he wouldn't return.

"But no, he did. He started circling low, low over the field. One ring. Another. He leans out of the cabin and waves at us, yelling something. But we can't understand him. Finally, we make out: 'Get rid of the cattle!' Engines weren't as powerful back then as they are now, you could still make something out.

"This is when we noticed that while he was flying, the horses and buffalo came back to their usual grazing spot in the middle of the field. We chased them off again, and Kuzminsky landed successfully. Cue music, trumpets—we carried Kuzminsky on our hands. An unforgettable day!"

"By the way, Lenin," Mikhail Arkadievich abruptly changed direction, "proposed that Mamontov's cavalry be stopped and chased off with the help of planes."

"Slander," said the Shimmering Party Worker, morosely spreading his arms apart, as if knowing ahead of time where this was going. "There's all kind of slander about him now."

"When I was in the Lubyanka," explained Mikhail Arkadievich, as if naming a place renowned for being uniquely suitable for reading books in general and Lenin's books in particular, "I read many of Lenin's tomes. Very many! And in them, there was such a note."

"What tome? What page?" quietly asked the Shimmering Party Worker, as if tired from all the slander.

"I don't remember," replied Mikhail Arkadievich, "but I remember for sure that I read it."

"Who cares about your first airplane over Mukhus!" suddenly cried an old man sitting at the other end of the table. "I personally saw the great Einstein with my own eyes!"

"Einstein?!" cried out the old men. "Ho! Ho! Ho! Ho!"

By the way, the popularity of Einstein's name among the people is astounding. And this popularity began long before the atom bomb. Even semi-literate people know that there lived a great scientist with that name. I think that the imaginations of the simple folk were rocked by the mere title of his teachings—the Theory of Relativity. I think many people decided that with the help of science, Einstein proved that everything in the world is relative. And the things that seemed sinful are also relative. Life became a bit easier.

Without admitting it to each other, and probably not even spending too much thought on the idea in general, they all gratefully came to love Einstein. This, I think, is where his legendary popularity came from.

By the way, I have two dear friends, both theoretical physicists and great lovers of literature.

"Can you explain to me in broad terms the Theory of Relativity?" I once asked one of them. "Only keep in mind that I'm an absolute moron in this field."

He instantly put this in his mind and kept it there.

"Hasn't Misha explained it to you?" he sounded surprised. "You should ask him. I'm just a theoretician. But he's a theoretician and a brilliant teacher."

Alright, I think, *I won't admit to being a moron anymore.* The next time I was with Misha, I asked him to explain the Theory of Relativity.

"Hasn't Volodya explained it to you yet?" he sounded surprised, but once he realized the situation, he got out a piece of paper and a pencil.

"I'll explain it with the help of a school exercise," he began. He laid out the parameters of the exercise and then quickly sketched out the solution, as if preserving my mental stores for the Theory of Relativity. But I felt with horror that my stores were insufficient not only for the Theory of Relativity, but for the school exercise too. And I didn't have the strength to admit it, so, pretending that our conversation had a simple, mundane character to it, I quickly explained to him my observations about the stylistics of Stern, which could be understood as a warm-up to the Theory of Relativity. He went along with the new topic so readily that I began to suspect something greater was amiss. I thought that not only was there something in Stern's stylistics, but something in his views that was worthy of the Theory of Relativity.

Evidently, my friend decided that after explaining the school exercise, I grasped the fundamentals of the Theory of Relativity on my own. Maybe after getting a handle on this theory, his students would begin discussing Stern or Dostoevsky. And he decided that everything was put in its place, that everything made sense now. I never touched the topic again.

Meanwhile, let's return to our old men, astounded that their countryman personally saw Einstein. Moreover, it later turned out that he had the unique opportunity to grasp the Theory of Relativity with the help of its author, who, being more of a genius than my friend, could have demonstrated the theory with the help of a few matches, but the absent-minded Einstein didn't have any matches within easy reach, and our countryman refused to let him borrow his box of matches out of pure pride, which, almost half a century later, he tried to present as highly developed vigilance.

Before retiring, the old man who was sitting at the opposite end of the table really did work at a closed atomic factory next to Mukhus. A relative of mine who worked there too once introduced me to him.

The old man used to be a superintendent and evidently once heard the physicists talking about Einstein. And he understood that he was a grand person connected to the creation of the first atomic bomb. The following can be explained less by the effect of wine than by the old complex of somebody who worked at a secret facility: where it's forbidden to speak about too many things, where too many things are fantasized.

"You what, went to America to see Einstein?" snarked the Shimmering Party Worker. "The freaking supply manager! They'd only let you go to Kengursk—to get lumber!"

"Supply manager . . ." mysteriously repeated the old man who personally saw Einstein—that's what it was called then.

"Why didn't you say anything until now?" exclaimed the Old Coot.

"I signed a nondisclosure agreement," explained the supposed supply manager, then added triumphantly: "Yesterday at exactly three in the afternoon, the agreement expired! After the war, when they organized the physicotechnical institute here, I went to work there and stayed there until my very pension. And so, in forty-six, three of the nation's biggest-name physicians and I, as the fourth, were sent to America to Einstein . . . To the town of Princeton!" he exclaimed happily, as if he had just played a trump card that was impossible to beat.

"Princeton?" repeated one of the old men, expressing communal surprise. "We've never even heard of such a town."

"And how could you have heard of it," smiled the supposed supply manager slyly, "when it was a secret, atomic town? It wasn't on a single map. Maybe now they've opened it up."

The old man folded his arms on the table as if he were a successful prime minister at a press conference, ready to field the journalists' questions.

"This man will be the death of me!" yelled out the Shimmering Party Worker. "Let him mourn my passing! The town of Princeton! As a member of the Party, I'm closing my ears. Let him tell whatever stories he wants."

"It *was* Princeton!" the supposed supply manager rushed to confirm, not giving the Shimmering Party Worker a chance to properly cover his ears.

The old man truly did dig his elbows into the table and close his ears with his hands. That said, when the other began his tale, Party principles entered into a fray with Party oversight in favor of the latter. And he lowered his hands.

"Tell us, Shaliko, tell us," the old men asked the supposed supply manager.

The old man's eyes sparkled with the purple light of inspiration. The small, balding, stout fellow was finally the center of attention.

"It's my first time telling this," he said, sheepishly scratching his bald spot. "Don't get mad if I lose track . . . Alright, so, they put me in with an unofficial delegation of Soviet scientists. We had to find out something from Einstein. You can guess what. Lifetime nondisclosure agreement! We fly in to New York and head off for this town, Princeton.

"By the way, Paul Robeson himself drove us. He was one of ours, plus he knew Einstein. We arrive.

"Can't say a bad word, we were received well. The table was set with everything, even Coca-Cola. He himself, though, like Churchill, only drank Armenian cognac. Smoking a pipe, drinking cognac. When we had a few, I gave the sign to our lead scientist: 'Go ahead.'

"And he goes ahead. He talks and talks and talks, but it didn't lead to anything. He refused. Robeson began to sing. He sings from his soul.

"*I don't know another country, where man breathes so freely.*

"Meanwhile, the lead scientist quietly translates for Einstein when Robeson sings in Russian. After Robeson's singing, our lead scientist took to it again. But he wasn't having any of it. 'If you want, I'll play my violin,' he says, 'but not another word about this. I gave my word to the president of America.'

"'The hell are we going to do with his violin?' I say. 'Let's go.'

"And so, we coldly (though still within the bounds of decency) said our goodbyes and went to our hotel. The next morning, I'm sitting in a park next to the hotel, and what do I see? Him. He's out taking a walk! I swear on my three grandkids—he's out for a stroll in an old set of pajamas. Can't you, a great scientist, buy one good suit here in America?! No, he just trundles along in his PJs."

Accompanied by all of the old men's laughter, excluding the Old Coot and the Shimmering Party Worker, the former supply manager stood up, moved his chair out of the way, and began demonstrating how Einstein walked. Everyone watched how Einstein "trundled." It was clear that, in his time, the supply manager watched films about Chaplin.

After demonstrating Einstein's trundle and definitively thereby definitively finishing off the Shimmering Party Worker, who could only grab his head in horror, the storyteller chipperly took his seat.

"So he's walking by me," he went on, "and he's holding his pipe. And suddenly, he stops right next to me. I thought he recognized me. I won't lie—he didn't. Turns out his pipe was out. He gestures with his hands: matches. 'No,' I say, 'you should have your own.' He didn't say anything. He just trundled off."

"Why didn't you give him a light?" exclaimed the Old Coot.

"I was afraid! The CIA could have been watching. Me *and* him. They'd have said that I passed him something in the form of matches. Try to prove your innocence then!"

"Listen," the Shimmering Party Worker beseeched the others again, "this man will be the death of me! What America?! What Einstein!? They only trusted you to go as far as Kengursk to get lumber! Lumber! Lumber! Lumber! They didn't even trust you to go to Zugdidi!"

"Princeton! America!" triumphantly cried the old supply manager. "And why is it that after the war, Stalin come down on the Jews? Remember—the fight against the cosmopolites? Joseph didn't stomach that sort of thing. That was his way of getting back at Einstein."

"Ha! Ha! Ha! Ha!" the old men laughed, and even the Old Coot gave up and joined in.

"Pour the wine," said Aslanych amidst cackles, pouring himself and Mikhail Arkadievich a glass. "Let's drink to our great adventurer. You, Shaliko, should have taken to America a barrel of Gudauta 'Isabella' and given it to Einstein as a present. He would have taken a sip and told you everything."

"The thought crossed our minds," explained the former supply manager importantly. "Don't think that you're smarter than everyone. But we were told that it was illegal to bring wine into America. Especially barrel wine."

The old men cheerfully took a drink and spiritlessly chased it down. And that was probably a concession to age.

"Now tell your story," the Old Coot said to Mikhail Arkadievich, helping his ear out with his hand. "You stopped on the Mikado."

"Yes, yes, gentlemen, it so happened," reluctantly began Mikhail Arkadievich, but gradually livening up. "Then Paris, taxi life, war, Hitler. But when the Red Army took Hitler down, I said to my friends: 'Our quarrel is over. We're going home, gentlemen, home! Since nobody could get on with Hitler other than the Bolsheviks, they must be right.' I genuinely believed that then. It's not good to bear your fatherland ill will.

"And some of us came home. The Red Square! Even Lenin's Pantheon managed to look alright in it, if you'll believe it. It was so intoxicating back then that that's how I saw it!"

"It's called the Mausoleum, not the Pantheon," the Shimmering Party Worker irritably interrupted him.

"Yes, the Mausoleum . . . At first, everything was great. We liked everything, but then the arrests started. They took me too. Forgive me, but what for? But the investigator just keeps nagging me: 'What is your assignment here, you White bandit?'

"'What assignment?' I say. 'I spent my whole life behind the wheel. Our quarrel has been ended by Russia's victory. We applaud you. We're patriots too.'

"'You better tell me, patriot' he yells, 'why you sang for the Mikado! Even Shaliapin didn't sing for the Mikado!' Concede, gentlemen, what a strange way to phrase the issue! I'm a poor immigrant in another country, I sing for whomever pays. Especially since I sang for the Mikado only once, and he seemed like a rather noble fellow. Yes! Someone of our own likeness.

"But every day, this guy harps on the same thing: 'Why did you sing for the Mikado, and what were you trying to tell him?' Eventually, I blew up: 'Stop playing with me, kind comrade! In my time, people of our circle wouldn't shake hands with the gendarmerie! They may have nodded at them, but never shaken hands!' And I showed him my hand, befouled not a single time by the touch of a gendarme. But if you can imagine, he just swats at my hand with his pistol handle. These two fingers still don't work very well."

Mikhail Arkadievich stretched out over the table the large, fine-tuned hand of an auto mechanic. The old men examined it with interest, twiddling with the injured fingers as if trying to rejuvenate them with their light gymnastics. Meanwhile, the owner of the fingers nodded proudly, showing them that they could even manipulate his fingers with greater gusto, that they didn't hurt at all.

Mikhail Arkadievich's injured fingers must have reminded the former soccer star of his erstwhile-injured toes, and the toes reminded him of soccer. And he immediately decided to share his recollections.

"Can what they do today even be called soccer?" he began. "They make a single goal and go about kissing each other. Phaw! In my time, you didn't go around kissing on the field. And in general, men kissing . . . It used to be that only drunks kissed. But now, it's the sober ones too!—mwah, mwah—everyone is kissing!"

"You're right about that," wheezed Mikhail Arkadievich, apparently taking no offense at the soccer player interrupting him. As he said this, he simultaneously eyed the Old Coot, who, possibly because of his poor hearing, was bending his fingers with unwarranted ardor. "It's a sign of society decaying. In kissing, men forgive each other their mutual dereliction of duty."

"Yes," agreed the former soccer player possibly without understanding him completely. "It used to be indecent. But now, everything is decent. In my soccer days, there were brilliant players—the Starostin brothers. Then Beria arrested them. He didn't forgive anyone their glory.

"And then, there was only one great soccer player—Boris Paychadze. Boris Paychadze is an era unto himself!

"Beria wanted to arrest him too. He was jealous of his glory as well. But he missed his chance. He thought: he's still a Georgian, he can run around for a bit. But then Stalin saw Paychadze play, and he was impressed. And arresting him became dangerous. What if Stalin asked, 'What happened to Boris Paychadze?' And Beria decided: I'll do it with Stalin's own hands. And he came to Stalin and said, 'I want to take Boris Paychadze! He's got loose lips.'

"Stalin raised his head, puffed on his pipe, and said: 'Alright, Lavrentiy, take Paychadze. But on one condition.' 'What condition, comrade Stalin?' 'You, Lavrentiy, will play in his stead. Deal?'

"But how is he supposed to play with that paunch of his?"

"Ha! Ha! Ha! Ha!" the old men laughed at the war chief's genial wit.

Only Mikhail Arkadievich and Timur Aslanovich didn't laugh. The former looked sullen, while the latter shot ironic looks at the storyteller.

"Boris Paychadze is an entire era. He played here once. He hit the most beautiful goal that I'd seen. He feints around a defender! Feint around a midfielder! Feint around another midfielder! And he slams it in from the penalty line into the right corner! Goal! And he himself flies forward like a rocket too! Why? We all jumped up in the stands!

"Apparently, as he was kicking the ball, he felt with his toes that he had misjudged by a few centimeters and knew that the ball would hit the frame! That's why he leaped forward! It rebounded! And he headbutted it right into the left! The stands erupted! Think of the ingenious brain you need to have, the brilliant toes you need to have to realize all that in the span of a second!"

"Ho! Ho! Ho! Ho!" the old men ho'd, astounded not only by Boris Paychadze's mental brilliance, but by his corporeal brilliance as well.

"Here's another story," the storyteller went on, happy with the first one's success. "It's 1950. August. Similar weather to what we have now. He played here. During halftime, the players drink lemonade in the corner of the stadium. There was a stand there. It had a window opening onto the stadium. Don't you remember?"

"Of course we do! That was where Misrop worked! Who doesn't remember Misrop?" the old men happily began talking one over the other, all looking to assert that they remembered fat, old Misrop.

"So, all the players are drinking lemonade. And Paychadze is drinking it too. But how!"

The storyteller snatched a bottle with a bit of water left in it, splashed it out off to the side, strictly leaned his head back, and held the bottle perfectly vertically above his head, just above his mouth. However, in honor of their memories of Paychadze, which had to be kept pure, he froze without touching the bottle to his lips, clearly showing everybody that he wasn't touching the bottle to his lips. In reproducing with absolute physical accuracy how the great soccer star sated his thirst, he somehow simultaneously impressed upon everyone that it was all just a game, a shadow, mere mimicry of the genuine thing.

"It was as if he was drinking the sky through the bottle—that's how Paychadze drank lemonade!" he exclaimed and contemptuously put the bottle back on the table, letting it know that it was by chance and just for a second that it was allowed to play such an important role, but was now returned to its pitiful, ordinary existence.

"Ho! Ho! Ho! Ho!" the old men came to as if they had understood everything.

"I didn't play anymore then," the storyteller went on, looking off into the distant scene, "but I was still young. Bold! And I went right up to Paychadze, put a hand on his shoulder, and said, 'Dear Boris, may you play for a hundred years more to the joy of the Soviet Union!'"

"And what did he say?" the Old Coot couldn't restrain himself.

"He tore the bottle away from his lips like this," said the former soccer player, and smoothly gestured with his hand, pulling the bottle away, underscoring the calmness and dignity of the movement. "He smiled and said, 'Hello, Zhora Gurgenidze!'

"I lost my mind! Was someone playing a joke on me, did someone tell him my name? But how? I didn't plan on going up to him, I didn't tell anyone about it!

"'How do you know my name?!'

"He didn't reply anything. He threw his head back again and drank his lemonade. I'm losing my mind, and he's drinking lemonade. He finishes it finally, looks at me, and says quietly: '1938. I was still just a punk then. My uncle and I had come to Mukhus and went to the soccer field. It was Mukhus playing against Armavir. One-one. Two minutes until the end of the match. Mukhus gets a corner kick. Some player takes it. He kicks! And he curves the ball from the corner into the goal! The stands erupt: "Bravo, bravo, Zhora Gurgenidze!" That was the first time I heard your name.'

"'Dear Boris,' I say, 'that was my star moment. Thank you, I'll tell my kids, my grandkids, my great-grandkids about this meeting!'

"'No, no,' he says, 'thank you. That was the moment I decided to become a soccer player.' That's the time I met Boris Paychadze."

"Ho! Ho! Ho! Ho!" the old men ho'd, astounded that their friend once fired up the heart of the great soccer star.

"They say Boris Paychadze died," added the old soccer player, barely holding back tears. "The great epoch of Soviet soccer has ended . . . Soon the Soviet Union will end too . . ."

"Enough sniveling," boomed Aslanych. "You lot grow sentimental a little too much . . . Great Georgia, great Paychadze . . . Sentiments always end in blood . . ."

"Next, what happened next?!" cried the Old Coot at Mikhail Arkadievich, as if he had stopped his retelling of his own volition.

"Next? Lockup. Magadan," Mikhail Arkadievich began again weakly, gradually getting into his tale. "Then exile to the upper reaches of the Yenisei. I became friends there with a veteran who had escaped from captivity and couldn't prove that he wasn't a spy.

"And suddenly, the radio informs us: Stalin is sick. Who could have thought! Cheynes-Stokes breathing! But none of us knows what that is. We rush to the local doctor. What is Cheynes-Stokes breathing? It's the end of the line, he says. Agony.

"We go outside. It's nighttime, the stars are out. The Siberian expanse. A cosmic kind of joy strikes us. 'We have to drink,' says my friend, 'or I'll die!'

"We recall that an exiled Latvian lives in the village. He peddles in moonshine. It's night, but we knock on his door. The poor guy must have thought that they'd come to take him away again. He didn't open the door for a long time. We're begging, but he just scuffles behind the door, grumbling. Finally, he opens it. We didn't say why we want to drink, but he could tell from our expressions. 'What,' he says, 'is it hopeless?' 'Yes! Yes!' we say. The Latvian warms up to us. He gives us a bottle. And then the radio brings us the long-awaited news: the dictator croaked!

"The iceberg had cracked and was on the move again. What hopes, what days those were! Immediately, the Twentieth Congress happens! Those who were left began coming back from the camps. That's when the Perestroika should've begun! Oh, Nikita, Nikita!

"And now what? By my ninetieth year of life, I've begun growing used to the Bolsheviks. Especially since the murderers were replaced by thieves. There have always been thieves in Russia. But now, democrats have begun popping up. And I notice that they have the energy of insolence, like the Bolsheviks did in 1918. They keep repeating: privatization, privatization . . . Let them return me my property, then I'll believe in them . . ."

"Why did you say that Stalin croaked?" said the Shimmering Party Worker, upset. "It's crude. Uncultured. He *was* the generalissimo. You could have said: died . . . was gone . . . left . . . departed . . . Russian is the richest language in the world. After everything that's happened, you're still the White bandit that you always were . . . 'Croaked . . .'"

"Croak is exactly what he did!" happily announced Mikhail Arkadievich. "They introduced that word during their revolution, and I'm returning it to them."

"And now, friends, fill your cups," boomed the old actor, pouring for himself and Mikhail Arkadievich. "My friend is right about a lot of things. I was just comparing the new ones with the old ones and was thinking about this.

"Some thirty years ago, the assistant secretary from the regional committee was here. A bandit among bandits. You all remember him. Circumstances related to my apartment forced me to go to him. I open the door. I walk in. He jumps up and makes towards me. He shakes my hand, sits me down, then sits down himself. He hears me out, promises to help, and walks me to the door. And he did everything he promised. Who am I? An actor. Yes, an extraordinary one—no need for false modesty. But what's it to him? He's never even been to the theater.

"And recently, I came to see one of the new democrats about something. My nephew is having difficulties with his job. Doesn't see or hear a thing I say. Looks right through me. He's a chatterbox! He made promises, but didn't do anything. I compared these two visits, the two chiefs of these two eras. And here's what I think.

"There used to be a system. A criminal system, but a system nonetheless. And people could get ahead on criminal talent. One of the main signs of criminal talent is the ability to sense a person's weaknesses and strengths.

"And when he saw me, he immediately felt my strength of spirit. But since he had never seen strength of spirit, he thought it was criminal strength. 'Oh,' he must have thought, 'what is this monstrosity that's come to see me? A mafioso disguised as an actor.'"

"Ha! Ha! Ha! Ha!" the old men laughed. One of them called out through the laughter:

"How could he have confused you when he was the chief mafioso himself?"

"He decided that I was part of a deep conspiracy and even more dangerous. The others had criminal instincts. But these new ones don't have anything yet other than the intoxication of power. When they develop a nose for decency, that's when we'll be able to talk about a new, democratic administration. But patience, friends, history isn't made quickly.

"There are worse things. The plague of nationalism is advancing on us from all sides, friends. People have gone mad, and there's nobody you could yell at: 'Silence! Sit down!'

"We old-timers, we've known each other forty, fifty years. Look at all of us: an Abkhazian, a Russian, a Georgian, a Mingrelian, an Armenian. Did we old, *old* Mukhusites ever war with each other over national affairs? Us— never! Jokes, jabs—of course! But we never had this plague between us. It was up above, but never between us.

"We were all united by the Russian language! Shakespeare came to me through Russian, and I carried him in my own language to my people! Will I ever forget that?

"And I'm confident that it will conquer this plague and once again unite our peoples. But if that doesn't happen, if this disease ruins us all, we'll die undefeated at a table just like this one. Let future generations say: 'There were, during the plague, these old men, and they held out!' Let's drink to that!"

The old men enthusiastically expressed their desire to die around a table just like this one and no other way. They drank cheerfully and even chased it down cheerfully, storing up their strength before the plague descended.

"Enough about politics," boomed the old actor irritably, as if somebody else had begun discussing politics in the first place. He pushed his glass aside, and suddenly grinned slyly and put his hand on Mikhail Arkadievich's shoulder. "Listen, Misha, you've seen half the world. You've known European women, Russian women, Caucasian women. Tell us, for God's sake, which is the best?"

"Promise you won't get offended, gentlemen?" Mikhail Arkadievich asked, puffing out his chest and pushing away the old actor's hand to ensure absolute freedom.

"We won't!" the old men responded in chorus, showing that they were willing to risk the reputations of their old women for the sake of the truth.

Mikhail Arkadievich looked over his companions with an eagle eye, evaluating the probability of resistance. He weighed everything out, then fired away:

"The best woman in the world is Japanese!"

"Japanese?!" the old men were blindsided—they hadn't anticipated a blow from this side at all.

"Just think, Old Coot, about your Sveta from Odesa!" boomed the old actor.

The old man had bowed over the table, head in hands, clearly anticipating an attack. The old men responded to the line with collective laughter, as if overjoyed that it was Sveta from Odesa who was farthest removed from Japanese women, which went a long way towards easing the plight of their own wives. Admittedly, geographically speaking, that was true: Sveta from Odesa was losing by about half the Black Sea to the companions' wives. Maybe even to Old Coot's own wife too.

"The best woman in the world is Japanese!" Mikhail Arkadievich exclaimed again, not giving anyone the chance to claim that they might have misheard something.

The old men laughed again, looking at the Old Coot, who was still prepared for an attack.

"As a lover or a mistress of the house?" yelled the Old Coot, his cry piercing the communal laughter of the old men, hoping to at least somewhat defend Sveta from Odesa with his specification.

"In all ways!" Mikhail Arkadievich said, destroying all hope. "A Japanese woman treats a man like a knight, and the man subconsciously adjusts to fit the image . . . It's a great tradition. It's pretty invigorating, you know . . ."

"It's the cult of the samurai!" the Shimmering Party Worker suddenly interrupted him. "And we beat those samurai on Lake Khasan,[58] and we'll beat them again!"

He triumphantly looked around the table, as if preparing to immediately go on a campaign against the samurai and searching for companions, but then, without any warning, Mikhail Arkadievich began singing in his slightly cracking, but still powerful voice. The old actor started booming in time with him, his voice like water flowing from a pitcher:

> From times forgotten, long gone by,
> From the fables of Iviron,
> From our famous ancestors,
> We've saved one word.
> It bears the beginning of our daring,
> A companion to fortune and grief.
> It has always sounded among us:
> Alaverdi, alaverdi!

Then, Aslanych began to sing my favorite Abkhazian drinking song "Scharda Aamta"—"Many Summers." And suddenly, that old devil, Mikhail Arkadievich joined in so heartwarmingly that I got the thought: what if at the turn of the century, the young Mikhail Arkadievich sang that song in a group of Abkhazian princes? But where are those young princes, where is he, where are they all? The other old men joined in too. The imbibed wine was nobly being transformed into song.

Suddenly, a man in sunglasses, a Japanese robe, and slippers on his bare feet appeared in the Amra's inner entrance, having parted the dejectedly waiting bathers as if they were weeds. He bravely and calmly walked by a few tables in the direction of the buffet. But then, that waitress jumped out of nowhere and blocked his path.

"No clothes, no service!" she declared boldly right in his face.

---

58 Lake Khasan was the site of a battle between Japanese and Soviet forces in 1938.

The man stopped and lazily looked her over as much as was possible in sunglasses. He had the air of a boss about him, but the waitress continued to block his path. It later turned out that he was such a big boss that the waitress hadn't even known what he looked like.

"No clothes, no service! Director's order!" she repeated.

And then, with inimitably calm insolence, the man took off his sun-blocking glasses as if he took off his bathing trunks. The waitress was taken aback, but not too much. He looked at her with the uniquely clear-eyed gaze of a very successful hustler.

"Dear," he said, "you're not old enough to service me with no clothes. I'm going to privatize all of this soon . . ."

"We have our orders," the waitress frowned, but didn't move an inch.

The man helplessly put on his sunglasses as if he once again put on his swimming trunks. But someone had apparently run to tell what was happening, and the director ran to the scene of action.

"Archil Archilovich," he cried out from afar, "you came yourself? Could no one else do it?!"

It was the same director that twenty-something years back had, before my eyes, similarly found out that Voroshilov with his entire entourage had unexpectedly arrived at the restaurant. He had to run down the restaurant deck to roll down to the tall guest, and his lame leg, unable to keep up with the rest of his obedient body, flailed after him. Another time, another clientele!

"My chauffeur would better be sent to retrieve death," said Archil Archilovich, grieving democratically. He shook his hand simply, showing that he wasn't offended for not being immediately recognized. "My friends from Moscow and I are sunbathing. Playing a little bit of Preferans. Got struck by a hankering for beer. But not this swill, obviously."

He nodded at the surrounding tables.

"You wound, Archil Archilovich," said the director, but immediately got a grip on himself. "Czech, Danish?"

"Czech," said Archil Archilovich, utterly democratizing.

"I'll bring it myself!" cried the director cheerfully at the retreating Japanese robe.

The director hobbled back where he came from with an expression of unusual delight on his face. And, as if afraid that someone might scare the delight off, he hobbled over to the Amra's railing and managerially looked out over the sea as it approached his establishment.

"Hey you, fisherman!" he yelled. "Don't you have anywhere else to catch fish?"

"What, can't spare the fish?" called out a voice from below.

"The fish isn't the problem," yelled the director, growing angry, "your dirty boat is! People on the beach want to look at the Amra, not at your tub. At least paint it. Let's go, let's go, up anchor! . . . 'Can't spare the fish!' What if I can't! I have the right. The fish around the Amra is our fish. We feed it with the patrons' leftovers. It's trusting. You try to fish out in the open sea! We'll see how good a fisherman you are then! Come on, let's go, up anchor!"

He went into a room behind the bar and emerged with a cardboard box covered by a fresh towel in his arms. Carefully propping up the oblong box from below with his hands, he walked out onto the deck with the expression of someone fresh from the maternity ward, holding his overdue first-born. And the happily hurrying, hobbling leg asserted the reality of the scene: lame, no one wanted to marry him until he saved up enough money, which took years and years. He approached the exit, the dejectedly waiting crowd parted, and he carefully descended downstairs where he once, before my very eyes, rolled like a boulder towards Voroshilov and his entourage.

I remembered the German and looked in his direction. Bah! He was finishing off his third bottle of champagne. Two bottles, like empty high-caliber shell casings, stood off to the side. The supposed wife and supposed translator looked similarly quieted and frightened. And it was now utterly impossible to tell who was the wife and who the translator.

Extinguished pipe in hand, he was darkly gazing off into the distance, searching for that second word that should be cried out to the country in order to return it into the womb of civilization. But the second word continued to elude him. And the German drank quietly and stoically, not like us, and searched. How many more bottles will he need?!

9

Lenin and Uncle Sandro

The thickset figure of my conversation partner once again appeared in the Amra's entryway. He crossed the deck in his quick, jubilant gait and sat in his seat.

"Everything's in order!" he said, grabbed the bowl of melted ice cream, drank it in a single gulp, and put it back down. "History is once again moving in sync with my watch. But don't ask me a thing: if you rush with words, you'll be late with deeds. What did I stop on? Right!

"In the beginning of the fifties, Stalin had the idea to be done with Beria, and then with the rest of the politburo. Every now and then, a tyrant is forced to refresh the general horror. And Beria, of course, realized this. And Stalin knew that Beria knew.

"But in the midst of his military victory, Stalin let the moment pass. The balance of power turned out to be in Beria's favor. And Stalin decided to disappear for a while. But where? Where could he crawl off to? To General Franco! Stalin did Franco an invaluable favor in his fight against the republican Spain. Under the guise of helping the republicans, Stalin bolstered their ranks with his own commissars, and they began arresting the cream of the republic. And thanks to that, Franco won and was deeply grateful to Stalin.

"Stalin had his own guard, which was outside the chain of command. Once, at night, he leaves one of two body doubles in his stead and secretly flies to Madrid. Franco receives him and hides him.

"Stalin remotely keeps tabs on everything happening in Russia and keeps in encrypted correspondence with both body doubles. The first tells him about the behavior of the members of the politburo, especially Beria. And the second tells him about the behavior of the first. As for who watched the second double, we don't know yet. Stalin steers them in the right direction.

"But then Beria kills the first double, believing him to be the real Stalin. Beria intentionally organized a stampede during the fake Stalin's funeral in order to weaken the cult of Stalin and lay the groundwork for the Twentieth Congress.

"The furious letter Stalin sent to the second double about the fake Stalin's outrageous funeral is still intact. All of Stalin's correspondence with the second double is still intact, actually. Stalin wrote to him that he would answer with his life for the first double's death. And the second double broke down. He knew the frightening combination of moves that Stalin was preparing in Madrid. And he came to Khrushchev on his knees and told him everything. That's why their letters survived.

"Khrushchev unexpectedly arrests Beria and executes him. Beria was such an egoist that he didn't even have a double. That made his arrest easier. Beria didn't expect it, but Stalin didn't expect it either. His whole strategy came crumbling down around him. Now he was getting responses to his encoded messages to Moscow not from the second double, but from who knows who, disguised as the second double. Stalin could tell by the heavy-handed cipher that he was being played for a fool. And Stalin said to Franco:

"'Now, this is going to be a long game. Freeze me like Lenin until a new revolution flares up. And when we're thawed out, Lenin and I will clash once more over the Hamburg score.'

"And Franco froze him. Then Franco died, and the Spaniards sold America the frozen Stalin for a billion dollars. That's why their democracy succeeded. But it won't last."

"Why does America need a frozen Stalin?" I asked.

He looked at me with such surprise that it was as if the whole world had long known the reason and I alone managed somehow to stay in the dark. But then, the proud wearer of the magenta shirt came up to us again. Head bowed humbly, he asked:

"Forgive me, but youth begs another question: what was Vladimir Ilyich doing January 20, 1917?"

My interlocutor suddenly narrowed his eyes slyly, nodded at the magenta shirt, and said:

"Playing a joke on an old man, are you. Well, as one great utopian once said: through play, they will learn. Now admit it: you, of course, meant January 19, 1917, didn't you?"

"Truthfully, yes," said the magenta shirt, looking at his feet.

"As I thought!" exclaimed my interlocutor and asserted haughtily: "Three things have never let me down: my head, my stomach, and my scrotum!"

The magenta shirt flinched but maintained a serious veneer. One of his friends crashed onto the table in laughter. The other, clearly the more conscientious of the two, hid his head under the table, leaving only his back visible, coursing with waves of laughter.

"Yes! Yes!" my companion went on, not noticing a thing. "That day, Vladimir Ilyich wrote a letter to Inessa Armand. But it was not a love letter. With indignation, but, of course, within the realm of gentlemanly behavior, Lenin rejects Inessa's attacks on Engels. Inessa criticizes Engels for being skeptical in his time of the idea of a universal strike. But in his time, the contemptible anarchists were the ones running around with that idea.

"However, history marched ever onwards, and Engels was no longer around. Time showed that a mass political strike is more than justified. If Engels had still been around, he would've realized that before Inessa did.

"Despite her femininity, Inessa didn't understand the dialectic of time. And neither did Bukharin, by the way. But that didn't stop Bukharin from being the Party's favorite. And if we're being completely honest, that's the reason that he was the Party's favorite—because he didn't fully get the dialectic. The thing is that the Party itself didn't fully get the dialectic, and therein lies the dialectic of its love for Bukharin.

"But you, of course, thought that it would be a love letter? Thought wrong! Lenin's love letters are in a safe location. Their time will come soon. The world will know the hundred and thirty fiery messages sent by the great revolutionary to his beloved! It's Dante! Petrarch! Pushkin! You must learn to love like Lenin! . . . But I can't talk about that! I can't! Go! Go!"

It seemed that the magenta shirt walked away feeling somewhat flummoxed. When my companion said that there were a hundred and thirty letters, I recalled the number he named during our first meeting. Now, it turned out there were three letters more. The correspondence must have been continuing, albeit not as actively as before. But then, I thought: who knows! So many years had passed since then. He must have still been quite able and could have easily found three more letters.

The circumstances of Inessa Armand's death are mysterious. According to some, she ended her own life in Kislovodsk, where Lenin forced her to go for rest. He wrote letters on the matter. He was very insistent. Was it friendly concern or something more? Those who propose suicide cite the contradiction between the official version of her death—cholera—and the fact that she was buried in an open grave.

My companion, clearly worked up by his monologue, turned to me. For the first time, he quietly poured the cognac himself. His powerful hand was shaking. Tears glistened in his eyes.

"Let's drink to the peace of her soul," he said, and then, forgetting about me, sobbed: "Inessa, your cold body has arrived from Kislovodsk ... I know, Inessa, it's your revenge!"

Then, abruptly sober again:

"Note that the word 'Inessa' has two s's, just like the word 'Russia.' I had to choose."

And again through the quiet tears of remembrance:

"She begged me to stay in Europe ... She had money ... A little ... But not enough ... Our own home in Switzerland and our children ... And music beneath her fingers ... Inhuman music ... I loved the children and the music so much ... But then, February ... That fool, Wilhelm, offered us gold ..."

Suddenly cheerfully, with pathos:

"I couldn't give up my last chance in life to prove that I was right, and not Plekhanov. And I did! And then, the irony of history and Koba! Who in Zurich could have thought about that then? But our meeting nears! Look out, *kinto*!"[59]

I thought he got too distracted and forgot to whom he was drinking. But he didn't forget. In keeping with Caucasian traditions, he poured out a little out of his glass to signify that he drank to the departed. He emptied his glass in one gulp, wiped his eyes with his palms, and looked at me with an expression of clear-eyed madness:

"Why does America want a frozen Stalin? What do you mean, why? ..."

But then, out of nowhere, Uncle Sandro came up to us. He was in an untucked, white shirt that was encircled by a Caucasian belt, which stressed his thin waist. The metal studs on his belt that remotely seemed to be silver glittered faintly. Let's also briefly note his breeches and light, Asian boots.

He appeared suddenly, but it later turned out that he was sitting to our left with the old men in their bender. However, I didn't notice when exactly he entered the Amra.

---

59 In Georgian, a *kinto* was a trader or restaurant entertainer in nineteenth- and early twentieth-century Tbilisi.

Uncle Sandro quietly and intently gazed at my companion with his bright eyes, which insolently refused to age. The other man responded with a similarly intense gaze, though at the same time, he tried to effect an expression of sharp, genially cunning curiosity—an expression with which we have been familiarized thanks to the many pictures with the invariable title, "Lenin Receives Peasants."

What's funny is that the title of the pictures never changes, even if they show Lenin having tea with just a single peasant. In my childhood, I remember my pedantic, childish logic noting the plural in the picture's title and forcing me to search and search for the other peasants, who must have been hiding somewhere in the war chief's office.

But unlike visual puzzles (for example, find the second rabbit), the second peasant, to say nothing of the others, didn't want to be found. And I remember that I made my peace with the thought that the rest of the peasants were there, but that they were waiting their turn outside of Lenin's office and outside the picture frame, which therefore meant that there was no error in the picture title. Oh, how I wanted to believe!

But the years went by. Newer and newer pictures cropped up in which Lenin continued entertaining newer and newer peasants. And in all those pictures, despite the monstrous bounty of peasants, Lenin's pose never expressed haste or (especially) fatigue. And his face continued to radiate sharp, genially cunning curiosity, and only the cup of invariable tea next to him was subjected over the years to greater and greater detail by the artists' hands, and it was often possible to divine that the tea was hot, maybe even unbearably hot (either that's steam above the cup, or it's Lenin's gingerly hovering fingers), and that caused some individuals to believe in the artist's unbelievable mastery, which smoothly flowed into astonishing audacity. The far-reaching insinuation was graspable! You see, Lenin's fingers are cautious, hovering gingerly, they're uncertain, unlike . . . That's right, you guessed it—unlike Stalin's fingers.

As the years went by, these pictures began to be infuriating, even though they never gave off the impression that eventually Lenin would get tired of this peasant, staring stupidly at his feet, seemingly from embarrassment, or especially this one, listening to him admiringly (Jesus Christ, he knows everything about us!), and that he, Lenin, would eventually take his eternally hot tea and splash it over the peasant's beard. To say nothing of the reciprocal burst of tea from the peasant into Lenin's mongoloid face or even of two streams of tea simultaneously crossing above his writing desk like two swords on Kulikovo Field![60]

No, no, never once did I get such an impression. I, in fact, *couldn't* have gotten it, because Lenin's face (sure, I'll repeat it) always radiated a sharp, genially cunning curiosity. His expression always immediately told all the peasants: I know, I know you'll try to pull the wool over my eyes, but I love you even still, since I'm your war chief and have plenty of wool of my own.

And in my student years, I was bent over Lenin's works—like I was bent over that ill-fated picture in my youth, searching for the missing peasants— only this time I was bent over his essays in search of some hidden—like those peasants—meaning, since the obvious meaning was too bland. Once again, I was searching with that same childish stubbornness, believing that the meaning was there, that it just had to be found. But when I didn't find it, I eventually decided that this meaning existed outside of the book's pages in life itself, in victory over said life. Which meant that it had to be in the text as well, since victory was achieved through the text.

But who knows, maybe the self-deception was a subconscious defense mechanism, since coming to terms with the possibility that there was and would be no meaning would have meant that I either had to explode, or else admit that I was a villain, bleating obediently at the tyranny's whim. And those were still frightening times, the times of Stalin . . .

However, carried away by these memories, I forgot about my companion. And he, meanwhile, continued gazing at Uncle Sandro with the aforementioned expression of curiosity. But for some reason, the expression wasn't coming to him so easily. Maybe the peasant wasn't right, or maybe something else was getting in the way. The situation got slightly tense. And I realized why. Both were silently insisting on their authenticity, but for some reason, with scandalous inevitability, one's authenticity meant the other's falsity.

"Have a seat, Uncle Sandro," I said peaceably, got up, and pulled up a chair for him. My tone, which ascertained Uncle Sandro's authenticity, simultaneously giving my companion a subtle reminder not to be too offended at the prototype of the literary hero, even if, on account of the author's laziness or absent-mindedness, he bears the hero's name in real life.

---

60 Kulikovo Field was the site of a battle between the Mongolian Horde and Russian forces in 1380.

It's too late to fix that mistake, since the book has long been in print, and it's obviously impossible to change the prototype's name, considering his venerable age and exclusive entanglement with his own name.

My companion sniffed derisively, making it clear that he not only understood me, but expressed his loathing of liberal attempts to smooth out contradictions.

Uncle Sandro ate quietly, not letting my companion out of his sight. His authenticity, maybe in light of his center of gravity having situated itself comfortably on a chair, had clearly strengthened. My companion felt that. And indeed, while Uncle Sandro was standing, it was easier to envision him evaporating into thin air.

"So this is Uncle Sandro," he nodded at Uncle Sandro. "And I thought you had invented him . . ."

"Him inventing me!" exclaimed Uncle Sandro cuttingly. "*You* invented *your*self! In my life, who *haven't* I met! The Prince of Oldenburg personally gave me a pair of Zeiss binoculars as a gift. As reward for my sharp sight. I would visit Nestor Lakoba as if I were a relative . . . Yes, Nestor," sighed Uncle Sandro, seemingly fully confident that he had taken the reins of our get-together, comfortably leaned back against the chair back and crossed his legs. His fingers carelessly, assertively latched on to his belt. It was clear that he was giving in to a stream of memories that he would waste no time in vocalizing. "I was the last person," he began, "to see Lakoba alive here, in Abkhazia. Discounting family, of course. That day, he left for Tbilisi and returned in a coffin.

"I was at his home when he was departing. He was worried, though he kept a tight grip on himself. Before going outside, he stopped in the doorway, took out his pistol, and shot at the ceiling.

"He always loved weapons, but we froze. We didn't know why he did it. But he, it turned out, was lifting his own spirits. He had a difficult conversation with Beria waiting for him, about Abkhazia's future, and he didn't know how the talk would end.

"He must have decided that if they tried to take him in Lavrentiy's office, he would return fire and take him down with the very first bullet.

"And he really did have a difficult talk with Beria, and they argued in the Central Committee. But Beria, *shaytan*, didn't lay a finger on him there. On the contrary, when Lakoba's chauffeur took him to his hotel, Lavrentiy sent his wife to invite him to their home and make peace over a bottle of wine. But Lakoba refused his wife. He didn't go. And then, Beria sent his mother, and she begged Lakoba to come by their home and drink with her son a bottle of wine, like they used to do when they were friends . . . Or rather, pretended that they were friends. And our Lakoba flinched—he couldn't refuse an old woman. He respected our ancient traditions and died because of it. The first and only glass that he raised in Beria's home turned out to be poisoned.

"No, the old woman knew nothing about it, I won't lie . . . Yes, Lakoba respected the traditions of our fathers, and they took advantage of it . . . And they caught you the same way, though, thank God, you're still alive. Though your mind has gotten a bit foggy," his bright eyes unexpectedly shot in my direction.

For a moment, my heart dropped at the possibility that he guessed what was . . . There was something . . . Then again, the end of his dictum most likely was aimed at the strangeness of my conversing with the man sitting across from me.

"But I'm talking about something completely different," Uncle Sandro went on, once again leaning against the chair back and thrusting his big fingers behind his thin, Caucasian belt. "I didn't just come to Lakoba's home as if I were a relative. I went hunting with Trotsky. I sat at the same table as Stalin twice. Rather, once at a table, and second time sat next to Stalin on a rug after a fishing trip. He sat on a chair, I sat on the rug. Specificity is important! I had gotten wet while fishing, and he presented me with his spare underwear. Special wool! To this day, they're in good shape!

"But I never once thought that I would meet with a fake Lenin. Lenin was bald in life. I guess it's with good reason they say that the dead's hair and nails still grow. Well, was it in the Mausoleum that you hair grew?"

My companion began shaking with restrained laughter.

"You'll understand everything soon, Sandro Habugovich, soon!" he assured him joyfully. "When we are victorious, I will put you on the Council of Elders. We neglected that last time. But allow me to ask you, how did you hunt with Trotsky? As far as I know, Lev Davydovich never appeared in your neck of the woods. Rubbish, Sandro Habugovich, all rubbish!"

At this point, Uncle Sandro roared with laughter, baring his powerful teeth, eyes flaring, and nodding at my companion, as if to say, "How's that scholar of history looking now?"

I was also surprised that somebody who had so thoroughly studied Lenin's life and surroundings missed that Trotsky had been in Abkhazia. Trotsky says so in his memoirs. But then, I realized why this was. In studying

Lenin's life, my companion had taken advantage exclusively of Soviet works. Trotsky's books had appeared in our country only in recent years, once he had already crossed beyond the pale.

"How could you know about it if you're Lenin?" said Uncle Sandro, stroking his mustache, which had been slightly fluffed out by his laughter. "You were in your grave when Trotsky had come here. You don't remember? Let me remind you.

"In Tiflis, Trotsky had found out about Lenin's death and sent a telegram to the Central Committee, saying that he'll come to the funeral. But Stalin calmly appraised how long a train took in getting to Moscow and replied by saying that Trotsky shouldn't come, that he wouldn't make it in time to the funeral anyway.

"In reality, Lenin was buried later, and Trotsky could have made it. But what good would Trotsky do Stalin standing next to Lenin's grave when he was busy dividing power between his own people?

"In a word, Trotsky got Stalin's response and went to Abkhazia out of grief to rest. Then he realized that he could have made it to the funeral, but it was too late.

"Later, when we met while hunting, he bristled and bristled at the bureaucracy that had mixed up the date of Lenin's funeral. But in reality, nobody had mixed anything up, and I already knew that. But he didn't. Back then, I was already mentally adroit.

"But Trotsky was a good shot. A lip-smacking good shot! One shot, and whatever he was aiming at was down for the count! But Stalin had gotten the best of him. And everything went downhill from there."

"Don't worry," my companion exclaimed, his expression dark either out indignation for Trotsky's treatment or for his own unlamented corpse. "There's a fight rearing! Sandro Habugovich, it's all ahead of us! But are you really that same Uncle Sandro? I thought he had made you up!"

"*I* made *him* up!" exclaimed Uncle Sandro, easily straightening in his chair. "He follows me like a rook follows the plowman. I plow, and he nibbles up everything I leave behind! And when he gets his royalties, he doesn't spare his uncle a single thought.

"But no worries. To each his own fate. Let me tell you a story. You two listen, and then let each say what he thinks.

"It happened three years ago . . . The stores' shelves weren't completely empty yet. There was still some food left. So, I'm bringing food back home on a bus. The bus is half-empty.

"There's a storekeeper sitting in front of me in a cream-colored jacket. This matters because I am telling you ahead of time what kind of jacket he is in. He has a store not far from my house. But I don't go there, because we have another store and buy what we need there. But I do know him a little, because he is my neighbor. He lives right there next to his store.

"If there's a ruckus outside or if shots are fired, he looks out of his window: is the store okay? But if he is already in the store when a ruckus starts up outside, he looks out the store window: is the house okay? Every now and then, he brings something from home to the store or something from the store to his house.

"And suddenly, a hale young man with the face of a ruffian enters the bus. I didn't like him immediately. He slowly looked the bus over and sat down next to the storekeeper. There were plenty of empty seats, but he sat down next to him. Why is it, I think, that he sat down next to the storekeeper when there are so many free seats?

"I keep my eye on him. Meanwhile, the storekeeper is in his cream jacket. It has pockets up top. And suddenly I see that bandit reach out with his hand for the storekeeper's pocket. But the whole time, he's staring forward as if there's something interesting there. He doesn't look where his hand is sneaking. But what's interesting is that the storekeeper is looking forward too, as if he doesn't see anything."

"Maybe he really didn't see anything?" I asked.

"No! Not a chance! He even thrust out his chest so that it would be easier for the other guy. A good goat thrusts out her udder like that to the goodwife. The way the guy looked had frightened him.

"And so, I look on. The bus is trundling along, and in the meantime, this guy unbuttons the storekeeper's pocket and takes out a pack of money. Not a big one, but a sizeable pack. Ten-bills. And he puts them in his pocket. And he still keeps looking forward. But what's interesting is that the storekeeper keeps looking forward!

"I'm enraged. The bastard will get off soon, and the storekeeper will just keep looking forward. I felt it rise up to my throat. I was beside myself. I jump up. I grab the bandit with both hands by his collar, drag him out into the passageway, and with all my might, smack him right in the neck. And he falls right at the doors. He's down. The noise! The din! Women are screaming. Nobody knows what is going on.

"The chauffeur brakes. 'Open the door," I yell. I don't even know why I do. The chauffeur opens the door. The guy tumbles out of the bus, then jumps up and runs away. I thought he was half-dead, but he ran off.

"The bus keeps going, and I explain to everybody what had happened. Everyone thanks me: 'Sandro is our defender!' And, of course, it's very nice to hear that.

"But the storekeeper is quiet. He just sits there modestly, as if he has nothing to do with what just happened. He's smiling slightly. Shrugging slightly. And some people are probably thinking that a mute-deaf man was just robbed and pity him the more for it.

"No, I think, he's a man, after all. He must be ashamed. I'm twice his age and wrangled with a bandit, defending his honor. While he was too scared. And there were lots of women in the bus, but he just shrugs and smiles abashedly.

"At the last stop, he and I get off. We head off in the same direction. We go. I ask him, 'How much money did you have in your pocket?' 'What money?' he replies. 'What do you mean? The ones the thief took out of your jacket!' 'I didn't have anything in there,' he says. 'I don't have the habit of putting money in my jacket. I have the habit of keeping money in my wallet.'

"And he takes out his wallet out of his pants and opens it like an accordion—it's full of quarters. I recognize people with an accordion like that in their pants by how they walk. The accordion plays! But I'm too preoccupied for that.

"'But I saw with my own eyes,' I say, 'a pack of red tenners!' 'No,' he says, 'I don't have the habit of keeping tenners in my pocket. I don't like it! No, I like trading, but I don't like keeping money in my pocket.'

"I start to lose it. 'What,' I say, 'have I lost my good sight in my old age? Am I confusing a red ten-bill with toilet paper?!'

"It's possible to confuse them now, but back then, it was still money.

"'Then,' I say, 'why did I smack him in the neck and he tumbled out of the bus?' 'You're a noble man,' replied the storekeeper, 'and the guy is probably a troublemaker. But he didn't take any money from me.'

"You bastard, I think, next time, when your store is on fire, I won't throw a glass of water in your direction. But I didn't say anything more to him and turned to go home. Maybe, I think, he's still ashamed as a man and therefore doesn't want to admit anything. He'll cool off overnight, I'll see him then and ask him.

"The next day, I go to his store. He's calmly vending his wares, as if nothing had happened. Then he leaves his customers, comes up to me, and says quietly from behind the counter:

"'I got Chinese stew meat. Once these leave, I'll give you some.'

"'No need,' I say. He clearly wants to bribe me. I'll be honest, if, in honor of my noble thrashing of that hooligan, he had set a table so that my friends and I could come eat, drink, and enjoy ourselves, I wouldn't have refused. And I wouldn't have told people that he puffed out his chest for the thief like a good goat sticks out its udder. It would have all been different. But he wants to hide the truth with Chinese stew meat. Ungracious!

"But I don't let him hide from the truth and once again ask him about the money. But he keeps insisting: I never put tenners in my pocket, and there was nothing there.

"Could I have lost my mind? Or maybe I erred? Maybe my eyes had grown weak in my old age? No, when my old lady asks me, I don't need glasses to thread a needle on my first try. And now you know why I got a pair of Zeiss binoculars in my youth. Maybe the storekeeper had lost his mind? No, he still keeps shop fine, no mistakes.

"And I ask him the next day, and the day after that: 'No! No! And no!' And I began loathing that idiot so much that I couldn't sleep at night. Why doesn't he admit it? Does he really think that I'll start taking halva or canned goods at his store for free? His store isn't anything special. And that's not the kind of person I am. Maybe he's still ashamed as a man? But what shame does that storekeeper have? He sells shapeless halva by the crate.

"Then what's the issue? No, I think, you bastard, I won't leave this alone. I find out elsewhere that he has a decent relative. He works in the airport as a dispatcher. An honest man. What else could he be? Good connections won't make an airplane to touch down or take off. For now. You *have* to be honest. I go to see him and tell him everything that happened.

"'What does he want from me?' I ask. 'I won't take water from his store for free. I won't go to his wife or his lover, if he has one, and tell her that he's a coward. Why doesn't he treat me like a man? Why won't he admit it? Get together a family council, explain to that idiot that he should come clean. I've sat at a table with Stalin together. I went hunting with Trotsky! But this guy treats me as if I were a vagabond with no clan to speak of, as if I could mistake a ten-bill for toilet paper.'

"'Alright,' he says, 'Uncle Sandro, don't worry. We'll get some relatives together in the next few days, and we'll get him to tell the truth.'

"'You do that!' I say and shake his honest hand. 'Otherwise, either I have to move or else burn his store in my old age! We can't just walk by each other as if nothing happened between us.'

"Four days later, I come to see the dispatcher again. He looks at me with such a sorrowful expression from afar, that I immediately understand: the storekeeper's plane had flown right by.

"'We,' he says, 'had a family council, Uncle Sandro. He refuses. What can we do? He said, "If you want to get rid of me, then get rid of me! Uncle Sandro is a noble man, but he made a mistake. My favorite cuh-ream jacket doesn't even *have* top pockets!" Honest, Uncle Sandro, my head hurt from his "cuh-ream" jacket!

"'He's an unpleasant fellow, even though he's a relative. Sorry, Uncle Sandro, but we couldn't accomplish anything with him. But if you want to fly somewhere, any flight in any direction—I'll get you a ticket. There's no kerosene, flights are being cancelled, it's tough to get a ticket. And if someone you know or if someone you know knows wants to fly somewhere—no problem! Tell them to just say your name. I know you won't send me any troublemakers. You'll send someone warm.'

"This guy was a piece of work too. Send him someone warm. One shells out money, the other sticks on wings. And who'll look after the airplanes? Me?

"I leave. What to do? I really might as well simply fly away from Abkhazia. But my soul is on fire. I can't calm down. And I remember he really did have a cream-colored jacket on. But I saw how the thief took money out of that jacket! Or had I really lost my mind?!

"As I walk, I carefully look at the people passing by. Independently of my will, my eyes are searching for cream jackets. I counted four people in cream jackets. And all of the jackets had top pockets! No, I think, you bastard, you won't fool Uncle Sandro! And then I see a fifth person in a cream jacket, but without top pockets! Think what you will!

"I go into his store again. He's vending. A few shoppers are there. He looks at me with quiet eyes, as if saying here I am, and here's my pocketless, 'cuh-ream' jacket.

"And it really is pocketless! Either I had gone insane, or he had managed to sew himself a new, pocketless, cream jacket. No, I can make out that the jacket isn't quite new. If I understand that, then I can't have gone insane? But since the jacket has no pockets, that means that the thief didn't sneak into it?

And since the thief didn't steal anything, that means I've lost my mind! And the storekeeper comes up to me and whispers over the counter:

"'Polish noodles. When these leave, I'll give you some.'

"I didn't say a word and walked out of there. I'm walking home. I have a grip on myself. But I have no idea who it is I'm gripping—someone normal or someone insane? If insane, how long can I keep a grip on him? And I also think that I need to come up with a new path to my home, because on this one, I could run into the shopkeeper. He might turn me into a criminal in my old age. So what, did he beat me, or did I lose my mind?

"And then, God sends me help in the form of his son. Just a kid, eight years old. Nimble. Doesn't look like his father. He was standing next to my fence, staring at the cherry growing in my yard. He didn't even notice me. And suddenly, I realized what to do. But he doesn't see me. His head is raised, looking at branches full of cherries.

"'Do you want some?' I ask. 'It's almost ripe.'

"'Yes,' says the boy, and points with his finger: 'that branch already ripened two days ago!'

"'Then let's go,' I say, 'you're not too late.'

"We enter the yard. I lift him up onto the tree. As soon as I let go, cherry pits start raining down on the leaves. He eats to his heart's content. Finally, I take him off the lower branch and put him on the ground.

"'Whenever you want,' I say, 'come eat some cherries. I know your dad. He is a good man. Brave! But a thief stole some money from your poor dad in the bus. I saw it with my own eyes.'

"'I know,' the boy replies, throwing his head back and looking at the cherry tree. It looked like he was regretting coming down so early.

"'How do you know?' I ask, trying not to get worked up.

"'Dad was telling mom,' the boy replies, his eyes scouring the branches. 'I heard from my room . . . Then he told her to cut the pockets off . . . And she did.'

"'On the cream jacket?' I ask, and my tone must have given something away, because the boy finally tore his gaze away from the tree to look at me.

"'No,' he says, 'on all of them. My dad has four jackets. One is black for funerals.'

"And here, I rushed.

"'What,' I say, 'your dad asked to bury him in the black jacket?'

"'Other way around!' the kid waved the question off. 'Dad goes to funerals in the black jacket.'

"Oh, he'll go too far, I think, then say:

"'How much money did the thief steal from your dad? Maybe you know?'

"'I do,' the boy nods. 'He took a hundred rubles. Dad told that to mom too.'

"'Alright, go on home,' I say. 'But not a word to your dad about our talk. He'd be hurt.'

"'I know,' says the boy and heads off home, looking back at the cherry.

"Alright. The next day, I go into that shopkeep's store. I waited until everyone else left. I even locked the door from the inside. The idiot grew scared. Maybe figured I'd beat him. But I didn't leave out his cuh-ream mother. I didn't leave out his cuh-ream father! I got his cuh-ream grandma and left some for his cuh-ream grandpa!

"I said everything I wanted to, I was so angry. But I didn't say anything about the pockets, of course. He could have guessed that I found out through his son.

"I exited the shop—I felt like I had been doused in Chegem water! My soul felt free! My head was clear! I even realized how the hundred rubles had ended up in his pocket.

"He probably took them out of the register as pocket change to pay the truckers when they brought him his goods. But they didn't bring him anything, and he forgot about the money. Small change! Which is why they ended up carelessly tucked away in his pocket, and why the mug of a guy noticed from afar that his pocket was bulging. Which is why he sat next to him.

"And what's interesting is that a week later, I'm at the barber's, when suddenly, the mug walks in there and, without noticing me, offers the barbers a pair of black market women's shoes.

"'What,' I say, 'you're into black market shoes now?'

"He looked around and immediately recognized me.

"'Yes,' he says, 'so that my neck goes unharmed.'

"He said it very amiably. And I liked that.

"'If I had known then what kind of man he was,' I say, 'I would have smacked him in the neck and not you. How much did you swipe from him?'

"'I don't remember,' he says, 'I think a hundred.'

"It all lined up. It turned out the pickpocket was the most honest of them all. The dispatcher was a piece of work too. 'Send him warm people.' He doesn't want the hot ones!

"You shell out money for him, he'll stick on wings for you. And the boy, by the way, even though it's been three years, he still comes by my yard. As soon as the cherry ripens, he's there. And then the apples, and the pears, and the figs. And every time, he says, 'I didn't tell dad anything then! And I won't tell him anything now!'

"The little devil! He grasped my character—I like the nimble-minded! But how long can that go on! Thank God I don't have to lift him up to the tree anymore. I'm amazed sometimes. First, I got the shopkeeper through his son, and now he gets me through his son? But no matter, if he doesn't calm down in a year, I'll make him climb that tree with a basket in his arms.

"And it turned out that the pickpocket was the most honest of them all. And to think that a whole month passed between the bus and the barber. And he could easily have said: 'I've never seen you before! Nobody has ever smacked my neck, and I never stole anything! I'm just peacefully selling these women's high-heel shoes!'

"And then I would have to once again prove what had happened. This is the world we live in now! The pickpocket turned out to be the most honest of them all. And now, you tell me why the shopkeep didn't admit that the guy had taken his money."

Uncle Sandro once again leaned back in his chair, slightly spread out his mustache, thrust his hands behind his belt, and began looking us over, chewing on his belt with his fingers. Pleased with the mental deftness he himself had demonstrated in his tale, it seemed like he now expected us to demonstrate our own acumen. Then again, judging by his expression, his hopes were low.

"At first, he was ashamed," I said, "and then he got stubborn."

His expression of irony didn't strengthen but didn't weaken either. It was the expression of an examiner. His gaze transitioned to my companion.

"Typical petit bourgeois hypocrisy," the other said loathingly. "I fought against such hypocrisy my whole life."

"Boloney," Uncle Sandro waved our responses off, apparently treating them as one. "I've pondered this for a long time and have finally realized the issue. Everybody wants to believe that he is living properly. And he decided to remove the pockets on his jacket not only because he was afraid of accidentally putting money in them again. He was most afraid that there would happen to be another noble person who would defend his honor free of charge. And he doesn't like that at all. Now do you understand why the Perestroika failed?"

"No," I said, taken aback at the sudden turn.

"But a single thief in the whole country changed his ways. And only thanks to me. You, meanwhile, go ahead and sit with your Lenin, who has more hair post-death than he had in life . . . I, meanwhile, will go to my old men . . . And you, when you write about what I said and receive money for it, you forget about your uncle."

"I won't forget, Uncle Sandro," I replied gloomily. It was impossible to reply more cheerfully. It's been going on for too long.

Uncle Sandro waved his hand, easily got up, and went to his old men in his light, triumphant gait. Now I understood that he had approached us to charm my madman just in case, and after he had accomplished what he set out to do, he lost all interest in us.

"What an inveterate human!" my companion exclaimed, delightedly looking at him and wiping his—since it's widely accepted to call it this—Socratic forehead.

By the way, this comparison is seemingly confirmed by vague rumors involving recurring hemlock.[61] But the thread does not end there—rather, it ends on the author of the comparison between Lenin's forehead and Socrates's, where hearsay has it hemlock played an important role too. Which leads me to say that there is no need to endlessly compare familiar foreheads with Socrates's. I can even hear a voice from above: "Leave Socrates's forehead to the Greeks. Worry about your own foreheads."

". . . I will definitely," my companion went on, "get him into the Council of Elders once we take power again. He is an exceedingly folksy fellow, even if he does lack an intuition for class. Come to think of it, why don't you write something like a double portrait of us: 'The Chief and the People.'"

"I'll try," I said.

Meanwhile, a person with a light blue bag in his hands approached us. He leaned slightly towards me and asked quietly:

"Do you need light bulbs?"

"What light bulbs?"

"Electric light bulbs."

I recalled that the wife of the cousin with whom I was crashing complained about how hard they were to obtain.

"Sure," I said.

---

61 Socrates was forced to kill himself by drinking hemlock.

I thought that the small transaction would make a nice break for me and would be a good lesson in private business for my companion.

The stranger carefully put his bag down on the floor, got hold of the zipper with two fingers, and smoothly swept it open. I looked inside.

At the bottom of the bag, carefully wrapped in cotton like they were gems, there glittered light bulbs of all sizes and shapes: egg-shaped, pear-shaped, plum-shaped. Nobly dim lamp bulbs glowed faintly alongside the more noble violet ones, which looked like exotic, imported fruits, or at least like eggplants.

Some of the light bulbs were in cartons used for selling eggs, when eggs were available to be sold, of course.

I took one light bulb from that very carton.

"The 'mignon' bulb," explained the vendor approvingly, and his hand caught up to mine to wipe the light bulb with a velvet ribbon he procured out of nowhere. The move resembled a doting mother combing the already-combed hair of a child shortly before parading him before guests.

Possibly continuing the mental comparison with the eggs, I examined the bulb in the light, as if trying to tell whether the yolk had transformed into an embryo yet. Alas, the tiny corpse of the tungsten thread lay at the bottom of the bulb, its gossamer form still twisting ostentatiously.

"It's burnt out," I said, putting the bulb back, feeling slightly guilty at making the revelation.

"Of course," he nodded confidently, "they're all burnt out. That's why I'm selling the 'mignon' at five rubles a pop."

"Who needs burnt out light bulbs?" I asked. The egg comparison was pursuing me: dank, rank.

"Anybody who works in any institution," he replied assertively. "You change out a burnt out one for a whole one, and then the government takes care of the rest."

He lingered a bit longer, then evidently realized that I don't have access to any institution, bowed, and put the light bulb into its nest. Farewell, "mignon!"

I examined the precious contents of his bag one last time as they disappeared beneath the seam of the zipper. Then I raised my head and took a careful look at the new Chichikov, selling the dead souls of light bulbs.

He was a middle-aged man in a faded, but tidy shirt and equally tidy, though even more faded pants, which were far removed not only from the height of fashion, but from the height of just about anything. However, his face, which had been thoroughly dried out by alcohol, expressed the modest dignity of a representative of maybe not the richest firm, but an honest one.

"And where's the troika-bird?"[62] I asked, absentmindedly looking around in space and time.

"Come again?" he replied drily but signaling a readiness to inject clarity into the situation, assuming that there were no hidden obscenities lurking within the question.

I suddenly became jovial. I sensed in all of this some grandiose and ultimately hope-bestowing symbol: the light of life, even if it was electric, was transitioning from Soviet institutions into private homes. These institutions once sucked the light of life from our homes. And now, the time of payment had come.

What was it that we saw earlier in our wildest dreams? We dreamed of how the last Soviet bureaucrat would leave the last Soviet institution, turning off the light and going home. No, it turned out that he doesn't turn the light off, he takes out the last light bulb and then leaves to go home, his pocket jutting out like it once had with the weight of quarter-liter vodka bottles. Also a source of light.

"Are the bulbs selling well?" I asked.

"Excellent," he explained eagerly. "This is my second bag today."

"Where do you get them?" I asked indiscreetly.

"That's a company secret," he replied dignifiedly.

"Do you sell anything else?" I asked.

"I have epaulets," he replied composedly.

"What epaulets?" I asked, as if I were someone who was explicitly interested in such merchandise.

The vendor grew excited and once again put his bag down on the floor.

"Everything from a major's to a general's," he said. He glanced at the sea and added: "Including those of an admiral . . ."

He reached for his bag, but I stopped him.

"No need for epaulets for now," I said, as if I had changed my mind, as if I was obeying some coherent internal logic. "Do you have weapons?"

He straightened and looked at me superciliously. His lips moved in an indignant monologue with the sound turned off. Nothing in the world looks

---

62 In Gogol's *Dead Souls*, the author utters the famous line, "Oh, troika, troika-bird, who came up with you?" before launching into a diatribe condemning Russia.

more comical than an expression of superciliousness on a face that has been dried out by alcohol.

"You may as well have asked about narcotics," he hissed finally, grabbing his bag. "We do not deal in anything illegal!"

With those words, he left us. I looked at my companion. The entire time I was talking to the vendor of burned-out light bulbs and self-styled generals' epaulets, his face expressed ever-increasing worry. Try as I did, I couldn't discern the cause of his disquiet. As soon as the vendor left, he almost screamed:

"Never forget, Ilyich's light bulb is unrelated! Ilyich's light bulb is unrelated!"

"Granted," I said, calming him down in order to finally get back to our semi-mystic chat.

"Why does America need a frozen Stalin?" my companion once again accurately pinpointed where he had stopped. "What do you mean, why? They know that a frozen Lenin is hidden in a safe house somewhere in Germany. At the appropriate historical moment, he will be thawed out. He will return to Russia, and the triumph of the global proletariat will be assured. But Stalin dismantled the global socialist movement. If they know that I've already been thawed out, then it's in the realm of possibility that they already thawed out Stalin too. The events in Iraq confirm this . . ."

"How so?" I asked.

"Saddam Hussein. You know who he looks like?"

"I don't get it," I said, even though I knew who he looked like.

"How hard would it have been for them to take Baghdad? Not at all. A UN resolution? To hell with it. Then why?"

"Saddam Hussein is a thawed-out Stalin?" I asked moronically.

"Phaw, how crude!" he replied. "Metaphysically—yes. But physically, no. The meta is what's most important—meta! Meta! Meta! They're using Hussein as an example for Stalin: this is what we'll do to your country if you revolt when we put you on the Russian throne. Stalin is useful to them. They're afraid of Lenin.

"Stalin won't necessarily be released looking like himself. There are plastic surgery options, because anti-Stalinist attitudes are still strong, though there are a lot of Stalinists too. But the people, once they believe that Lenin is alive, will rise up, and we will triumph."

"And what if the revolution doesn't pan out?" I asked. "The authorities are aware of the ease with which you took over the Winter Palace in 1917."

"We'll throw ourselves into battle, and then we'll see," he said firmly. "And if the revolution doesn't succeed and they don't kill me, then back I go into cryogenic storage until a new revolutionary uprising. Hey, listen, let's both go into cryo if we don't win right now. I'm confident you're one of us. I wouldn't want to lose you in the future. What do you say?"

"I'll think about it," I said seriously.

"Think on it, think on it," he replied, clamming up frostily. "As you wish."

"Given our Russian disorderliness," I said, softening the cause of my uncertainty, "our scientists would freeze us and then forget to thaw us out."

"Worry not! Not a chance!" he flared up. "There are underground German scientists here—they're the ones who thawed me out. They're experts, they know what they're doing!"

I thought about it, thought some more, and said:

"What if the revolutionary uprising doesn't happen for a long time? You could spend the whole twenty-first century in cryo . . ."

"So what?" he suddenly spread his hands, gave a sly wink, and leaned in. "You'll have a unique chance to look into the twenty-first century! You're a writer, aren't you at all curious?"

"Of course I am," I agreed, and then added, whining nostalgically: "But I won't be able to return to my own time, will I?"

"That, I can't promise you," he said strictly. "You have a regressive imagination. You're constantly looking backwards. That's obvious from your works too. You have to always be looking forward!"

I thought about it, thought some more, and said:

"Do you feel anything during cryo?"

He raised his head, closed his eyes, and blissfully leaned back. It was reminiscent of how people would lean back at the barber's in an attempt to catch a squirt of cologne. Then he opened his eyes, sat up, and said contemplatively:

"It was the sweetest time of my life. The whole time, I felt like Inessa was nearby. A thousand and one nights next to Inessa! True, for a time, I felt an unpleasant rattling in my ears. After I was thawed out, the scientists figured out that the rattling was connected with the bombings in Hamburg. But everything else was fantastic—life beneath the northern lights."

I thought about it, thought some more, and said:

"While frozen, would it be possible to dictate to someone your impressions?"

"Hogwash!" he exclaimed, and then added, without hiding his disgust: "You were clearly the patient of a farcical hypnotizer: I see a flowering meadow, a string of dancing girls, and the like. It's a deep extrication from the external world. Only your imagination is at work, like in a dream. At first, it's an aggregate of meaningless events. Then you correct these meaningless images. I left in my imagination only my work on the Leniniana and conversations with Inessa."

"What was there more of?" I asked, business-like.

"Enough of both," he replied, and then added haughtily: "God send the same to all."

"In cryo?" I asked.

"In general," he said.

I thought about it, thought some more, and said:

"Is your love for ice cream at all connected to your time in cryo?"

He looked at me with suddenly glossed-over eyes. Then he looked off to the side, then back at me. I again sensed his train of thought clambering up and fumbling, clambering and fumbling. I didn't think that this question would cause him such difficulty and was ready to apologize when suddenly, growing red and meeting my eyes with agonizing suspicion, he forced out:

"That . . . that's an improper question . . . That's an idiotic question . . ."

I nodded, completely agreeing with him. He went on much more confidently:

"It's absurd! I thought through twenty-four scenarios—there is no answer. What, did you think that they use an IV to drip ice cream into your body while you're frozen?"

"No, of course not," I said, "it's foolish, my brain was out in the cold."

"Out in the cold?" he asked in surprise. "Why out in the cold?"

I accidentally said those words. His eyes glazed over, and his mind once again began clambering and fumbling.

"What if I were frozen for a month?" I said in order to return his train of thought into its proper place. "And then we'll see?"

"For a month?!" he started. "But that's unprofitable! Cryo is too expensive a delight!"

"Well, I'll think about it," I said dimly.

"So be it, think on it, think on it," he nodded and then added acidly: "If it's not too much of a burden for you."

He turned towards the sea and even started purring some Neapolitan song, as if reminiscing about Capri and the companionship of a more worthy writer-interlocutor.

I was very tired of the fantastic madman, but for some reason, right at this moment, when he had had the last word, it would have been awkward to leave him. And he always had the last word! For crying out loud!

And suddenly, something unexpected happened. A small and festive family appeared in the Amra with a little girl in a white dress and a wide, black belt. They were clearly locals. The man greeted the diners several times and came up to the woman selling ice cream. The girl noticed by companion even though his back was to her, probably because of his sailor shirt, dropped her mother's hand, flared out her dress, and ran at him, yelling:

"Grandpa Lenin! Grandpa Lenin!"

Smiling tenderly, the various diners' gazes accompanied her. Some, probably newcomers, stood up to get a look at whomever she was talking about. The girl's mother and father were smiling too. My companion readily turned around at her voice and spread his arms to catch her. Shuffling in her little shoes, the girl ran up to him and immersed herself in his hug. My companion jumped up and tossed her into the air a few times, tightly and accurately catching her with his powerful arms every time.

The girl trustingly flew into the air, blinking from the resistance of the thick sea air, smiling in delight from the flight. One of the Amra's diners was quick enough to snap a photo and eternalize the touching scene.

He finally sat her down on his knees. The girl was beaming. My companion was beaming too. The girl, overflowing with goodwill, looked at me and said:

"Enthoy your meal, mister writer."

I looked triumphantly at my companion, letting him know that my renown was no less than his own. He pretended not to understand me. But then I made a mistake. I asked the girl:

"How do you know that I'm a writer?"

"Daddy said," the girl smiled. Still beaming, she waved in the direction of her father.

My companion let out a dry, caustic laugh, alluding to the thoroughly formal quality of such renown. Meanwhile, the girl's father was walking away from the ice cream seller. He held three bowls of ice cream in each hand.

It looked like he was holding a bouquet of magnolias in each hand. It was obvious that one of them would be brought to my companion.

Rushing to head off the girl's parents, our waitress ran up to us.

"You're at it again," she hissed, her voice full of bitter reproach. "You think I didn't hear what the child shouted?"

"My dear, what do I have to do with anything?" my companion said mockingly, deftly holding the girl on his knees and patting her on the head. "Out of the mouths of babes comes the truth. I didn't even call myself Ulyanov."

"Leave it, for God's sake," the waitress said wearily, and gave me the check. I paid and ceded my seat to the girl's father. The waitress managed to clean the table, making room for the new bowls of ice cream to bloom in place of the old ones.

I said goodbye to my companion. He nodded carelessly in response and, looking at the bowls of ice cream, started whispering something to the girl on his knees. I doubt that the new portions of ice cream had so caught his attention. More likely, he was doing what children do when they have a fight and attempt to underscore their closeness with another.

At the same time, the girl's father bid me farewell much more warmly. He said goodbye with a note signaling a degree of involuntary guilt at having stolen my interlocutor. In defending his family's comfort, his demure smile seemed to say: at least we get a Lenin like this—most people don't get any kind of Lenin.

I was leaving the Amra. The setting sun was casting lilac pink flecks onto the bay. Fishing boats were making for the mouth of the river like a herd of cattle returning home after a day out in pasture. I once had a boat on the river too, called Chegem.

Half a lifetime passed from my village, Chegem, to my boat called Chegem. I didn't even really notice the second half, in Moscow. Maybe because I passed it in recollections about Chegem.

Now there is neither the village Chegem, nor the boat. Time has washed Chegem away. And after I moved to Moscow, my boat was washed away by floodwaters. Maybe I should not have left? But Moscow turned out to harbor enough time to reminisce about Chegem for a fairly long time. So, it's all for the best in this best of all possible worlds.

The peaceful, bronze bodies of sunbathers could be made out beyond the river on the beach of the military resort. Eternity and peace wafted from the distant, blue-hued mountains. But for complete peace of mind, I had to call Moscow. I called in the evening and made sure that the manuscript was where it was supposed to be. And I definitively came to the conclusion that new times had come—this is of no use to anybody anymore. It's amazing that I didn't realize this right away.

About the Translator

Alexander Rojavin is a multilingual intelligence, media, and policy analyst specializing in information warfare. He is currently editing a book on modern Russian cinema as a key battlefield in the Kremlin's information war (forthcoming Routledge). At the same time, literary translation has always been one of his first loves.